The End of Desire

A ROWAN GANT INVESTIGATION

BOOK THREE OF THE MIRANDA TRILOGY

A Novel of Suspense and Magick

By

M. R. Sellars

E.M.A. Mysteries

This book is a work of fiction. Names, characters, places, and incidents either are the product of the author's imagination or have been used fictitiously. Any resemblance to actual events or locales or persons, living or dead, is entirely coincidental, except as noted.

The name *Velvet Rieth*, is used with permission, and is loosely based on an actual person. While some characteristics of the individual's persona are accurate, the character portrayed herein does not necessarily reflect the actual personality or lifestyle of the aforementioned.

THE END OF DESIRE: A Rowan Gant Investigation
A WillowTree Press Book
E.M.A. Mysteries is an imprint of WillowTree Press

PRINTING HISTORY
WillowTree Press First Trade Paper Edition / October 2007

For information, contact WillowTree Press on the World Wide Web:
http://www.willowtreepress.com

ISBN 10: 0-9678221-6-5
ISBN 13: 978-0-9678221-6-7

Cover Design Copyright © 2007 Johnathan Minton

Cover Photography: Johnathan Minton

Cover Model: Ms. Mickie Mueller

Author Photo Copyright © 2004 K. J. Epps

10   9   8   7   6   5   4   3   2   1

PRINTED IN THE U.S.A.
by
TCS Printing
North Kansas City, Missouri

Books By M. R. Sellars

<u>The RGI Series</u>

HARM NONE
NEVER BURN A WITCH
PERFECT TRUST
THE LAW OF THREE
CRONE'S MOON
LOVE IS THE BOND
ALL ACTS OF PLEASURE
THE END OF DESIRE

<u>Forthcoming In The RGI Series</u>

BLOOD MOON
MIRANDA

<u>Other Publishers (Anthologies)</u>

COURTING MORPHEUS (Apex 2008)

ACKNOWLEDGEMENTS

This is the part where I gush about the folks who make all this possible. "This" being all of these words I hurl at paper and hope like hell at least some of them stick. This list is certainly not comprehensive. There are many, many folks who make the Rowan Gant series possible, not the least of which are those of you who buy them each time I write a new one. However, the folks listed here have been directly responsible for support, insurance, research, ideas, steak, crackers, beer, assorted boozes, chips and dip, various candies, donuts, ice cream, and sometimes even a shoulder to cry on when things aren't going the way they are supposed to in my world. For that, I owe them at the very least a kudo or two here... After all, as my dear friend Tish would say, "It's a moral imperative."—

Dorothy "Donut Radar" Morrison: *Tour Buddy Extraordinaire*

Sergeant Scott "Big Scary Cop Guy" Ruddle, SLPD: *'Nuff Said*

Roy "I Concur" Osbourn: *A Source Of Much Information and Amusement*

Kristin "Don't Call Me Kirstin" Madden: *Adopted Little Sister*

Trish Telesco, Christopher Penczak, Edain McCoy, Charlotte Bailey, Gail Wood, Maggie Shayne, and all you other crazy WIP's—you know who you are.

Velvet Rieth: *Sleazy Motel Investigator Extraordinaire. Love the eye patch!*

Gil Rieth: *I'll Pass on the Whole Stun Gun Thing.*

Anastasia and Seitz: *Officially Endorsed "Murv Stalkers"*

Dr. Amy Miller, Adrienne, and Dawn over at St. Louis Skin Solutions

Coldie, Crystal, Layla, SinGin, Moonfire, and Lord Bastard: *The Team That Makes the RGI Forum and Fan Club Actually Happen*

Duane "Three Beer" Marshall, Angel, Randal, Scott, Andrea, Rowan, Lori, Beth, Jim, Dave, Rachel, Doug, Duncan, Kitti, Boom-Boom, Kevin, David, Bella, Shannon, Denessa, Annette, Boudica, Imajicka, Owl, Breanna, Anne, Heather, Kathy (all of them and their various spellings), Marie, Lin, Jerry, Mark, Christine, Rollie, Hardee, Z, Mickie, and probably twenty or thirty more...

All of my good friends from the various acronyms: F.O.C.A.S., H.S.A., M.E.C., S.I.P.A, etc. (And even the acronyms that have since disappeared...)

Patrick and Tish Owen: *Family Forever*

My parents: *You know... I wish you were here.*

Scott "Chunkee" McCoy: *World's Greatest Publicist*

Johnathan "Are We There Yet" Minton: *Cool Pictures Dude*

My daughter: *Stop Growing Up So Fast.*

My wife Kat: *Insert Mushy Stuff Here.*

The gang at CAO for the *MX2* and entire *Brazilia* line of cigars

Coffee, Green Tea, Joss Whedon, TISM, Crocs, Pop Rivets, 11½ Inch Fashion Dolls, Vodka, Tonic, Limes, the Mexican place around the corner, Asparagus, Hans Grüber, Compost, John McLane...

And, as always, everyone who takes the time to pick up one of my novels, read it, and then recommends it to a friend.

For *Browncoats* everywhere.
Keep on doing the impossible…

AUTHOR'S NOTE:

While the city of St. Louis and its various notable landmarks are certainly real, many names have been changed and liberties taken with some of the details in this book. They are fabrications. They are pieces of fiction within fiction to create an illusion of reality to be experienced and enjoyed.

In short, I made them up because it helped me make the story more entertaining—or in some cases, just because I wanted to do so.

Note also that this book is a first-person narrative. You are seeing this story through the eyes of Rowan Gant. The words you are reading are his thoughts. In first person writing, the narrative should match the dialogue of the character telling the story. Since Rowan (and anyone else that I know of for that matter) does not speak in perfect, unblemished English throughout his dialogue, he will not do so throughout his narrative. Therefore, you will notice that some grammatical anomalies have been retained (under protest from editors) in order to support this illusion of reality.

Let me repeat something—I DID IT ON PURPOSE. Do NOT send me an email complaining about my grammar. It is a rude thing to do, and it does nothing more than waste your valuable time. If you find a typo, that is a different story. Even editors miss a few now and then. They are no more perfect than you or me.

Finally, this book is not intended as a primer for WitchCraft, Wicca, or any Pagan path. However, please note that the rituals, spells, and explanations of these religious/magickal practices are accurate. Some of my explanations may not fit your particular tradition, but you should remember that your explanations might not fit mine either.

And, yes, some of the magick is "over the top." But, like I said in the first paragraph, this is fiction…

For behold, *I* have been with you from the beginning,
and *I* am that which is attained at *the end of desire*.

From
The Charge of the Goddess
As attributed to Doreen Valiente

Thursday, November 24
3:09 A.M.
Room 7
Southern Hospitality Motor Lodge
Metairie, Louisiana

PROLOGUE:

Annalise Devereaux felt like she was suffocating.

Not the literal asphyxiation one experiences from lack of oxygen, but a metaphorical suffocation brought about by the absence of something else entirely. A something else that was just as important to her as the air she was now breathing.

And, metaphorical or not, the agony she suffered because of the void it left was no less real.

At the root was the feeling she harbored deep inside. It was the unquenchable thirst that drove her to do unspeakable things for no other purpose than self-gratification. It was the force that made her no longer Annalise, but Miranda.

It was also the thing that now brought her pain.

The inner sensation was no longer a mere tickle; nor was it the insatiable itch she had grown to know so well. It wasn't even a mere compulsion. In fact, it had surpassed her very need to breathe in order of importance, making itself the top rung on her ladder of survival. And, with that, it had turned to a raging fire that could not be quelled.

Still, that didn't stop her from trying to snuff out the flame.

But, for everything she did to feed the hunger, to douse the burning, to satiate the desire—simply to breathe—she still felt as if she was gasping. As though she was barely clinging to life in the face of that which had become all consuming.

The truth is, it felt as if someone was actually taking it from her, breath by breath. Literally stealing the force that fueled her will to live; and in her mind it belonged only to her, and her alone.

She knew all too well that her current situation had everything to do with Saint Louis. Everything that had happened there had been wrong, and although the reward had been sweet for a time, the price paid was too high. Two sacrifices so close together, both of whom would be missed. Doing that had been beyond dangerous; it had been reckless. She knew when it was happening that it was a mistake, but she'd had no choice.

She had demanded it, and Annalise had to do as *She* said.

But, *She* would also never take responsibility for the mistake. The blame would fall to *Her* servant, to Annalise. With blame came penance, which must be paid by the servant. It now seemed that penance was sharing her reward with another—the reward that kept her from suffocating as she was right now.

The identity of the other remained a mystery. And perhaps it always would. But the fact remained that she hated her for taking what didn't belong to her. Even though *She* was giving it to the other freely, in Annalise's mind, the other was still stealing.

Call it greed, but she had already tasted it all, and for her, half simply would not do. She intended to take it back.

Annalise allowed her anger to feed her lust as she looked down at the man beneath her. He had been easy enough to coax here to the small motel room. All it had taken were some kind words, a cheap bottle of rum, and the promise of a bed for the night. It was a better deal than he would have had otherwise.

In the end, the hardest part had been getting him to shower.

He was still struggling against the bonds that held him securely to the bed. He pretty much had been ever since he'd realized this wasn't just a game.

It had been nothing to get him into this position. She'd started him on the pint of rum as soon as she had picked him up. Of course, as always the bottle contained more than mere alcohol. So, by the time he'd had several healthy swigs, followed by the shower, he was "medicated" enough to be pliable. But then, they always were.

The vagrants along Airline Highway were easy prey. Even better, they were rarely, if ever, missed. When they disappeared no one asked questions. No one wondered where they might be. No one, except maybe the others like them with whom they spent their pathetic lives each day and night. But, no one listened to them. And, just like her chosen sacrifice, none of them even mattered. Like all men, they were there for her amusement, and because these wretches led such an unremarkable existence, they were perfect for those times when the need arrived unannounced.

She just had to be careful which ones she chose. But then, Miranda did the choosing, and *She* was always careful.

Except for Saint Louis.

Annalise stared into the man's face. His fear was making the rum and Diazepam cocktail wear off quickly, which was exactly what she wanted. She needed his fear and his pain, for with them came his undying love. And, these were the currency that brought the reward.

She could see a newfound sobriety in his watery eyes as he peered back at her, silently pleading. She could barely hear his hoarse moans and squeals through the several loops of duct tape encircling the lower half of his head, securing the washcloths she had stuffed into his mouth.

At the moment, she was kneeling astride his chest, resting her weight primarily on her knees, which pressed down hard upon his upper arms. It wasn't so much that she needed to do so for a practical purpose. There was no way he could escape the ropes with which he'd been tied. But, the position made her feel even more in control, and she was certain that it brought him pain. It was a demonstration of her power over him, for her own benefit as much as his.

Leaning slightly, she reached to the side table and picked up a cigarette then placed it in her mouth. With a flick of her thumb, she sparked a butane lighter to life and carefully touched the flame to the tobacco. After taking a shallow drag, she allowed the smoke to slowly roll from her mouth between crimson glossed lips and inhaled it deeply through her nose. Regarding her victim with little concern, she exhaled slowly, took a second drag, and then repeated the process.

She felt him relax slightly, and so she allowed herself to smile. She didn't take a third drag from the cigarette. Instead she put it out.

Annalise caught her breath, feeling her arousal as she slowly twisted the smoldering butt against the man's cheek. His muffled screams were music, and as he arched between her thighs, it made the wave of pleasure intensify, causing her to emit her own involuntary moan.

By the time she crushed out a second cigarette against his flesh, and then a third, Annalise was no longer in control of her own actions.

It was all *Her*. It was all Miranda.

Her face spread into a wicked grin as she shifted backwards and settled her weight onto his belly so that his chest was now fully exposed. A haunting, almost ethereal tone surrounded her words as she spoke to him.

"Now, little man. Let's see how much you love me."

As she spoke, she flicked the lighter to life and adjusted the flame to full. Before she had finished the sentence, she was holding the bright yellow fire against his bare nipple, reveling in the scent and sound of his crisping flesh and smiling as he squirmed between her thighs.

So the sacrifice began—as did payment of her reward.

Unfortunately, someone else, somewhere else, was receiving half of it.

Half that she wanted back.

M. R. Sellars

Saturday, November 26
4:17 P.M.
Room 7
Southern Hospitality Motor Lodge
Metairie, Louisiana

THE END OF DESIRE: A Rowan Gant Investigation

"Manager said da' do-not-disturb sign was on da' door all day yestuhday, an' t'day," the uniformed cop said. "Room was only paid up ta' t'day though, so dey came in ta' clean it an' dat's when dey found 'im."

The older homicide detective to whom he had been speaking jotted a note then gave him a nod and asked, "Did the manager say who paid for the room?"

His words were structured with the generic speech pattern of any randomly selected Midwestern location, audibly setting him apart from the natives of the Crescent City.

"He said da' podna paid for it, cash money."

"Partner?" the detective asked. Just as his lack of accent set him apart, his question marked him as a very recent transplant. "Did you get a description?"

The uniformed cop raised an eyebrow and gave the detective a confused stare. After a brief pause he nodded toward the victim on the bed and repeated, "Da' podna. Cap over dere paid for it."

"Who?"

"Da' victim," a slightly younger detective interjected as he entered through the motel room door. Obviously he had heard at least some of the exchange. "Ya' gotta excuse Country dere. He never learnt a secon' language."

The older man turned, peering over his glasses at the source of the new voice and said, "The victim?"

"Yeah, you rite," the younger man replied with a nod.

The uniformed cop glanced over at him and grinned, "Hey, cap. How's yamamma'n'dem?"

"Dey good," he replied, giving the other man a slap on the shoulder. "Ya' gonna be home later? I'll pass by ya' house."

"Naw, I prahmis' Jawn ah'd he'p out wit 'is maw-maw house."

"Yeah? It bad?"

The uniformed man gave his head a sad shake. "Ya' you rite, it's bad. She still waitin' on da bastuhds ta' bring da' trailuh."

"Gawd. Well you tell 'em hey from me."

"F'sure."

A lull fell in the conversation, and the newly arrived detective turned his attention to the older man. "Well... Dere ya' go."

"Uh-hmmm...Okay," the transplant muttered then glanced back to the patrolman. "Sorry about the miscommunication there."

"So'kay, cap," he replied.

"Okay, well thanks. I guess I'll catch up with you if I need anything else."

The cop simply nodded then turned and made his way out of the room, which was quickly becoming crowded, even though there were only two crime scene technicians, the victim, and the two detectives occupying the space.

The younger detective offered his hand and said, "Bailey. Joe Bailey."

The older man took it and answered, "Tim Fairbanks. But, everybody just calls me Banks."

"You got it, Banks," the younger man replied. "Everybody jus' calls me Joe. Where ya' stay at?"

"I've got a hotel room over at..."

"No...I mean where da' ya' live? Where are ya' from?"

"Oh. Kansas City. Homicide division. I had some vacation time coming and not much to do, so I volunteered through the FOP to come down here."

"We can use da' help. Glad ya' here."

"Thanks. Just got here a couple days ago. That's kind of obvious, I guess."

"F'true. Doin' okay so far?"

"Pretty much. Although, there have been a few times when I thought I was going to need a translator," Fairbanks sighed.

"Like jus' now?" Bailey replied. His own voice had the clipped affectations of the region but was nowhere near as thick as the uniformed officer where his dialect was concerned. He grinned at Fairbanks then momentarily poured it on for effect. "Ya' get used ta' it. Ya' jus' stick 'round awhile dere, cap, an' ya' learn how ta' tawk rite like us."

"Yeah," Detective Fairbanks chuckled. "So I've been told."

The two men shuffled around to get out of the way as a crime scene technician excused himself with a grunt and skirted past them. After a moment, Detective Bailey shook his head and let out a low whistle as he inspected the scene.

"Gawd. Ya' evuh seen such a thing, cheef?"

The question hung waiting in the thick air. It almost seemed as if it was held aloft by the cloying odor of sweet watermelon, cigarette smoke, and burnt flesh that still permeated the motel room even though the door had been wide open for some time. While Bailey's tone was more rhetorical than anything, the query still seemed to beg an answer.

Fairbanks grunted, "You mean this week, or ever?"

Detective Bailey chuckled.

"Actually, I was serious," Fairbanks offered.

"F'true?"

"Yeah," he continued with a nod. "I've seen something a lot like it. Of course, there wasn't any blood and the guy wasn't dead."

"Ya' lyin'?"

"No." He gave his head a shake. "True story."

Bailey whistled again. "Where ya' see dat?"

"A few years back when I worked a vice detail, we raided a sex club. I hit my assigned door, and when I came through it, this hooker had a buck-naked john all trussed up to the bed. Pretty much just like this guy is." He dipped his head toward the scene in front of them. "The pro was all dolled up like a Catholic schoolgirl, and she was beatin' the hell out of him with a yardstick."

"No way. F'true?"

"Yeah," he nodded again. "Trust me, I'm pretty vanilla. I couldn't even begin to make up something like that. I have to say, it appeared that they were havin' a pretty good time of it too—before I interrupted them, of course. Especially him, from the looks of things, if you know what I mean."

The younger cop shook his head slowly and grinned. "Gawd! Dressed like a Catlick schoolgirl, huh? Sick bastuhd liked dat did 'e?" After a short pause he nodded toward the victim. "F'sure, I don't think dis one here enjoyed it so much."

Fairbanks bobbed his head. "Yeah, I'm inclined to agree with you."

"Well," Bailey began, "I sure don't think we're talkin' about jus' your av'rage hooker did dis though."

"That was my thought too, what with the level of torture and all. Are you thinking maybe gang retribution or something on that order?"

"Naw, I doubt dat. Not da' kinda gang you mean, anyway. Dere's more goin' on here than ya' think."

"Why do you say that?"

"Lookit 'is chest," he offered, pointing.

Detective Fairbanks pushed his glasses up on his nose and leaned in to look. After a moment of inspection, an intricate pattern became obvious even through the wide swath of dried blood and random burn marks covering the dead man's skin. The longer he looked, the more it revealed itself, until it formed what appeared to be a crosshatched heart pierced by a long dagger or sword.

"So our killer is a bit of an artist, then?"

Bailey let out another of his trademark whistles. "Cheef, dat's not jus' art. Dat dere is a *veve*. Air-zoo-LEE Don-toe. Whoever done dis did more than jus' kill dis guy. Dey put a *gris-gris* on 'im."

Fairbanks looked closer at the intricate incisions then leaned back and sighed. Shaking his head he muttered, "Yeah. Okay. I'm definitely gonna need a translator."

Thursday, December 1
1:12 A.M.
Room 16
Airline Courts Motel
Metairie, Louisiana

THE END OF DESIRE: A Rowan Gant Investigation

CHAPTER 1:

The last time I had been to New Orleans I was with Felicity, and we had come here on vacation… Well, it was actually a working vacation on her part, as she had been hired by an architectural magazine to shoot pictures for an upcoming layout featuring several of the more artful buildings in the city. Still, there had been plenty of time for relaxation, which was more than I could say for my current visit.

Back then, we had stayed at a plush hotel in the French Quarter on someone else's tab and spent our days doing what amounted to sightseeing, even though my wife had a camera to her eye most of the time. Of course, that wasn't particularly unusual for her whether she was working or not. It was more or less a by-product of her reputation as one of the top freelance photographers in the country. But, in the end the only real difference between us and the other tourists snapping pictures was that Felicity knew what she was doing and was being well paid to do it.

Me, on the other hand, I was just along for the ride. Still, she didn't let me off the hook too easily. This meant that I spent a good part of the time playing the role of her pack mule—tirelessly plodding through the streets behind her, toting her padded, lens-laden bags, and at her demand, handing over a freshly loaded camera body or switching out the optics. But, I didn't mind. We were together, which was the most important thing to me; and besides, I was getting to see the sights with both eyes.

Just as our days were spent wearing down the soles on our walking shoes, our evenings generally consisted of tossing back hurricanes of all varieties. Frozen, on the rocks, in fishbowls…pretty much any way the restaurants and bars served them. Okay, to be honest the hurricanes actually started around midday with a trip to a random bar, but who was watching a clock? This was New Orleans, and that is how things were done in The Quarter.

But, like I said. That was then. This was now, and now was very different—on many levels.

I shook off the memory and gave myself a mental shove back into the here and now, a process easier imagined than done. My brain stumbled a bit, regained its footing in the present but refused to fully surface from the pleasant remembrance. Of course, I'm sure that as much as I needed the normalcy of the thought, it was also being fueled by a simple mnemonic.

Hurricanes.

Hurricanes in a glass…

Hurricanes on the gulf…

I'm certain the residents of the area would agree that the former were certainly preferred to the latter. Especially after the three seemingly back-to-back storms that had so recently rained destruction down upon this magickal city, Katrina being the worst of all.

Even though the sun had already set, gazing out the windows of my rental car as I drove from the airport to my motel in Metairie a few miles outside the city proper, the aftermath had been evident. In fact, the motel itself might have even seen its own share of damage. Looking around, I couldn't be entirely sure if that was the case or if the Airline Courts had always been in such sad shape.

Storm damage or not, the accommodations certainly wouldn't garner a rating in the Michelin guide. In fact, I can pretty much guarantee that a large amount of work would have been required to simply bring them up to standard with the most basic building codes. However, under the circumstances, I suppose I had no right to complain. The room was mine, and there didn't appear to be any leaks over the bed. The bathroom was a different story, but I could work around that. I hoped.

Given the short notice, I was actually surprised that I had found a room at all. After my first few calls, it seemed that anything with four walls and a roof was occupied by someone holding a Federal Emergency Management Agency ID card. They had been crawling all over the city in response to the disaster, though if you asked around, the opinion was that they hadn't arrived soon enough and were accomplishing even less now that they were here.

Upon making it to the Airline Courts however, I was more than just a little amazed that they had accepted a reservation at all. Especially once I saw the sign in the smallish lobby that advertised their hourly rate, as well as individual condoms for a dollar apiece. Of course, profiteering knew no bounds, and the price I was paying for the all but condemned space definitely spoke to that fact.

Again, I shook off the thought and tried to keep my mind from wandering. I was tired. Actually, no, I was exhausted, and on top of everything else that was happening in my life at the moment, I'm sure the fatigue had a lot to do with the sluggishness of my brain. I was fully aware that I was having trouble staying focused, and that was something I couldn't afford right now. The problem was, whether I could afford it or not, I was too worn out to do anything about it.

I padded over to the side table in the corner and picked up my bottle of water. The mere removal of those few ounces of weight caused the piece of furniture to shift and rock onto one of the back legs, making the lamp that adorned its surface thump against the wall. It was obvious that not only was the rickety hunk of pressboard and chipped laminate unbalanced, but also the room itself wasn't even close to level. I pressed on the surface of the table with a very slight touch of my fingers. It rocked forward and then back as soon as I removed my hand, causing the tassels—those that remained anyway—on the torn and discolored lampshade to swing back and forth. Why I had bothered with the exercise to begin with I couldn't say—nervous boredom I suppose or maybe just my mind wandering yet again. Whatever the case, I did it twice more but didn't find enough amusement in it to continue past that.

As if in reply to the clunk of the lamp, a somewhat spastic thump began against the opposite side of the wall, random at first, then falling into an increasing, though halting, rhythm. It was accompanied by muffled words of encouragement—of the x-rated variety—as well as some thoroughly unconvincing moans.

I glanced at my watch. A few minutes from now the disharmonic symphony would stop, and shortly after that would be punctuated by the sound of the toilet, followed by the room door opening and closing. The flushing toilet would follow that once again, and then the whole process would start over. If I was lucky, there might be fifteen minutes of semi-peace in between.

Of course, there was no mystery at all about what was going on. In fact, my room was probably the only one in the complex not seeing that sort of action tonight, though I'm sure it normally did. It definitely smelled like it.

Letting out a heavy sigh, I looked down at the overpriced bottle of water in my hand, then twisted the cap from it and took a swig. Wandering back around to the end of the bed, I rooted through my carry-on and extracted a container of aspirin. Popping the cap, I poured some into my palm, nudged the excess back into the neck of the bottle, then tilted it and allowed a couple of them to fall back into the pile again. I didn't count them so much as look at the size of the heap resting in my hand to judge the self-prescribed dosage accordingly.

The exercise was probably futile in and of itself. I knew the pain in my head wasn't one that could be remedied with over-the-counter medications—or prescription drugs either for that matter. It was born of an ethereal source and for the most part would remain staunchly unaffected by the pharmaceuticals of the mundane world.

I also knew my stomach was going to hate me—fact is, it already did since I'd been more or less living on the bitter analgesic and coffee for close to a week. Now that I thought about it, I would probably need to avoid any serious injuries as well, lest I bleed out, given the amount of salicylate coursing through my system and thinning my blood. Still, aspirin itself seemed to be the only thing that would at least take the edge off, and I had to do something in that respect. Right now my head was pounding just as it had been ever since the plane touched down. Actually, it had been for the past few weeks, but arriving here had made it thud even harder. If I was going to stem my exhaustion, I was going to need to dull the pain enough to get some sleep. Something else of which I was severely lacking.

Of course, that might not even be possible with the continuous traffic next door. I suppose I should be grateful that this room was at the end of the complex. Otherwise there was no doubt in my mind that the strictly adult soundtrack would have been in stereo.

I popped the handful of pills into my mouth, gave them a quick chew and then took a swig of water and swished them around before swallowing. My hope was to get them into my system a bit faster than they would by simply swallowing them whole. The acrid bitterness caused my mouth to pucker involuntarily, so I took a fresh pull from the water bottle and swished again, trying to rinse the residue if not the taste from my tongue.

Replacing the cap, I regarded the drink silently and wondered to myself if I should have picked up a bottle or two of antacid to use as a chaser instead. I didn't get much time to ponder the thought, however, as my cell phone began to trill, softly at first then ramping up in volume as it continued its quest for my attention.

Turning, I wandered back to the dumpster refugee that was masquerading as the side table and scooped the device from its surface, making the piece of furniture rock yet again. Glancing quickly at the incoming number on the LCD, I flipped open the phone and put it up to my ear.

"Yeah, Ben," I grunted.

"Your goddamn finger broken?" he replied, more annoyance than concern bolding his words.

"Do what?"

"You were s'posed ta' call when ya' got there. I been sittin' here waitin' all friggin' night."

I glanced at my watch again. It was definitely after midnight, so I couldn't logically dispute what he'd just said, on either count. Technically it was morning, and besides, he was correct. I had in fact made that very promise.

"Oh, yeah," I replied as I reached up and rubbed my forehead. "Sorry about that."

"Yeah, well, ya' oughta be," he countered.

"I'm a grownup, Ben. I can ride an airplane all by myself. I've done it several times, believe it or not."

"Don't be an ass, Row. That's not what I'm talkin' about. It's not like this is a normal trip, an' you know it."

He was correct yet again. There's very little one can consider normal about catching a last minute flight bound for a distant city to go in search of a serial killer. Especially one who has most likely been dead for better than 150 years but just happens to be up to her old tricks again because the wrong person decided to play with the wrong kind of magick for all the wrong reasons. It wasn't as if I was with the FBI, or even a cop. But, I did have a vested interest because that "wrong kind of magick" had been deeply affecting my life and, more importantly, my wife's for almost a month now. It was time for it to stop, and I was willing to do whatever it would take to make that happen.

"Yeah, Ben, I know…" I muttered in reply. "But when is the last time you recall anything being normal in my life?"

He answered without missing a beat, "Nineteen seventy-two."

"I'm pretty sure you didn't even know me in nineteen seventy-two."

"You're right. Anyway, I was just guessin'. Actually, I'm bettin' you've prob'ly never had a normal day in your life, period."

"It feels that way," I sighed. "But, there was a time…"

"Yeah, Row, I know there was…" he agreed, his voice trailing off as it lost some of its edge.

My friend was agreeing because he had been around when things were sane. While 1972 was pushing the limit, we truly had been friends for more years than I could remember. So he was well aware it wasn't until I started hearing the voices of the dead that things began to get weird. And, while it seemed like a lifetime, especially to me, that affliction had only come upon me somewhere around a half dozen years ago.

What with me being a Witch, I suppose that most would think I should be used to such things as communicating with the departed. After all, that's exactly the sort of thing Witches were "supposed to do," right along with riding brooms and sprinkling bat wings into bubbling cauldrons. To be honest, I sometimes thought that the Hollywood myth about WitchCraft would be a much easier way to live than I did at present. Riding a broom would definitely save me the aggravation of traffic.

Of course, while the "double, double, toil and trouble" aspect is a disproportionate fiction, Witches do tend to be more open to accepting the unexplained without going to great lengths to debunk it. Magick is certainly a part of our lives, and we know that it is very real. But, by the same token, we also know that real magick isn't what you see in the movies and on television.

So, while I wasn't particularly surprised by the fact that I could hear the dead, or even that they sometimes chose radical measures such as stigmata with which to communicate their distress to me, it definitely didn't make me see it as the norm. No, I knew for a fact that I was the odd man out. Very few people, Witches or not, get stuck dealing with this sort of thing. I just happened to be one of the unlucky ones and, because of me, so was my wife.

And there, in the proverbial nutshell, was the root of the whole problem I faced at this moment in time. My wife. Even as I stood here, she was back in Saint Louis, warming a bed in the psych ward of a hospital—which I suppose was better than the jail cell she had occupied only a few days before, after being accused of at least two brutal murders. Those charges had been dropped, but the nightmare was far from over.

In truth, it was only just beginning because it turned out the thing that went bump in the night was a half sister that, up until a few days ago, my wife didn't even know she had. And that sister was up to her eyeballs in Voodoo and hoodoo. Of course, that wouldn't be such a big deal, except for the fact that she had apparently taken a perfectly acceptable religion along with its associated magickal practice and perverted both of them into something vile and grotesque. While her take on that was probably 180° opposite mine, I'm betting that her victims would probably agree with me. In fact, judging from the pain in my skull, I knew for certain they did.

But opinions weren't important right now. What was, however, was the fact that whatever she had unleashed was no longer using her alone as a vehicle to inflict pain and death, it had been trying its damnedest to use my wife as well.

I even had the freshly healing wounds to prove it.

Still, why Felicity had been sucked into this, other than a familial connection we didn't even know she had, was something of a perverse mystery in its own right. And, solving that mystery was what brought me here, now, to this seedy motel room in the burbs of New Orleans, with nothing more in my possession than what I could quickly stuff into a single overnight bag and my carryon backpack.

"Row? You still there?" Ben's voice drifted into my ear, breaking me out of the semi-dream state into which I'd managed to sink.

"Yeah, sorry," I mumbled. "Drifted for a minute there."

"*Twilight Zone?*" he asked.

That was his personal catch phrase to describe any time that I would experience an ethereal event, especially one that would push me into a trance or something even worse, such as a seizure. The first few times he had witnessed it happening to me he had been frantic, not that I had reacted much better. These days, however, he just took it in stride—as much as one could with that sort of thing, anyway.

"No… Just tired," I told him. "So, did you just call to chew me out for not calling you first, or was there something else on your mind?"

"Little of both, I guess," he grunted.

"Okay, if you're finished with your lecture, are you ready to move on to the other?"

"What the hell is that?" he asked, confusion in his voice.

"Ummm…I don't know. You called me, remember?"

"No, White Man. I mean what's that fuckin' noise?"

Apparently my next-door neighbor had another transaction waiting in the wings, either that or one of her co-workers had been in the queue. I'd already identified the voices of two separate bad actresses operating out of the same room. At any rate, it appeared my hoped for fifteen minutes of peace wasn't going to happen, at least not during this particular hour.

"Exactly."

"Exactly what?"

"Just like you said, it's fuckin' noise, Ben," I told him, echoing his raw terminology. "Let's just say there is a lot of nightshift work here at the Inn."

"Jeezus, Row... You aren't gonna...you know..."

"Come on, I think you know me better than that."

"Well couldn't ya' get a decent room somewhere else?"

"Believe me, I wish I could. Right now I just need to be happy it has a roof and electricity."

"So you at least got a TV?" he asked.

"Actually, no. I don't think the people who normally use these rooms are all that interested in TV. Why do you ask?"

"Just wonderin' what you're doin' for entertainment?"

The non sequitur queries were really starting to aggravate me, so I snapped, "I'm not here for entertainment, Ben, and you know that. Now, are you going to tell me whatever it is you had on your mind or not?"

"You sittin' down?"

"No. There isn't a chair, and I'm not so sure I want to use the bed from the looks of it. I'm not even sure where I plan to sleep in here now that I think of it."

"Yeah, great. Well hold on ta' somethin' anyway."

"Come on, Ben. What's with the melodrama?"

"Payback's a bitch."

"What?"

"You kept me waitin', I'm just returnin' the favor."

I shook my head and let out a heavy sigh. "I already said I'm sorry. What more do you want?"

"You gettin' pissed at me yet?"

"I think you can safely say that I am, yeah. Why?"

"'Cause that's what I wanted. Like I said, payback."

"Then I think you can consider the debt cleared," I told him. "Now do you actually have something to tell me, or is this all just part of your grand plan?"

"Actually, I do have somethin'. Figured you mighta heard it on the news, but I guess not…"

"I haven't seen any news since I left Saint Louis, so you guess correctly."

"Yeah, well like I said, brace yourself. It looks like your evil sis-in-law is at it again."

CHAPTER 2:

I was suddenly feeling very ill. Under different circumstances I would have blamed the acidic churn in my gut on the healthy dose of aspirin I'd swallowed only a few minutes before. However, the sour nausea was accompanied by hollowness in the pit of my stomach that told me this was a different kind of sick. It was the queasiness that bore its way into your intestines at right about the moment you realized you had seriously screwed up.

Whether I wanted to admit it or not, my impromptu trip here to New Orleans had been born only partly of logic and reason. The majority of the impetus was pure emotion that I had been all too willing to ascribe to gut instinct without really giving it any serious thought. What I realized now was that any of the calculating and planning I had done was probably nothing more than the inner ramblings of someone on the verge of a nervous breakdown. The truth is, I probably belonged in a hospital bed in the psych ward right next to my wife's.

Of course, this was nothing new. I had always acted on impulse, and even when I was wrong, fate somehow allowed me to come out on top. But, my luck in that arena couldn't last forever. It was bound to change at some point, and I feared that time had now arrived. I'd let haste guide my actions and doing so led me here, almost 700 miles due south of where I apparently needed to be, with no one to blame but myself—which is exactly what I was doing at this very moment.

"Okay…" I finally said as I let out a heavy sigh and desperately tried to process everything that was bouncing around inside my skull. "Let me get off here and see if I can find a flight back right away. I'll call you back as soon as I know when I can be in Saint Louis."

I received no response. I waited a moment and wondered if I'd lost connection due to problems with cell towers in the area. I even pulled the phone from my ear and glanced at the LCD to check the signal strength. Finding it well within limits, I spoke again, "Ben? Are you still there?"

"Ya'know," he finally replied, "I could be a total ass and just let ya' do that." He let out a heavy breath, which told me he'd been at the other end all along. He'd just been thinking, most likely rocked back in his chair with his free hand massaging his neck as he had a tendency to do whenever pondering something serious. After another brief pause he added, "Hell, I should let ya' do it 'cause ya' had no business goin' down there anyway."

"What the hell are you talking about, Ben?" I asked.

"Simple, White Man. Much as I'd prefer your happy ass was in Saint Louis where I can keep an eye on ya', the murder didn't happen here. It happened there."

"Here?"

"Yeah, there. In New Orleans."

"Where here?" I demanded.

"Ain't important, Row. It's bein' investigated and they're keepin' us in the loop."

"Fine. That's lovely. I'd expect nothing less. Now, where did it happen?"

"I'm not tellin' ya'."

"Why not?"

"'Cause if I do, you'll try ta' find a way ta' get into it."

"How do you know that?"

He half chuckled. "How? 'Cause I know you, that's how. Besides, if that ain't your plan, whaddaya need to know the particulars for?"

I couldn't dispute either point, so I asked, "Yeah, so what if I do? Maybe if I check out the crime scene, I can pick up on something they can't see. You know how that tends to happen with me."

"Yeah, I do. But, the scene's a week old."

"A week?!" I exclaimed. "Why in the hell are we just now hearing about it?"

"NCIC backlog, Row," he explained. "Not to mention a hurricane and a flood which I'm sure you noticed. NOLA PD is swamped. Too much crime, not enough time or coppers for that matter. It just got entered, and that's only 'cause a fresh volunteer from KC is down there, and he remembered somethin' about one of our bulletins that made 'im do a little diggin'."

"Well, I've pulled impressions from old crime scenes before. So that's not really an issue."

"Doesn't matter."

His stonewalling was really pushing me to the edge, but I knew I wasn't getting anywhere with the direct approach, so I changed my plan of attack, "Well, are you certain it's her?"

"Until they finish processin' evidence, no. And with things the way they are down there, that could take awhile. But I did talk ta' the copper workin' the case myself. The victim was male, found in a room at a no-tell motel just like the two here, and he was tied ta' the bed kinky-sex style. From all indications, he was tortured ta' death, which we know is 'er favorite pastime. Still waitin' on autopsy results, somethin' else that could take awhile, but from what I understand she worked 'im over good. He also said they found hair that sounds like it could be a match. And, if that ain't enough, she carved one of 'er pictures inta' his chest."

"A *veve*?"

"Yeah. The heart-shaped one."

The hair on the back of my neck prickled at the mention of the symbol. It was definitely one of her calling cards.

"It figures," I mumbled, and then launched into an appeal, "Listen, Ben, even if the scene is a week old, maybe if I just had a look?"

"Uh-huh, how 'bout no."

"Dammit, Ben."

"Jeezus, Row, just give it a rest. Hell, what makes ya' think they'd even let ya' into the scene anyway?"

"Easy. You could call them back. I mean I'm already here after all. Don't you cops have some kind of fraternal code about helping one another out?"

"That's just for speedin' tickets."

"I'm serious, Ben."

"I know ya' are, but even if I did call, I'm gonna tell 'em what? My buddy the Witch is in town and wants ta' come by and look at the gore fest? It don't work that way and you know it," he told me. "On top of that, what you do in Saint Louis doesn't necessarily fly elsewhere. Shit, it doesn't always fly here and you know that too, in spades."

"Then what about Constance?" I pressed, "She's federal. What if she made the call?"

I was talking about Special Agent Constance Mandalay of the FBI. She was also a good friend, not to mention that she and Ben had been in an on again, off again relationship ever since his divorce. Even so, I didn't feel guilty about asking him to get her involved in this because she was already in it up to her neck anyway. It wasn't as if I was asking him to use his personal influence over her, not that he really had any based on what I'd witnessed of their relationship.

"Not happenin'," he replied. In my mind's eye I could see him shaking his head as he spoke. He continued before I could object again, "Look, Row, like I said. It's bein' investigated. The MCS and the Feebs are in the loop. There ain't shit you or I can do about it, and so there's no need in you tryin' ta' get in somewhere that you're not welcome."

"So what's to keep me from checking the newspaper and finding the location?"

"Nothin'," he grunted. "Except maybe the fact that they didn't run a story on it."

"How do you know?"

"I asked."

"Why?"

"Because I wanted ta' know how easy it was gonna be for you ta' get inta' trouble."

"Well, why didn't it make the papers?"

"Victim was a street person, and there's plenty of other shit goin' on down there right now. It just wasn't considered newsworthy."

"Okay, so what if I just go to the local police myself?" I countered.

"Knock yourself out," he harrumphed. "But I can tell ya' right now you'll just be wastin' your breath 'cause I already told 'em ya' might try that. Look, Row, you ain't packin' a badge, so you're just another civilian ta' them. The coppers down there are short-staffed and under siege for fuck's sake. They ain't got time ta' deal with ya'." He paused briefly to allow the comment to sink in, then continued, "Besides, I thought you were s'posed ta' be down there chasin' a ghost, right?"

"A *Lwa*," I corrected. "They're deified spirits within Vodoun religious practice."

"Yeah, well that's just another friggin' word for ghost in my book."

"Uh-huh. And I also wouldn't exactly call it chasing. I'm just looking for her history. It's really more like genealogical research if you want to know the truth."

"Chasin' or not, it's what ya' went down there for, right?"

I drew in a deep breath. I really couldn't argue with him too much because it really was the reason I'd come here. After a bloated silence, I huffed out my agreement almost as one word, "Yeah, I guess."

"Then that's what ya' need ta' concentrate on. You do the Witch stuff, and let us do the cop stuff."

Even though I knew continuing to argue with him was futile, I decided to press my friend just a bit further on the subject. "So, tell me something. If I can't help then why did you even bother telling me about this, Ben?"

"Figured since you were there, ya' had an off chance of hearin' about it anyway. Thought I'd see if I could get to ya' first."

"But…"

He cut me off. "No but's, Row. It was a judgment call."

"So how'd you make that call?"

"How else? I flipped a friggin' coin."

"What a novel approach."

"Like I said. Judgment call. Heads I tell ya' what I can and deal with ya' bein' pissed, or tails I don't tell ya' and still deal with ya' bein' pissed 'cause I didn't. For me it was lose-lose no matter what I did."

"Glad to know I'm worth so much consideration," I grumbled.

"It was a no-brainer, Row. I got bad guys ta' catch. Better I spend my time thinkin' about that instead of whether I want ya' torqued at me now or torqued at me later."

"Yeah, I know you're right," I conceded.

"If you wanna know the truth," he offered. "I didn't actually flip a coin. I was gonna tell ya' anyway."

"Why, because you figured I'd probably already heard about it?"

"No... Actually, 'cause I'm a bit worried about ya'."

"Don't tell me, let me guess. Because you're afraid I'm going to go looking for her?"

"Jeezus, White Man, I keep tryin' ta' tell ya' I ain't stupid. Hell, I know you're gonna go lookin' for her. What I'm afraid of is that you're actually gonna find 'er."

I had to give Ben credit; he definitely knew me as well as anyone could—except for my wife, of course. I was definitely going to look for Annalise, and finding her was my ultimate goal. I had absolutely no idea how I was going to accomplish this, but I knew where I was going to start. Therefore, I had no more hung up with him than I was heading out the door in search of a way to get into the local crime scene. What I was going to be able to do at almost 2:30 in the morning was yet another mystery, especially considering the fact that I didn't even know exactly where the crime scene was located. However, I had an idea, and since I wasn't going to be able to sleep for a variety of reasons, I decided I might as well get started.

I had no doubt my friend was correct in his assessment that I wouldn't be welcomed with open arms, so the head-on approach wasn't even an option. Especially since I wasn't going to get any support from him or Constance where that was concerned. This was something I would have to do on my own, with subterfuge. As my wife had recently pointed out, I wasn't a very good liar, so that was yet another hurdle I would need to face. Unfortunately, deceit was going to be necessary because the truth was simply too insane to be believed.

I had just pulled my door shut when my next-door neighbor stepped out of her room and, not paying attention to where she was going, stumbled directly into me. She jumped back with a yelp, teetering on a pair of platform heels that looked a half-size too big. Regaining her composure, she shuffled then leaned against the doorjamb. I wasn't sure if she was doing it for balance, or if she was trying to look alluring. Maybe it was both, although she wasn't accomplishing the latter—in my eyes at least. Either way, she simply looked me over and smiled.

I muttered, "Sorry," then gave her a nod and started for my car.

"Gotta light, Mistuh?" she asked before I'd made it two steps.

Even though it was against my better judgment, I stopped and looked back at her. In the dim swath of yellow spilling from the overhead light, I could see enough of her face to tell that her vacant eyes were fixed with a substance-induced glaze. I didn't really want to know which substance. Her vinyl skirt was too short, her top too tight, and her makeup too thick. She looked like she was in her late forties, but something about her felt like she was maybe all of fifteen.

I rummaged quickly in my pocket, withdrew a book of matches and tossed them the short distance to her. She missed the catch even though my aim was dead on, so she stooped to pick them up. While she was doing so, I took a quick glance around to make sure I wasn't being set up for a mugging or some such and then hurried on to my vehicle.

As she stood again, she let out a hoarse giggle and called after me, "Ah won't bite, shuga. Unless tha's what ya' wan' me ta' do."

By now I had the car door open and since I had originally backed in was just getting ready to turn and slip into the driver's seat. Out of reflex, I shook my head while saying across the top of the sedan, "No thanks."

I heard her reply as I was pulling the door shut.

"Ya' sure ya' not lookin' fuh comp'ny, bay-bee?"

If she said anything after that, I didn't hear it because the windows were up, the engine was running, and I was already pulling out of the parking space.

CHAPTER 3:

Ben had given me something to go on whether he realized it or not. It was tenuous, I admit, but it was something. He'd told me they found the victim in a motel room, specifically, the no-tell type. So, that was where I would start my search.

When I first set out, I even gave serious consideration to the fact that the murder might have happened right where I was staying. In fact, I was less than a mile up Airline Highway when I literally thought about turning around and going back, imagining for a moment I might be able to exchange some cash for information from my next-door neighbor. That sort of transaction would probably make me her easiest client of the night. Of course, that would all hinge on whether or not she actually knew anything, and she hadn't struck me as the type to stay up on current events that weren't a part of her immediate future. Besides, at the rate she'd been going, she had most likely already found someone in need of her particular brand of personal services by now, and I would have to wait until I could catch her between clients. In my mind, standing around waiting for that to happen wasn't exactly an enticing prospect considering the fact that I was sure to be faced with extricating myself from another sort of proposition yet again. On top of that, it didn't sound particularly safe either. But, in the end it wasn't fear or even the distaste that kept me from making the U-turn. There was a niggling hunch in the back of my head, and it kept telling me that I needed to look somewhere else. So, I listened to it.

I had seen the crime scenes in Saint Louis; therefore, I knew the types of venues the killer chose. While they were certainly establishments of the hourly rate persuasion, they were more along the lines of seedy in a quaint, un-redecorated sense—things like outdated, mismatched furniture and paint or wallpaper that hadn't been in style for over twenty years. But, the important point was that they were clean. They definitely weren't anything on the order of the squalid hole where I had taken up temporary residence.

There was a gut feeling I had about Annalise, or maybe it was her alter ego, Miranda, for all I knew. Perhaps both. It was the product of an ethereal connection I'd made at the second Saint Louis crime scene, and all I could say was that I had picked up an impression. That impression had now formed itself into a theory. To me, it seemed she saw herself as above such a place as the Airline Courts. In fact, I was dead certain she perceived herself as above most everything and everyone.

Even so, she still picked motels well known for clandestine meetings of a sexual nature for her kills. There could be a handful of logical reasons for this, not the least of which was the fact that she could almost count on absolute privacy, given the nature of the business. But, logic wasn't what drove a serial killer. Something the experts liked to call a stressor was the motivational culprit.

So, while the logical reasons may well be factors, if my feeling was correct, she was choosing them for an altogether different, and very specific reason—that being nostalgia. My guess was that, in typical serial killer form, she was attempting to recreate something from her past, possibly even her first kill.

The question that remained for me was which one of them was responsible? Based on the period of the motels, it almost had to be an event in Annalise's life, since everything so far indicated Miranda had been dead for better than a century and a half. But then, why was Miranda seizing on it?

Of course, that was just another part of the big, scary puzzle.

I'm sure my theory wasn't new. The FBI profilers had more than likely come up with the very same idea, or something close. However, mine was based on observation and a quick brush with the *Twilight Zone*, as my friend would say. So, when all was said and done, I had no credentials to back it up; therefore, it was really just a mental stab in the dark. Still, it was all I had to work with, and right or wrong, it narrowed down my possibilities significantly.

Or, so I thought.

That last assessment changed the moment I pulled into a combination gas station/mini-mart and thumbed through the hotel listings in a tattered phone book. Even after discounting all lodging that was obviously upscale or I knew to be a reasonably respectable chain that didn't fit the image I had kludged together, there was an exorbitant number of local motels that I didn't know enough about to confidently exclude. In fact, I gave up on my cursory count when I hit 50 and there were still more to go.

What started out in my head as a promising slip up by Ben had now turned into a daunting task that my exhausted brain wasn't at all interested in tackling. It then crossed my mind that my friend hadn't actually slipped up. He probably already knew how overwhelming it would be.

Of course, even if the list had only been a dozen or so locations as I had hoped, I still had yet to figure out how I was going to determine which one actually was the scene of the homicide. Calling the numbers and asking if they'd recently had a murder in one of their rooms didn't present itself as a terribly attractive or even productive option. Nor did driving to each one and hoping for a psychic impression to tell me when I'd arrived where I needed to be. Given the way my head already felt, I probably wouldn't be aware of one if it happened anyway.

I still had an option though. Ben had told me they didn't run a story in the paper, but I wasn't entirely sure I believed him. He could have been lying, which was something he was more than willing to do if he felt it was in the best interest of the person he was trying to protect, namely me.

If that was the case and it actually had been reported in the newspaper, maybe it would point me to the correct place. I knew that idea was full of if's and maybe's, but it was really my best option at this point. However, it was also something that wasn't going to happen at this hour. It would have to wait until well after sunrise when I took my planned trip to the New Orleans Public Library because the paper I needed would be nearly a week old, and that would probably be the only place I could get my hands on it, if at all.

I actually felt my shoulders fall in a physical response to the realization. The growing weariness had been held at bay by sheer will, and that was now crumbling in the face of failure. The extra high dose of aspirin I had taken wasn't helping either. While it was only doing a little to dull the edge on my headache, it was definitely going a long way toward enhancing my exhaustion. I caught myself yawning as I stood at the payphone and knew what little energy I had left was draining from me as if someone had just pulled a cork to let it out.

Now that I had to postpone this nocturnal quest, my thoughts were relegated to returning to my motel room, so I could at least try to get a few hours sleep. I ripped the pages from the phone book and stuffed them into my pocket, just in case, then turned and started back toward my car. Before I made it as far as the front bumper I stifled two more eye-squinting yawns.

I stopped in my tracks and sighed heavily, rubbed my forehead for a moment, then turned and aimed myself at the door of the mini-mart. If I was even going to make it back to the motel in one piece, I was going to need a cup of coffee.

"I jus' started 'em fresh," the man behind the counter offered as he watched me head for the coffeemakers. "Dey should be ready in jus' a coupl'a minutes."

"Thanks," I replied, giving him a nod as I continued over to the stand where the brew was streaming from a stained filter basket into an equally soiled carafe.

Using what I saw as a judge, it was a safe bet the coffee wasn't going to be top-notch, so I pulled one of the large cups from the stack and started prepping it with sugar packets. After dumping in six, re-examining the size of the vessel and adding another three, I began rooting through a tray of flavored creamers. After finding a half-dozen that matched, I lined them up then started peeling back the tops and dumping them in.

The fatigue had now worked itself into every nook and cranny of my being, so by the time I picked up the fourth creamer, my hands had decided not to operate in accordance with what my brain was telling them to do. Before I could manage to tear back the foil top, I fumbled the small plastic container, and it fell from my hand then rolled across the aisle floor. I turned and knelt down to retrieve the escapee, and when I did, my eyes caught a silvery glint of light bouncing from a somewhat familiar shape.

Wrapping one hand around the fugitive condiment, I pushed my glasses up onto my nose with the other and continued to kneel there, staring at the object. The gratuitous trinket section was positioned immediately across from the coffee; probably some marketing guru's brilliant idea for how they could move high-profit-margin, cheap plastic toys by catching junior's attention while the parent was getting a cup of java. I had no doubt that it was effective to some extent because it now had my undivided attention.

Of course, I was focused on a particular item. Dead in the middle of all of the junk was a peg which held several blister cards, each of them containing a toy police badge, whistle, and plastic handcuffs. Ben's earlier comment rolled through my foggy brain, "You ain't packin' a badge, so you're just another civilian ta' them."

He was correct. But now, like some fateful sign, here was a badge, and it even looked pretty convincing given the short distance between it and me. It wouldn't stand up to any manner of scrutiny, that much was for certain, but if it was just a quick flash it might work.

"Ya' okay over dere, cap?" the man called out.

"Yeah," I answered and, realizing I'd been staring at the toy just a bit too long, offered up an explanation. "I just dropped a creamer, and I didn't want to leave a mess over here for you to have to deal with."

"Dere ya' go," he replied, a thankful note in his voice.

I sighed and looked away from the toy rack then muttered a personal admonishment under my breath as I stood, "Yeah Gant, impersonating a cop. That'd be really bright, wouldn't it?"

Stepping back over to the low counter, I finished adding the creamers to the cup then poured in the just finished coffee on top. I was happy to see that it blended to a milky brown instead of the sickly grey I'd faced before at other such establishments.

Wandering over to the checkout stand, I placed the cup on the counter then dug in my pocket for my wallet.

"Dat gonna be two-sixty," the man told me.

I tossed three ones in front of him.

"You gotta silvuh dime?" he asked.

I shoved a hand into my pocket in search of the change but found nothing but the car keys and the crumpled pages from the phone book.

"No, sorry," I offered with a shake of my head. "Don't worry about it. Just keep the change."

"Awrite," he replied, giving me a quick nod.

I picked up my coffee and started for the door but halted as the thought of the phonebook pages in my pocket began bludgeoning my grey matter. Then, without thinking anything through, I seized on one of the names I remembered seeing, turned back to face the man, and said, "Mind if I ask you something? I just drove in and I'm looking for the Keys Motel?"

"Dat's no problem," he replied, pointing past me. "Ya' jus' go down Airline a coupl'a miles and dere it is."

"Great, thanks," I offered with a weak smile then let out a nervous chuckle which I'm sure was more a product of the lie I was telling than any sort of acting skill. On the heels of the laugh I added, "You know, I heard there was a weird murder that happened there recently. You hear anything about that?"

"Naw, somebody told ya' wrong on dat," he told me, shaking his head and jerking his thumb in the opposite direction. "Da' murder happened ovuh for da' Suthun Hosp'tality. Dat's back up da' road."

"Really?" I returned with a nod. "My wife will be glad to hear that. The story kind of spooked her a bit, you know."

"Yeah, you rite."

Adrenalin instantly dumped into my system, and my fatigue momentarily fled, along with anything I had that might have resembled good sense. I should have turned and left right then and there, but the impulse that had made me ask the questions was stuck in overdrive, and it didn't care what trouble I might be making for myself. Instead I headed back in the direction of the coffee counter, my sights set on the toy rack as the lie took on another layer.

"F'get somethin'?" the man asked.

"Sort of," I said over my shoulder. "I saw something over here I think my kid would really like."

CHAPTER 4:

True to what the man at the gas station had told me, the Southern Hospitality Motor Lodge was just up the road. Its lighted sign became apparent shortly after I pulled back onto the main thoroughfare, and within moments I was swinging into the almost full parking lot. Once I found a space and nosed my car into it, I shut off the lights, then the engine, and proceeded to visually scan the front of the small motel.

From the outside, it definitely fit the image I had in my head as the kind of place Annalise would select for a kill. It looked clean but far enough out of date to be a throwback to the mid 1960's, perhaps even earlier. I suspected the interior decor would reflect that as well, even if it had been partially updated at some point.

The office itself was located at the street end of a single level building that extended for several units before eventually connecting with an L-shaped two-story addition. In the far corner where they joined, I could see a large yellow X flapping gently across a room door. Unfortunately, this was something that had become an all too familiar sight for me in recent years, and I could almost certainly guarantee that the black lettering on the bars of the wavering X spelled out CRIME SCENE - DO NOT CROSS, or if not exactly that, something very close.

Before leaving the lot of the mini-mart, I had ripped open the blister card containing the toy, pulled out the thin, stamped metal badge, and tossed the rest into the garbage receptacle near the payphone. Since it was positioned toward the far end of the building, I hadn't had to worry too much about the attendant seeing me throw away the bulk of my recent purchase, which I am betting would have raised a bit of suspicion.

Now that I was sitting here in the darkness, I pulled my wallet from my back pocket and emptied it, save for my driver's license which I left in the display slot on one side. I was counting on the fact that being a Missouri issue would make it look different enough to appear like an official law enforcement ID. The rest of the contents, credit cards, cash and the like, I stuffed into my jacket pocket and zipped it closed.

Fumbling with the toy badge, I undid the pin and forced it through the inner layer of my wallet opposite my license, managing to stab myself in the fingertip twice while doing so. Once I succeeded in finally getting the fake shield decently positioned and secured, I simply sat back in my seat and stared at it. Out here in the darkness, it looked pretty good—to an untrained eye, maybe even like the real thing.

I practiced flipping the improvised ID case open, giving a silent count, then snapping it back shut, trying to instantly master what I'd seen Ben and the other cops I'd worked with do so many times in the past. My big problem was that I was going to need to look convincing but still only show the badge long enough to create a belief that I was official. If I was asked to let someone see it up close, I was in trouble.

If it weren't for the fact that I was so nervous, I might have considered trying to throw a little magick behind the ruse. It was really all just the power of suggestion combined with a bit of inner energy to create what, in the parlance of WitchCraft, was called a glamour. In short, it was an illusion. A way of making someone believe they were seeing something that wasn't really there. I actually had more than half the battle won already, given the physical appearance of the toy. But, casting a glamour involved affecting someone's will, and while I wasn't so white-light as to have a problem with that, I did seem to be having issues controlling my own will at the moment, much less someone else's. Applying magick to the situation just seemed like a very bad idea, especially magick born of anxious energy. Of course, everything about what I was planning to do fell smack into the middle of the bad idea category, so it probably didn't matter.

At one point it even dawned on me that some of the most

notorious serial rapists and killers in recent history had used this very trick to gain the trust of their victims. This type of musing wasn't new to me. I'd had thoughts like it before. In fact, I often wondered if my unfettered psychic connections to both the victims, and at times the criminals themselves, were doing irreparable damage to my psyche. This was, however, the first time that such contemplation left me afraid that due to that possible damage, I might be becoming just like them.

I sighed and tried to forget about the knot of fear that my wandering brain had just created in my already churning stomach. I had enough to worry about without tossing that in on top of it.

The time had been pushing 3:45AM when I shut off the car, and by now I was sure to have been sitting here for a solid fifteen minutes, maybe even longer, prepping the phony badge and trying to work up the courage to actually use it. I looked across the lot at the office. It was dark except for the pink neon glow of the NO VACANCY sign in the window. This wasn't necessarily a bad thing, and I hoped that it just might work to my advantage.

I took one last sip of my coffee and swallowed hard before settling it into the cup holder and getting out of the vehicle. Though the temperature had been mild earlier, and I am certain that it hadn't suffered any significant change, I felt a damp chill run the length of my spine. It hit me like a rush of excitement in fact, and that worried me. However, I pressed on across the quiet lot.

Arriving at the office door, I reached out and gave it a tug, only to find that it was locked just as I had hoped it would be. It would definitely increase my chances of being able to pull this off if I could hang here in the shadows where the darkness could obscure the telltale giveaways surrounding the lie.

I hesitated for a moment, then reached up and rapped my knuckles hard on the glass pane of the door. I waited as thirty seconds stretched into one minute, and then that folded itself into two. Seeing no movement inside, I hammered my fist against the door again. This time a dim light switched on and was visible through the doorway behind the small check-in desk. I stood watching my reflection in the mirror on the back wall and waited. A short moment later, a disheveled, middle-aged woman in a housecoat appeared through the opening and squinted at me. Immediately shooting me a disgusted look, she pointed at the glowing NO VACANCY sign and started to turn.

I thumped the heel of my palm against the door once again to get her attention then flipped open my wallet and pressed it against the glass. Up until this point I could have turned and walked away, no harm, no foul. But now I was committed, and in the back of my head I was telling myself that was exactly what I needed to be, committed— although my inner voice was using a vastly different sense of the word.

The woman squinted at me again, and I watched her closely as my heart raced. Her face sagged, and then her posture seemed to relax somewhat as she started through the opening and out around the desk. It then came to my attention that I was holding my breath, so I let it out slowly and took in a fresh lungful of air as I waited. She continued across the lobby toward the door, and when she was within a few feet, I slowly pulled the wallet away, flipped it shut and tucked it into my jacket pocket.

A moment later the deadbolt clicked, and she pushed the door open.

"How can I help you, officer?" she asked through a tired yawn. While her voice was definitely cloaked with the hallmark cadence of the region, her accent seemed to hail more from the mid-South; therefore, she lacked the clipping of syllables I'd learned to expect from natives of the area.

I felt a fresh chill traverse my spine, but this time it wasn't a sense of excitement. It was more a sense of fear—but not for myself. I was afraid for her and the fact that she had so willingly believed I was a cop without closer inspection of my credentials. I tried my best not to let it show and instead simply pasted on what I believed to be an official looking expression.

"Sorry to disturb you, ma'am," I launched into my spiel. "My name is Gant, I'm a special investigations consultant with the Major Case Squad in Saint Louis, Missouri."

I had considered using an alias but figured I would just stumble over it if I did. Considering the amount of deception I was forcing myself to engage in all at once, I thought keeping it simple would be my best course of action. Besides, if I did this correctly, I could get away with a majority of planned misdirection and only a little actual falsehood. In fact, so far I hadn't lied so much as tested the elasticity of a not quite current truth. I was, in fact, a consultant to the MCS, just not lately. Splitting hairs, I know, but I was trying to work within a scheme that would keep my anxiety at bay, otherwise I knew I would never be able to pull this off.

"I'd love to help you, hun, but cop or no, I still don't have a vacancy."

"Actually, ma'am, I'm here on official business," I continued. "There was a homicide here last week, correct?"

"Yes, and I've been paying for it ever since," she grumbled. "Fortunately, it hasn't kept the Feds from renting the rooms."

"So I see," I acknowledged, pointing toward the neon sign. "Well, the reason I'm here is to look over the scene."

She cocked her head then asked, "But I thought you said you were from Missouri, hun?"

"Yes, ma'am," I replied with a nod. "I can't really get into any details other than to say we have a couple of cases in Saint Louis that appear to be related to this one."

"Like maybe a serial killer, you mean?" she pressed.

"I really couldn't speculate about that," I replied, shrugging as I shook my head. "I'm just here to look at the crime scene."

She reached up with her free hand and rubbed her eyes, then shot a quick glance at her watch. Looking back to my face, she asked, "This couldn't wait until morning?"

"I know." I shook my head apologetically. "But the lieutenant sent me down here for a quick look. I just got in a little while ago and drove straight here. My flight back home leaves at ten so I only have a few hours."

"They don't give you much time to work, do they?"

"That's just how it happens sometimes."

"All right then, hun," she said. "Let me get my shoes, and I'll take you on down to the room."

"You know," I offered. "I've really disturbed you way too much already. If you just want to give me the key, I'll go have a look and then drop it back through the mail slot when I'm done. That way you can get back to bed."

"Okay," she said, giving me a quick nod. It sounded almost as if there was a note of relief in her voice. "Let me get it for you."

She turned and headed back around the check-in desk, rummaged beneath it for a moment, then returned to the door with a key that was attached to a bright red, diamond-shaped piece of plastic, which was emblazoned with a large number 7.

Handing it to me, she pushed the door open a little farther and pointed down the length of the building. She stifled a yawn then said, "Room seven. All the way down in the corner, hun. Can't miss it with that damn tape up."

My face must have betrayed the sudden flutter in my stomach as I took the key. Room 7 had been the ongoing theme with Miranda. It was the number on the doors where both Hobbes and Wentworth were killed in Saint Louis. And, it had even been the room at the no-tell palace where Felicity had taken a potential victim when under the *Lwa's* control.

"Something wrong, hun?" the woman asked.

"N…no," I half stammered, catching myself and quickly trying to come up with a plausible excuse for my sudden reticence. "I was just thinking that seven wasn't such a lucky number for the victim."

"That's a fact," she replied with a shallow nod. "Odd enough he specifically asked for it too."

I wasn't surprised by the comment. The desk clerk where Wentworth was murdered had said the same thing. He had explicitly requested room 7.

"Yeah," I agreed. "Odd that it was even available. When I called down here it took forever to find some place with a vacancy."

The words were out of my mouth before I even realized what I was saying. I had just managed to contradict my entire fabrication with a single slip of the tongue. A fresh spasm hit my stomach, but I tried to ignore it and nonchalantly turn my head toward the distant room in hopes that I could hide any expression it might involuntarily evoke.

A second later I sighed then turned back to her and said, "I'm sorry. I've really kept you long enough, ma'am."

If she had noticed my slip-up, there was nothing in her face that said as much. She simply pointed to the mail slot in the door and replied, "It's no problem, hun. You can just drop the key in here when you're finished."

"Will do, and thank you very much. Again, I'm sorry I had to disturb you at this hour." I was doing my best to recover from my stumble and sound official, so I added, "Now, make sure you lock the door behind you."

She simply nodded in reply, but I waited until she was back inside and I heard the click of the deadbolt before I turned and headed toward the room.

"Dammit! Stupid. Stupid." I muttered the admonishment to myself as I walked.

Concerned that I might need to simply veer toward my car instead of continuing on with this insanity, I cast a furtive glance back over my shoulder. Fortunately, I didn't notice anything unusual, such as her spying on me from the window, so I mutely worked at convincing myself she was half asleep and had completely missed the gaffe.

It didn't take me very long to cover the distance between the office and the far corner of the building, and though I made it a point to walk at a modest pace, my heart was thumping hard against my ribcage by the time I arrived at the door.

I stood there for a minute, simply inspecting the surroundings. The physical characteristics of the building made room 7 an obvious choice even over and above Miranda's penchant for the number. The way this particular end of the structure terminated, there was an open stairwell leading up to the second story of the addition. That dead space would have acted as a sound barrier to dull any errant cries from her victim. Still, there was a room on the opposite side of this one and, given the limited availability of lodging in the city lately, it almost had to have been occupied by someone. Had that been the case, surely the guest would have heard something.

I gave my head a small shake then reached up and massaged my temples. I was tired, I had a headache, and I had just lied my way into a crime scene. My brain was launching into rampant speculation while ignoring the facts. It remained that a murder had occurred in room 7, and no one had reported anything suspicious, so I needed to stop over thinking the situation and just do what I came here to do.

Glancing back toward the office, I still didn't see anything to raise any alarms. Turning in place, I saw nothing on the parking lot to worry me either. Giving up and deciding I must be in the clear, I stuck the key into the lock.

The moment metal touched metal, I felt the chill on my spine once again. This one, however, was just like the first, carrying with it not fear but a feeling of excitement. As sick as it seemed, the sense of elation literally felt like the passionate rush of anticipated sexual release, and it coursed through me, branching out to touch every nerve. At that instant, there was no doubt in my mind that Annalise and Miranda had been here.

I closed my eyes, drew in a deep breath, and then let it back out slowly as I struggled to ground myself, mentally fighting to maintain a solid earthly connection and not allow the cries of the dead to drag me across the veil. Then, opening my eyes once again, I twisted the key in the lock and pushed the door open, tearing the tape seal between it and the jamb in the process.

Ducking beneath the yellow crime scene tape, I stepped into *her* world.

CHAPTER 5:

I froze in place, an involuntary physical pause brought about purely by things felt, rather than seen.

I had only taken a single step across the threshold and then come back upright before hitting the invisible wall. Now, as I stood there motionless, the incandescent bulbs in the walkway overhang were spilling illumination inward through the open door at my back. The light edged in past my form, revealing random bits of the room in narrow swaths, making it appear far more eerie than I suppose it would have under less horrific circumstances. Of course, it didn't help that my own distorted shadow fell along the floor down the center of the oblique display and then disappeared into the otherwise blue-black darkness, adding an urgent sense of foreboding to the overall picture.

Of everything permeating the unmoving air, to me, sex was the most palpable. But, it wasn't the same stale funk of peddled intercourse and spent prophylactics that oozed throughout my lodging back at the Airline Courts. In fact, sweet watermelon, cigarette smoke, and what might have been a hint of burnt flesh were actually what formed the base of the obvious olfactory signature here. However, raw, uninhibited sex was definitely the high note, and in that way, it rose above everything else.

Simply being the accent, however, wasn't good enough for it where I was concerned. It hit me hard and didn't let up. Even at a week old, the assaulting pheromones seemed fresh enough to have been released into the atmosphere only a moment before. Unfortunately for me, my awareness of things ethereal served only to amplify their effects several fold, and no amount of grounding could stop them.

But, even then it went deeper still. Intertwined with the base physicality were two very distinct emotions—love and fear. And, even given the opposite natures of the two, it was obvious to me that they were not mutually exclusive. Though starkly different, the feelings wrapped around one another and then wove themselves tightly into the sex itself. On the surface, they seemed symbiotic, feeding on one another in an endlessly growing spiral of depravity.

I blinked hard in the darkness then forced myself to relax and simply observe. I didn't know how long I would be able to actually accomplish that feat, but for now it worked, and that was enough to allow me to move once again. Taking a pair of steps farther inward, I twisted in place, carefully shut the door, and then flipped on the light switch before turning back to scan the interior.

It looked much as I had imagined it would. Cheap paneling covered the walls, leading upward from dark institutional grade carpeting and ending at an off-white acoustically textured ceiling. A single light fixture clung to the center of that light-colored plane, spreading luminance downward from a pair of medium wattage bulbs.

A full bed all but dominated the narrow room, jutting out from the wall to my left. It had already been stripped of linens, but the vinyl mattress cover showed several rusted smears of varying size and shape that I suspected were the product of blood that had soaked through the sheets. Along the wall to my right was a low dresser with a television perched on its marred top.

Also to the right of center, on the back wall was a doorway leading into a small room housing a vanity-style sink and dressing mirror; left of that, on the perpendicular wall I could see what was most likely the door to the shower and toilet. Oddly, in the far left corner of the main room, a table lamp and telephone sat on the floor between two outdated chairs. A small, round table that looked like it might have originally made a home beneath them was sidled up close to the head of the bed.

I stepped slowly through the space, negotiating the tight area between the foot of the mattress and the short bureau. All the while I was fighting against feelings of arousal. Under different circumstances I am sure I would have considered it a pleasant sensation, but at the moment it seemed sick and twisted. It kept hammering at me, gaining ground with each shuffling step I took.

I paused again and took a deep breath, focusing instead on the pounding headache I'd been trying so hard to forget. The pain wasn't exactly what I would call welcome, but it was preferable to the sickening idea of being turned on by what had happened here, and that was the ethereal sensation I needed to deny.

Extreme arousal was almost too mild a description for the feeling that had been coming over me as I stood out on the walkway, and now that I was directly exposed to the scene, the excitation was taking over. Though I was alone and had no need to speak, what little of my rational self that remained wanted desperately to put what I was feeling into words. However, try as I might, nouns, adjectives and any other modifier for that matter had become all but meaningless. I could think of no way to accurately convey the sensation with simple syllables. Even the verbal theatrics of an adult film didn't seem as though they would do it justice.

I had felt something very similar to this at the crime scenes in Saint Louis and had thought it close to overwhelming then. I had even experienced it all first hand the night Felicity had tried to kill me while under Miranda's control. However, each of those instances was merely a faint hint in comparison to now.

I'm sure that at the other scenes the sensation had probably been masked by a host of conflicting energies occupying the room, namely evidence technicians and cops. As for the night of my direct encounter, I was too busy dealing with my own fear to take much notice of anything else.

This, however, was different. It was the first instance in which I had been alone and unthreatened in *her* world. Although, whether or not I was truly unthreatened remained to be seen.

Even as I concentrated on the aching in my skull, an intense and very pleasant tickle slowly undulated through my groin. I instantly caught my breath and even felt myself rock slightly as my knees seemed to buckle momentarily. Even though it was a shock, the level of pleasure the sensation carried with it was unlike anything I had ever felt before. I felt sick to my stomach at the thought of what had caused it, but at the same time it felt so amazing that I found myself consciously wishing it would happen again.

Out of reflex I looked down. Even though no one was here but me, I couldn't keep from making a self-conscious check to be certain I wasn't embarrassing myself. Surprisingly, given the nature and intensity of the sensation, what one would assume to be the affected body part appeared to be at rest, and nothing was out of place.

But, then, when I gave it some thought, I suppose it shouldn't have been such a surprise after all. There was something about the sexual energy that was alien, and having been down this road before, I knew exactly what it was. The arousal was patently feminine, just as the fear was wholly masculine.

I simply stood there for at least a solid minute, maybe even two, struggling to center my thoughts on the ethereal migraine and deny the other sensation. If my ploy was truly working I couldn't say, but since there was no repeat of the tickle, I pressed forward.

Continuing around the end of the bed, I made my way over to the table. Its surface was crusted with reddish-brown smears of dried blood in various patterns just like the mattress cover. One recognizable outline was almost certainly that of a knife or maybe even a pair of scissors. Others were not so defined, some of them large, some of them small. I had seen what Miranda had done to Officer Hobbes back in Saint Louis, so I knew mutilation was a big part of her sick turn-on. Therefore, it really wasn't a stretch for me to imagine a severed body part or two from the victim being responsible for the more generous stains.

Here and there, around the edges of the table, a silvery glint of bi-chromatic fingerprint powder glimmered in the soft light. A basic effort to go through the motions, I assumed, because I'm sure the police didn't really expect to find anything by way of a usable print here.

Thus far I had been observing a hands off policy, making it a point to look but not touch. I wish I could say the decision was because I didn't want to disturb anything given that the scene had apparently not yet been cleared. However, noble as it sounded, that idea had become moot the moment I pushed open the door. I had broken the seal, so if the police needed to return in search of further evidence, I had already rendered anything they might find inadmissible because I had contaminated the room, thereby breaking the chain. I wasn't really certain whether what I had done was a misdemeanor or a felony, or even what penalty it carried. But, I was definitely hoping I wouldn't be finding out anytime soon.

To be painfully honest, the real reason I was keeping my hands to myself was self-preservation because I feared my inherent predisposition for uncontrolled psychometry. Simply being in this room had already bombarded me with more than I was sure I could handle, the most recent sensation being a case in point. Actually touching something could put me into a spiral, sending me through an ethereal event from which I might not recover.

It's not like it hadn't happened before. Over the years I'd almost died more than once while channeling homicide victims. I wasn't too keen on it then, and I definitely wasn't interested in becoming one of Miranda's fatalities by proxy now.

Squatting down, I brought myself to eye level with the bed. I don't know what I thought I was going to see from that angle, but one never knows until he tries, so I did. I panned my gaze across the tableau and tried to visualize what had gone on here one short week ago. Having had what amounted to my own firsthand experience, I expected it would be relatively easy to do. What I didn't expect, however, was the visualization coming upon me with a vengeance.

In front of me, there is a nude man tied to the bed, a standard clothesline rope criss-crossing beneath the metal frame and securing tightly to his wrists and ankles. An extra loop of the rope is visible around his neck. The reason for it becomes clear as I watch him struggling against the bonds. Each time he pulls against them, the noose tightens and he begins to choke. I can actually hear the distant echoes of him gagging, muffled though they are, as his mouth is covered with a wide swath of duct tape which is wound about his head and lower face.

I watch as, with each desperate twist or pull, the rope bites deeper into his throat, forcing him to cease his fight. A look of suddenly realized terror is filling his eyes, and between each bout of choking himself, he lets out a nasal whine.

I know that seeing this should disturb me, but it doesn't. Not in the way that it should.

What actually does disturb me is that I feel no compassion as I watch him. No empathy. But, even that isn't the worst of it. If I was feeling nothing at all, perhaps I could make sense of my uncharacteristic disregard by attributing it to a forced clinical detachment.

But, unfortunately, that isn't the case.

I am feeling something.

I am amused.

Worse than that, the tickle has returned, and I am becoming increasingly aroused by his plight.

Though the immediate feelings I had sensed upon entering the room had been a combination of both killer and victim, my primary concern for my own safety had been in regard to him. Not *her*. While I'd had my brushes with channeling killers, they were always alive when I had done so. Though I knew that this one, or at least part of her, wasn't, I hadn't considered it as fully as I should have, and now that changed everything.

The dead were the ones who spoke loudest in my head, and they were the ones who most often tried to pull me deeper into their world in an effort to make me understand. I suppose I couldn't blame them for trying to get their points across any way they could. Dead or not, everyone has a story to tell, and it helps if someone will listen.

But, this one didn't just want someone to listen. She wanted someone to control. Though I could feel the victim and hear his anguish, he was a bit player on this mental stage. Miranda had a far stronger presence, and she intended to dominate the scene now—just as she had done then.

That was one of the problems with channeling. It didn't really matter what you as the channeler wanted or even what you personally found to be distasteful. You were simply a conduit, and it was all about the likes and dislikes of the one flowing through you.

I definitely didn't want Miranda this close to me, but it was too late. She was already inside my head, or I obviously wouldn't be feeling the things I did. It was this realization that I clung to, using it as a shield against her onslaught and denying her control over me. My gut feeling was that I needed to cut and run right away because I no longer feared becoming her victim, I was afraid of becoming *her*. Given the pure insanity of that very thought, I was starting to believe all of this wasn't just a risky move—it was a flat out mistake.

But, I also knew that if I left now, I would leave empty-handed. All the deception and trespassing I had engaged in so far were only worth the gamble if I was going to have something to show for them in the end. I had to keep going until I found something tangible that would help me locate—and stop—both of these killers.

Of course, a raging psychosexual event that might possibly leave me blithering in ethereal bliss was definitely not the result I needed, especially when one considered the imagery that would bring it about. Unfortunately, that seemed to be where this was all heading, and very quickly at that.

Since running wasn't an option, I decided maybe I should find a different way to approach all of this. But, before I could do that, I was going to have to back out of the path I had already taken.

I started to stand up but found I was once again frozen in place, unable to make myself move. I chose to try the same thing I had done earlier—I blinked hard and willed the image to go away

But, when my eyes fluttered open, it remained. In fact, it seemed even more tangible than it had before. It looked real enough to reach out and touch, and I even found that I had to stop myself from doing just that.

Trying again, I drew in a deep breath, shut my eyes, then slipped my thumb and forefinger beneath the rim of my glasses and pinched the bridge of my nose. After a moment, I let the breath slowly out through my mouth and allowed my hand to fall. With trepidation, I opened my eyes once again.

He still hadn't gone away, and now it was even worse—*because he had company.*

CHAPTER 6:

The new arrival in question was a petite redhead, and it was visibly obvious from what I saw happening in front of me that she was this poor man's worst nightmare. Unfortunately, he was not alone in that, as she was mine too.

I had a sense, within the vision at least, that a good deal of time had passed between what I had been witnessing moments ago and what I was seeing now. It appeared that the man was still alive, but judging from the visible wounds, blood, and burn marks on his face, I could only surmise that Miranda was well into his torture at this point.

As I watched, conflict stormed through my brain in the form of internal voices locked in a heated debate. One of them was demanding in no uncertain terms that I close my eyes or look away immediately. It was telling me I should do whatever it takes to break this connection. I knew in my gut this was the voice I should be listening to, but it was only one of the three bickering inside my skull; and, the other two were ganging up on it.

The second voice was countering that if I didn't watch what was being offered, everything I had risked would be for naught. It was telling me I might miss a vital clue that would allow me to stop her. While that had once been a valid point, I wasn't so sure if I believed it anymore.

The real problem was the second voice's partner in all this. It was the one that worried me most. It came to me as little more than a murmur of support for the heretofore failing argument; however, I wasn't completely fooled. I could sense that it had its own agenda with a horribly dark intent. But, even more frightening than its intent was the power it seemed to carry with it. I only wished that I had recognized that fact a bit sooner because it wasn't until it had all but assumed control that I realized the source—it had joined forces with the sickeningly pleasant tickle that had been set loose in my body, and together they were drowning out all good sense and reason. As I had feared, Miranda was trying me on for size.

Even as I fought to maintain control, my tenuous grip on my perceived reality faltered, and the vision stepped in to take its place.

Though I can see her only in profile, I swear that my wife is in front of me at this very moment, sitting astride the bound man. She is positioned such that she is pitched backward; her arms are outstretched behind her, straining and rigid. Her hands are clamped firmly to his thighs as she supports herself. Her back is arched, and her chest is rising and falling at a quickened pace. I can hear her panting just as I can hear the man's muffled squeals of agony.

She has one stocking-clad leg extended in front of her, bent slightly at the knee, and I see the muscles of her calf flexing as they keep a tight rhythm with her panting breaths. Her foot is pressed against the man's upper arm, pinning it against the headboard. Her calf is flexing because she is slowly twisting her stiletto heel into the flesh of his bicep. The end of the spike disappears into the deep depression it has created, and blood is oozing from the wound.

Colors bloomed as realities once again shifted, and I found myself back in the motel room alone. The roller coaster ride of channeled visions was tossing me haphazardly about and depositing me wherever its whim desired. Not particularly unusual as such ethereal events go, but I didn't think I would ever get used to it.

I blinked.

I remembered Ben telling me before I ever boarded the plane to come here that he was looking at a picture of Annalise and that she was a dead ringer for Felicity. I suppose, however, that simply hearing someone say something like that makes it easy to discount their opinion. Even though I hadn't seen the picture myself, I was positive that I, of all people, would have no trouble telling the two women apart. After all, I had been married to one of them for almost fifteen years, so surely I would know my own wife.

However, at this moment my personal perception was no longer crystal clear on that point.

Without thinking, I muttered aloud, "Felicity?"

Her name tumbled into the room wrapped in a question. I knew the woman I had just seen in front of me couldn't possibly be my wife, but the image was truly beyond uncanny.

As if triggered by my question, the light overhead bloomed, and I once again found myself with at least one foot in a different plane of existence.

I can hear my own voice echoing in the room as I utter my wife's name.

Though her breathing never alters from its frantic pace, the woman suddenly jerks as if startled. Pushing herself forward, she sits up, still straddling the man. She stops twisting her heel then drops her foot down to the bed, and her victim is given a momentary reprieve from his agony. Cocking her head to one side, she appears to be listening intently, as if she hears my voice as well.

Slowly she turns toward me.

I study her face as she looks through me, creasing her brow. I can begin to see the differences in her features, but not at first glance, or even the second for that matter. I takes a long moment before I am certain that I am not looking at my wife.

I remember hearing it said that everyone has a doppelganger somewhere on the planet. Whether or not that is a scientific fact I cannot begin to say, but given the vision now staring me in the face, I am inclined to believe it. This woman can almost pass as Felicity Caitlin O'Brien's twin.

She turns, and showing little concern for her victim, she drags her now bloody heel across him as she climbs from the bed. She slowly saunters toward the window at the front of the room and stands there, still listening for a repeat of the sound.

Though not fully nude as is her victim, she is scantily dressed.

What little of her wardrobe there is consists of black lace and patent leather. Her red hair cascades in a loose spiraling fall down her back. It feels hot in the room, and I can see that her exposed ivory skin is damp with sweat. It glistens in dim light as she remains still except for the rise and fall of her shoulders as she breathes. On her left shoulder, I can see what appears to be a tattoo of a stylized triskele.

I have seen it before. It is the mystery veve *from the previous crime scenes.*

After several minutes she reaches out and slips a finger between the slats of the blinds. Slowly, she presses down, opening a small gap through which she carefully peers.

I watch her as she tilts her head from side to side until finally she is satisfied that no one is there. Turning, she saunters back to the bed and looks down at the bound victim.

"Don't worry, little man. It was nothing," she says to him in a sweet drawl. She takes a moment to flip an errant shock of hair back over her shoulder then adds with a feigned pout, "Of course, that nothing *interrupted me, so I guess we'll just have to start over."*

Sliding one knee onto the bed, she dips forward and scoops something into her hand before bringing the other leg up. Kneeling next to him, she smiles sweetly and holds up a stun gun.

"Ready?" she asks.

He begins to buck against the bonds, a scream caught behind the duct tape gag and diverting to exit in the form of a short, nasally whine through his nose before being unceremoniously cut off as he chokes.

"Good," she giggles. "So am I. Just remember, I love you."

With a wicked grin, she leans forward and presses the business end of the device against his bare genitals and squeezes the trigger.

I buckle and begin falling backward as I feel his pain.

But what's worse is that I also feel her pleasure.

In that moment everything shifted, and the three-dimensional quality of the vision flattened then faded in a bloom of light. I could instantly sense that I had stepped back into my own world, but both the sensation of pain and arousal remained.

Though I had felt myself falling, I found that in reality I hadn't moved at all. I was still squatting next to the bed, staring directly ahead, just as I had been at the beginning. I did notice, however, that I was holding my breath. I let it out with a heavy sigh. My eyes were itching and dry, so I closed them, but the moment I did so I feared I would regret the action. It seemed that blinking was getting me into a lot of trouble right now. Still, I knew that sitting here forever with my eyes closed wasn't going to get me anywhere, so I steeled myself in preparation for the onslaught of another round and allowed them to flutter open.

This time, the vision was still gone.

Letting out another sigh, this one of a semi-relieved nature, I rocked back on my heels and stood upright. Reaching to my face, I removed my glasses and rubbed my eyes. Slipping the spectacles back on, I gazed around the room. Everything was just as it had been when I entered. Nothing had changed, no matter how real the things I had just witnessed may have felt.

Making a slow half turn exactly where I stood, I finally wandered back to the small room housing the vanity. Removing my glasses once again, I twisted on the faucet and cupped my hands beneath it. Bending over the sink, I first pressed one handful of water against my face and then another. After a third, I turned the water off and leaned forward with my knuckles on the vanity as I stood there dripping into the basin.

The phantom pain in my groin had faded away, but the sense of arousal had only grown stronger. It was still distinctly feminine, however, and was as odd to me as it was pleasant. Of course, it also made me feel terribly ill.

"Gods, Gant..." I muttered to myself. "Just get the hell out of here while you're still sane."

"Gant?" her honey dipped drawl floats into my ears. "So that's

who you are."

I am still standing at the basin, and I know the voice has come from behind me. Without bothering to dry my face, I pick up my glasses and slip them on then turn to look out into the main room.

She is perched on the edge of the bed, on the side nearest me. But, she has changed. Her hair is dark auburn and piled atop her head in a soft swirl reminiscent of a long ago era, which matches the high-necked Victorian dress she now wears. What I see of her face is stern, and far more oval shaped than before.

She is seated next to the headboard, and I can still see the man sprawled out behind her. He appears the same although there seems to be far more wounds on his body than there had been before.

She flickers like a frame jumping on a movie at the theater.

Her hair is once again fiery red and long. She is back to being a scantily dressed mirror image of my wife. She uncrosses her legs and re-crosses them in the opposite direction, stretching one out as she does so. She smoothes her stocking carefully then regards it with little emotion.

"Damn," she says, her voice flat. "A run."

She still hasn't looked in my direction, and I begin to think that perhaps I was simply hearing things. I begin to turn away.

"Where are you going?" she asks.

I stop and furrow my brow.

"Yes, I'm talking to you, little man," she continues, still without looking at me. Instead she seems to be intent on the items she has piled on the small table next to her.

"Me?" I ask calmly.

"Yes, you."

"How? You aren't even really here."

"You tell me," she counters. "It's your vision, now isn't it? Ah, there it is..."

She smiles and holds up a scissors-style cigar cutter.

"Right now I think I would prefer to believe you're a figment of my imagination," I tell her.

She shrugs. "If you want to believe that."

"You left it up to me."

She counters with a question. "Yes, I did. But you aren't that stupid, now are you?"

"No." I shake my head. "Unfortunately, I don't suppose I am."

She giggles. My answer is obviously amusing to her. Canting her head to the side but still not looking in my direction she says, "You belong to her *don't you?"*

It is a statement as much as a question, however, I ask, "Her who?"

"The her *who is taking what is mine," she spits. "Felicity, I believe is what you said."*

"I have no idea what you're talking about."

She carefully trims the end from a cigar then sets it alight. Silence flows between us as I watch her. A thin stream of blue-white smoke comes from between her pursed lips as she blows on the glowing tobacco and inspects to see that it is burning evenly. Placing the lit end in her mouth, she then exhales slowly through it, sending a cloud of pungent smoke billowing from the end. I know all too well that she is "smoking it" for her Lwa.

After a moment she pulls it from her mouth and rests it on the edge of the table.

Again, there is a theatrical flicker, and the stern, auburn-haired woman is in her place.

"You're lying. I think you do know," she says as if there had never been a lull in the conversation.

"Why do you think that?"

"Because you feel it."

"Feel what?"

She finally looks up at me and smiles thinly, her dark eyes piercing. Reaching to the side, she takes hold of the victim's hand. He is securely bound so he is unable to pull away, but a horrified squeal begins behind her as he struggles, only to be interrupted by her careful method of bondage. I hear a metallic snick and watch as she slips the cigar cutter over his pinkie finger at the second joint.

"The same thing we are going to feel when I do this," she says and punctuates the sentence by bearing down and squeezing the cutter closed.

The stir that had been wriggling deep inside my body flared in that exact instant. No longer was it simply extreme arousal; it was now tickling nerve endings I didn't even know I had. The result was a pleasure so intense as to be literally excruciating in its scope. I now knew the true meaning of having something feel so good that it hurt.

The room began to spin and then everything went completely black.

I opened my eyes and the acoustically textured ceiling filled my field of view. I felt spent in a way I had never experienced before, and to say I was confused wasn't doing my current state any justice. I was completely addled. I was in agony deep inside, but it was a pain born of emptiness. An ache that called out, begging to be filled by the pleasure once again.

With a groan, I started to sit up but felt a firm pressure pushing me back down. I fell back and my head thumped against the floor.

I blinked.

Now I not only saw the ceiling but Annalise as well. She was leaning over me, one high-heel encased foot pressing down on my chest and holding me to the floor.

"Tell Felicity I want it back," she said. "All of it."

In that moment everything shifted, and the three-dimensional quality of the vision flattened then faded in a bloom of light. I was still squatting next to the bed, staring directly ahead as I had been at the beginning. I did notice, however, that I was holding my breath. I let it out with a heavy sigh. My eyes were itching and dry, so I closed them, but the moment I did so I feared I would regret the action. It seemed that blinking was getting me into a lot of trouble right now. Still, I knew that sitting here forever with my eyes closed wasn't going to get me anywhere, so I steeled myself in preparation for the onslaught of another round and allowed them to flutter open.

The vision was still gone.

I stood up, rubbed my eyes, then turned and started back toward the small room housing the vanity. I had only made it two steps when I caught myself and came to a halt.

An unbelievably intense feeling of *déjà vu* overwhelmed me as recent memories flooded in. Though the hollowness still ached deep inside, my rational brain pushed through the fog and assumed control once again. I decided not to bother with a repeat of the trip to the sink that I wasn't even sure I had really made. I simply needed to get out of here before leaving became impossible.

Turning, I headed toward the front of the room, skirting around the end of the bed then reaching the door in two quick steps. Any sense of stealth and caution to which I had earlier subscribed was now depleted. I pulled the door open and stepped out into the night, almost forgetting to tug it closed behind me. Starting up the walk, I broke into a jog, trying to put distance between the scene and me as fast as I could.

I gave my watch a quick glance and figured that I'd only been in the room for a little over twenty minutes. It had seemed like much longer, but that was the way of things with ethereal visions. They seemed to run by a clock all their own.

Nearing the office, I fished the room key out of my jacket pocket and popped it through the mail slot, barely stopping as I did so. Turning, I started on an angle across the lot toward my car.

I had only made it a few steps when the authoritative voice hit my ears.

"FREEZE! POLICE! LEMME SEE YA' HANDS, RIGHT NOW!"

CHAPTER 7:

My arms were starting to go numb.

Of course, since my hands were still cuffed behind my back, I don't suppose I should have been surprised by that fact. I shifted slightly forward in the metal chair then rotated my shoulders as much as I could manage in an attempt to jumpstart the circulation. While I was leaning, I extended two fingers on my right hand, grasped them with my left, and held tight. It was a trick Ben had taught me long ago to relieve the pressure of the cuffs on my wrists. At the time, I hadn't really understood why he assumed I would need such knowledge. It wasn't like I had a tendency to get myself arrested. However, I was grateful for the arcane tip now since it afforded at least a small amount of relief from the biting restraints.

I glanced around at the blue-green walls in search of a clock. I was guessing that I had been warming this chair for better than an hour, but my sense of time was so screwed at the moment it might have been no more than fifteen minutes. By that same token, it could easily have been half a day. I simply didn't know. Twisting slightly in my seat, I looked back over my shoulder to inspect the wall behind me and found nothing but another sea of nauseating blue-green. I'd already engaged in this futile exercise more times than I could count, so why I was bothering again I had no idea. There was nothing for me to see, other than the sickening color and the one-way mirror across the room in front of me. For all I knew, someone was on the opposite side of it watching me. In fact, I would bet hard money on it.

Settling back in, I hung my head and spent some time staring at the worn, grey carpet. It was patterned with more than its share of stains, the origins of which I didn't even want to speculate over. But, when you have little else to do, your brain will tend to entertain itself however it wants, so it set about trying to identify the oddly shaped splotches of its own accord, regardless of my feelings on the subject.

As I sat staring at what I had decided was most likely the fossilized remains of a coffee spill, I could hear one of the ballasts on the fluorescent light fixture above me humming toward extinction. It wasn't terribly loud just yet, but I suspected it would be in the not too distant future. Hopefully, I would be out of here by then and wouldn't be around to hear it when it finally died. Of course, given my current predicament, there were probably worse places I could be.

The officer who had brought me here referred to the building as *The Bureau.* I hadn't seen much of it, but judging from what I had glimpsed, I assumed this was where the detectives were based as opposed to the uniformed officers. That wasn't much of a surprise either. Given that I had cajoled my way into a sealed crime scene, it stood to reason that I had raised more than a few eyebrows in all the wrong places. I'm sure I had probably managed to make myself a suspect of some sort.

My sleep-deprived brain mulled that over for a moment before forcing me to let out an involuntary harrumph. So far, Felicity had been accused of the murders, new evidence pointed to the real killer being a half-sister she never knew she had, and now I was up to my neck in the wrong side of the investigation. I suppose there was nothing quite like keeping it all in the family.

I had just set my sights on identifying a different stain a foot or so over from the first when the relative silence of the interview room was broken by the sound of the door swinging open. I looked up in the direction of the noise and saw a disheveled looking man enter then push the door closed behind him. He appeared to be somewhere around my own age, maybe a few years older, and from the looks of him, I would have guessed he was running on nearly the same amount of sleep as me.

He didn't say anything initially. Instead he simply took the few steps over to the metal table that was positioned in front of me and stood there silently reading something in a manila folder. After several languid moments, he shut the folder and tossed it onto the surface of the table.

"Get up and face the back wall," he grunted.

I slowly rocked forward in the chair and stood, then made the quarter turn in place, finding myself once again staring at a panorama of putrid blue-green. It was a good thing my stomach wasn't bothering me at the moment, or I might have added another stain to the carpet.

I heard the rattling of metal against metal and felt the pressure encircling my left wrist ease up, then the strain on my shoulders as well. After another rattle, I could feel the bracelet being removed from my right.

"Thanks," I muttered, not sure if I should say anything or simply remain quiet.

He didn't acknowledge my gratitude. Instead he simply said, "Sit down and keep your hands on the table in front of you where I can see 'em."

I complied and waited.

The detective pulled out the somewhat matching chair on the other side of the table and took a seat. He remained mute as he shuffled the file folder over in front of himself then settled in against the backrest. After a long pause he reached into his pocket, withdrew something, splayed it open and tossed it on the table in front of me. It was my wallet, complete with the toy badge pinned inside.

"Care to explain that, Mister Gant?" he asked.

"It's a long story," I offered, knowing the comment was stupid the moment it exited my mouth.

"I'm not going anywhere," he replied. "Neither are you."

Keeping with my established pattern of inane answers, I said, "You wouldn't believe me if I told you."

"You'd be surprised," he grunted. "I've heard it all."

"I doubt you've heard this one."

"Try me."

At this point I figured I had little to lose, so I sighed and answered with a tired drone in my voice. "I'm trying to stop a killer."

"Really? I thought that was a job for cops," he harrumphed then nudged the fake badge. "But, wait, you're a cop, right?"

"Obviously you know I'm not," I replied.

"You're not?"

"Look, Detective…?"

"Fairbanks."

"Detective Fairbanks. Do you think you can dispense with the sarcasm?"

"Why? Does it annoy you?"

"Honestly, yes."

"I guess we all have something that gets under our skin," he offered. "Personally, sarcasm really doesn't bother me much. What really gets to me is people who pretend to be something they're not."

"Let me guess. Especially when they pretend to be a cop."

He leaned back in his chair, regarding me with a cold stare, then nodded and said, "Yeah. That'll do it."

"In my defense," I explained, "I never actually said I was a police officer."

"No, you didn't," he replied as he leaned forward and flipped the file folder open. Peering through the glasses resting on the end of his nose, he read aloud, "Special investigations consultant with the Saint Louis Major Case Squad is what you said."

He looked back up at me and waited.

"Yeah," I agreed. "Something like that."

"Uh-huh. See, the problem is this," he nudged my wallet again, "You flashed a fake badge in order to gain entry to a crime scene, and that shows intent. So, no matter what you said, you were impersonating a cop. It's kind of one of those actions speak louder than words things."

I knew my argument had been lame when I made it, but I was too tired to think of anything else. Besides, lying is what had landed me here in the first place, so making up a new fabrication probably wasn't my best course of action.

"What if there's an element of truth to that story?" I asked.

"What, so now you're telling me that you actually are a cop?"

I shook my head. "No. But I actually am an independent consultant for the Major Case Squad in Saint Louis."

"Really?"

"Sometimes."

"Define sometimes."

"It largely depends on the case and who happens to be running it."

"So, which is it right now? Sometimes yes, or sometimes no?"

I didn't answer.

"Yeah. That's what I thought."

Once again my mouth overrode my brain. "Look, Detective Fairbanks, you're right. I impersonated a police officer. But it's not like I did it to assault anyone, or to get free donuts or something."

"Free donuts. That's funny." He wasn't laughing.

I shook my head again. "Sorry. I haven't had much sleep in the past few days."

"Welcome to the club."

"Okay, so, other than annoying you, what kind of mess have I managed to get myself into?"

"That would be up to the judge," he told me. "Impersonating a law enforcement officer and violating a sealed homicide crime scene could get you five. Maybe a little more if we throw the donut comment in on top of it."

I let my head hang for a moment as I felt my shoulders fall. "I suppose I should call my attorney then."

"That would probably be a good idea, unless you can give me a damn good reason why you shouldn't be charged."

I wasn't sure if he was just stringing me along, or what. However, I looked upon his comment as an invitation to get myself out of this debacle. Not having a reasonable explanation that didn't sound utterly insane, however, I took the only course of action I could think of and played a card I wasn't even sure I was truly holding.

"Any chance you could call Detective Benjamin Storm in Saint Louis?" I appealed. "I'm sure he could clear some of this up for you."

"Storm," he muttered as he leafed through the papers in the file folder then stopped at a handwritten page of notes. "Would that by any chance be the same Detective Benjamin Storm who said, and I quote, 'Jeezus H Christ. Fuck me. Just throw the book at his sorry ass'?"

Obviously, I wasn't holding the cards I thought I was. I nodded and said in a flat tone, "Yeah. That would be him."

"Yeah. We found his card in your personal effects."

"Maybe if you called…"

He cut me off, "Special Agent Constance Mandalay with the FBI Saint Louis field office? Storm said you'd probably toss her name out there too."

"Sounds as if you two had a pretty in-depth conversation."

"Yeah, we did. A couple of them, in fact. Nice guy."

"At the moment I guess that assessment depends on which side of the table you happen to be sitting."

"I guess I can understand why you'd think that, but actually, Mister Gant, you owe him big."

"How do you figure?"

"Easy. Besides warning me that you'd probably make a nuisance of yourself—which was dead on the money, obviously—your friend filled me in on everything that's happened to you and your wife in the past few weeks."

"Everything?"

"Of relevance," he replied with a nod.

"Then you should know that I'm doing all this to help her."

"That's what Storm says. And, fortunately for you, according to him there really is an underlying truth to your story, just like you said. He did, however, stress to me in no uncertain terms that you are *not* here in an official capacity with the Major Case Squad…or any other branch of law enforcement for that matter. The way he explained it, you're here of your own volition, and you're supposed to be on a quick fact finding trip, nothing more."

"That was the original plan," I agreed.

"Of course, it would appear that you got a bit overzealous in your search and deviated just a bit."

"Maybe so, but if you…"

He interrupted me again, "Gant, just agree with me and call it good, okay?"

I paused as what he said filtered through to my temporarily dense grey matter, and then I nodded. "Yeah. Okay."

"So, after his understandable initial reaction to my more recent call, he calmed down and had a change of heart about havin' me throw the book at you. Actually, he even asked if I could do him a favor and cut you some slack."

"And you said?"

"I told him I'd think about it, but I wanted to have a one-on-one with you first."

"Which, I take it, we've pretty much just had."

"Pretty much."

"How did I do?"

He shrugged. "You proved to me you're a bit of an asshole, but under the circumstances I think I'm willing to understand why that might be the case."

"Reach any other conclusions?"

"Yeah, actually I have."

We sat staring silently at one another for several heartbeats. Finally, I cleared my throat and asked, "Do you plan to share?"

He flipped the folder shut then scooped up my wallet and sat back in the chair. While he fiddled with the clasp on the toy badge, he said, "Storm said you told him you have a return flight to Saint Louis Saturday afternoon."

"That's true."

"I'd suggest that you exchange your ticket for a flight leaving today. The earlier, the better."

"So, you're telling me to get out of town?"

"Pretty much," he said with a nod as he stood up and tossed the empty wallet in front of me. "You can pick up the rest of your personal effects at the desk."

"At the risk of getting myself in deeper," I said. "What about the fact that I violated a crime scene?"

"You're a lucky man, Mister Gant. To be perfectly honest, you didn't violate much. The scene was officially cleared yesterday. The motel staff just hadn't made it around to cleaning up yet."

"I see, so no harm done."

"I wouldn't say that," he returned. "You managed to waste my time, and that's another one of those things that tends to bother me."

"Sorry about that."

"Yeah. Sure."

A quick impression from the motel settled into my gut as I stood from my chair. However, instead of being the horror that had gone on behind the door of room 7, it was the sick fear I had felt for the woman at the office when she had been so willing to open the door.

"Detective Fairbanks, is there any chance you could do me a favor?"

"I'm fairly certain I just did. Storm didn't tell me you were greedy too."

"I'm not. It's not really for me," I pressed. "It's for the lady who runs the motel. Is there any chance you could go have a talk with her?"

"I did." He tapped the folder. "Or did that slip past you?"

"I mean about something else."

"What?"

"Safety, I guess. She was just too trusting. I mean, she just opened the door to the office and didn't even ask to see my credentials up close. What if my aim had actually been to assault her?"

"Then you'd be at the morgue right now sporting a toe tag instead of here talking to me."

"What do you mean?"

He shook his head and chuckled. "Mister Gant, while your concern is commendable, the woman you are so worried about is a retired cop from Tennessee. She had you pegged as an imposter from the word go, and she was packing a Glock in her housecoat. The only reason she didn't just shoot you before calling us is that she knew we'd probably want to talk to you first."

CHAPTER 8:

My rental car had yet to be impounded according to Detective Fairbanks, so it was supposed to still be sitting on the parking lot of the Southern Hospitality Motor Lodge where I had left it. I had been allowed to use a phone to call a cab while I was waiting for my personal effects, and since it took several minutes to get me officially signed out, by the time I was at the curb, my wait was relatively short.

I set about the task of getting my credit cards and other odd items situated back into my wallet after I had told the driver where I was going and then settled back in the seat. I quickly checked my cell phone and noticed it was off, so I thumbed it on and laid it in my lap as I continued to arrange my life in the worn fold of leather. The phone started vibrating and warbling the instant it latched on to a signal.

I knew the familiar tone was alerting me to voicemail, but that could wait. When it finally stopped, it was only briefly before starting into the upwardly stair-stepped trill of an incoming call. I shoved my still disorganized wallet into my pocket then picked up the chirping device and glanced at the screen. The display showed that the caller was Ben. Apparently, Detective Fairbanks hadn't wasted any time letting him know I'd been released.

My thumb hovered over the talk button as I debated whether or not I really wanted to listen to my friend read me the riot act at this particular moment in time. According to the digital clock in the corner of the LCD, it was already pushing 10 A.M. I knew I would have to deal with him eventually, but right now I wasn't sure I was in the right frame of mind to take the flak. Fortunately, the internal deliberation was rendered moot by my hesitation, and the call defaulted to voicemail.

I let out a sigh and then proceeded to punch a speed dial number before tucking the device up to my ear. The phone at the other end rang twice then was picked up by a hospital operator.

"Doctor Helen Storm, please," I asked.

"Whom should I say is calling?"

"Rowan Gant."

"Hold please."

The strains of some unidentifiable instrumental piece flowed into my ear for the better part of three minutes before the line clicked and a fresh voice came on.

"Good morning, Rowan," Helen said. "I was expecting you to call much earlier."

Ben's sister was sometimes harder to talk to than he was. Not because she would become as undone as he, but rather the opposite. Being a psychiatrist, she had far more effective ways to let you know you had screwed up. However, I assumed she wouldn't have any reason to do so in this case. On top of that, I wasn't calling her about me; I was calling about my wife. Felicity was currently under her care, for several reasons; not the least of which was that she was the only one I trusted where that was concerned.

"I was unforeseeably detained," I replied.

"I know. Benjamin called me earlier."

"Lovely," I mumbled. Obviously my assumption had been wrong. "So, I guess he's ready to kill me by now."

"He certainly is not happy. However, for the most part he is understandably concerned about you and what you are getting yourself involved in," she continued. "As am I."

"What's new about that, Helen? You've been concerned about me since the day we met. I doubt that's going to change anytime soon."

"I suppose you are correct about that, Rowan," she replied. "However, there are those times when I am even more concerned than usual. Such as now, for instance."

"I appreciate it, but I'm fine."

"I sincerely doubt that you are."

"Is that my friend or my analyst saying that?"

"Both."

"Yeah. I'm not surprised."

"Have you been getting any sleep?"

"Sure. Plenty."

"You are lying, Rowan. I can hear in your voice that you are exhausted."

"Listen, Helen," I said. "I didn't call to talk about me. How's Felicity doing?"

"She is holding her own at the moment," she replied. "She has good moments and bad. Right now she is in a mild depressive state, but that is to be expected under the circumstances."

"Has she had any more of the episodes?"

Episode was the only generic term I could muster for what I meant. Helen had actually witnessed Felicity under the control of Miranda before I left for New Orleans, so she knew exactly what I was talking about.

"Fortunately, no."

"Good."

"Is there a reason she might have?"

"I'm not sure…" I allowed my voice to trail off for a moment. "All I can say is that I think I might have riled up the *Lwa* just a bit."

"How so?"

"I can't really get into any details at the moment. Let's just say Miranda and I had an encounter."

"You found her?"

"Not physically, no, but…" I left the alternative unspoken.

Helen sighed and a fresh measure of concern threaded into her voice, "Rowan, you do realize that you are making my case for me. You are not going to do Felicity any good if you manage to lose touch with yourself in the process."

"I know that, Helen."

"You need to be careful."

"What makes you think I'm not?"

"I know you too well. You are there alone, and you do not have anyone to stop you from taking unnecessary risks."

"Yeah," I muttered. "I suppose you do know me. Well, I am. Being careful, that is."

"I hope you are correct, however, I suspect that what you perceive as being careful is a far cry from fact."

"You don't have to mother me. I know what I'm doing," I returned, even though I wasn't sure I believed the statement myself. Rather than allow it to go any further, however, I changed the subject. "So, like I said, I called about Felicity. Not me. Is there any chance I could speak to her?"

"Yes, there is. In fact, I suspect hearing your voice might help her mood," she replied. "Hold on for a moment, and I will have the switchboard transfer you to her room."

The music filled the earpiece once again, though this time I thought I might have recognized the tune. I didn't get much of a chance to place a title with it, however, as I was treated to a much shorter wait than when I was originally placed on hold. The song was abruptly cut short, and I heard my wife's voice in its place.

"Rowan?"

"Hey..." I said, trying to inject some liveliness into my tone. "How's my favorite redhead?"

"Okay."

"Just okay? Helen says you're doing pretty good."

"Aye," she muttered, her singsong Celtic lilt coming through. "Helen should know, I suppose."

"Yeah, that's what she gets paid for."

She fell quiet, but I could hear her breathing softly at the other end. After a long pause I asked, "Are you still with me?"

"Aye," she mumbled. "I'm here."

"Would you rather not talk right now?" I asked, trying desperately to keep disappointment from invading my voice.

"No," she replied then corrected herself. "I mean... I do want to talk. It's just... It's just that it's so good to hear your voice right now."

"Yours too," I told her.

"What about you then?" she asked. "How are you?"

"Me? I'm fine."

"*Breugadair.*"

The accusation actually made me smile. Even though she had just called me a liar, the fact that she was interjecting Gaelic into her speech meant that she was much more her old self than even she realized.

"What makes you think I'm lying?" I asked.

"I'm depressed, Rowan, I'm not stupid."

My voice softened. "Can't get anything past you, can I?"

"Of course not."

"Well, you don't need to worry about me. I'll be fine."

"Aye, you haven't been sleeping, have you?" She wasn't really asking, she was telling.

It was obvious that my powers of deception were more than a bit anemic lately, but then, according to my wife they always were. I decided not to even make an attempt at denying the observation.

"Not enough," I admitted. "But, like I said, you don't need to worry about me. You need to worry about you."

"Worrying about you is part of what makes me who I am."

"Same here," I told her. "But you need to concentrate on feeling better. I'm responsible for getting you into this, and I'll get you out of it."

"How do you figure that you're responsible, then?"

I closed my eyes and gave my head a slight shake. I knew immediately that I had said the wrong thing, but there was no way to take it back.

"That's not important right now," I told her.

"Aye, it is to me."

I let out a cautious breath as I tried to choose my words. "Let's just say that if I had never become involved in Ariel Tanner's murder investigation all those years back, we'd probably be having a much more normal life. Maybe all this wouldn't be happening."

This wasn't a new thought for me. It was simply one that I usually kept to myself. But, it had weighed on me for quite some time. Had I never opened the door to that other realm by insinuating myself so deeply into that first investigation, maybe the dead would be speaking to someone else instead of me. And, if that were the case, Felicity wouldn't be sitting in the psychiatric wing of a hospital because an out of control *Lwa* was using her as a horse.

"Aye, *Caorthann*," my wife soothed. "You had no choice. Ariel was your friend."

"I'm supposed to be cheering *you* up," I finally muttered.

"You are…" she replied, and I could actually hear the smile in her voice.

"I'm glad you think so, because I don't feel like I am."

"How is it down there?" she asked, switching the subject without acknowledging what I had just said.

On reflex I looked out the windows of the taxi at the piles of detritus as I spoke, "Not as bad as we saw on TV, but it's still not good."

"Are you keeping your wards up?"

"Yeah. I am."

When she replied, her voice was still illuminated by the somewhat bright tone that had made me smile a moment ago. "*Cac capaill.* You're lying again. You haven't been able to shield yourself for more than ten minutes in years. I know coven initiates who ground better than you."

I allowed myself a grin at the comment, complete with the Gaelic profanity. Knowing Felicity as I did, I took the curse as yet another positive sign.

I felt the car slowing and looked up. We listed briefly as the driver swung the vehicle into the motel's lot in a tight arc and then eased us up in front of the office.

"Hold on, honey," I said into the phone as I fished out my wallet.

I did a quick mental calculation of the tip and stuffed some bills into his hand with a quick "keep the change," then stepped out of the vehicle and started across the lot to my own car. The trip had put a dent in my traveling cash, but I wasn't hurting yet. Still, I figured plastic was probably going to be my best choice to pay for my meals from this point on.

"Okay, I'm back," I said after returning the phone to my ear.

"Have you been eating?" she asked, still bent on taking care of me by long distance.

I didn't think she needed the worry, but it seemed to be giving her something to focus on. So, if it made her feel better, I wasn't going to argue.

"Aspirin and coffee."

"Rowan…"

"I'll get something later. I promise."

"Something healthy."

"You got it. Something healthy."

"So what are your plans today?" she pressed.

I glanced at my watch and saw that it was 10:20.

"I'm going down to the main branch of the library to check their archives. If I'm lucky I'll be able to pick up a lead on Miranda from some of the genealogy records. I don't know if it will do any good, even if I find something, but maybe."

"Aren't you supposed to be meeting up with Doctor Rieth to have a look at the cemetery?" she asked.

"That isn't until tomorrow. She's still in Baton Rouge right now. But, I have a map so I might go out there myself this afternoon."

I stopped at my rental car then pulled the key out of my pocket and unlocked the door. I opened it but didn't get in right away. I just stood there watching the traffic out on Airline Highway.

"Please don't," Felicity appealed.

"Why?"

"Just… I don't know. Just don't go alone. Please wait until tomorrow when Doctor Rieth is with you."

"Okay," I answered softly. "I can do that. Don't worry."

"Promise?"

"Yes, honey. I promise," I said, unconsciously nodding as I spoke. "Truth is I should probably go back to the motel and grab some sleep once I'm done at the library."

"Aye, I think you should."

Silence fell between us. I turned to slip into the car, and my eyes caught the sight of a maid's cart outside the door of room 7. Some of the furniture was already resting in a pile near the entrance to the open stairwell on the left.

"I'm loving you right now," my wife finally said.

"I'm loving you too," I replied.

"Well..." she began hesitantly. "I suppose I should let you go."

"Yeah, I guess you're right. I still need to figure out how to get to the library from here."

"Call me later? When you wake up from your nap..."

"Absolutely."

"I love you."

"I love you too, sweetheart."

I waited to fold the cell phone in half until I heard the click at her end. I hated to end the call just as much as she, but I really did need to figure out where I was going, and get there.

It took a moment for me to realize I was still staring in the direction of room 7 as the maid and a man who could have been a maintenance worker went in and out the door at random intervals. I absently wondered how soon they might have the room ready for rental and even considered going over to the office to ask. Of course, the lady behind the desk probably wouldn't be particularly interested in renting it to me after what had happened a few hours ago.

Besides, I also remembered what Detective Fairbanks had said. While I'm sure he was well aware I had no intention of leaving New Orleans just yet, I suspected another run-in with the local constabulary wouldn't go nearly as well as the first. I knew I was going to need to fly beneath their radar for the rest of my visit. Occupying a room at a motel run by the person who had turned me in didn't strike me as falling into that category.

But, even if that hadn't been the case, staying here would probably be a very bad idea. Even though my current digs were far less than desirable, I had to take another important point into consideration. They could replace everything in that room except the ghosts. They were there to stay, and I wasn't all that keen on spending any more time with them than I already had.

I shook my head and started to get into the car. As I slid into the seat and closed the door, I noticed a figure standing in the doorway of the office. It was the owner, sans housecoat this time, although I'm betting she was probably still well armed. She stood sipping from a cup and watching me through the window with a determined stare.

I decided to check my map when I was a little farther down the road.

CHAPTER 9:

It had been heavily overcast when the police turned me out, but any precipitation was sporadic. Now, however, it was falling steadily. Not pounding, by any means, just a steady rain. At least it waited until I was indoors.

I had just finished yet another perusal of the microfilm drawers in the archives division of the New Orleans Public Library. Now, I found myself gazing out the window at the small third floor courtyard, watching the water spatter against the windows. Even up here, the sharp smells of mold and mildewed carpet were prominent as they jetted out through the ventilation system.

The condition of the library itself was enough to make a person heartsick. The flood that had come in the wake of Katrina had inflicted more than its share of damage on the building and its contents. The signs were everywhere, including the water level marks on the walls.

But, it wasn't merely the physical toll that evoked painful emotions. This repository of the written word was now only a part-time library. The rest of the time, it was a temporary federal office housing the FEMA response teams.

Armed officers waited at the entrance, bringing you in single file through metal detectors as if you were entering an airport concourse. The main floor now housed very few books. Instead, harried people with government ID's occupied the better part of it, each of them systematically interviewing survivors of the disaster, cataloging their losses and shuffling paperwork—but providing little or no relief. The overwhelming sense of despair I could feel from the people I had seen waiting, government forms clutched in their hands, was almost more than I could bear at the moment. Had I not been focused on my own task, I firmly believe I would have sat down in the middle of the floor and wept for them.

Even with an entire floor of the building between them and me, I could still feel it.

I shook off the anxiety then gathered my steno pad and two square boxes containing rolls of microfilm from the top of the metal cabinets. Making my way around the end of the stacks, I headed back toward the center of the dogleg in the L-shaped room. Earlier it had been almost dead up here, but now there was plenty of quiet activity. I wandered up the rows of microfilm readers, checking all the way to the back of the farthest stand, but found them all occupied. Letting out a sigh, I trudged over to a table and pulled out a chair. I hoped my wait wouldn't be overly long.

"Excuse me...Sir?" a young woman's voice broke through the calm room. She wasn't being loud by any means, but given the relative quiet, her words were hard to miss.

I looked in the direction of the voice and saw a very young-looking blonde motioning to me with one hand as she used her other to rewind a roll of film.

"Yeah?" I grunted.

"I'm done here if you need the machine," she offered.

As I had noticed with Detective Fairbanks, her voice held none of the clipped affectations I had become used to hearing since I had arrived in the city. It made her seem almost as out of place as I felt. But, given the fact that she was young, as well as casually dressed in jeans and a hooded sweatshirt, I figured she was probably a college student from out of state.

"Yeah, thanks," I said in a tired drone, giving her a shallow nod.

I pushed the unused chair back beneath the table then walked over and stood next to the reader and waited patiently. The young woman removed the spool of film then tucked it back into a box. Gathering up her notebook, she hefted her backpack from the floor and slipped it over one shoulder before stepping aside and giving me a smile.

"You kind of have to coax it a bit sometimes," she told me. "It sticks every now and then."

I nodded. "Yeah. I had to use this one earlier. Thanks."

"Soooo…Genealogy?" she asked.

"Huh?" My question came out more as a grunt than a word.

I wasn't really paying attention. I already had my own spool of aging film in my hand and was pushing it onto the feed spindle when she made her query. Truth is, my mind was wandering, and it had settled on the fact that I hadn't done research by microfilm since I was in college myself, which was longer ago than I really wanted to think about.

"I was just wondering if you were maybe doing genealogical research," she pressed on, apparently unfazed by my woolgathering expression. "You know, investigating your roots. That sort of thing."

"Yeah," I said, glancing back and giving her a tired nod. "Yeah, I guess you could say it's something like that."

I turned back to the task at hand and pressed the plastic spool inward until I felt it snap. Then I tugged on the free end of the film and started to thread it beneath the glass.

I couldn't help but feel the girl was still standing behind me. I wondered for a moment if I should reach back and check on my wallet. But, malicious energy wasn't what seemed to be coming from her. Actually, it felt more like a bizarre mix of curiosity and arousal. Of course, with everything that was bombarding me, I didn't even want to hazard a guess as to whether or not those feelings were coming from her or somewhere across the room. Instead I just tried to ignore her and hoped that she would go away.

"Yeah, I figured as much," she finally said. "I've been watching you."

Obviously, ignoring her wasn't going to work. I glanced back over my shoulder again. "Yeah? Why's that?"

"Well, I mean…" She paused for a moment then shrugged. "You look kinda old to be a student."

"Thanks," I replied, my voice flat.

Turning back to the machine, I fished the loop of brittle film through the guide plate and hooked it onto the take-up reel.

"Oh, that wasn't meant as an insult," she said, backpedaling.

I replied without turning this time. "No big deal. I wasn't offended. I realize I'm old as compared to you. That part of my brain still works."

I felt something touch me, and I looked down to see that she had leaned in close, actually bringing her ample chest against my arm. I had the distinct impression the physical contact wasn't an accident. She proved that out by dropping her voice even lower and infusing it with a sultry sweetness.

"The truth is, I really like older men...a lot...know what I mean?" she whispered as if sharing a secret.

Now the hairs on the back of my neck were no longer at rest. I stopped what I was doing and hung my head for a moment then sighed.

Finally, I said, "Please tell me you aren't trying to pick me up."

I could hear the nonchalance in her voice as she replied, "Well, hey... You're kind of cute. I was thinking maybe we could go get a cup of coffee or something and see where things go from there?"

I turned to face her and she eased back, flashing me a shy smile that was too brazen to truly qualify as coy.

"I'm betting I'm old enough to be your father," I said.

"Yeah, probably. So what? That's the point."

I opened my mouth to comment on that observation but decided against it. I certainly had no right to judge whatever her proclivities were. Instead I bolstered my objection with, "I'm also happily married."

"Yeah. Okay. But, she isn't with you right now is she?" she countered. "You've been alone since I've been here."

"Actually, she's the entire reason I'm here at the moment, but that's not the point..."

"Hey, I won't tell if you won't."

"Look, young lady..."

"Erika." She interrupted me then thrust out her hand. "And you are?"

I ignored her gesture but returned with a sigh, "Rowan."

"Rowan. That's an interesting name. I like it." She continued holding her hand out waiting for me to take it.

"Thanks," I replied, still ignoring the offered appendage. "So, listen, Erika, you've got to know that you're playing a dangerous game here. You have absolutely no idea who I am."

After a silent pause, she finally allowed her hand to fall back down to her side. "Yeah. Well, that's part of the turn-on too."

"Uh-huh. Well, I could be some kind of sicko for all you know."

"You look pretty safe to me."

"Most sociopaths do," I told her. "And, I've actually got some experience in that area."

"Really? How so?"

"Trust me, you really don't want to know."

She paused again and gave me a once over as if she were sizing me up. "Okay. So, tell me. Are you a 'sicko'?"

"Again, that's not the point."

She pursed her lips, thrusting the lower one out in an exaggerated pout while giving me an obviously practiced come-hither gaze. "So what is it then? Are you just not into blondes?"

"Listen, Erika, is this some kind of game show? Is there a hidden camera somewhere? Because, honestly, I don't have time for this."

She chuckled. "You're funny too."

I held up my hands in mock surrender as I huffed out a heavy breath. "All right, look, I'm flattered... At least I think I am... Anyway, this just isn't going to happen. Understand?"

She blinked and shook her head. To me, her expression looked as if reality had just walked up behind her and given her a swift kick.

"You're serious," she said, a wisp of incredulity in her voice.

"Yes. Yes, I am."

"You really don't want to…"

"No. No, I don't."

"Well… Okay. It's your loss."

"I'll just have to take your word for that."

"Well, you know…" she began, as she opened her notebook and

started pulling a pen from the spiral binding. "I could give you my number in case you change your mind..."

It was my turn to do the interrupting, "That isn't necessary. I won't."

She looked at me curiously then shoved the pen back down and closed the notebook. "Okay. Well, never know until you try." With a shrug she added, "Good luck with whatever you're doing there, I guess."

"Yeah. Thanks. You too."

With a shake of her head, she finally walked away.

I took in a deep breath and shook my own head as I let it out. This was the second time I had been propositioned in as many days. Even less if you considered that the first had actually been fewer than twenty-four hours ago. Granted, that one had been a hooker, but I had to wonder just what it was about me that was attracting the overtures.

Turning back to the machine, I decided to put it out of my mind and get to work. If the rest of the day continued along the same lines as my morning, I still had a lot of searching ahead of me. Even then I was beginning to wonder if I would ever find what I was looking for, especially since I didn't really know exactly what that was.

Cocking my head over against my shoulder, I stared at the image on the marred base of the film reader. Winding the celluloid slowly, I located a reference frame. I glanced over to my steno pad and read a note I had scrawled across it then returned my gaze to the dimly luminous image and started winding the lever. The film stopped moving after a moment, so I gave the side of the machine a hard rap with my knuckles to re-engage the slipping gears then started winding it again. After a few seconds I slowed, advancing the film frame by frame until I found the date I had written in my notes.

Using both hands, I twisted the projection head and turned the image of the better than 150 year old newspaper 90°, which would allow me to hold my head at a less painful cant. Sitting down, I adjusted the magnification and began turning the focus ring. It took me a minute of fiddling to get it to a point that was at least readable, though a long way from what one could call sharp.

Picking my way through the scratches and dropout, I scanned the almost undecipherable blobs, trying to make sense of the vernacular of the day. I was on the verge of giving up when something caught my eye.

Reaching up, I pulled on the positioning bar and centered the frame. Tilting my head up, I focused on the words through the lower half of my bifocals. Tracing beneath them with my finger, I read silently to myself, although I could feel my lips moving slowly as I digested the words.

When I finished, I went back to the top of the paragraph and read them all again. It was at that point my heart skipped a pair of beats and vaulted into my throat.

CHAPTER 10:

It took reading the small, almost hidden public notice for a third time before my heart let itself slide back down into my chest. Even at that, it kept racing, fueled by a fresh dump of adrenalin.

I sat back in my chair and let a hot breath escape slowly through pursed lips, then rubbed my hand across the lower half of my face, ignoring the sharp stubble that by now must have had me looking like a bum. Pushing my glasses up, I closed my eyes and pinched the bridge of my nose between my thumb and forefinger, simply sitting there and allowing the information to soak fully into my grey matter. Whether I was suffering from a bout of subdued elation or exhaustion-induced insanity, I didn't know, but I heard myself let out a small chuckle.

When I finally opened my eyes, I looked to make sure the words were still displayed on the base of the reader and hadn't merely been a figment of my exhausted imagination. Finding that it was quite real, I muttered to myself, "Miranda, you bitch."

I leaned forward then snatched up my pencil and scribbled a couple of quick notes. Scooting the chair back, I stood, and with a rapid spin turned the crank until the film had rewound completely onto the spool. Popping it off the feed shaft, I made my way quickly across the room to the microfilm imaging station. My timing was fortunate, and there wasn't a wait for this more sophisticated piece of equipment.

Loading up the roll, I quickly advanced it to the noted page. When it was centered to my satisfaction, I punched print, and a moment later the large format laser printer nearby hummed to life. I zoomed in and bracketed off the text then printed enlarged versions of it as well, just to make sure I had myself covered where readability was concerned.

Less than five minutes later, I was returning the spools of film to the tops of the storage bins where they belonged and then collecting the rest of my belongings.

"I made these three copies," I said to the archive librarian behind the desk as I splayed them out on the counter for him to see. "What's the damage?"

"A dollar-fifty," he replied. "Did you find what you were looking for?"

"Yeah, you could say that," I answered absently, digging through my wallet and extracting a pair of dollar bills. "An interesting part of it, anyway."

"Let me get your change," he said as he took the money.

I didn't wait. I had already folded the papers, stuffed them into my backpack, and was three steps toward the elevator by the time he finished the sentence.

"Keep it," I called over my shoulder, not bothering to look back or even slow down.

I now had a brand new piece of the puzzle. I just had to figure out where it fit and what to do about it.

"Why the hell haven't you been answerin' your goddamn phone?!" Ben demanded.

He wasn't going out of his way to contain his anger, but right now I didn't care. As long as I held the phone far enough from my ear, I was good.

"I was in a library," I told him calmly. "So I had it turned off."

I was telling the truth, for the most part anyway. My cell phone had really been off the entire time I was in the library. However, the real truth was that I had switched it off much earlier. The minute I pulled off the lot at the Southern Hospitality motel, in fact. Primarily, because I expected he would constantly be trying to get hold of me, and I wasn't yet ready to be bothered.

My expectations were dead on because as soon as I was outside and punched the power button, the device began chirping with voice mail alerts. Five minutes later, when I reached where I had parked my car, it was warbling with an incoming call.

This time, however, I was still riding on the adrenalin high of my new discovery, so I gave in and answered it.

"Yeah?" he barked. "So why the fuck didn't ya' just set it ta' vibrate?!"

"Because I was busy and wouldn't have answered it anyway," I replied. "And, with you calling every ten or fifteen minutes you would have worn out my battery."

He grumbled something unintelligible but refrained from direct comment on my candor. Instead he launched directly into admonishing me. "Sonofabitch, Row. What were ya' thinkin'? Do ya' realize how much shit you coulda been in with that stunt?"

"Not answering my phone?"

"Goddammit, stop bein' an asshole. You know what I'm talkin' about. The shit you pulled impersonatin' a copper!"

"Oh, that. Well, yeah, I think Detective Fairbanks made that pretty clear."

"Yeah, well imagine my friggin' surprise when I got the phone call this mornin'."

"Are you sure 'surprise' is the right word?"

"Pissed off works too."

"Uh-huh. That's what I thought you really meant. But, we both know you expected me to do something about getting into the crime scene."

"Yeah, but I didn't actually think you'd be able ta' find it. Dammit, White Man, I never woulda dreamed you'd go that far."

"Neither would I," I admitted. "Trust me, I didn't know I had it in me."

"This ain't a joke, Row."

"I know that, Ben. But, remember, we're talking about Felicity here. You should know by now, I'm going to do whatever it takes where she's concerned."

"Obviously," he replied. "So, I guess you realize I owe this copper a big one now, don'tcha?"

"I figured as much."

"We ain't just talkin' a box of cigars or somethin' either," he added.

"I kind of figured that too. And, by the same token, I owe you as well. But, I think I've pretty much been running a tab for a while now anyway."

"Yeah, you can say that again."

"Well, do me a favor and don't call in your markers just yet. I might need an extension on my credit line first."

"How's that? Fairbanks told me you were s'posed ta' be gettin' outta town, ASAP."

"I'm not done here yet."

"As far as he's concerned, ya' are, and I gotta agree with 'im."

"I'll be home Saturday, just like I originally planned."

"You're gonna get your ass in deep shit again, Row, and I ain't gonna be able ta' get ya' out of it."

"I'll be fine if I'm careful."

"Like ya' were this mornin'?"

"More careful."

"Jeezus…" he muttered. "You're a fuckin' piece'a work, ya' know that?"

"So you've told me several times."

"Well? Was it worth almost gettin' locked up?"

"I don't know for sure just yet, but I think so."

"Did'ja end up goin' all *Twilight Zone*?"

"Back to back episodes with no commercials," I replied.

"Jeezus…" His tone switched to one of concern. "So, you okay?"

"Other than a lingering gender dysphoric psychological issue, just fine."

"Gender what, psycho who?"

"Don't worry about it."

"Well, I think ya' had lingerin' psych issues before ya' ever went down there."

"Thanks for the vote of confidence."

"Uh-huh," he grunted. "So spill it. Whaddid ya' see?"

"A seriously twisted mirror image of my wife named Annalise."

"You saw 'er?"

"Hell, I did more than that. I talked to her."

"Was it la-la land talked to, or like for real?"

"In the vision," I explained.

"How the fuck did ya' talk to 'er?"

"I think it has something to do with the fact that the *Lwa* is a spirit, so we're obviously dealing with a dead person here. And, as we know, I tend to have conversations with dead people."

"So ya' didn't talk ta' evil sis, ya' talked ta' the ghost."

"Actually, I'm pretty sure I talked to both of them."

"See, now that's just even more fucked up than usual, Row."

"You think I don't know that?"

"Well? Whaddid she…they say?"

"She told me she wants it back. All of it."

"It?"

"Unless I missed my guess, I think she was talking about sexual gratification."

"You wanna explain that one? You ain't sayin' you had some kinda la-la land sex with 'er are ya'?"

"No," I replied, shaking my head out of pure reflex. "Of course not. I'm pretty sure she means the sexual gratification she gets from torturing and killing her victims."

"Okay. So does she think you have it or somethin'?"

"No, but she definitely thinks I know who does."

"Felicity," he grunted.

"Yeah."

"Why?"

"At the risk of sounding glib, she didn't say. In fact, I got the impression she doesn't even know who Felicity actually is, but unfortunately she knows her name. And, mine too."

"Whaddaya mean? How?"

"Long story short, I was talking to myself…"

He interrupted me. "I thought you were talkin' ta' her?"

"This was before I was talking to her," I said with an exasperated sigh. "Just let me finish. So, I happened to say my own name aloud, and she came back with something like, 'oh, that's who you are.'"

"Fuck me… How much weirder is this gonna get, Row?"

"Weirder, I don't know. Clearer, that's a different story."

"How so?"

"You sitting down?"

"Awww, Jeeeezzzz… Yeah. What?"

"Listen to what I found at the library…"

I reached over into the passenger seat and pulled the printouts from my backpack. Unfolding them, I shuffled through in search of the largest image. While I did so I asked, "First off, have you ever heard the story about the Lalaurie family in New Orleans?"

"Can't say as I have."

"Okay, then let me give you a little background. Back in the early eighteen-thirties, Doctor Louis Lalaurie, his wife, Delphine, and their daughters moved into a mansion on Royal Street in the French Quarter. They quickly became prominent in the community and were soon very well known for their social gatherings.

"Now, remember, this was during a time of slavery, and they definitely owned their share. More than their share, actually. They had a house staff consisting of dozens. But, before too long people started noticing that slaves seemed to come and go a bit more often than normal, and that raised some suspicion.

"Then, in April of eighteen thirty-four, the reality behind those suspicions came to light when a fire broke out in the kitchen and swept through a good portion of the mansion. After the blaze was put out, the people who had been fighting the fire discovered a secret room behind a barred and locked door in the attic. When they entered, they found more than a dozen slaves, both male and female, in various horrific states. They were all either chained to walls or to makeshift operating tables. Many had open, festering wounds where limbs had been amputated or organs removed. Several of the men had been castrated, and it is said that one man even had a hole bored into his skull and a stick protruding from it."

"Jeezus, Row…" Ben groaned. "Are you sure you ain't talkin' about a friggin' horror movie or somethin'?"

"I know. It sounds like one, doesn't it? But, here's the rub. One of the initial theories was that Doctor Lalaurie had been conducting medical experiments on the slaves. However, according to the story printed in the New Orleans Bee, it was determined via witnessed accounts that the wife, Delphine, was insane and that it was she who was responsible for inflicting the tortures on them."

"Damn. So did they hang 'er sorry ass?"

"No. Following the discovery, she fled New Orleans in a somewhat spectacular escape, and where she ended up is a bit of a mystery."

"So you think maybe the ghost of this Delphine woman is really Miranda?" he asked.

"No, but close. Listen to this," I replied then shifted the papers so I could read him the notice. "*Found Drowned. The coroner held an inquest yesterday on the body of a woman named, Miranda Blanque, sister of Delphine Lalaurie, aged forty-three years, who was found floating in the Mississippi opposite the third municipality. It appears that on Sunday night last, she was seen to have jumped into the river. Verdict accordingly.*

"That was from the front page of the New Orleans Bee, September eighteenth, eighteen fifty-one. The tomb that Doctor Rieth is taking me to see is that of one Miranda Blanque, date of death, on or around September fourteenth, eighteen fifty-one, which would have been that Sunday."

"Jeezus, Row…"

"Yeah, Ben. I think maybe insanity runs in that family."

"No shit," Ben muttered, then spoke up and huffed, "Okay… I hate ta' rain on your parade, but where does all that get ya'?"

"It gives us a pretty good idea why Annalise has been doing the things she has," I explained.

"Yeah, but we're still talkin' about a dead person here, Row. I can't arrest a dead person. Besides, what it all comes down to is that Felicity's evil sis is the one that's really doin' the killin'."

"I know that. But, Miranda is the one driving her to do it."

"Yeah, so? Miranda's still dead. We need ta' be lookin' for a *live* homicidal bitch."

"Yes, *you* do."

"Whaddaya mean?"

"I mean Annalise is your problem, not mine."

"Come again?"

"Look, Ben, I've been told at every turn to stay out of this. By your superiors, by Detective Fairbanks this morning, and at least a dozen times by you over the past few weeks. So, that's what I'm doing."

"I thought ya' said you'd been at the library?"

"I have."

"Well, the way you're talkin', it sounds more like ya' been hangin' out in a bar gettin' trashed. In case you haven't noticed, you're up ta' your ass in all of this no matter what anyone has said."

"I can't help it if our investigations overlap."

"Now you're just bein' an asshole again, White Man."

"Call it what you want, but I'm not here looking for Annalise. I'm looking for Miranda."

"Oh, so now you're a friggin' ghost cop, are ya?"

"Sure. Why not? Obviously somebody has to do it; I guess it might as well be me. Look at it this way—I'm giving you what you want. I'm staying out of your way."

"Fuck me," he spat then paused. A second later he added, "Like I said before, I think you've lost your goddamned mind. When's the last time you got some sleep?"

"You're the third person to ask me that today," I said. "It's starting to get a little old."

"Been awhile, huh?"

"That's irrelevant, Ben. This whole thing got personal the minute Miranda decided to use Felicity as a horse. You don't really think that's going to stop just by finding Annalise and locking her up do you?"

"Shit, I don't know," he huffed. "I ain't mister Voodoo guy. It's all just one big freak show as far as I'm concerned. Hell, I sometimes wonder if I'm a half bubble off for believin' any of it."

"You've seen too much not to believe, Ben."

"Yeah, and that's the problem..." he sighed. "So, tell me... What're ya' gonna do now that ya' think you've found 'er?

I puffed my cheeks then blew out a heavy breath before answering. "I haven't figured that part out yet."

CHAPTER 11:

*T*heir reprieve had been too long, and I was growing impatient. I needed to be satisfied and these constant interruptions were making that need even harder to bear. If that little bitch in the kitchen knew what was good for her, she would get on with her work and stop pestering me.

I started back up the stairs, pausing only for a moment when I thought I heard my name being called yet again. The tickle deep inside was growing, and it was all I could do to stand there in silence, waiting. But, I heard nothing other than the sound of my own heart as it began to race faster with anticipation. Turning, I gathered my dress in front of me and started back upward, my shoes striking with a deliberate thump against the wooden planks. Before I was even halfway through my climb, I could hear their muted sobbing filling the short voids between my footfalls.

My excitement welled in a warm rush that traveled all the way into my stomach, forcing me to catch my breath in a sudden gasp.

They feared me. I could feel it. I could even taste it on the air as I began to take shallow breaths through my parted lips. This was how it should be. Their fear and their pain were my pleasure. It was how they showed their love for me. And, it belonged to me—as did they.

I stopped at the top of the stairs, standing perfectly still for a short moment. The tickle was becoming the itch that would soon be exploding through me, making my knees go weak and my passions flare; but I knew that at this moment it was only the beginning. Very soon that itch would be everything. And, all that I needed to make it happen was just on the other side of the door.

I unlocked the barrier and pushed it open. A small swath of dim light fell across the room. The door creaked on the un-oiled hinges as it swung wider. I entered slowly, savoring the promise of what was to *come before turning and pressing the door closed in my wake.*

They were moaning, at least those who could. Some of them were even sobbing quietly. Their misery fueled my desire. I stepped with determination across the room, the soles of my shoes clacking lightly against the floorboards.

I stood near him in the darkness. I could hear him mumbling, and it sounded as if he was praying. I smiled to myself at the very thought, imagining that his prayers were not to God, but to me as his Goddess.

I started to step away, but my foot hit something soft that made me almost lose my balance. I felt it move as I shuffled then heard it whimper as I thudded against it again. One of them was on the floor. I couldn't tell if it was a woman or a man, but that mattered little. I gathered my dress up and stepped on it. The thing let out an animal-like wail, but I ignored its pleas, and instead I reveled in its misery. After a moment I continued across the room.

The shutters clunked as I swung them open, allowing the afternoon light to spill in. It was growing late, but the illumination seemed bright in the shadowy room. I glanced around at the others. Most had provided me with fruitful entertainment. Those that did not were no longer here. But, my sights this day were not set on them. I was here for the new arrival.

I moved deliberately back across the plank floor, returning to my station near his head. He was chained to a low table—nude and bound at the wrists and ankles. He was pristine but for a few telltale signs of the lash. Looking at him, prone and helpless, I felt the itch ignite my entire body.

It was time.

I shuffled over to a small table and wrapped one hand around the handle of a bone saw then gathered a cloth rag into the other. With excitement welling in the pit of my stomach, I stepped quickly back and stood over him. Forcing his mouth open, I stuffed the filthy cloth into it then took hold of his hand and pressed the serrated edge of the saw against his wrist just below the shackle.

"Now," I said, my voice dripping with sweetness. "Let us see how

much you love me, little man."

I was just preparing to draw the toothed blade through the first layer of his flesh when the door opened. I looked up to see my sister standing there, a frown creasing her face.

"Miranda," she admonished. "I should have known I would find you here."

"I need it, Delphine," I told her between short, panting breaths. "I need it now."

"Our guests will be here in less than two hours."

"I know," I appealed. "I promise this will not take long."

She stood staring at me, and I at her. The itch had overwhelmed me now, and I could feel myself trembling. I needed release, and I was certain she knew it. I had seen her in this very same state more than once.

"Delphine, please..." I begged.

She slowly pressed the door shut then turned and walked toward the table. The corners of her mouth twisted into a knowing smile as she knelt and took his hand from me.

"Get some rope to tie it off first," she said softly. "We would not want him to die just yet."

I awoke to the sound of my travel alarm chirping from its position atop the rickety nightstand.

I was sprawled out on the bed in my room at the Airline Courts. Contrary to what I had told Ben earlier, I had actually chosen to sleep on it. Although, I hadn't bothered to turn it down, nor did I get undressed. I suppose that somewhere in my exhaustion, I had come to the conclusion that as long as I had a few layers between me and it, the creeping crud wouldn't be able to get to me.

My mouth was dry, and my heart was thumping hard in my chest. I felt more like I had been running laps than sleeping. My head was killing me, not that such was unusual these days, but for some reason, between lances of pain I was seeing an image of a saw. I didn't know exactly what it meant, but it was seriously disconcerting because each mental flash of the serrated blade left me with that bizarre feeling of feminine arousal deep inside.

I rolled over and stretched out, grabbing the twittering alarm clock and switching it off. I had set it for 6 P.M., and the digits were displaying 6:07. Apparently it had taken several minutes for it to get my attention, which was a testimony to how tired I really was. I placed it back on the nightstand, causing the dilapidated piece of furniture to rock and thump against the wall. Rolling back, I pushed myself up and sat on the edge of the bed.

I needed to call Felicity. Not only had I promised her I would, but I needed to hear her voice again too. Something else I needed to do was eat. The diet of aspirin and coffee was starting to take its toll, and I was actually feeling the need to fill my stomach with something solid. Unfortunately, that bizarre tickle combined with the phantom memory was causing the very thought of food to make me nauseous.

After several minutes of holding my head between my hands, I rocked forward and stood. In an almost catatonic stupor, I dug through my overnight bag and pulled out my shaving kit then trudged into the bathroom to make an attempt at washing away the last eighteen or so hours of my life.

M. R. Sellars

Friday, December 2
3:07 P.M.
St. Louis Cemetery #1
New Orleans, Louisiana

CHAPTER 12:

Obeying the blinking signals on the car leading me, I turned right onto Saint Louis Street, continued along the short jog, and then made a quick left and almost immediately pulled to the curb. I shifted my vehicle into park then took a moment to rub my eyes. I was awake, but I still felt like I could use more sack time, several days worth, in fact. That was the problem with sleep. Once you had gone without it for as long as I had, you played hell trying to get caught up. And, it seemed that the more you got, the more your body wanted. Not that I had managed to get all that much, but it had apparently been enough to give my body a taste of what it was like—which wasn't working in my favor at the moment.

Last night I had tried to crash again after speaking to Felicity and then making a quick run to a drive-thru and tossing down a less than stellar burger. Unfortunately, my slumber was really no more restful than the afternoon nap that had preceded it. I couldn't even blame the nocturnal activities of my neighbor for that fact either. No matter how hard I tried to program myself with pleasant thoughts, the repetitious nightmare wasn't about to leave me alone. Without fail it interrupted each cycle before it was even fully started, effectively keeping me from getting any true rest. I don't suppose I would have minded that so much if I had learned something useful in the process. However, I never actually remembered enough of the details to know if the repeating terror was important or just my subconscious desperately trying to rescue itself by casting out the sick memories.

It wasn't until the sun was already peeking through the small window of my room that I managed to drift off for any extended period of time. As it turned out, that was only for a few hours before I was jarred awake by Doctor Rieth calling my cell phone. Given the fact that I probably would have slept right through our planned meeting, I suppose it had been for the best.

I finally stopped rubbing my eyes then reached over to the passenger seat and rooted around in my backpack. After a moment I pulled out a small, point-and-shoot digital camera. I stuffed it into my jacket pocket then shoved my hand back into the pack and retrieved a fresh bottle of aspirin I had picked up earlier this morning.

My headache was bearable for the moment, but the persistent dull ache had started ramping up a few minutes ago and had gradually increased the closer we got to our destination. Since I had a minute I figured it might be a good idea to see if I could head some of it off at the pass. I had just broken the seal on the bottle when Doctor Rieth knocked on the window.

She was in her mid-fifties and stood average height. In truth, she looked much like the photograph on her book jacket. Shoulder-length hair that occupied a hue somewhere between blonde and strawberry. Her features were pretty, but her expression seemed to change little. Except for a quick smile upon our initial face-to-face meeting a little earlier, she had worn a sober mask that spoke to her academic ties. Still, her eyes betrayed untold wisdom that I suspected was born of experience, both good and bad.

I quickly tossed a few of the aspirin into my mouth and swallowed them dry, causing a lump to rise in my throat. Then, I left the bottle in the console and climbed out of my vehicle.

"Headache?" Doctor Rieth asked across the top of the car.

"Yeah," I answered with a nod, choking the pills the rest of the way down.

"How many aspirin did you take?" she pressed.

"Probably not enough," I told her as I hooked around the front of the rental and joined her on the sidewalk.

She shook her head. "You know, that probably isn't very good for you."

"Yeah. It says that right on the bottle."

"All right then," she replied. "I'm not your mother."

"Thank you for recognizing that fact, Doctor Rieth. Most of my friends don't."

"I thought we had agreed to dispense with formality?"

"You're right," I said with a nod. "Thank you, *Velvet*."

"For what it is worth," she continued. "I would suspect their concern is what makes them your friends."

"Uh-huh. That's the argument they use too."

She gave me a nod then turned and started walking down the sidewalk. The high walls surrounding the cemetery were rife with signs of their advanced age. However, it was also obvious that great care had been taken to maintain them over the years, and they even appeared to be an eternal work in progress.

The entrance itself was a gaping mouth, and its teeth were iron gates that were now propped open. There was something altogether eerie about the invitation they presented. I wondered if it was just me, or if Velvet viewed it in the same way. If she did, her expression didn't let on.

We covered the relatively short distance between our vehicles and the entryway in a matter of a half-minute, both silent as we walked. I made the turn as we reached the gate, starting through without really slowing down. However, before I managed to cross the threshold, the good doctor's arm shot across my path, barring my way. I stumbled against my momentum then caught myself and took a step back.

"What?" I asked.

"What are you doing?" she asked in reply.

"Well… I thought I was going into the cemetery, but I guess I was wrong?"

She shook her head. "You need to give them an offering first."

"Oh," I replied, unsure of what else to say.

She gave her head another shake then asked, "Do you have any change with you?"

I shoved my hand in my pocket then dug around and extracted all of the loose coins I managed to find. Holding them in my palm, I used my index finger to spread them out and display them to her. "This enough?"

"It's really not as much about the amount as the effort and respect," she told me as she nodded at my hand then showed me the similar pile in her own. "Just let them know you have a gift for them and ask permission to enter."

"I can't say that I've ever done this before," I offered, a hint of embarrassment in my voice.

"Have you gone into cemeteries before?" she asked.

"Yeah, of course."

She sighed. "Then I suspect you've offended a few ancestors."

"Great."

"Don't worry about that now. You'll all get over it," she told me with a quick shake of her head. "Just do it right this time."

"Anything special I'm supposed to say?"

"No, just speak from the heart. Tell them you're bringing a gift and ask permission. It's not hard. It's like showing up at a dinner party with a bottle of wine and knocking on the door."

"And then I just walk in?"

"You'll know what to do," she said and smiled for the second time since we'd officially met. "Believe me, if they don't want you to come in, you'll know it."

"Okay," I replied, unable to keep the apprehension out of my voice.

I stood next to her before the opening and tried to gather my thoughts. I had absolutely no idea what I should say, but after looking through at the closely arranged rows of tombs, I began to speak.

"Greetings…" I said then hesitated.

I glanced over at Velvet in search of reassurance but found little, as her eyes were closed and her lips were moving in a silent greeting to the spirits.

I turned back to the opening and started again, speaking softly but still aloud, though I'm not sure why. "Greetings. My name is Rowan, and I've come to visit you…for…well, for some very important reasons. I've brought you this token…"

I wasn't sure quite what else to do at this point, so I held out my hand to display the coinage.

The day was pleasant with the temperature resting in the upper fifties. With the sun shining there had been no reason for anything more than the light jacket I had donned when I left the motel. However, a slight chill ran up the length of my spine causing me to shiver involuntarily. It lasted only a moment and was then followed by soothing warmth that flowed over my entire body. My anxiety was instantly replaced by comfort.

Just as Velvet had said, I knew in that moment that I was welcome.

"Put the coins over here," Velvet told me, stepping forward and placing her own in a receptacle just past the gate.

I followed suit, and though she hadn't verbally instructed me to do so, I mimicked her overt motion that made the coins clatter noisily. Still, I glanced over at her with a raised eyebrow.

She recognized the question in my face and immediately explained. "You want them to hear it. They need to know you are actually leaving the gift you promised."

I simply nodded.

Apparently, she felt at home in the cemetery as it seemed to be loosening her staunch expression more than a little.

"Rowan," she said with a slight smile. "You can talk here. It's okay. Just keep your voice low."

"Okay," I answered with a nod. "I just wasn't sure."

"Well, you can. Oh, and in case I forget, don't just walk out the gates. When we leave, we'll say goodbye, thank them, and then back out."

"Back out? Like walk backwards?"

"Yes."

"Okay. You're the expert."

Velvet looked up and to the right, pointing as she mumbled something to herself. A second later she took hold of my arm and pulled gently to guide me.

"The tomb should be this way, near the back."

With a nod I followed along, letting her lead the way down the narrow paths. We hadn't been picking our way through for more than a minute or so when the pain in my head made a sudden leap in intensity. I stumbled but managed to catch myself as a hard stab of agony drove deep into the base of my skull.

"Are you all right?" Velvet asked, concern in her voice.

"Something's wrong," I told her, reaching up to rub the back of my head.

"We're almost there. Are you going to be able to handle this?"

I nodded carefully, the pain still clawing at my grey matter. "I have to."

We started forward again, rounding the corner of a large family tomb. Velvet was in the lead, and she suddenly halted then looked back at me.

"Someone's here," she whispered.

I stepped forward then looked up and past Velvet. Standing thirty or so yards down the narrow row was a petite woman with fiery red hair cascading down the center of her back. She had her forehead pressed against the stone face of the tomb in front of her.

I stopped dead in my tracks and stared.

As if the woman could sense she was being watched, she pushed back from the tomb and slowly turned toward us.

There was the distance to consider, not to mention that there were oblique shadows falling across her from the closely spaced stone mausoleums. But, the resemblance was as beyond uncanny as it had been in the vision.

I had spoken to Felicity less than two hours ago, and I knew for a fact that she was still resting comfortably in Saint Louis, *Missouri*, under Helen Storm's care. But, if I hadn't known that, I would have sworn she was standing here now, staring directly at me.

A faint look of recognition flickered across the woman's face, but was quickly obscured by the creased lines of abject fear.

"Is that…?" Velvet asked, her voice barely above a whisper.

"Annalise," I replied, my own coming out as a dry croak.

I'm not sure how many heartbeats it took before the two of us were no longer frozen in place, but Annalise was the first to thaw. She turned and bolted down the alley, taking off like a sprinter from a starting line.

She had a healthy head start, but I was already in motion and closing the gap.

CHAPTER 13:

"Call the police!" I yelled over my shoulder to Velvet as I darted forward.

Annalise had everything on her side at the moment. Not only did she have a lead of several yards, but she had youth as well. She was also in better shape, which was obvious just by looking at her. Rounding out the advantages, it was a sure bet she was more familiar with this maze of tombs than I could ever hope to be, which was something that could play against me at any moment. All she had to do was duck between a stand of the structures or turn down an alley, and I could be lost.

However, I had something I was hoping would trump everything she had stacked in her hand. Determination.

I didn't take time to look back and see if Velvet was doing as I asked. She knew the whole story about why I was here, and I had filled her in on Annalise when we had met for lunch earlier. She was well aware of how serious this was for all concerned, so I had to hope she was on top of it.

To my surprise, my quarry didn't run very far, and she was now slowing suddenly as she veered left toward the outer wall of the cemetery. I was still too distant to understand why, but I pushed myself harder, intent on seizing the opportunity that had been presented. Another ten steps and her reasoning became clear. I could see an opening in the wall leading out to a side street. I hadn't realized there were multiple entrances to the cemetery, but as I suspected, she knew her way around.

Or, so I thought.

Her own footsteps came to an abrupt halt as she literally slammed her body into the iron gate blocking the side entrance. I heard a creak combined with the heavy metallic rattle of a chain. As I continued running, I saw her push hard against the unyielding barrier then heard her shriek at the top of her lungs.

She threw her petite body against the gates yet again, making them bow outward. Wedging her shoulder into the newly formed gap, she tried to force her way through the small opening. The delay this caused gave me the break I needed, and I pumped my legs even harder, quickly covering the remaining fifteen or so yards.

I didn't put on my own brakes until the last minute. Instead, I grabbed at the first thing I could reach which was the gate itself. I wrapped my hand around one of the upright bars and used my momentum to yank it back, narrowing the already slim gap with her still in it. The frame pivoted inward with a rusted groan, pinning her in place less than halfway through. She let out a pained yelp as the bars compressed across her forearm and wrist, driving in against her chest and shoulder.

Catching her breath, she glared at me then spit in my face before screaming, "Bastard! *Va te faire, vous fils d'une chienne!*"

I wiped my cheek with the back of my hand then glared back. Her voice was the same as I'd heard in the vision, however, there was no sweetness in her drawl this go around.

Now that I was so close to her in the flesh, I was even more taken aback by how much she resembled Felicity. There were definite differences, but they were far from glaring. I had assumed the vision had been filling in blanks using my conscious memory as a pattern, but I apparently hadn't given the ethereal enough credit for its accuracy.

Unfortunately, that preciseness was about to become my downfall. Her appearance was literally so disconcerting that I not only hesitated, but also unconsciously eased up on the gate, which in effect allowed her freedom of movement. That was a mistake that cost me dearly.

I knew I was probably already too close to her, but as usual I hadn't thought far enough ahead to even consider her response to being cornered. The moment the pressure against her forearm backed off, she jerked it free and twisted toward me. In a flash her hand was up to my face, and her nails were latched on, digging into my flesh with extreme prejudice. I let out my own yelp of pain as I could feel my skin starting to tear. I reached up to grab her wrist but was a half second behind. She ripped the sharp claws downward, taking a good hunk of the skin from my right cheek with them.

I staggered back, still clinging to the gate. I used my weight to yank on it but was again too far behind the curve. Unable to thread herself through the small opening, she pulled back out of the gap and twisted away before she could become trapped yet again.

Swinging forward, I grabbed at her as she continued turning in preparation to run. I managed to catch her upper arm but was unable to actually get a grasp on anything but the sleeve of her jacket, which slipped immediately from my fingers. Still, I managed to knock her off balance enough that it caused her to stumble against the corner of the opening in the wall.

Leaping, I half tackled her from behind, wrapping my arms around her torso. She screeched and struggled as I locked my forearms across her chest and fought to pin her arms.

"RAPE! HELP! RAPE! NINE-ONE-ONE! RAPE!" she screamed.

"Give it up, Annalise!" I shouted over her shrieking. "The cops are already looking for you. They know what you've done! It's over!"

My comment only served to renew her vigor as she fought against me. Bending her knees, she pulled her lower half up at the waist and placed her feet against the wall in front of her. Kicking away from it hard, she caused me to stumble backward and careen into the opposite wall, still holding her in a tight clench. She continued to squirm, and I was thrown completely off balance. We both crashed onto the concrete, although given that she was on top of me along with the manner in which the air burst from my lungs, I am fairly certain I cushioned the majority of her fall. Still, I refused to let go as she struggled to break free.

However, the jarring impact had allowed her to slip farther down in my grasp, and while I was trying to deal with the burning pain in my cheek and the fresh ache running up and down my back, a brand new attack made itself known. Her elbow slammed hard against my ribcage as she fought to inflict as much damage as she could in her bid for escape. The sharp pain hit a second time as she drove it in again, kicking and screaming all the while. When she tried to bring the appendage in for a third strike, I twisted against her, which caused it to glance along my side instead of landing a direct hit. Unfortunately, although the move saved me from another blow to the ribs, it allowed her to wriggle down even more.

In an instant, crushing agony tore into the top of my left wrist, and I let out a scream. A muffled shriek came from her throat as she bit deeply into my arm. Once again I could feel my flesh tearing as her teeth sunk through skin and tendon. My hand jerked with a spasm, and my arms loosened out of reflex. She instantly scrambled upward, and through my watering eyes, I caught a glimpse of her mouth smeared red with my blood. I rolled and pulled myself to my feet as well, but she was already sprinting away.

I flashed a quick glance back to my right looking for help but didn't see anyone. I had no idea where Velvet had gone, but apparently I was on my own. I started after Annalise, following her up one of the wider "alleys" toward the center of the graveyard. Once again, she was well in the lead.

Darting to the right, she disappeared, and I pressed myself even harder to catch up. Focusing on the point where she ducked from sight, I brought myself in closer to the row of tombs and veered in the same direction. Coming up on the opening, I thrust my hand outward and used it to buffer myself against the structures as I took the turn at a dead run. My wounded appendage thudded against the wall, and I felt a fresh twinge of pain shoot up my arm. I fought to ignore it, but I could feel myself wince as I let out a yelp.

I was starting to pant hard as I fought for breath, but I pushed forward, covering the short distance and hooking around the opposite end of the row of tombs. The area opened up; however, there were two wide alleys, one to the left and one to the right. Acting purely on instinct, I veered to the left and continued running. As I shot past a large crypt, I caught a glimpse of her in another passage to my right, running in the general direction of the front gate.

Skidding on the walkway, I changed my direction and took after her. We zigzagged between tombs, her managing to stay a few paces out of my reach, but with me gaining on her each step.

As we crossed a main alley, she continued straight on and slipped into a narrow gap between two crypts. I started to follow but could tell immediately that I would never be able to fit my frame through the opening, so I whipped to the left and shot around the end of the row. I could already hear her frantic footsteps ahead, so I didn't even bother making the second 90° turn to go toward where she had cut through. Instead, I kept going forward. She was still ahead of me, but her shortcut hadn't given her the edge she needed. In fact, it had worked just the opposite, and I was now barely within reach. Lunging, I launched myself through the short space between us and tackled her as she shot out in front of me.

Once again we both went down hard on the concrete, but it was obvious from the way she kept moving that her leather jacket was affording her more protection than my thinner cloth garment was giving me. Still, she screeched as we rolled, and I did the same. I'm not certain if it was from pain or anger on her part, though I suspected it was both.

She rolled over in a flash and kicked at me as she scrambled back against a tomb bearing a brass plate and more than a few X's scribed on its surface. I wasn't certain, but I thought I saw the name Marie Laveau inscribed on the plaque before Annalise's body obscured it from my view. A plate full of coins scattered everywhere when she knocked it from its pedestal. It was soon joined by candles and vases full of flowers that she upset as she continued scrabbling away from me.

I came up to a kneeling position and lunged toward her again, but she twisted out of my way. When she rolled back toward me, her hand was wrapped around the heavy glass container of a seven-day candle. Out of the corner of my eye, I saw it arcing toward me, so I threw my arm up and twisted, catching the brunt of it against my shoulder. I heard a wounded animal screaming then realized that it was me.

She scurried backwards, kicking me as she moved, then climbed to her feet and started running again. I dragged myself up and started after her, stumbling against the tombs as new and altogether unpleasant agonies joined the old. Slipping along a walkway, I shot out onto the main alley that ran parallel to the front wall. Looking to the left, I saw that she was already hooking to the right and out the front gate.

I ignored ceremony and rushed headlong behind her at a renewed sprint. The souls of the departed were just going to have to cut me some slack this time.

CHAPTER 14:

I exited the gates and shot across Basin Street in front of the cemetery without even bothering to check traffic. Fortunately, there was none to speak of. Annalise had widened the gap between us due to that last scuffle, and no matter how hard I was pushing myself, I no longer seemed to be able to gain on her. In fact it was all I could do to keep from falling farther behind. My only saving grace was the fact that she wasn't moving as fast as she had been before either, and it even looked like she might be faltering because I could see that she was holding on to her side as she ran.

I knew exactly how she felt. I wasn't sure if there was a single point on my body that wasn't ravaged by pain at the moment, and I knew it was slowing me down. I was also well aware that the pains weren't just from the damage she had inflicted. My legs were getting heavier, and my lungs were burning as I gasped for breath. A sharp pain was piercing my ribcage with each labored gulp of air, and I was even starting to feel lightheaded. The extreme exertion was taking its toll on my already exhausted system.

I kept my eyes focused on Annalise as I covered the half block to North Rampart. She was already out into the middle of the street dodging traffic as I ran off the curb. The sound of a blaring horn pierced my ears then mixed with the squeal of tires against pavement. I jerked my head in the direction of the noise and saw the oncoming vehicles. It felt as though my heart seized in my chest, and I was frozen with fear. I don't know how, but I still managed to jump forward. A compact car skidded at an angle, and I felt a whoosh of air at my back. I elected not to look because I didn't want to see how close I had just come to being road kill.

Another horn blared, and yet another. Rubber squealed on asphalt, and a truck slid to a halt in front of me, stopping only inches away and to my left. I jerked to the side and started to go around it when a loud crash met my ears. I caught a flash of the truck lurching forward out of the corner of my eye and jumped back instead. I felt myself thump against the first car that had barely missed me and watched as the truck was pushed several feet by the vehicle that had just rear-ended it, finally halting exactly where I would have been had I continued around it. I slid sideways between the truck in front of me and the compact car at my back then shot forward hooking around the end of the pileup I had just caused. I should have been scared out of my wits, but at this point I actually found myself feeling like a confused squirrel on his way across any given street.

Ahead of me, Annalise was dealing with her own self-inflicted obstacle course. I watched as she ran directly into the side of a station wagon that had only a split second before screeched to a halt in front of her. She bounced against the front quarter panel, stumbled, then regained her footing and continued on. As she swivel-hipped around the front end of the vehicle, she glanced back at me for a split second then tore off across the asphalt.

I launched myself into the mess once again, running a serpentine course between vehicles that had ended up stopped at oblique angles. Traffic was coming to a halt quickly; however, there were still a few cars in motion, and we both had to dodge them as well. Horns were still honking, some at us, some at other cars as confusion ran rampant through the mid-afternoon drivers. Some of those who had been directly involved in the accidents were out on the street screaming at us as we darted past them.

If I hadn't been smack in the middle of this insanity myself, I'm sure I would have been looking around for the movie cameras. It was simply that surreal.

The various obstructions had caused our pace to slow somewhat, but it didn't allow either of us to actually catch our breath. I had managed to close in by maybe a pair of steps at the most, so Annalise was still well ahead of me when she hit the curb on the opposite side of North Rampart. Our trajectories had been thrown off with all the zigzagging, and she now veered to the left. Anticipating her move, I barreled across trying to angle myself so that I could continue down the cross street where I assumed she was heading.

Though it still appeared to me that she was holding her side, she seemed to have gained a second wind. She sprinted across the mouth of Saint Louis Street, but instead of turning down it as I expected her to do, she continued along the sidewalk parallel to North Rampart. Because of my angle and momentum, I overshot the sidewalk and had to double back a few paces, instantly losing any gain I had picked up. Making the quick turn and whipping back around the corner of the building, I leaped across the curb and fell in behind her, still several paces to the rear.

My heart was racing so fast it felt like a single drawn-out thump inside my chest. I was wheezing air in and out of my tortured lungs as fast as I possibly could, but the oxygen apparently still wasn't making it to my brain because the lightheadedness I had felt a moment before was now becoming dizziness.

Over the sound of the blood rushing in my ears, I thought I heard music trilling nearby. Some portion of my tipsy brain still managed to recognize the tune and forwarded a message to the appropriate quadrant telling me that it was my cell phone. I ignored this new bit of information and kept running. I couldn't tell what Annalise was going to do next because she was merely following a straight line at the fastest pace she could muster. I tried to stay focused on her and anticipate her moves, but she had fooled me once already, so I wasn't sure how confident I was in making another guess. The problem was that I think she was well aware of her edge because at the last minute she feinted left then veered suddenly right onto Toulouse.

However, at the same instant she was making the turn, a man was coming around the corner from the opposite direction. She slammed headlong into him, causing him to stumble back against the wall of the building as she tripped and rolled to the ground. I tried to yell to the man to hold her there, but I couldn't catch enough breath to form the words.

He was already helping her scramble up to her feet a second later when I made it to them. I reached out to grab her, and she quickly twisted away, once again screaming "RAPE" as loud as she could manage while doing so.

The man immediately grabbed my arm and shouted, "HEY!"

I tried to wrench away from him, but he had his fist twisted into the cloth of my jacket. Annalise didn't wait around to see what was about to ensue; she immediately turned and bolted down the street into the French Quarter.

I pulled hard, trying to break free of the man, but he appeared to be dead set on protecting her from me, shouting once again, "HEY! Whaddaya think you're doin'?!" Then, with a sudden look of surprise in his face he added, "GAWD!"

What the final exclamation was all about I didn't know, but I decided his apparent shock might work to my advantage. I seized on the fact that he was pulling against me and that I could use the opposing force as additional leverage. Yanking back, I then suddenly pitched forward and launched myself into him. Taken completely by surprise, he slammed backwards against the wall. He was by no means incapacitated, but it jarred him enough that I was able to twist and pull free of his grasp. I started away before he could make another grab for me, but I still sucked in a quick breath and wheezed it back out at him as, "Cops…Call cops…"

Huffing hard, I ran in the direction Annalise had taken, but by now she was completely out of sight. Fortunately, I didn't hear any footsteps behind me, so when I reached the first cross street, I slowed before glancing first left then right, but I saw no sign of her. I thought about flipping a mental coin and heading one direction or the other, but something didn't feel right about the tactic. Instead, I picked up my pace and decided to jog farther along Toulouse, heading deeper into The Quarter.

Going ahead and crossing Burgundy Street, I entered the second block. It actually made sense that she would have continued along this path as it would afford the easiest way to disappear. The sidewalks were littered with debris that had been removed from hurricane-damaged buildings. There were even several refrigerators and other appliances blocking the walkways, many of them inscribed in indelible marker with what appeared to be derogatory statements about FEMA and the executive branch of the federal government. With delivery trucks and other vehicles on the road as well, it made for a maze in which hiding places were beyond plentiful.

If the inanimate objects weren't enough, the farther in I traveled, the more activity I encountered. There were people going about their daily routines, which now included a large amount of rehab. The majority of them were intent on their jobs hauling trash out of buildings, and paid me little to no attention, although I did get an odd glance or two. I guess they weren't used to seeing people jog through The Quarter.

My somewhat slower pace was actually allowing me to catch my breath, but the dizziness remained, and it was starting to make me nauseous. My throttled-back jog also wasn't doing anything positive for my anxiety. As long as Annalise had been within my line of sight, I had felt like there was a chance to catch her. Now, I was beginning to wonder if I was simply wasting my time. Even if I was, I couldn't give up quite yet. But, I also knew that running full out down the street wouldn't allow me to see her if she was hiding just around a corner.

In a way, this all should have been funny, but I definitely wasn't laughing. It had barely been one day since I had told Ben that Annalise was his problem and not mine. I suppose when I said that, I had simply been spouting empty words because when it came right down to it, she was just as much my problem as anyone else's. Maybe even more. While Miranda was definitely at the root of this evil, I knew all along I was dealing with both of them, and it was a no-win situation. I had to find Miranda to find Annalise, but I had to find Annalise before I could do anything about Miranda.

I stopped in the middle of Dauphine as I crossed, glancing quickly up and down, but still saw no sign of my wife's doppelganger. Continuing on across, I began running into more people, some of them possibly tourists from the way they were acting. However, instead of ignoring me as most of the workers had, the odd looks became far more frequent, and some of the individuals even made it a point to step out of my way.

The dizziness had grown worse, and I could no longer maintain a jog. Now, I was merely plodding along while sending my barely focused gaze to search both sides of the street, not that it was doing any good. My head was pounding as the world tilted and spun, and I wasn't sure any longer if I would even be able to pick her out of the crowd if I was staring directly into her face.

An older couple darted out of my path as I began to stagger, their own faces stretching into horrified masks right before my eyes. I turned to look at them then stumbled and fell against the wall of the building next to me. I knew Bourbon Street couldn't be much farther, but when I looked up, the signature light post at the corner seemed as though it was a mile away.

I slumped against the bricks as pedestrians continued going out of their way to walk around me, even stepping out into the street to do so. I hung my head and closed my eyes, trying to breath deeply and force the nausea to pass, but I wasn't having much luck. When my eyes fluttered open, I noticed a small splotch on the sidewalk. For no other reason than to try focusing my eyes, I stared at it. The edges of the blot began to sharpen, and a moment of clarity overtook my vision. In that second I noticed a droplet of red as it fell and struck the blotch with a wet splat. Directing my gaze toward the source, I noticed a ragged flap of flesh peeled back from the top of my wrist and a swath of the same crimson flowing across the back of my hand.

I felt myself sinking as fatigue overwhelmed me, and I slid downward against the wall. Voices were echoing in my ears, and I struggled to understand them with little success. I tried to push myself back up to my feet but couldn't seem to make my legs work.

I rolled my head back and saw lights flashing. My mouth watered as a fresh round of nausea attacked my stomach. I could feel my lips moving as I tried desperately to ask for help but found myself unable to make the word come out.

Everything began to spin and go dark.

Trilling music began playing softly. I knew it was my cell phone demanding my attention once again, but I couldn't make my hand move to retrieve it. It continued stepping up in volume but was suddenly drowned out by the sound of a car stopping nearby.

The last thing I remember hearing was a rush of radio static followed by a voice echoing in my ears as it said, "I got 'im. Corner a Too-Loose an' Bourbon. Better send da' paramedics."

CHAPTER 15:

"Apparently kitten has claws," Velvet said, giving me a once over as she walked in.

"Isn't that some kind of makeup or something?" I grunted. "I think my wife has some of it."

"I believe it might be a shade of nail polish," she replied. "But, I was actually talking about your face."

I had to lift my head slightly to see her because at present I was lying back on a table in a treatment room of a hospital. Earlier, when a nurse had been asking me for insurance information, she mentioned that I was at Charity Campus or something of that sort. My brain had still been a bit muddled at the time, so I hadn't really registered much. Not that I would have really known where it was to begin with. All I knew was that it seemed like I spent a lot of time in places like this whenever I got involved in an investigation. It was a wonder my insurance carrier hadn't dropped me yet. If they didn't this time, I was sure they would be raising my premiums. That was something they always did without fail.

"Yeah, that," I muttered, reaching up and brushing my fingers against the gauze bandage now covering the wounds. I felt a tug on the back of my hand and gave it a glance. I had pretty much forgotten about the IV line taped securely to it. I gave it a half-hearted wiggle to reposition the tubing then laid my hand back across my chest. "Teeth too."

"How is the arm, by the way?" she asked, nodding in the direction of the other appendage which was now wrapped in its own windings of sterile dressing.

"Not bad right now. But, I can already tell the local is wearing off."

I had lost track of how long I had been here. I'd been drifting in and out for a while although I had officially regained consciousness at right about the moment they were preparing to slide me onto the treatment table upon arriving in the emergency room. Since my most recent memory at that point—other than the disembodied voice—had been that of chasing after Annalise, my body seemed to think it was something I needed to continue doing. I was told that it had taken both paramedics and a nurse to keep me from coming off the gurney at a dead run.

"Do you know if they've found her yet?"

"Not that I've heard, but I'm not really in the loop."

I shook my head as best I could since it was resting against the pillow, and with a full load of sarcasm muttered, "Fucking wonderful."

"Tough little bitch, isn't she?" she stated as much as asked.

"Reminds me of my wife," I replied but didn't expand further.

"That's some wife."

"You have no idea." I sighed then tried to reposition myself a bit so that I wasn't talking at the ceiling. "So, where did you go back at the cemetery? I looked up and you were just gone."

"I left my cell in my car. I ran back to call the police like you said."

"Oh."

"Feeling abandoned, were you?"

"Maybe a little," I admitted. "It's not like we know each other all that well. A lot of folks wouldn't have wanted to get involved...especially after listening to my outlandish story and then hearing her scream 'rape.'"

"I was already involved," she told me. "I took you there, remember? Besides, I'm not like a lot of folks."

"I'm getting that impression... And, believe me, right now I appreciate that more than you know."

It grew quiet in the room except for the noises of the staff out in the hall. I rested my head back against the pillow and stared at the ceiling for a long while, contemplating the acoustic tiles as I tried to ignore the various aches that hadn't benefited from a hypodermic full of local anesthetic. After a minute or two, a curious thought flitted through my brain, and I rolled my head to face Velvet once again.

"How did you get in here anyway?" I asked. "I seem to recall a cop standing outside the door when the doctor left earlier. It looked like he was guarding it or something."

"I told him I was your wife," she replied.

"You did what?"

She smiled. "Calm down, I'm only kidding."

"Okay…I just didn't figure you for that sort of levity."

"I have my moments," she replied. Then, she shrugged and continued, "Actually, it didn't seem to be a problem. I just asked if I could check on you, and they let me right in. Maybe it was because I already gave a statement and…"

She was interrupted by a quick knock then the door swinging open. A petite, dark-haired woman clad in scrubs came in then shut the barrier behind her.

"Oh, hello," she said, noticing Velvet. "I'm Doctor Miller… You are?"

"Doctor Rieth," Velvet replied, shaking her hand.

Doctor Miller canted her head to the side and furrowed her brow.

Before she could say anything else, Velvet offered, "I'm a different kind of doctor." She nodded in my direction and added, "Actually, I'm only here because I'm a friend of Rowan's. I was just keeping him company."

Doctor Miller gave her a quick smile, "I see. Well, I need to go over a few things with Mister Gant, so…"

"Say no more," she told her before she could finish the spiel. "I need to go get a cup of coffee anyway." Glancing in my direction, she added. "I'll see you in a little while."

"Yeah," I returned. "Do me a favor and have a cup for me while you're at it."

"Will do."

After Velvet left, the doctor turned her attention back to me.

"So, how are you feeling, Mister Gant?"

"Pretty much like I was run over by a truck," I replied.

"The way I understand it, you almost were."

"Yeah, there is that."

She opened a chart and scanned the papers inside. "I wanted to ask you something. You mentioned earlier that the only medication you had been taking lately is aspirin?"

"That's right."

"How often?"

"I don't know," I replied. "A few times a day I guess."

"How many is a few?"

"I don't know… Six… Maybe eight."

She frowned. "What dosage?"

"Just a handful."

She looked at me and frowned even harder, "Seriously?"

"Well, not a big handful. I guess maybe six or seven. Or ten or twelve. Depends on when I was taking it and how bad I hurt."

"At a time?"

"Yeah."

"Eighty-one or three hundred twenty-five milligram?"

"Whatever regular old aspirin is. Three twenty-five I guess."

"Why?"

"Chronic headache."

"Have you seen a doctor about it?"

"Trust me, it's not that kind of headache."

"Really. What kind of headache is it then?"

"You wouldn't believe me if I told you," I sighed.

"So, you haven't been taking the aspirin on doctor's orders?"

"Not unless I'm now a doctor."

"Honestly, I had you pegged as more intelligent than this, Mister Gant. You do realize that OTC meds are still drugs, don't you? Self-medicating is extremely dangerous. Especially the way you were doing it." She huffed out a disgusted breath before continuing, "Did you even bother to read the directions on the bottle?"

"Of course. Take two, yadda, yadda…"

"Mister Gant," her tone remained serious. "Do I have to spell this out for you? The reason you collapsed is that you are severely dehydrated and have dangerously low blood pressure; both of which are symptoms of severe salicylate poisoning."

"So, what you're saying is I overdosed on aspirin?"

"To put it simply, yes. Given the amount you said you were taking, I'm surprised you aren't in much worse shape."

I let my head fall back on the pillow. "Doc, you have no idea."

"What do you mean?"

I lifted my head back up. "I mean I just let a killer get away because of a goddamned headache. You can't imagine how that feels."

She thumbed through the papers in the file then looked back at me with a confused expression. "Are you a police officer?"

"No," a new voice answered for me. "But, he likes to pretend he is."

Doctor Miller turned and at the same time, I looked over toward the door. Neither of us had noticed the new arrival until now.

"Detective Fairbanks," I said with a dispirited sigh.

"You done with him, Doctor?" he asked, flashing his ID.

"Actually, I'd like to admit him for observation. Will that be a problem?"

"If it's all the same to you, I'd rather not stay," I interjected.

"You shut up," Fairbanks instructed, glancing at me. "Right now you're in custody, and what you want doesn't matter." Looking back to Doctor Miller, he continued, "If you need to keep him, that's no problem, as long as he doesn't go anywhere. But, right now I do need to talk to him if you don't mind."

"Be my guest," she replied. "I'll go get the paperwork started."

The detective waited for her to leave then looked back at me with a stoic expression. After a moment of playing stare down, he said, "I thought we had an agreement. So I'm sure you can imagine my utter dismay at finding out you were still in town."

"You didn't really expect me to leave, did you?"

"Yes, actually I did."

"Well, sorry about that, but I wasn't finished here yet."

"What? You just aren't happy with your visit until you cause a multi-car pileup on one of the busiest streets in the city?"

"That was unfortunate," I replied.

"Unfortunate?" he harrumphed. "I was thinking more like unconscionable. You're just lucky no one got hurt. Although, I wouldn't be surprised if you end up getting sued by a couple of people, and I wouldn't blame them a bit if they do."

"I was chasing the killer," I said.

"That's what your friend out there told us in her statement," he agreed with a nod. "But, tell me this—how do you know you were chasing a killer and not just some frightened woman who thought you were going to rape her or something? We have at least two eyewitnesses who claim they saw her running from you screaming just exactly that."

"You wouldn't..."

He held up a hand to stop me. "Yeah, I know, I wouldn't believe you if you told me. That seems to be your excuse for everything."

"It's not an excuse, it's the truth."

"Yeah, whatever. Sounds like an excuse to me."

"If I told you, you would think I'm insane."

"Hell, Gant, I already think you're insane."

"Look, you said you'd talked to Ben, and he filled you in on this case."

He nodded. "You mean this case that you aren't actually working? Yeah, he did."

"That's not the point. What I'm trying to tell you is that the woman I was chasing is Annalise Devereaux. She's your killer."

"No, Mister Gant, she is a person of interest to the Major Case Squad in Saint Louis," he corrected.

"Call her whatever you want, I'm telling you she killed two men in Saint Louis, at the very least one here, and who knows how many more. She's been implicated in..."

He cut me off. "You aren't telling me anything I don't already know. We cops actually know how to work telephones. Some of us even go so far as to use fax machines and email you know."

"Then why wasn't someone watching the cemetery? If you knew about her then all of this could have been avoided."

"Mister Gant, in case you haven't noticed, we have our hands full around New Orleans. Hell, I'm just down here as a volunteer. I was actually expecting to shuffle papers for a few weeks to help out, but I ended up on the streets working a homicide, and somehow that managed to get me hung with you. All I can figure is that I've done something to piss off God because my life normally doesn't go like this."

I ignored the sardonic remark and told him, "I'm not the one you need to worry about."

"Right," he nodded emphatically. "We need to worry about the mystery woman you chased through traffic."

"Annalise Devereaux."

"So you say."

"She hasn't come forward and pressed charges, has she?"

He shook his head. "No."

"She won't."

"Statistically, you might be correct. Whoever she is, she's probably scared shitless to even come out of her house after what you did."

"That's not the reason. She won't come forward because she's..."

"...Annalise Devereaux, evil killer woman. I know. You've told me. So what? You still assaulted her."

"What I was going to say is that she knows you're looking for her."

"How?"

"I told her."

"You told her we're looking for her?" he asked calmly, although his expression didn't fit his tone.

"Yes."

"Mind if I ask why? And, don't tell me I wouldn't believe it if you told me."

"I don't know," I told him.

"Well that's new and different," he hmmphed. "Assuming that you are correct, and this woman actually is Miz Devereaux, did it cross your mind that telling her we're looking for her might make her harder to find?"

"Not at the time, no. Besides, don't you give that sort of info to the media so it can be broadcast on the news?"

"Not always. And, definitely not right away," he replied. "This time was one of those definite not yet situations."

"Well...I guess I screwed up then."

"You guess? Holy crap, Gant, you're just a goddamned joy to have around, aren't you?" he said, his sarcasm expanding to fill the room. "Do you do this sort of shit to Detective Storm too? Because if you do I'm surprised he hasn't killed you yet."

"Ben and I work together a little better than you and I seem to."

"We aren't working together, Gant. You're just getting in the way and being a huge pain in my ass."

"I don't have a choice."

"Really? How's that? What did I ever do to you?"

"I'm trying to help my wife. You already know that."

"Yeah, I do. I'm just not entirely clear on how chasing after *a person of interest* in a murder investigation you have *nothing to do with* is helping your wife."

"I can't really explain it."

"Don't tell me, let me guess—I wouldn't believe you if you told me."

Instead of responding to his sarcasm, I simply replied, "You're just going to have to trust me on this."

"I did that once already, and look what it got me."

"Listen, Detective Fairbanks..."

"No, Gant, *you* listen. You've been in town less than forty-eight hours and you're already vying for your own position next to Katrina as the worst natural disaster ever to hit this city. You rank somewhere on the order of an empty-handed FEMA bureaucrat at this point, so nobody is really interested in what you have to say."

"Fine," I spat. "So what now? Am I under arrest?"

"If I had my way, you sure as hell would be," he barked in return. "But apparently Storm isn't the only friend you have in high places, so technically you're in protective custody."

"Constance?" I asked.

"I have no idea who," he replied with a shake of his head. "But, based on the call we received, somebody at the FBI has a vested interest in you for some unknown reason. Hell, we've actually been looking for you for them since this morning."

"Looking for me?"

"That's right. Apparently, the feds would like for you to come home."

"What's that supposed to mean?"

"It means, as much as we'd like to bury you under the jail right now, we aren't going to. But, as soon as the doctor cuts you loose, I'm personally sticking your ass on a plane back to Saint Louis and letting them deal with you."

CHAPTER 16:

Initially, I was adamant that I had no intention of allowing them to admit me to the hospital. However, my argument didn't last long. To his credit, Detective Fairbanks did give me a choice, limited as it was. The way he explained it, my options were to get on the first airplane bound for Saint Louis, to stay at the hospital until the doctor released me, or to spend the remainder of my time here in New Orleans inspecting the inside of their lockup. Since I was already dwelling on his bad side, I had no doubt he was serious.

Unfortunately, after a short exchange with Doctor Miller, he retracted the option of immediate travel home, which had been my preferred choice. And, since I was technically in police custody, there was no room for me to negotiate that point. Apparently, disliked as I was, they were still intent on me not dying until they were in the clear. I had no doubt this was based solely on an issue of liability rather than any true concern for my continued well-being.

So, while I was no fan of hospitals, the idea of spending the night in jail was even less appealing; therefore, the decision became an instantaneous no-brainer. At least I was going to have a clean bed in which to sleep for a change.

I was also told that my rental car had been impounded, which I'm certain wasn't going to sit well with the company that owned it, but there wasn't much I could do. And, of course, it didn't stop there. They took the key to my room at the Airline Courts in order to collect my luggage and anything else I had felt comfortable with leaving there unattended. I was, however, assured they would be returned to me, as well as the rest of my personal effects, upon my release and once I had been escorted to the airport.

Since the police had already taken Velvet's statement, and they didn't see her as the threat they saw me, she was free to leave. She had graciously offered to hang loose for a while once I was settled in, however I was well aware she still had an hour or so drive ahead of her to get back to Baton Rouge. As much as I would have appreciated the company, I felt as though I had disrupted her life more than enough already, so I urged her to go home. Eventually, she gave in, though only after I promised to contact her if I needed any further help. It seemed I had made at least one friend while I was here.

Now, to occupy the void, I had been trying to watch TV. I managed to catch the last half of a re-broadcast episode of *Firefly* on a cable station, but after that, all I seemed to be able to find were so-called "reality shows" that were worse than a waste of time. After running up and down the gamut of channels, I switched it off. Dragging myself out of the bed for the third time since arriving in the room, I made my way to the bathroom to empty my bladder. They were still running IV's into me at full bore. While I had insisted after my second trip to the toilet that I must be fully re-hydrated by now, I was informed that I was being flushed out. A catheter was offered if I felt the repeated trips were too annoying, but I declined, promising instead to fill the sample cups each time I went. Fortunately, that seemed to satisfy them.

I finished executing my duty and had just rolled the IV stand back into place next to the bed before sitting down when a nurse came into the room.

"How are you feelin', Mistuh Gant?" she asked.

"About as good as can be expected," I grumbled. "By the way, I just left you a present in the bathroom."

"For me? Why, thank you. Ya' shouldn't have," she replied in a bubbly voice.

"You're way too cheerful," I told her.

She ignored the statement and went about checking my IV then my pulse and blood pressure. When she was finished, she asked, "Do ya' need anythin'?"

"Not that I can think of," I replied.

"All right then, my name is Adrienne, and I'll be takin' care of you this shift. If you need anythin'…"

I held up my hand and interrupted her, my voice somewhat astringent. "Just press the call button, yeah, I know…" When I finished the comment, I sighed heavily then said, "Look, Adrienne. I apologize. That was rude. This just hasn't been a particularly wonderful day for me, so my mood isn't what you would call good."

"I understand," she said with a smile.

"Thanks."

"Besides, dawlin'," she added, grinning. "Dawn already warned me you were a grouch."

"Yeah, making friends and influencing people. That's me."

"I'll just pick up your specimen an' I'll be back ta' check on ya' later. Okay?"

"Looking forward to it," I told her as I twisted around and lay back on the bed.

She headed out, stopping by the bathroom as she went. When she came out I called over to her, "Hey, Adrienne. You wouldn't happen to know what time it is, would you?"

She glanced at her watch. "Ten to eight."

"Thanks."

"No problem."

When she was gone, I sat back up on the bed and reached over to the telephone. I dialed for an outside line then started punching in the toll free line and pass code of my calling card. Once I heard the fresh dial tone, I stabbed in a number I'd come to memorize over the past week. After a pair of rings, the operator came on the line.

"Felicity O'Brien's room, please," I asked.

"Whom should I say is calling?"

"Her husband, Rowan Gant."

"Mister Gant, please hold," she replied.

After a short wait the line was picked up.

"Rowan?" Instead of hearing Felicity's voice, I was greeted with Helen Storm's issuing from the handset. She seemed calm, but her tone held an underlying note of concern. "We have been trying to reach you for hours."

"Is something wrong?" I asked immediately, my own concern rising to the surface. "Is Felicity okay?"

"At the moment, she is fine. However, earlier today she experienced a somewhat bizarre psychotic episode."

"Miranda?" I asked.

"I am not certain. All I can tell you is that for a period of several minutes, she believed someone was chasing her, and she was doing everything in her power to get away. At one point she actually bit one of the staff. Afterwards, she was frantic, asking repeatedly to speak with you."

I sighed heavily as I hung my head. "It was me."

"You? What do you mean?"

"I mean she was trying to get away from me," I said then explained further by filling her in on the details of the afternoon.

"At this point I would say the question is, are you okay?" she said when I finished.

"I'll be fine," I told her. "But, unless I find a way to stop all this, Felicity isn't."

"You do not know that, Rowan."

"Yes I do, Helen," I replied. "This connection between her and Miranda…or her and Annalise…or both…I don't know…whatever it is, it's getting stronger."

"But, this is the first episode she has experienced in several days."

"Maybe so, but just look at what triggered it."

"The chase?"

"Not exactly. The fear."

"A strong emotion."

"Exactly. I think that is what's driving all of this. I just don't know what's making the connection, other than the fact that Annalise and Felicity are related."

"Do you think that could be it?"

"I'm positive it has something to do with it, but if it was the only factor then I think Felicity would have started experiencing this before now. If the evidence in all of the unsolved murders adds up, Annalise has been at this for at least two years, maybe more."

"Perhaps what triggered the connection was her visit to Saint Louis," she suggested.

"Proximity? Maybe so, but then why hasn't the connection faded now that she's no longer there?"

"Maybe once the connection was made that was all it took."

"I'm not willing to entertain that option."

"Why not?"

"Because if it's true then there's nothing I can do to save my wife."

"You cannot be certain of that, Rowan."

"Helen, I've read everything about Voodoo and hoodoo I can get my hands on. I've even had lengthy conversations with a published expert on the subject. But, I still don't know enough about how it works to be sure of anything."

"What did Doctor Rieth have to say about this?"

"Pretty much the same thing she said before I ever came down here. She agrees with me for the most part. While the familial tie is almost certainly fueling this, something from the outside has to be working on Felicity as well. It isn't completely unheard of for a *Lwa* to jump from one horse to another, but it isn't typical or even common. The faithful invite them in, which is what allows the possession to take place. Popping into someone uninvited isn't their preferred method of corporeal manifestation. And, that's not even taking into account that a devout practitioner of Vodoun can go an entire lifetime without ever being a horse. So, for this to be happening to a non-practitioner, something external almost has to be involved."

"However, you have stated yourself that Miranda is not a typical *Lwa*."

"That's true, but she's still a spirit. She's going to take the path of least resistance. If they didn't, everyone would hear them..." My voiced trailed off at the end of the sentence, then I added, "Just like me."

"And, Felicity," Helen reminded me. "She is a Witch as well, and she has demonstrated her own propensity for communicating with the dead."

"Yeah, I know," I breathed. "But we both know that isn't the normal way of things. Besides, I'm pretty sure it's my fault that she's been cursed with that affliction."

"You cannot constantly take blame on yourself for the things over which you have no control, Rowan," she admonished. "We have had this discussion before."

"We'll have to save my therapy session for later, Helen. Right now I have to figure out why my wife is being randomly possessed by a sadistic dead woman."

"Were you able to find anything at the cemetery?"

"Besides Annalise? Actually, I didn't even get a chance to look at the tomb. I had it in my head to go back and check it out, but that's pretty much not happening at this point."

"Can someone check for you?"

"I'm sure I can get Velvet—Doctor Rieth—to do it," I said. "But, I really hate asking her to do that even though she's offered. I've imposed upon her enough as it is."

"She might be your only option."

"True. But, to be honest, I'm probably grabbing at straws anyway. Felicity didn't know about Annalise until recently, and by all indications, Annalise has only recently become aware of Felicity—although I'm fairly certain it is only cursory. I don't get the impression she knows any specifics. So, the odds of her being responsible for any intentional *gris-gris* directed toward her are pretty low."

"Who would be responsible then?"

"That's the big question, Helen. People don't work magick on someone without a reason. I'm not saying that the reasons are always pure, by any means, but just picking someone at random and working magick on them isn't terribly effective."

"So, what other options are there?"

"Just what Velvet mentioned originally. Felicity has something that belonged to Miranda, or possibly Annalise. Something like a piece of jewelry maybe, or it could even be the other way around. Of course, we can obviously rule out Miranda being in possession of any corporeal items falling into that category, so if that were the case, it would have to be Annalise who has something of Felicity's."

"And, you have had no luck in that area of investigation?"

"Not really. One would think it would have to be something obtained recently, but Felicity can't remember purchasing or selling anything over the past few months. Of course, that doesn't mean that Annalise didn't somehow come by a piece of jewelry that Felicity sold on an auction website or something in the past. These things do change hands."

"Could it have been a gift Felicity received, perhaps?"

"Thought of that too. No luck there either."

"Well, Rowan, if your theory is correct, there has to be something that has bound the two of them together."

A fresh stab of pain struck deep inside my head, as an all too obvious word echoed in my ears. But, it wasn't an agony borne of the chronic ache to which I had grown accustomed. It was an emotional pain brought about by a truly horrific realization.

"Rowan? Are you there?" Helen asked.

"I have to go," I said quickly.

"Rowan? Is something wrong?"

"I'll explain later," I replied, rushing to get the words out. "Take care of Felicity. I'll be there soon."

She was still talking to me when I hung up the phone.

Twisting left then right, I located the control pendant on the bed and stabbed the call button with my thumb. I was already up out of the bed when Adrienne came through the door.

"What can I do for ya' Mistuh Gant?" she asked.

"I need to speak with Doctor Miller."

"She's not on duty this evenin'. I can get the physician on call. Are you feelin' okay?"

"Get her on the phone then," I instructed, ignoring her question.

"And, tell her she needs to get Detective Fairbanks over here right away too."

"Is something wrong?"

"Yes, there is," I replied, my voice rushed. "Very wrong. But it's something I can't fix here. I have to get back to Saint Louis right now."

CHAPTER 17:

I was escorted directly to my gate at New Orleans Louis Armstrong International Airport. The only problem I had with that fact was that it happened ten hours later than I wanted. The delay, however, wasn't for a lack of me trying to get out of town; that much was certain.

As I suspected would be the case, Detective Fairbanks turned out to be the least of my problems. He was in as big a hurry to be rid of me as I was to go, so he took next to no convincing where my being allowed to leave was concerned. He didn't even ask why I was in such a rush. Of course, I had a feeling he knew the answer I was likely to give and simply didn't want to hear it again.

Still, he insisted Doctor Miller make the final call, and she was definitely the hard sell, especially since I was doing this all by phone. Unfortunately, by the time she grudgingly agreed to my release, it was too late. There wasn't a single Saint Louis bound flight to be had, no matter what I was willing to pay, where I was prepared to sit, or how many connections I was content to make.

Once again time was presenting itself as my enemy; but for this skirmish my luck no longer held, and I was unable to beat the clock. The best I could manage was to change my existing reservation, and since the airline with the earliest departure time happened to be the one for which I already held a ticket, that was easy enough done. Beyond that, I was still stuck in New Orleans for the rest of the night, which didn't sit well with me at all, a fact I was all too happy to share.

In response to my severe agitation, the physician on duty insisted on prescribing a sedative. I didn't want it; however I was told that my wants weren't the issue, but my obvious needs were. I suspect the needs to which he referred were less mine and more theirs, as I wasn't being shy when it came to making my displeasure with the entire situation somewhat vociferously known.

Therefore, much to my chagrin, whether I liked the idea or not, I ended up sedated. The only choice I was given was whether I wanted to take it orally of my own volition or be held down for an injection. I opted for the pill. I'll admit it was probably a good thing he forced the issue because the fact that I was trapped here wasn't helping me cope with the personal demon I had only recently loosed upon myself. I sincerely doubt it would have allowed me to sleep otherwise. What little I did manage, however, certainly wasn't restful. Even a drug-induced slumber couldn't stave off the all too real nightmare that was now raging inside my head.

The next morning, true to his word, Detective Fairbanks intended to see me off personally, so he showed up at the hospital early. I was already showered and having fresh dressings applied when he arrived. As it was, the paperwork for my release took longer than anything else.

Our ride to the airport was conspicuously silent, and it really didn't change much after reaching our destination, save for an occasional grunt to direct me here or there. Fairbanks saw me through the check-in process step by step. He didn't physically turn over the bulk of my personal effects until my bags were checked and he had my boarding pass in hand. I don't know if he did it for dramatic effect or if he really believed I might bolt and wreak more havoc in the city. I decided knowing the answer wouldn't accomplish anything for either of us, so I didn't bother to ask.

At the security gate, he handed me off to a uniformed officer and instructed him that I was to be his sole duty until I was in the air and heading north. Then, with only a scowl in my direction to serve as a farewell, he was gone.

The officer walked me through security and dutifully waited until I was on board the aircraft. If he followed his orders, he probably also continued to stand there until the airplane had taxied out to the runway at the very least. I'm betting he did—because the instruction hadn't sounded at all like a joke.

According to my watch, we were wheels up right on time at 7:40

A.M. I still had a little over two hours ahead of me before I was going to have my chance to grapple directly with a monster of my own making.

I just hoped that it wouldn't be too late.

M. R. Sellars

Saturday, December 3
9:43 A.M.
Lambert Saint Louis International Airport
Concourse C, Security Gate
Saint Louis, Missouri

THE END OF DESIRE: A Rowan Gant Investigation

CHAPTER 18:

Impatience had ruled over me for the entire trip, and it was only getting worse now that I was on the ground. Since my flight had arrived at one of the farthest gates it possibly could, I had been faced with plenty of distance to cover on foot. Any other time that wouldn't have bothered me a bit, but in this instance I viewed the walk with nothing but disdain. Of course, it wasn't so much the walk itself as the added delay because it had taken almost fifteen minutes for me to jog up the crowded concourse. I was absolutely certain I could have made it in half that time had it not been for constantly becoming stuck behind people who were more interested in window shopping and visiting than actually moving.

"Rowan!"

The voice issuing the call was unmistakable. Ben was only a few feet ahead as I started through the exit on the security checkpoint, and while I really hadn't expected to see him here, I also couldn't say I was terribly surprised. I'm sure he wanted his turn at chewing me out and simply couldn't wait to get started.

I had actually caught sight of him even before he called my name over the flow of moving bodies. He was hard to miss. Standing six-foot-six tends to make you stick out in the crowd. Being an exceptionally tall Native American even more so. Throw in the fact that he had his badge displayed on a cord around his neck, he may as well have been waving a flag. My intention had been to slip through with the rest of the crowd, hoping to pass by unnoticed. Unfortunately, he saw me before that could happen. What's worse, my reflexes betrayed me by making me look up in his direction at the sound of my name.

Now, I really had no way to avoid him. I was just going to have to keep moving so that he couldn't derail me.

When I neared, he let out a quiet exclamation. "Holy fuck…"

As his voice trailed off, he reached up with a large hand and smoothed his salt and pepper hair, sliding the paw down to the back of his neck where he allowed it to rest. His dark eyes were wide as he stared at me, and I had a feeling whatever admonishment he had originally intended to hurl my direction was momentarily on hold.

"What are you doing here?" I asked, switching my backpack to the opposite shoulder as I continued walking past him at a brisk pace while veering to the left.

"Fairbanks called an' said you were on your way," he replied, catching up in a single, long-legged stride and falling in step with me.

"Figures," I said with a shake of my head then glanced over and added, "I guess he was afraid I'd turn around and come right back, so he'd better send a welcoming committee."

"What the fuck happened to ya'?" my friend asked, ignoring the comment.

"What? Didn't he fill you in?"

"He had plenty ta' say about ya', yeah. Other than the stuff I won't repeat, he said ya' went a couple rounds with some woman then chased 'er across traffic and caused a coupl'a friggin' wrecks… But he didn't tell me ya' actually got hit by one of the cars."

"I didn't," I told him. "And, it wasn't just some woman. It was Annalise."

"Wait a minute… Are you sayin' Devereaux did this to ya'?"

"Yeah."

"You mean a five-foot-nothin' woman kicked your ass?"

"Yeah, Ben, she did," I replied, voice cold. "Then she got away, and your buddy down there didn't seem all that interested in finding her. So, do me a favor and save the jokes. I've got something kind of pressing I need to take care of right now."

I was angling toward the exit, so he grabbed my arm and tried to guide me to the right. "She kick ya' in the head too? Baggage claim is this way."

I pulled away and continued toward the far exit, which led out to the taxi stands. Without looking back I said, "I'll get it later."

I hadn't made it a full step before his hand clamped down on my shoulder, and he stopped me dead in my tracks. "Whoa... What the fuck? Where's the fire?"

"You wouldn't believe..." I started immediately but caught myself before I could finish the sentence.

I suppose Detective Fairbanks was correct. The phrase really had become my personal mantra while I was in New Orleans. In the matter of only two days, I had become accustomed to hiding what I knew and, more importantly, how I knew it. All for fear of being seen as a lunatic, and now, because of that fact, the sentence seemed to tumble from my mouth at the slightest provocation.

And, apparently my brain was too occupied at the moment to adjust to the fact that I was back on familiar ground, talking to someone who wouldn't think I was completely nuts. Of course, standing here now and forcing myself to consider this new reality didn't necessarily change my mode of thinking. I wasn't so sure this was something I was ready to tell Ben either. Even if he wouldn't think I was insane, I wasn't certain I wanted to waste time explaining right now.

I sighed, "Look, Ben, I just need to get home. There's something very important I have to take care of."

"What?"

"I'd really rather not say."

"Rather not, because it's somethin' stupid and ya' think I'll stop ya', or rather not somethin' else?"

"Something else."

"So ya' aren't about to go get yourself inta' some more shit?"

"No," I replied with a shake of my head. "If anything I'm planning to get out of some."

He stared at me for a moment, searching my face. I'm sure he was looking for some physical indication as to whether or not I was lying.

"This way," he finally said, giving my arm a tug. "I'm parked on the upper level of the garage."

Ben's driving didn't bother me for a change. In fact, given that speed limits, in his way of thinking, were more a suggestion than anything else, I actually welcomed it because we arrived at my house quicker than I would have by taking a cab.

I was out of the van before he even had it in park, intent on my single-minded task. It had been cold when I left Saint Louis, and that hadn't changed a bit. Snow had even visited the city, leaving an inch or so of white covering the landscape. My coat was hanging open, and a stiff wind was snaking into it as I strode up the driveway, but I ignored the chill.

I could hear footsteps behind me as Ben broke into a short jog to catch up.

"Yo! White Man… Where're ya' goin'?" he called out.

I didn't respond. I simply unlatched the gate and continued on, first passing by the back deck then the detached garage with a determined stride. Ben was alongside me now, but other than the fact I was aware of his presence and could feel his concern, I wasn't paying any attention to him whatsoever.

Pressing on, I stalked across the pristine blanket of my back yard, my breath condensing in opaque clouds as I huffed the cold air quickly in and out. The dull thud in my head had never left, but it now morphed beyond the chronic throb and burst into acute stabs at the base of my skull. The sickening ache increased with each step and began spreading through my body like electricity seeking ground. My stomach was starting to churn, and I fought back a wave of nausea that was creating a bitter tickle in the back of my throat.

The onslaught continued, and by the time I made it three-quarters of the way across the yard, it had grown so intense that I literally stumbled. Unable to maintain my balance, I fell to my hands and knees. A sharp lance of pain shot up my wounded arm, and it buckled, sending me face first into the snow.

"Jeezus, Row… Are you okay?" Ben asked, fresh concern rimming his voice as he reached down to help me up.

Though I knew he was right next to me, his voice sounded hollow and distant. I started pushing myself up, but as the pain phased through my body, the nausea took hold, and I pitched forward again, expelling the remnants of my hospital breakfast in a steaming lump. I gagged a second time but only vomited a small stream of bile for my trouble. I could feel myself hovering dangerously close to slipping across into the world of the dead, and I knew Miranda was standing on the other side waiting for me with ill intent. The worst part, however, was that I knew for certain this whole thing was my fault and no one else's.

I steeled myself and sucked in a deep breath, holding it for a moment as I sought my mental footing once again in the corporeal plane.

"Holy shit…" Ben exclaimed. "Rowan… What's wrong?"

His voice sounded normal once again, but the pain wasn't letting up. I pushed against the ground and lifted myself to my knees. I felt my friend slip a hand under my arm to help as I climbed to my feet and began my march toward the back of the yard once again.

"Dammit, Row! Talk to me," Ben demanded.

I still didn't respond. I had to remain focused; otherwise, I feared I would succumb to the force that was now attempting to stop me. I picked up my pace and covered the last several yards with Ben still holding my arm as if he feared I was going to fall again. Arriving at the door of Felicity's potting shed, I shrugged away from him and grasped the handle with my good hand. I gave it a quick tug, but it only moved outward a pair of inches before resisting my attack. Looking down, I saw the padlock seated firmly in place.

I knew the key was inside the house, but I didn't feel as though I had time to go in after it. I needed to do this now. I pushed the door inward then yanked it hard, leaning all of my weight back with the motion. I heard the sound of the wood beginning to splinter as stress took hold of the screws anchoring the hasp. The door came out another couple of inches and stopped. I pushed it in and yanked again, and then a third time. On the fourth try, the aging boards splintered and the door swung open wide with a loud crack.

Stepping in through the doorway, I grabbed a shovel then immediately turned and came back out. Continuing around my dismayed friend, I waded out into the decorative garden at the very back of the yard and set my sights on a large mound of snow-covered rocks.

I was just slipping the point of the shovel beneath one corner of the largest of the sponge rocks when Ben grabbed my arm. I looked up at him and could see the concern in his eyes had turned to something almost resembling fear.

"Are you gonna tell me what the fuck's goin' on here?!" he demanded.

"When I'm done," I managed to croak. I could feel hot tears beginning to stream down my face.

"Dammit! You're actin' like ya' lost your friggin' mind, White Man," he pressed.

"I'm trying to save my wife, okay?!" I shouted. "Now, either help me or get the fuck out of my way!"

Before I finished the sentence, I was already looking back down and shoving the business end of the garden implement deeper under the large rock then lifting. The decorative stone broke loose as I leaned my weight into the improvised lever, then it rose slowly upward, teetered for a second and rolled away with a heavy thump. I instantly began driving the point of the shovel against the frozen ground, breaking up the hard soil and scooping it away as fast as I could with only one good arm.

"Jeezus, I must be nuts," Ben grumbled as he reached out and yanked the shovel from my hand and started about the process of digging. "What're we lookin' for? A quicker way ta' hell?"

"A metal box," I replied. "About a foot down."

"A foot? Is that all?" he replied, heavy sarcasm in his words.

He continued to dig, ramming the shovel down hard and tearing at the earth. After several minutes, we both heard a hollow clunk as the spade struck home. He worked the point in beneath the box and pried one end up from the depths.

I was already kneeling next to the hole, tearing at the surrounding dirt with my hand. As soon as I could get a grasp on the unearthed rectangle, I wrenched it from the ground and fumbled with the clasp. Popping the latch on the small toolbox, I yanked it open.

There, just as it had been when I placed it there several weeks ago, was a fashion doll. Its ivory complexion and fiery red hair were visible through the clear cellophane that enveloped it. A dark purple ribbon criss-crossed around the poppet holding the plastic wrapping securely in place.

"You buried a fuckin' doll in your back yard?" Ben asked, a mix of confusion and incredulity in his voice.

Looking up at Ben, I said, "It's her."

"Her who?"

I could already hear an angry wail screeching in my ears, getting louder with each heartbeat.

"I'll explain in a minute," I told him, rushing the sentence from my mouth as fast as I could speak. I held my hand out toward him and asked, "Do you have a pocketknife?"

He dug his hand in his pocket and withdrew a lock blade, but before opening it he peered at me with curious concern.

"Just give it to me, Ben!" I shouted. "Now!"

The banshee scream was deafening now, and I was starting to lose my grasp on reality once again.

My friend opened the pocketknife then handed it to me, though I could still see reluctance in his eyes. I snatched the doll from the box and flipped it over. Holding it against the ground with my wounded hand, I slid the sharp blade beneath the ribbon with my other and then drew it upward. The sharp edge sliced cleanly through the criss-crossing purple bands, and they fell away.

The world bloomed in front of me and settled to a muted shade of reality. The scream was fading from my ears, echoing the word "no" as it disappeared into nothingness. I let go of the poppet then slowly twisted around from my kneeling position and sat back in the snow. Pressing the blade lock with my thumb, I slid the back side of it across my thigh and snapped the knife closed. Holding it out toward my friend, I let out a heavy sigh.

"That's it?" he said as he took it from me.

"That's it," I replied.

"Okay… So whaddid you just do?"

"I broke a binding."

"Broke a binding…" he repeated.

"Yeah."

"That some kinda Witch thing?"

"Uh-huh."

"Shouldn't there've been sparks, or flyin' monkeys or somethin'?"

"Only in the movies, Ben…I've told you that a…"

He cut me off. "I was kidding."

"Sorry," I breathed. "I'm just not in a very humorous mood right now."

"Yeah, no shit… Okay… So, what happens now?"

"I get cleaned up and go see my wife. Maybe even bring her home."

"Good plan, but I was talkin' about with the Witch thing."

"Nothing, Ben. It's over. I'm done."

He let out a harrumph and shook his head. "Ya'know, the way you were actin' I woulda thought you were disarmin' a bomb or somethin'."

I hung my head and sighed again. "That's closer to the truth than you can possibly know."

CHAPTER 19:

S oft light was filtering into the room when I awoke.
I hadn't yet opened my eyes, but I could definitely tell it was no longer dark. My brain was shrouded in the warm fog that hovers in the void between wakefulness and deep slumber. Somewhere in the back of my head, I knew the pleasant confusion would be wearing off soon, even if I would rather it did not. I tried to embrace the sensation, but as always it was fleeting, and my grey matter was already telling me it was time to get on with the day.

A momentary panic gripped me as flashes of memory were revealed through the rapidly dissipating haze. My heart fluttered, and although I feared what I might see, I slowly opened my eyes. The sudden palpitations began to settle as soon as I focused on my surroundings and saw the familiar trappings of my bedroom at home. I felt myself relaxing the moment I realized I wasn't in a hospital room or even a sleazy motel hundreds of miles away.

However, no sooner had it faded than it flared in a second attack when I rolled over and found myself alone in the bed. It dawned on me that there was a huge gap missing in my memory. I had absolutely no recollection of getting into the bed in the first place. I concentrated on what I could remember. In the forefront was the fact that I had checked Felicity out of the hospital and brought her home.

Fortunately, that thought, combined with my nose, caused the burgeoning wave of anxiety to die out before it ever managed to fully take hold. The aroma of freshly brewed coffee was drifting through the house, locked in a battle with the smell of frying bacon as they both fought to overtake one another. That was all it took to remind me the month long nightmare was over.

My stomach rumbled, expressing its displeasure regarding the fact that I still hadn't eaten since the previous morning. Given that I hadn't even managed to keep that particular meal down long enough to digest, the growling was not at all unexpected. It wasn't that I hadn't had an opportunity to eat; I just hadn't been especially interested in food, until now that is.

Throwing back the covers, I rolled up to sit on the edge of the bed. I rubbed my eyes then fumbled around on the nightstand for my glasses. Once I had them seated on my face, I stood and trudged into the bathroom before heading out to the kitchen.

"What are you doing up, then?" Felicity asked when I finally came around the corner a few minutes later. The background Celtic lilt in her voice was a welcome sound in my ears.

"Am I not supposed to be?" I asked.

"I was trying not to wake you," she replied, walking over then slipping her arms in around my waist and laying her head against my shoulder.

I wrapped my arms around her and hugged tightly. "Pinch me so I know I'm not just dreaming this."

"It's okay," she whispered. "You aren't."

"That's good. I don't think I could handle it if I was."

"How did you sleep?" she asked.

"Good," I said, pausing a moment before adding, "I think."

She pulled back and looked into my face. "You think?"

"I don't know," I shrugged. "I don't remember much after... Well, much after sitting down on the couch last night to be honest."

"That's because you fell asleep while we were talking."

"Sorry. I didn't mean to."

"It's okay."

"So, if I fell asleep on the couch then how did I end up..."

"In the bedroom? I managed to get you up and guide you in there. You know, you actually follow orders very well when you're asleep."

I let out a half chuckle. "Yeah. I bet you enjoyed that."

"It was amusing."

"I don't remember."

"Aye, well it's probably a good thing you don't," she said with a small grin. "Like I said, you follow orders *very* well."

"Excuse me?"

"I'm joking."

"Yeah, so you say."

She grinned again.

"I really am sorry. I finally get you home, and then I pass out on you. Not exactly a homecoming to remember I don't suppose."

"It's okay. You needed the rest."

"Bacon's burning," I told her.

"Ooops!" she said, slipping out of the embrace and hurrying over to the stove.

I stepped over and pulled a mug from the cabinet then filled it with coffee. After a swig I leaned against the counter and offered, "I still shouldn't have fallen asleep on you."

"Aye, it was obvious you needed it, Row. You were snoring loud enough to wake the dead."

"Trust me, they don't need my help for that." I took another swallow of coffee then topped off my mug and slid hers across the counter so she could reach it.

"Thanks," she said with a smile.

"So, what about you?" I asked. "You're the one we need to be worried about here. How are you feeling?"

"Fine."

"You sure?"

"Yes. I'm fine."

There was something in the way she answered that told me otherwise.

"I'm not convinced."

She didn't respond. Instead, she focused on placing the finished bacon on a paper towel covered plate and then laying fresh strips into the skillet. When she was finished with that task, she simply continued staring at the pan, occasionally nudging the sizzling meat with a pair of tongs.

"Felicity?" I pressed.

She let out a sigh then looked up at me. "Aye, I'm fine. I really am."

"Honey, you're sounding less convincing every time you say it."

Her shoulders drooped, and she gave her head a barely perceptible shake. "I know."

"So… Would you like to tell me the truth?"

"I'm not sure what that is, Rowan."

"Well, what do you think it is?"

"That's the problem. I'm not even sure what to think, either."

I silently digested the comment for a short span then asked, "Is it because I did the binding on you?"

"No," she shook her head to punctuate the reply.

"Are you sure?"

"Yes, I'm sure about that at least. I'll admit I'm not happy you did it, but I do understand why. The truth is I don't have the right to be angry with you over that. If you recall, I once did the same thing to you for the very same reasons."

"That didn't give me license to do it though."

"No, it didn't. But, I would be a hypocrite if I held it against you."

"Okay… Then, is it something else I did?"

"No. I think it's probably more the things that I did."

I shook my head as I said, "You didn't do those things. Miranda did. You had nothing to do with it. If anyone is to blame for that, it's me. This never would have happened if I hadn't done that binding."

"A binding shouldn't have caused that, Rowan. Unless you were intentionally binding her to me, which I would find hard to believe."

"I agree. And, no, I certainly wouldn't have done it intentionally. But, it still happened, so that means I fucked it up somehow."

"How?"

"I have no idea. But I must have, otherwise we wouldn't be standing here having this conversation."

She took a moment to flip over the bacon strips and nudge them about the pan again. Finally, she looked up and said, "It's not just the things I did, Rowan. It's everything."

"Everything covers a lot of area, honey."

"Aye, it does," she agreed. "What I mean is, everything that's happened. The arrest... The time in the hospital... The fact that I suddenly have a half-sister-cousin or whatever who just happens to be a twisted killer. Who, by the way, is the product of my father screwing around on my mother with my aunt, which isn't something a daughter really needs to find out about her dad. How do I reconcile that?"

"I don't know," I admitted. "But, we find a way, and we do it together. And, if we can't do it alone, we have Helen to help out."

"I'm... I'm just a little overwhelmed right now."

"I pretty much got that," I soothed.

"Aye," she sighed. "Maybe I should just get us all booked on one of those stupid tabloid talk shows."

"They'd never go for it," I told her, trying to interject a bit of humor. "You aren't nearly strange enough for them."

"You don't think so?" she quipped, her voice suddenly taking on a demanding edge. "How about if after we tell them all that, we clue them in that I'm a repressed, closeted dominatrix Witch whose husband has only just discovered after almost fifteen years of marriage that she'd really like to put a dog collar around his neck and explore a few sexual fetishes with him in the bedroom? Do you think maybe that would pique their interest?"

I could tell by the look on her face that she had run directly into a wall of regret the moment the last word flew from her mouth. I paused, trying to think of what I should say. My delay in responding didn't seem to help the matter because she hung her head and stared at the floor.

"You have me there," I finally returned. "I think that just might get their attention."

"This isn't a joke, Rowan," she said.

"I know it isn't," I replied softly. "I'm sorry. I wasn't making fun of you."

"No... I'm the one who should be sorry," she muttered, turning back to the stove without looking at me. "I shouldn't have just blurted

that out. You're probably having enough trouble with it already…
Especially after what you've been through."

"What I've been through?" I asked, a bit of incredulity creeping
into my voice. "You're worried about me?"

"Of course," she mumbled. "And… I'm worried about us."

I placed my coffee cup on the counter then stepped over to her.
Wrapping my arms around her from behind, I gave her a gentle
squeeze. Her body was rigid, and I could feel the tension knotted up
inside her.

"Aren't we a pair?" I mumbled. "Me worrying about you, you
worrying about me, us worrying about us, and neither of us
accomplishing anything other than driving ourselves nuts…"

"Pathetic, isn't it?" she whispered.

"No… I'm pretty sure it's just what makes us who we are," I
whispered in her ear. "And, just so you know, *us* is fine, sweetheart."

"You're sure?"

"Positive," I replied. "And, I seem to recall we've had this talk
before. Your proclivities in that area didn't come as a big surprise, and
they aren't a problem. You never needed to keep it a secret, especially
for so long."

"There were times I almost told you," she said in a low voice.

"Well, you finally did and it's all good. You had nothing to worry
about. You're just going to have to be patient with me."

"About what?"

"That particular game. I've never played it, so you're going to
have to fill me in on the rules."

"Aye, so I haven't so totally freaked you out that you're going to
leave me?"

"Do you really think you can get rid of me that easily?"

After a moment she whispered, "I love you."

"And I love you right back. Warts and all, my little *repressed
dominatrix Witch*."

I felt her beginning to relax, and I gave her another reassuring
squeeze.

"Why don't you get out a couple of plates," she said. "Breakfast will be done as soon as I scramble some eggs."

"You got it," I replied.

A moment later, as I was digging silverware from the drawer, I glanced over at her and said, "Dog collar, huh? So, would I have to bark?"

She didn't look over at me, but even in profile I saw the corner of her mouth turn up as she said, "Only when I tell you to."

Tuesday, December 6
9:07 P.M.
Baton Rouge, Louisiana

THE END OF DESIRE: A Rowan Gant Investigation

CHAPTER 20:

Darkness had become light, and light had become darkness once again.

Annalise hugged herself tightly as she lay naked in the empty bathtub. It had started out filled with hot water—as hot as she could bear it in fact. But that had been almost an hour ago. She had long since drained it but hadn't been able to bring herself to climb out.

Her first emotion had been fear, but that had quickly given way to confusion. The man, Rowan, had called her by name. He said they knew. But, how could they? How could they possibly know she was the one responsible for all the things she had done? The only answer that would come to her tortured mind was—Saint Louis.

At least she was safe from them for now. Annalise Devereaux didn't live here. Behind these walls, she was someone else.

But, there was someone who knew where she was. *She* always knew. And, from *Her* she could never be safe.

Annalise let out a low moan and shivered as she tried to curl into an even tighter ball. The air in the room was cool against her skin where her still damp hair laid in twisted strands across her shoulders and back. She had finally found the energy to pull a towel down from the rack and was using it as a makeshift blanket, but it wasn't enough to completely cover her.

She knew she should get out, dry off, and change into some clothes, but she didn't have the strength. This had been going on for five days, and the increasingly hotter baths had become her only refuge. But now, they were no longer working. Simply moving was a struggle, and it only seemed to be getting worse.

Miranda was being a bitch.

The desire had been welling in Annalise for too many days now, but Miranda wasn't talking. And, without Miranda, she had no way to appeal to *Ezili* for comfort.

She was forsaken.

She was being punished.

At first, the tickle had been a pleasurable annoyance, but that pleasure didn't last for long. Miranda never came to her. She knew she was there in the shadows, waiting.

Watching her, but never touching.

Never joining.

Never making her whole.

Very soon the tickle became the all-consuming itch, but still Miranda only watched. As always, with the itch came the need, and the need remained unfulfilled. Without Miranda, Annalise could only go so far. Miranda was in control of the gift, and it was being purposely withheld.

Annalise had been denied any form of release, and that just made the need stronger. And as it grew, the need soon became an ache.

No matter what she did, or how she tried to quell the fire on her own, it remained. Blazing through her body like a rampant fever. And now, the ache had turned to blinding pain.

"Why are you doing this to me?" she whimpered aloud, her voice thin and cracking. "I've done everything you've asked..."

She felt her plea was falling on deaf ears. *Ezili* could not hear her, and Miranda was the hand of punishment. *She* didn't care that Annalise was suffering. It was exactly what *She* wanted. Besides, *She* wasn't being denied. *She* was taking her own pleasure in Annalise's torment.

It all came back to Saint Louis. *She* had tasted the fresh sweetness of the other. The one called Felicity. But, that sweetness had suddenly been taken away.

Someone had to pay, and that someone was Annalise.

On the heels of her whimper, the pain intensified. She knew Miranda was testing her to see just how much she could take—and delighting in every moment of her pain. She would have cried if her body had been able to produce tears, but they had long since run out.

She could only close her eyes and whine.

"Everything," she whispered through clenched teeth. "Everything you've asked..."

She held no expectation of a reply other than the sound of her own dry sobbing, as it had been her only answer each time she asked. Even so, she simply didn't have the energy to be surprised when the familiar voice finally echoed inside her head.

"No..." Miranda said. "Not everything..."

M. R. Sellars

Wednesday, December 7
4:19 P.M.
Saint Louis, Missouri

THE END OF DESIRE: A Rowan Gant Investigation

CHAPTER 21:

Ben and I were standing on the front porch of my house. Even though it was cold, something about being inside right at this moment made me feel closed in. Trapped. Even though he was my friend, I couldn't help but feel cornered by him right now. I'm not certain that being out here really made that much difference in the way I felt, but I would take anything I could get.

We stood in silence for a moment. The frosty air moved around us on a gentle breeze, making the wind chimes in front of me tinkle lightly. I reached out and gently grasped the cold metal tubes, causing them to fall silent once again.

"The Feebs coordinated with NOLA PD on that homicide. Got a definite match on the hair found at the scene," he offered.

"That's good," I said, as I carefully let go of the chimes.

"They've been watchin' the cemetery, but so far she hasn't showed."

I didn't answer.

"Theory is she's too spooked to go back right now."

I still kept my mouth shut. I heard my friend sigh hard then shuffle in place. After a long pause he spoke again. "They think maybe they've connected a couple of unsolved homicides from last year too. All homeless types. Jury's still out on 'em though, 'cause they don't have the exact signature she's usin' with her victims now. But, enough shit matched up ta' make 'em wonder. The behavioral guys at Feeb central are checkin' it out."

I remained shrouded in my self-imposed reticence, simply staring out across the yard.

"You even listenin' to me?" Ben finally asked.

"Yeah. I'm listening," I replied.

"But ya' ain't talkin'."

"No. I'm not."

"Look, Row, I'm tryin' ta' tell ya' she's gone completely off radar."

"I pretty much got that, Ben."

"Okay. So, I'm lookin' for help. Got any la-la land happenin'? You wanna throw me a bone here?"

I glanced in his direction. "I think you already know the answer to that question."

He huffed out an exasperated breath then stared into the yard for a moment. Eventually, his hand moved up to smooth back his hair then slide down to rest on his neck.

"C'mon Row… You seen anything at all? A nightmare? Ya'know, any kinda spooky shit that might give us some insight on this?"

"No."

"I don't believe ya'."

"That's your prerogative."

"Jeezus…" he muttered. "This ain't some kinda game, White Man."

"You don't have to tell me that, Ben. I know it isn't."

"Well, would ya' tell me if ya' did see somethin'?"

"I don't know."

"What kinda answer is that?"

"The best I can give you right now."

"Okay. So the Feebs dug up some background on 'er," he said, as he dropped his hand down and sent it inside the folds of his coat to retrieve his notebook. "Think that might help jog some *Twilight Zone* stuff?"

"Don't bother, Ben. I don't want to hear it."

He stopped with the notebook halfway out of the inner pocket, stood there for a moment, and then stuffed it back in with a heavy breath to punctuate his frustration.

"What's gotten inta' you?"

"A little bit of sense maybe."

"Come on, Row…" he eventually mumbled.

"Besides, the way I understand it I've been banned from this case… And, any other investigations for that matter."

"Technically, yeah, but I'm just tryin' ta' keep ya' in the loop. What they don't know ain't gonna hurt 'em."

"It's not them I'm worried about."

"You really aren't gonna talk about it, are ya'?"

"No."

"What's the real reason?"

"In case you don't recall, I quit."

"Bullshit. That's what you said, but you didn't mean it."

"Yes, I did."

"No, you didn't."

"I'm not going to have this argument with you." I shook my head for emphasis. "Shouldn't you be happy about this, Chief? For years you've been telling me to stay out of everything. *Let the cops do the cop stuff,* I believe is what you said. Well, you've convinced me. I'm letting you cops do your jobs. I'm not getting involved."

"You already are, Row."

"Not anymore."

"So you're sayin' you've just switched off the *Twilight Zone* shit, and that's the end of it? I thought you said it doesn't work like that."

"No, it doesn't," I muttered.

"So then you do still see shit, don'tcha?"

"Only if I look," I said then paused before adding, "And, I try not to."

"Yeah, but you do anyway. I know you."

"That's not the point."

"Then what is?"

"Not what. More like, who."

"Felicity?"

"Uh-huh."

"So, Firehair wants you to quit?"

"She didn't come right out and say it. Not lately anyway. But, she's good with the decision, and that's really all that matters."

He exhaled a long, slow breath. "You blame me, don't ya'? Both of ya' do."

"No, we don't."

"You gotta. I got ya' into all this when I came to ya' about the Tanner homicide."

"No." I shook my head, again using the exaggerated motion to punctuate my answer. "What you did was ask me some simple questions about WitchCraft and Wicca. I'm the one who got myself in too deep. I'm the one who let it take over my life."

"So, what're ya' gonna do?"

"Take my life back."

"Yeah, sounds good in theory, but I mean what about the *Twilight Zone* stuff. If you still see the crap then what're ya' gonna do?"

"I'll just have to live with the nightmares."

"Do ya' really think you can?"

"I already do, Ben. Every single day."

"Yeah, but can ya' live with the thought of not doin' somethin' about what ya' see?"

Once again, I didn't answer. Instead I just looked away and stared out across the lawn.

Ben pressed on. "Okay, so, what about Firehair? She sees shit too."

"Don't remind me."

"But..."

"There aren't any but's," I interrupted. "Face it. You don't need me. All I ever do is visualize the horrors that sick, twisted people exact upon others. It's not like I can make them stop what they're doing. I wish to hell I could, but I can't."

"That's not true, Rowan," he offered with a shake of his head. "You've helped stop the bastards more than once. You've saved innocent lives."

"Tell that to Randy and Starr," I spat, blatantly naming the two members of Felicity's coven who had been tortured and murdered by a serial killer bent on my demise. His primary reason for what he did to them was so that he could draw me out into the open, and I'd been living with that guilt ever since.

"That wasn't your fault."

"Your sister keeps telling me the same thing. Maybe someday I'll fool myself into believing it too."

"You're bein' too hard on yourself, White Man."

I let out a sarcastic chuckle that I simply couldn't contain. "You're kidding, right?"

"Come again?"

"Forget everyone else for a second, and take a good look at me, Ben. I'm a fucking wreck. Felicity isn't much better. She just hides it better than me. And, the real truth is she'd be just fine if it wasn't for me."

"How do ya' figure?"

"Easy. For six years I've let magick control me instead of the other way around. And, because of that screw up, I brought all the crap down on her as well. I'm supposed to live by the rule of *harm none*... Well, I haven't been doing a very good job of it... It's time for me to stop. Stop hurting her, and stop hurting myself. End of story."

"Ya' really think any of that's gonna change if ya' keep everything bottled up inside?"

"I don't know, but I have to try."

"You aren't selfish like that, Row."

"Maybe it's time I started being a little selfish."

"It ain't you... Listen, I..." Before my friend could get the rest of the sentence out of his mouth, his cell phone trilled. "Jeez... Hold on a sec..."

He dug the device out of his coat pocket, flipped it open, and then pressed it up to his ear. "Yeah, this is Storm... Uh-huh... Yeah... Yeah, I'm gonna be there... Yeah, just talkin' ta' Row... Yeah, about work... Dammit, Al, let's not go there... I'm serious... Yeah, I said I'd be there... Uh-huh... Okay, I will... Later."

After folding the phone and stuffing it back into his pocket, he looked over at me with a mildly pained expression. "That was

Allison," he said, referring to his ex-wife.

"Something wrong?"

"Other than the fact that she's still pissed at me for ever draggin' you inta' this sorta shit? No, not really. The offspring's in a school play tonight, and I promised ta' be there, so I gotta go in just a bit. Oh, and she said ta' tell you hi."

"Tell both of them hi for us."

"Yeah, I'll do that," he replied then paused. "Look, Row... If ya' happen ta' do that la-la thing... Ya'know, if ya' go all *Twilight Zone* and see somethin'..."

I cut him off before he could finish the thought. "I wouldn't wait by the phone, Ben, because I won't be calling. Not about that. I'm serious. I'm done."

"Yeah," he said with a nod. "Okay. But, if ya' change your mind..."

"Don't worry, I won't." I switched the subject before he could press me again. "Before you go, are you and Constance doing anything the seventeenth?"

"Dunno, why?"

"Felicity and I were wondering if you two might be up for dinner or something."

"Yeah, maybe. I'll check."

"Just dinner with friends. Nice and normal. No shop talk."

"Yeah, I get it."

"Just let us know."

"I will. Okay... Well... Guess I'd better get goin'."

"Look, Ben... I'm sorry..."

"Don't be," he breathed. "You're right. You didn't sign up for this shit, it just kinda happened to ya'. It ain't your problem."

"Thanks for understanding."

"Yeah. No problem."

I could tell he wasn't happy with the situation, but at the same time I also knew he didn't truly fault me for the decision.

"So, I'll talk to you later?" I asked.

"Yeah. Later."

He started to leave, but before he reached the bottom of the stairs, he turned and looked back up at me. "Oh, by the way. Speakin' of Constance, she's been checkin' on that thing for ya'. You know, the secret Feeb call to the NOLA PD."

"Did she find anything?"

"Nada. Whoever called 'em from the bureau ta' get you released ain't talkin'."

"That doesn't make sense."

"No, it don't. She's gonna keep on it, but it pretty much looks like she's at a dead end. Apparently you got another mystery on your hands."

"I think I'll just call it good and leave it alone."

"Yeah, well let's hope it has the same plan about you."

M. R. Sellars

Wednesday, December 7
11:46 P.M.
Room 3
Continental Motel
Baton Rouge, Louisiana

THE END OF DESIRE: A Rowan Gant Investigation

CHAPTER 22:

Annalise stared at the limp body. She was on her knees, straddling the man's stomach where he lay on the floor.

"I hate you, Rowan Gant," she growled, her voice thick with anger.

He had started twitching uncontrollably after the first blow. Following the second, all movement stopped, and she felt his chest lower slowly as the air sighed from his lungs. She raised her arm over her head again, feeling the cold derision knotting into a ball at the pit of her stomach.

"I HATE YOU," she repeated, as she swung the tenderizing mallet down hard for the third and final time.

She heard a mushy thump and the splintering of bone.

Blood was now soaking through the black fabric of the hood wherever the pulpy remnants of his face came into contact with it. The sticky wetness made the cloth glisten in the harsh, overhead light of the small room. She sat back and allowed herself to smile as she watched it spread.

There was no impending reward behind this kill. No tickle, no itch, no physical gratification. She didn't love this man as she did the others. He was a tool for her to use. He was nothing more than an object. And now, the object had fulfilled a purpose.

Annalise pulled herself up to her feet and stepped over to the bed. She could still feel the anger coursing through her body as she reached into her bag then withdrew the brand new twelve-inch butcher's saw. She tore off the paperboard sleeve and carefully removed the blade guard before turning back to the body on the floor.

One cross wouldn't be enough, and there was still much to do.

Thursday, December 8
2:46 P.M.
St. Louis, Missouri

THE END OF DESIRE: A Rowan Gant Investigation

CHAPTER 23:

The headache had come on me in the middle of the night, which meant I had been wide-awake since a little after one in the morning. The cause of the pain, however, was a mystery to me. I had become so accustomed to the ethereal pounding in my skull that I couldn't always distinguish between it and a plain old migraine, but this one was definitely bizarre. It had some of the same hallmarks as the chronic ache I experienced when someone or something from the other side wanted to have a sit down with me. However, those had a tendency to come at me from the back. This one was a full-bore frontal assault. In fact, my entire face hurt.

I glanced at the clock on the microwave. It was pushing three o'clock in the afternoon, and the vexation had been coming and going all day. I'd barely managed to get any work done at all, and I had a client who was starting to get more than just a little anxious.

"Screw it," I muttered to myself, then reached out and snatched a bottle from the counter.

After removing the lid, I poured a pile of aspirin into my hand and stared at them. I started to pop the analgesics into my mouth but stopped in the middle of the motion then lowered my hand and stared at them again. With a sigh I scooped the pills back into the bottle and replaced the cap. I had poisoned myself once already, so I didn't need to get back into the habit of eating these things like candy.

I glanced at the clock again. It hadn't changed.

I tried to manage a quick mental calculation and failed miserably. Felicity had called earlier to tell me she wasn't going to be home until after seven because she was stuck on a photo shoot, and apparently a foul-up had them running behind schedule.

I tried to do the calculation again and came up with a different answer. I gave it a third go, using my fingers this time and came up with four hours before she would possibly be home. I didn't guess there was any need for me to do anything about starting dinner just yet. I sighed, mulled over my options for a moment, then reached over and yanked open the freezer door. I rummaged around for a bit then pulled out an icepack. I figured my best bet was to lie down for a while and hope the ache would subside.

I was a half dozen steps from the couch when the telephone rang. I paused for a second then continued toward the sofa. The answering machine was on; it could get it.

The telephone pealed again, demanding to be answered. As much as I wanted to simply sprawl out on the couch and ignore the thing, I knew it was entirely possible Felicity was calling to check on me or to give me a schedule update. Maybe they had made up some time, and she was going to be home earlier than expected. I gave the sofa a longing glance then turned and headed for the phone. For good measure I went ahead and stuck the icepack against my forehead. Continuing across the room, I stepped around both dogs who were stretched out for an afternoon nap in the most inconvenient locations they could manage.

I glanced at the caller ID through bleary eyes and saw that it wasn't Felicity after all. It was Ben. I considered just turning around and heading back for the couch, but I was already standing here, so I figured I might as well answer it.

"Hello?" I grunted into the handset after settling it against my ear.

"Hey, White Man," Ben returned. "You sound like shit."

"I feel like it," I replied. "Headache."

"Which kind?"

"That's the question of the day. Actually, I don't know."

"No shit?"

"No shit."

"That sucks."

"Can't argue with you there," I said. "Look, no offense, but I was just about to sack out for a bit."

"Sorry 'bout that," he replied then fell silent.

"Well? Was there something you needed?"

"Yeah, for one I wanted ta' let ya' know Constance and I are good for dinner on the seventeenth. Need us ta' bring anything?"

"Not really," I replied. "We weren't going to do anything too elaborate."

"Ain't it time for that Witch Christmas thing or somethin'?"

"Winter Solstice. Yule," I agreed. "Middle of the following week. Normally we'd celebrate the weekend before, but Felicity's coveners had a hell of a time getting their schedules to jive this year, so they're all doing individual celebrations."

"Oh, okay. Makes sense," he replied.

There was an overwhelming aura of preoccupation surrounding his voice, and that told me he had something else on his mind. The question about Yule had really been little more than a stall tactic while he decided how to work whatever that something else was into the mix.

I decided to give him a hand.

"What's going on, Ben?" I asked. "I have a feeling you didn't call just to RSVP."

"No, I didn't," he replied. "Actually, this is kinda an official call."

"Official how?"

"I need ta' talk to ya' about Annalise Devereaux."

"Unless you're calling to tell me she's in custody, I don't really have anything to say. You already know that."

"Unfortunately, no. She went completely off radar after your little run in with her. Up until now."

"That's not what I wanted to hear, Ben," I replied.

"Yeah, I figured ya' wouldn't be too excited 'bout that."

"Why do I get the feeling the 'up until now' part has something to do with this call?"

"Because you're psychic?"

"No, actually I'm not," I replied.

"Yeah, I know. Look, Kemosabe, I wouldn't call if it wasn't important."

My voice went flat as I spoke, "Important how? Because I seem to recall telling you I was done, Ben. More than once."

"Yeah, but I still don't think ya' meant it," he replied.

"Yes, Ben, I did, and I'm not going to bother giving you all the reasons again."

"Yeah, well ya' need ta' talk ta' me about this anyway."

"No, I don't. I'm staying out of this."

"I'm afraid you can't. That's why I called."

"What do you mean I can't? Listen closely, this is me hanging up."

I had the phone halfway to the cradle when I heard him bark, "Don't be an asshole, White Man! I really need ya' ta' listen to this."

Ignoring the insult, I put the phone back to my ear and demanded, "Why, Ben? Why do you want to drag me back into this?"

"Did I say I wanted ta' do it?"

"Well, why else would you be making this call?"

"You ready ta' shut up and listen?"

"Fine. What about her?"

"She killed again…"

"I can't say that surprises me," I told him.

"Yeah, didn't figure it would," he replied. "But, she added a new twist you need ta' know about."

"What's that?"

"She carved *your* name in the victim's chest. Accordin' to the M.E., it appears she did it before she killed 'im."

"My name?"

"Yeah, Row. *Your* name… And, there's more."

"What?"

"The victim's head was covered with a black cloth bag that was filled with dirt and some kinda dried leaves."

Before Ben could continue I interjected, "And, the torture was only cursory, nothing to the extent of her other victims. But, when she killed him she did it by bashing his head in with a hammer or something similar."

Ben fell silent at the other end, but I could hear him breathing. I had thought my ability to surprise him had run out long ago, but in this case it seemed to be operating full force.

"I'm right, aren't I?" I asked.

"Think maybe that's why ya' got the headache?"

I didn't answer.

"Okay, so what's it mean, Row?" he asked. "It some kinda Voodoo curse?"

"Hoodoo actually, but yeah. It's a cross," I explained, recalling the particulars of the magickal working from my recent research. "It's old folk magick. She's seeking revenge against me for something. Everything that happened in the graveyard maybe. I don't know. Normally the person hexing would use a black china figurine instead of a living human, but we already know she doesn't operate within normal parameters."

"That fits. Victim was an African-American male," he offered.

"I think you'll find the leaves are from a blackberry bush. The dirt most likely came from the graveyard. She probably has bags of it sitting around."

"She tryin' ta' kill ya' with Voodoo?"

"More or less," I replied. "When did this happen?"

"Last night. Medical examiner estimated the time of death at sometime Wednesday evening. The records at the motel where he was found pretty much back that up, although no one saw Annalise, as usual."

I grunted, "Middle of the week. I guess that would make sense."

"What?"

"Nothing really. I'd have to look up the actual cross to be certain, but I remember something about executing it over a seven-day period, starting on a Saturday. I was just speculating that she might have chosen Wednesday since it's basically in the middle. I'm guessing she didn't want to sit in one place for seven days taking a hammer to a decomposing corpse."

"Okay, so tell me what ya' make of this part then. She amputated both his hands. Both of 'em were still at the scene… Well, kinda… They were missin' all the bones."

"Hold on a sec…" I told him.

I tucked the phone between my ear and shoulder then tossed the icepack over onto the coffee table. It wasn't doing much good; besides, my brain was now far too occupied to focus on the pain. I hated to admit it but Ben was correct. I was never going to be able to distance myself from this sort of thing, no matter how much I tried.

Stretching the cord out, I stepped over and scanned the next set of shelves, systematically moving stacks of books which were two and three deep until I found the volume I was searching for.

"You still there?" Ben asked.

"Yeah, hang on," I told him as I flipped to the index of the selected text, noted the page number for crossings, and began thumbing back through. "Okay…here it is. My guess would be she's going to use them for some more *gris-gris*. There's a crossing here that calls for drying chicken bones, crushing them up, then using them as a component for a curse."

"I'll let Baton Rouge PD know that," Ben replied.

"So, is that where the body was found?" I asked.

"Yeah… Motel just like all the others, 'cept it was room three instead of seven."

"Sacred space."

"Come again?"

"Three would be a number equated with protection. She wanted a safe place to do the cross."

"Stickler for detail, ain't she?"

"It's all part of working magick."

"'Kay, we're back ta' that. So if she's tryin' ta' kill ya' with magic, what happens when it doesn't work? I mean, it ain't gonna, is it?"

"I don't know."

"You mean you don't know what she'll do if it doesn't work, right?"

"I mean I don't know on either one, Ben."

M. R. Sellars

Monday, December 12
10:02 P.M.
The Whine Cellar Bondage Club
Private Playroom C
Bridge, Illinois

CHAPTER 24:

Annalise reached over her head and grasped the suspension cuffs, which were securely attached to an overhead beam, then gave them a tug. You never knew what the state of the equipment might be in some of these clubs. Not all of them were maintained as well as they should be. But, this place actually appeared to be properly cared for. In some ways it even reminded her of her own.

She gave the hardware a second tug, and the shiny chains rattled against one another. The metallic clinking noise made her heart race with anticipation.

Steadying herself, she looked down at the mostly nude man lying spread-eagle in front of her. She had only just finished locking him into the floor-mounted restraints moments before. He stared back up at her, adoration in his eyes.

"Did I say you could look at me?" she demanded.

"No, Mistress," the man whispered.

His display of subservience ignited the tickle deep inside. This was the first time she had felt the desire in several days, and to her relief, it was actually pleasurable. Not like it had been before, when she was being punished. Still, the sensation gave her a moment's pause. Those days of torment had been almost more than she could bear, and the thought of facing it again frightened her more than anything.

But, this time it would be different. Miranda promised release. *She* had promised the reward.

Using the suspension cuffs to maintain her balance, Annalise stepped up onto the man's bare chest and twisted slowly, rocking back on her stiletto heels and digging them into his flesh. He groaned as she swayed back and forth, walking in place on his prone body.

And, the tickle continued to flare. She knew the itch wouldn't be very far behind.

This particular sub was a trample fetishist whose kink was being used as a woman's doormat. In fact, he even went by the name "mat." Annalise had always found this particular display of dominance enjoyable, just as she did now. However, truth be told, tonight she had been more in the mood to mete out a good flogging. There was certainly no shortage of bare backs here that she would have relished marking with the sting of braided leather. From what she had seen in the club proper, it was obvious that there were several who would have gladly submitted to that torture as well. However, Miranda had said no. She had a specific purpose for Annalise being here, and "mat" was it. *She* had yet to tell her why. Only that for the moment, she was to seek him out, and him alone.

It had been a long drive to get here from Baton Rouge. With restroom breaks and fuel stops, almost eleven hours to be exact. Annalise had been up and on the road several hours before dawn. She knew full well she should be exhausted, but she wasn't. She hadn't even napped after checking into her hotel. She had merely freshened up, changed into suitable attire, and brought herself here to do Miranda's bidding, though she was still at some loss as to what that bidding was.

Stepping hard, she continued grinding her heels into the man beneath her, reveling in the way his soft flesh gave way to her weight. He moaned as he tensed against his bonds. She wasn't far behind him in the endorphin rush. The tickle had become the itch, and her breaths were now coming in shallow pants.

"Thank you," the man gasped. "Thank you for coming back, Mistress Felicity…"

Annalise stopped moving.

She stood there, frozen in place at the sound of the name—the name of the other.

After a moment she shifted her weight then slipped the toe of her shoe beneath his chin and lifted, rolling his head so that she could look directly into his face.

"What did you call me?" she asked, her tone this time far more inquisitive than demanding.

"I'm sorry, Mistress..." the man apologized meekly. "Mistress Miranda."

"No," Annalise said firmly. "Tell me what you called me."

He continued looking up at her but didn't answer.

She carefully stepped down from his chest then lowered herself until she was seated on his stomach. Smiling sweetly, she reached out and grasped one of his nipples between her thumb and forefinger. Pinching hard, she began to twist and pull the tender flesh.

"I said," she growled, emphasizing each word. "Tell... Me... What... You... Called... Me."

The man tensed and groaned heavily, his face screwed into a mask of pain.

"Yes... yes... Mistress..." he stammered through the grimace. "I... I said, Felicity... I... I'm sorry... I shouldn't... I shouldn't have used... your... real name..."

Annalise eased off on the nipple, but not without giving it a final rough tweak. She remained sitting as she continued staring blankly into his face. Now she knew why Miranda had insisted she come here in search of him in particular. He must have a connection to the other.

The itch faded quickly upon the revelation, completely bypassing the tickle in reverse and becoming no more than a hollow numbness in the pit of her stomach. Anger welled inside her, and she felt her cheeks flush with its heat.

"I don't understand," she murmured. "Why do you think I'm her?"

"Mistress?"

"Why do you think I'm her?" she said again, louder.

"Mistress? But I don't..."

She didn't hear the rest of his answer as it was drowned out by the voice inside her skull.

"You will... When it is time..." Miranda said.

"This is why?" Annalise muttered under her breath. "She is why

I'm here?"

"*Yes...*"

"What, Mistress?" the man breathed.

"Shut up!" Annalise spat.

"*Mark him...*" Miranda's voice echoed again.

"No," Annalise said aloud. "I won't."

"*Punishment or reward, Annalise... You decide.*"

"All you want is her!" Annalise complained aloud. "What about me? I've done everything for you! The reward belongs to me!"

"*There is enough for you both... Now mark him...*"

"Mistress?" the man questioned again.

"I thought I told you to shut up!" Annalise barked, flashing him an angry stare.

"*Show him how much we love him...*" Miranda demanded. "*I promise, you will be rewarded...*"

"Damn you..." Annalise muttered. "Goddamn you..."

"*I am already damned... As are you... Now do as you were told...*"

Annalise huffed out a heavy sigh. She knew she couldn't truly disobey. If she did, the punishment would come again. She feared that perhaps this time it would be even worse.

Reaching back, she slipped off one of her pumps then turned it in her hand so that she could use the tip of the sharp heel as a stylus.

The tickle returned, spreading out through her stomach, forcing the anger to flee, giving way to pleasure.

Pressing the heel-tip against the man's bare chest, she pressed down and began to drag it in a languid arc. He yelped at the new pain, tensing just as he had done before.

"Relax, little man," Annalise whispered. "I'm just showing you how much we love you..."

Tuesday, December 13
8:19 A.M.
Saint Louis, Missouri

CHAPTER 25:

Normalcy had returned. Well, normalcy so far as I could consider my life normal. Several days had passed since Ben's call about the homicide in Baton Rouge, and I'd heard nothing about it since. In addition, other than my painfully lucid nightmares, which had greatly lessened in frequency, my afflictions were keeping a low profile. I still had a bit of the chronic ache in the back of my skull but nothing like the blinding migraine I had faced before. Since I'd rarely been without the twinge for several years now, it was easy to ignore.

At any rate, Felicity and I had fallen back into our routines, and though we were unable to ignore everything that had happened or that a killer was still at large, we decided not to let it consume our lives as it had in the past. For the time being at least, we were making a go at being just plain average, even if it was in large part a lie. So far, we seemed to be having a relative amount of success on that front, at least as far as the outside world was concerned.

I took a drink of my coffee then glanced up at the clock on the microwave before bringing my gaze back down to my wife. As usual, she was in the middle of dumping what had to be the fourth or fifth heaping spoonful of sugar into her own cup.

"What time is your meeting?" I asked.

"Ten thirty," she replied. "Why?"

I shrugged. "Well, for one thing, you were out of bed before me, and you're already dressed. It's not even half past eight yet."

"That a problem?" she quipped with a smile, rattling the spoon around the inside of the ceramic mug as she added hazelnut-flavored creamer to the already overly sweetened brew.

"Can't say that it is. I'm just not used to you being on time, much less early."

I dropped my eyes back to the newspaper. Most everything on the front page had fallen into the category of depressing, so I was perusing the daily comics in hopes of finding a chuckle or two instead.

"Aye, well I'm not actually there yet," she said.

"You have a point," I agreed without looking up.

"By the way, do I look okay?"

"You look great, as usual."

"Rowan," she admonished. "You aren't even looking at me."

I lowered the paper and gave her a quick glance. She was clad in a dark grey, pinstripe business suit. Her hair was swept up off her shoulders and pinned in place, cascading into a neat fall down her back. It also didn't escape my notice that she'd seen more than just a cursory visit with her makeup table.

"You look great. Just like you did five minutes ago when you asked me the same thing."

"I already asked?"

"Uh-huh. Twice actually… This time makes three."

"But, you're sure I look okay?"

"Yes," I told her with a nod then looked back down at the comics. "You look wonderful."

"I was thinking maybe I should wear a skirt instead of slacks. What do you think?"

"Okay."

"Well, do you think that would be too much?"

"I don't know. I guess that would depend on who you're meeting with and how short the skirt is," I chuckled.

"I'm serious, Rowan." She offered the words with a heavy note of exasperation in her voice.

I folded the paper and laid it aside then brought my eyes up to meet hers, giving her my full attention. "All right… What's up? I've never seen you this nervous about work before."

"I'm not nervous."

"Yeah, right."

"Okay, fine. I'm a little nervous."

"Why?"

"I'm not usually dealing with the stigma of an arrest and a stay in a psych ward."

"I don't understand. You've done several jobs since you got home. Why is there a problem now?"

"Those were established accounts who already knew me. This is the first meeting I've had to pitch to a potential client since all that happened, you know. It's different."

"Yeah, okay. But, I really think you're getting yourself worked up over nothing, sweetheart," I reassured her. "You'll be fine. You always are."

"I wish I had your confidence about that."

"Okay, let me ask you this—Did you approach them looking for work or did they call you?"

"They called me."

"There you go."

"There I go what?"

"If anything that was in the news about your bogus arrest was going to affect their decision, I doubt they would have even called you in the first place. Obviously it isn't a factor."

"Maybe they just haven't heard about it yet."

"Only if they were living under a rock."

She frowned hard. "Thanks a lot."

"Seriously, Felicity. I really think this is a non-issue."

"Maybe you're right."

"I know I am."

"I hope so."

She took a sip of her coffee while staring thoughtfully into the space just over my shoulder. I watched her for a moment then picked up the paper again and unfolded it.

"Black, maybe?" I offered as I began to scan the cartoons.

"Black what?" she asked.

"Black skirt," I replied. "Understated, professional. And, black goes with everything, right?"

"So you think I should change, then?"

"No, but you do. I can tell by the way you're staring off into space."

"I'm going to go change."

"What a surprise," I mumbled.

She didn't reply to my last comment. Instead, she simply placed her coffee cup on the counter then turned and headed out of the kitchen. Her footsteps hadn't even faded around the corner when the dogs began barking in the back yard. The chime of the doorbell followed quickly, as if to add urgent punctuation to their ruckus.

"I'll get it," Felicity called out.

I heard her as she shuffled quickly to change direction, and that was soon followed by a click when she unlatched the deadbolt on the door. Before I had a chance to find where I had left off on the comics page, however, a somewhat disturbing noise hit my ears, and it took the form of my wife's voice wrapped in an altogether annoyed tone.

"*Damnú!*" she exclaimed. "I thought I told you to leave me alone!"

I had already tossed the paper onto the counter and was out of my seat when I called out to her. "Felicity? What's wrong?"

I hadn't even taken my first step when I heard a heavy thud on the floor along with a muffled male voice. Both of these new sounds caused my heart to jump in my chest, and I darted out of the kitchen. I wasn't sure what I was expecting to find, but my brain was so conditioned to the horrific that a sense of semi-contained panic had already set in. In a fraction of a second, it had taken it upon itself to fill in the blanks with all manner of possible unpleasantness.

What I did see when I rounded the corner, however, was the last thing I had imagined, and it gave me enough pause to stop me dead in my tracks. My wife was still fully upright and was trying to back away from the now open door. Unfortunately, her ability to affect the maneuver was being severely hindered by an altogether familiar looking man who was bowed down in front of her, arms locked around her ankles as he murmured half intelligible praises in between each fervent kiss he bestowed upon her feet and shoes.

"What are you doing?!" Felicity barked as she tried to pull her foot out of his grasp. "Stop it!"

My initial fear for her safety immediately shifted to annoyance. Brad Lewis, the man currently molesting my wife's feet, was the same individual she had almost trampled to death while under Miranda's control. Fortunately, he hadn't pressed charges over his injuries, primarily because he was beyond just your average submissive fetishist who got a thrill from the abuse. So far beyond in fact, that by all indications, he was psychologically addicted to it.

Unfortunately, however, that which saved Felicity from both criminal charges and a civil lawsuit had quickly turned into a very different sort of problem. Lewis had fixated on her, and for a period of several days made a major nuisance of himself with repeated telephone calls. She had finally stopped trying to reason with him and took advantage of her repressed persona along with his desire to serve a Domme by literally ordering him to stop calling. The tactic had seemed to work, as the unwanted contact stopped cold following that one-sided conversation.

Until now, that is.

Calls were one thing, but this was a whole new dimension. Prior to this point, he hadn't been bold enough to actually come to the house—at least not that we knew of. Now, not only was this frightening in a sense, it made me angry.

My momentary bewilderment wore off, and I started forward, but Felicity was already taking her own measures to deal with the groveling stalker.

"*Damnú!* Get... Off... Me!" she shrieked, yanking one foot free as he was focusing his attention on the other.

Squatting quickly, she grabbed a handful of his hair and began pulling his head upward as she stood. Given the burning glare in her eyes, if I hadn't been as angry about his intrusion as was she, I would have almost felt sorry for him.

Before I covered the few steps between us, she had him back up into a kneeling position in front of her with his head held back so that his face was upturned. In a flash the open palm of her free hand struck his cheek with a loud crack. I was just grabbing him by the shirt collar when she slapped him hard again.

"Felicity!" I barked. "Don't you think that might just be encouraging him?!"

"*Is cuma liom sa diabhal!*" she shouted. "I'm pissed off!"

The spate of Gaelic was a new one on me, so I wasn't entirely sure what she had said. However, the English portion of the sentence left nothing to the imagination, not that her actions hadn't already spoken volumes.

"All right, get out!" I demanded as I hooked one hand under his arm while keeping the other twisted into the back of his collar. I was trying to pull him toward the door, but Felicity still hadn't let go of his hair.

"But, Mistress…" he whined.

"*Dún do bheal!*"

He was obviously completely unfamiliar with Gaelic as he half whimpered again, "But, Mistress…"

"I am *not* your Top!" my wife shouted back into his face. "I thought I made that clear!"

"B…b…but, last night…" he stammered.

"*Tá tú glan as do mheabhair!*"

That one I knew, and it roughly translated into something about him being crazy.

"She's right. You're delusional," I growled then glanced at Felicity. "I think it might be time for a restraining order. I'll hold him. You call the police."

"But… Last night… At *The Whine Cellar*… Where we met… You were there. Don't you remember?"

"Aye, now I know you've lost your mind," she harrumphed, finally letting go of his hair and stepping back.

"But you were!" he insisted. The whimper in his voice was starting to fade and now even seemed to be taking on a bit of agitation.

"She was here all night," I countered. "She never left the house."

I quickly repositioned my grip on him for a better hold. I was beginning to worry that his mental state was going to make this a bigger problem than it already was, and I wanted to be prepared if this became any more physical than it already had.

I shot Felicity a firm glance and said with emphasis, "Honey, I really think you'd better call the police now."

"You marked me!" Lewis contended. "You said I was yours... That I could serve you... You said that you loved me!"

"I did what?"

His free hand started to move, so I immediately let go of his collar and did the only thing I could think to do. I slipped my arm around his neck, placing him in a headlock. From looking at him, he definitely appeared to be in better shape than me, so I felt I needed every advantage I could get where leverage was concerned.

Even with my tightening grip, however, he didn't stop. But, instead of reaching for my wife, as I had feared he was about to do, he grasped the front of his own shirt through the wide opening in his jacket and ripped hard.

Buttons bounced across the floor with a sharp, plastic clatter, and I heard Felicity gasp. From my present angle I couldn't see what she was staring at, but the look on her face told me it couldn't be good.

"What?" I asked her. "What?"

Instead of answering, she brought her hand up to her mouth and closed her eyes as she took another step backward. Since he was no longer struggling against me, I loosened my grip just enough to peer over his shoulder.

Even though it was upside down and less than perfectly scribed, the design was unmistakable. The welts were an angry red and were scabbed over in the places where blood had seeped out of the deeper scrapes. The wounds were obviously recent, and that supported the time frame of his story to some extent.

I felt a familiar hollowness well in the pit of my stomach as I stared at the pattern. Among the bruises and fresh high heel marks covering his chest, scraped deeply into his skin was a checkerboard heart pierced by what could only be meant as a dagger.

"Felicity," I breathed carefully. "Call the police, then get Ben on the phone."

CHAPTER 26:

"This is seriously fucked up," Ben said. The tone of his voice was flat and more than just a little introspective.

My friend had arrived while the local police were still taking our statements. After he spoke with them for a few minutes, then made a quick phone call, they left, taking Lewis with them. As usual, the neighbors got an eye full of the goings on. I was beginning to think we might need to move, but who was I to take away their source of entertainment?

Now, some half hour later, we were sitting at the breakfast nook in the kitchen, contemplating our cups of coffee.

It was just the two of us at this point. Felicity had been slightly shaken but not enough to keep her from being determined to attend her scheduled business meeting—even though I objected. In a way, I suppose it was a good thing she ignored my protests. She probably needed something to take her mind off the whole situation. The truth is, I wished I had something to divert my own attention from it, but I also wasn't naïve enough to believe it would matter even if I did. My attempt at embracing denial was no longer working. It was painfully apparent that forces beyond my control simply wouldn't allow it.

"Believe me. I know that." I replied after a thick pause. "I guess it could've been worse though. It's not like he actually assaulted her or anything."

"Yeah, Row, I'm afraid he did."

"Not really. All he actually did was slobber on her shoes."

"While she was wearin' 'em," Ben added. "Simple battery is any form of unwanted physical contact, so by law what 'e did qualifies as common assault, Kemosabe."

"Yeah, that's what the other cops said too." I shrugged. "What I meant was I just usually think of assault as something a bit more malicious. He didn't actually attack her with any intent to do harm."

"Yeah, a lotta people think like that. Of course, then there're the ones that think they've been assaulted if someone looked at 'em cross-eyed. But this ain't one of those situations. It was assault any way you slice it... But, technically you're right. As assaults go, it was minor. No more than a misdemeanor... You could probably throw trespassing in on 'im if ya' wanted. But, anyway... Firehair's gonna be pressin' charges I assume?"

"Under the circumstances, I'd like for her to at least get a restraining order, but it's a touchy situation since he could still file charges against her for the incident at the motel... And, I think that would qualify as something a bit worse than what you were just talking about."

"Yeah. That'd be more like aggravated assault with intent."

"Yeah... Exactly... So... There it is..." I let my voice trail off without saying anything further.

"Uh-huh," my friend grunted. "I know what ya' mean. At least they're gonna hold 'im for a bit, what with the mark on 'is chest an' all. Ackman and Osthoff are on the way over ta' ask 'im a few questions."

"There is that," I finally said. After another lengthy pause, I added, "But, I get the feeling that really wasn't the 'fucked up' you were talking about, was it?"

"No," he replied with a shake of his head. "Not really."

"Didn't think so."

"Sorry."

"Sorry for what?"

"That ya' can't get away from it."

I sighed. "It's not your fault."

"That doesn't keep me from feelin' for ya'."

"Yeah. I suppose it doesn't... Thanks."

"Not a problem." He waited for a measured beat then added, "I guess we got our answer."

"What answer?"

"What Annalise was gonna do if she couldn't off ya' with the hocus-pocus."

"Oh… That."

We sat in silence for a minute. I absently spun my coffee mug in place on the table, fiddling with it for no other reason than to expend the nervous energy I had pent up inside. I could feel Ben watching me, and I was fairly certain I knew what he wanted to say. It wasn't very long before he proved me correct.

"You wanna talk about it now? The case I mean."

"Do I want to? No," I replied with a shake of my head. "But, obviously she isn't leaving me much choice in the matter."

"Yeah, guess not," he grunted. "So… Ya' done any *Twilight Zone* since we last talked?"

"No, actually. A few nightmares, but nothing of consequence."

"What about that headache ya' had? That still with ya'?"

"It pretty much went away."

"Ya' lyin'?"

"No."

"Whatcha do? Burn a candle or somethin'?"

"Something like that."

"So then her kung fu ain't as good as yours?"

"I'm reserving judgment on that at the moment."

"You're still here."

"The war isn't over yet."

"Yeah. Wunnerful… Okay… So, back to the land of normal people… Ya' got any theories? Like what she might do next?"

"I have no idea."

"Now I know you're lyin' on that one, 'cause I got a theory myself. Since that hocus-pocus didn't work, she's gonna try ta' kill ya' the way regular fruitcakes do."

I gave him a barely perceptible shrug. "Maybe."

"Ain't maybe, Row. It doesn't take a trip inta' la-la land ta' figure it out. Why else would she come back here?"

I just shook my head in response.

"Ya' think this is about what happened in New Orleans?"

"Maybe." I shrugged again. "That was my first thought, but after mulling it over for a bit I think it's probably more likely to be about what I did when I got home."

"What? Ya' mean the thing with the doll?"

I nodded.

"How the fuck could she know about that?"

"Miranda. If she's really here to come after me, it has to be because of her. I don't think Annalise would chance it on her own. She really doesn't have a solid reason."

"Nutcases don't need reasons, Row. Do ya' think she's got a logical reason for what she's been doin' so far?"

"In *her* mind, yes. I think that in her view of reality, she sees what she is doing as perfectly logical."

"'Zactly. In *her* twisted-ass mind. So, what's ta' keep 'er from havin' some fucked up reasoning tellin' 'er ta' come after you?"

"I don't know. I mean… Yes, you could be right, but I really don't get the feeling Annalise is particularly stupid. She knows it would be dangerous for her to come here looking for me, even if she does have a vendetta. Miranda has to be behind it. Controlling her. Making her do it."

"Well, I dunno about that, but you're right about one thing. She ain't stupid."

"Is that just an opinion, or do you know something I don't?"

"Besides the fact she's got a doctorate in psychology? Yeah, a little."

"She has a doctorate?"

"Yeah," he grunted, as he reached into his pocket and dug out his notebook then flipped it open. "Got some background on 'er if ya' wanna hear it. I've had it for a while, and I tried ta' tell ya' about it the other day but you said you didn't wanna talk about the case anymore."

"*Mea culpa.*"

"Yeah, whatever," he said as he flipped through the pages then settled on one. "So, anyway, here it is in a nutshell. Near as we can figure from what we've been able ta' piece together, Devereaux started out life as Mary Kathleen O'Brien. But, about two months after birth those records suddenly stop. It's like she never existed..."

"But, if the records stop..."

"Hang on, I'm not finished. Ya' see, that's just all part of the big soap opera. Apparently the birth mother had a friend try ta' adopt 'er. When they caught on to what was up, they changed 'er name ta' Cynthia Anne Smith and shipped 'er outta state to a different orphanage in Mississippi."

"How'd you figure that out?"

"I didn't. The Feebs did."

"Well, how did they manage to make the connection?"

"Dunno. Maybe they leaned on a nun or somethin'. So anyway, she bounced around foster homes for about six years, startin' from when she was just a few months old until she eventually ended up in yet another orphanage."

"That had to be rough on a kid. Any idea why she wasn't adopted out as a baby?"

Ben shook his head. "No one's sayin'. Rumor has it that as she got older she was in and outta trouble here and there though. At least, that's what they managed to pick up from the files, such as they were. Anyhow, she finally got adopted by the Devereaux's when she was around eight." He flipped through the pages of the notebook. "Yeah, here it is, Scott and Andrea Devereaux. Older couple from Tupelo, Mississippi. Old enough to be more like grandparents, actually."

"That's odd, isn't it?"

"Yeah, a little. But, they wanted a kid and they had money. A lot of it... Big numbers followed by lotsa zeros if ya' know what I mean. An' apparently they donated quite a bit to the orphanage where she was livin'."

"So, after they adopted her, they changed her first name as well as her last? That seems like a cruel thing to do to an eight-year-old kid. That's had to screw with her sense of self identity."

"Yeah, tell me about it. Guess it's no wonder she's so fucked up."

"So, have you been able to contact them?"

"Nope. Both deceased. Have been for quite a few years. And, there weren't any other livin' relatives, so they left the whole shootin' match to guess who?"

"Annalise."

"Bingo. Speakin' of that, it seems the address she used for her driver's license might've been kinda bogus. The place actually exists and all... Or, it did before the flood... And, she even owned it... But accordin' to one of the neighbors NOLA PD managed ta' track down, they don't think she actually lived there. A lawn service came by and kept the place up, and the guy said he noticed a car there a couple of times late at night, but he never saw anyone actually livin' there."

"Do you think she was planning ahead for the eventuality of getting caught?" I asked.

"Possibly. That, or she was usin' it in the middle of the night or somethin'. Who knows? Doesn't really matter much 'cause since the flood, it's totaled. If there was any evidence there, it's gone now.

"So, anyway, on the doctorate thing... She attended three separate colleges. Not sure why the moving around, but in the end she did her post-grad work at George Washington University in DC, which is where she got the doctorate. She didn't really put it to use though. Not professionally anyway because after she got it, she worked as a VP for her dad's company. But, that only lasted about a year."

"What happened?"

"Dunno. Apparently she just up an' quit. But, after the parents kicked, she sold off a lotta property as well as the family business. Been a lot of turnover there, so nobody really remembers much about 'er. However, after that, even though she didn't need the money, she spent some time working as a pro-dominatrix."

"That really doesn't come as a big surprise."

"No, it doesn't. She even owned one of those fetish clubs for a while 'till it got shut down." He flipped a page in the notebook and scanned down the page. "Yeah, here it is, *Gwendolyn's Keep*."

"Another pseudonym..."

"Yeah... Back then she was callin' 'erself, Mistress Gwen. Regular identity crisis with this one."

"Any idea why she was shut down?"

"Yeah, actually. That took some diggin', but it seems one of 'er clients filed assault charges. Said she took the 'game' a bit too far. Accordin' to the police report, she fucked 'im up good. Lessee... Yeah... Whole lotta stitches, a broken hand, broken nose, and several bad cigarette burns."

"I guess there's no surprise there either."

"Yeah, well her contention was expressed consent, which didn't necessarily fly. So, the club got closed down and there was a big stink. Almost went ta' trial, but she had the money ta' make the whole situation go away. The nasty rumor is she not only paid off the client but a coupl'a local officials as well because they were lookin' real hard at criminal charges. Anyway, after that she pretty much just dropped off the map. Not even a parkin' ticket since. Pulled a Garbo. Total recluse. No friends or acquaintances ta' speak of. She just pays 'er taxes, donates to a coupl'a charities for the write-off, and that's about it."

"Well, I think we know better than that."

"True story."

"Of course, with all that money, I suppose it isn't hard to disappear if that's what you want."

"Yeah, that's a fact... Of course, right now 'er bank accounts and credit cards are bein' tracked, but somethin' tells me she's prob'ly got a stash we don't know about... Maybe even whole 'nother identity or two... Hell, I'd bet my paycheck on it." He flipped the notebook closed then stowed it back in his pocket. "Okay, I showed ya' mine. Your turn."

"What do you mean?"

"I mean this whole Miranda thing. You seem ta' think she's the real reason evil sis-in-law would come back... So, explain it to me. Why would this dead chick be after you?"

"Oh, that... Well, it's simple really. When I severed the binding, I took Felicity away from her."

"So she's really after Felicity, not you?"

"Probably. But, my bet is that Miranda wants Felicity alive and well so that she can continue using her as a horse. Annalise, on the other hand, based on what I picked up from that vision, would rather that not be the case. So, she's going to be severely conflicted."

"Could be good for us if she is. Might cause 'er ta' make a mistake that'll let us get a bead on 'er," he offered then thrust his chin toward me. "So technically, you're safe."

"I wouldn't say that. I'm a roadblock for both of them. I'm the one who took Felicity away. I know that didn't sit well with Miranda at all. And, since I'll also protect my wife at all costs, Annalise isn't going to be terribly happy with me either. Neither of them will."

"So you're pissin' em both off."

"Essentially, yes. That would be my guess. Therefore, I'm expendable as far as both of them are concerned."

"So, ain't you worried about Firehair out runnin' around by herself?"

"At the moment, no." I shook my head. "Miranda exercises too much control over Annalise. She isn't going to let Annalise come after Felicity. If anything, she'll probably attempt something magickal again. I'm just not sure what."

"Somethin' with the bones?"

"Possibly, although that would be more curse oriented and more likely directed at me. If I had to speculate, I'd say she'll probably try to re-establish the bond between them."

"How?"

"At this point your guess is as good as mine."

"Well, I hate ta' say it, but there ain't much I can do about the *Twilight Zone* shit, Row."

"I know."

He sat staring off into space for a moment then exhaled heavily. "Okay. I'm gonna call and see if we can put somebody on the house. Then I'll check with Constance and see if the Feebs can put you two up in a safe house."

"I don't think that's necessary, Ben," I said. "Besides, we tried that before, and if you recall it didn't end very well."

"That was a different situation."

"Maybe. But I still don't think it's necessary, and even if it is, I'm not willing to take that chance. I need to stand my ground."

"No, you don't."

"I'm not going to argue the point, Ben."

"Jeezus… Well, why don't you an' Felicity at least come crash at my place 'till we can get a handle on this."

"I need to stay put. But, maybe I can talk Felicity into getting out of harm's way."

"Yeah, right. Like she's gonna go for that."

"Yeah, you're probably right."

"Ain't no prob'ly to it. I've been down this road with you two before. She's more stubborn than you if that's possible."

"Believe me, that's already on my mind."

Ben's cell phone began trilling, so he fished it out of his pocket and flipped it open. "Yeah. Storm… Uh-huh… Yeah… Hold on, he's sittin' right here. I'll ask 'im…"

"What?" I asked as he cupped his hand over the mouthpiece.

"Has Felicity got a necklace with a half a coin or somethin' like that on it?"

"Yeah," I replied with a nod. "It's an heirloom she got from her mother."

"Was she wearin' it today?"

"Probably. She almost always is."

"Yeah. That's what Lewis just told 'em."

"What's that got to do with anything?"

"He's still insistin' it was Felicity he was with. Swears he can't be makin' a mistake 'cause she was wearin' the same necklace last night when he hooked up with 'er."

"Dammit, Ben, we aren't going there again, are we? Felicity didn't…"

He cut me off. "Calm down, Row. It's all good. I just had ta' ask. We know the guy's a wingnut."

He removed his hand and returned his attention to the phone. "Yeah, Row says 'e thinks she wears it all the time, so she prob'ly had it on this mornin' when the fruitloop showed up... Yeah, that's my thought too... Wait, hold on... What, White Man?"

I had been waving at him to get his attention.

"If you're looking for something to distinguish them from one another, ask him if the woman last night had any tattoos. Annalise has a triskele on her back, near her left shoulder."

"How do ya' know that? Wait... Forget I asked..." He moved the phone back up to his mouth. "Ya' catch that? Yeah, left shoulder. Yeah... I'll hold..."

"So?"

"So cool your jets," he told me. "We ain't comin' after Felicity. The guy's certifiable and we know it. Ackman's gonna ask 'im about the tatt."

After a moment he repositioned the phone and said, "What's that? Yeah. Thought so... Okay, I'll be over in a few. Later."

I watched him as he folded the phone and stuffed it back into his pocket.

"You were right. Lewis says she had the BDSM tatt on 'er shoulder. That somethin' you got from a visit to the *Twilight Zone*?"

I nodded. "Yeah."

"Well, odds are he's just so fixated on Firehair that he's sayin' anything 'e can to make us believe there's a relationship there, so I wouldn't worry about it. So, look... I gotta run. I need ta' hook up with Ackman ta' go check out that club."

"Do you want me to come with you?"

"No." He shook his head. "What I want is for ya' ta' pack a bag, grab your wife, and hightail it over ta' my place. I can give ya' my spare key."

"I wouldn't count on that happening."

"Yeah, I know. So, we go for number two on my wish list instead.

You stay right here with the door locked, and call me if any ooga-boogas pop in and give ya' a message."

Other than a particularly angry resurgence of my chronic headache, the rest of the day passed without incident. But, as they say, all good things must come to an end. Unfortunately, for me, the good things always seemed to reach that end far too quickly.

M. R. Sellars

Wednesday, December 14
1:17 A.M.
Unit 103
Blue Moon Apartments
Saint Louis, Missouri

THE END OF DESIRE: A Rowan Gant Investigation

CHAPTER 27:

"Why?" Annalise asked aloud.

"It is not for you to ask..." Miranda told her.

"But, I've had this all my life."

"And, that is why you must use it now..."

"But..."

"Do not argue, Annalise... Do as you have been told..."

Annalise stared at the necklace in her hand. It was a small half-coin suspended from a delicate gold chain. She fingered it gently, feeling the uneven edge where it had been cut like a puzzle piece. This was all she had of her true history. A gift from a mother she had never known. She had always imagined that somewhere the woman who had given birth to her was wearing the other half around her neck and thinking of the daughter she had given up.

There was a time in her life when she had felt nothing but animosity for that woman. But, in recent years her feelings had changed. She knew there had to have been a reason for her mother to make the choice she did, right or wrong. She wanted desperately to believe that she regretted that decision each and every day and was somewhere out there looking for her.

"But, my mother..." she objected again.

"Ezili is your mother, Annalise..."

"Yes, I know that, but..."

"Annalise!" Miranda's voice scolded. *"Do as you have been told!"*

She jumped involuntarily at the harshness inside her head. Fear gripped her at the thought of punishment, but this time her defiance was not so easily dismissed.

"I can't..." she muttered.

"You can, and you will..." Miranda instructed.

"No."

The word came from her mouth as no more than a whisper, but she knew that didn't matter. It took only a thought for Miranda to know.

She felt her muscles tense as the odd euphoria of possession began to overtake her. She tried to repeat the word, but nothing more than a gasp would exit her lips. She struggled against the cold embrace of the spirit, but her will had been broken long ago. It was only a moment before she felt herself being drawn into darkness as the *Lwa* entered her body.

As her vision tunneled, she watched her hands moving of their own accord, anointing the necklace with the dead man's blood then placing it into a small glass bottle.

The last thing she remembered before disappearing into the void was the overpowering scent of cloves.

CHAPTER 28:

I had just finished spreading butter onto some slices of whole wheat bread before layering them with Swiss cheese and shaved, smoked ham. I already had a frying pan resting on the stove waiting patiently for me to ignite fire under it so that I could go about the business of grilling the sandwiches for lunch.

Felicity was hard at work in her basement office. Her meeting had gone well the day before, and it was almost a foregone conclusion that she would be signing a contract with the company. However, she still had other obligations to fulfill, so she was presently involved in applying her own brand of technological magic to some digital photographs she had taken for a different client.

It was actually a slow day for me. I had spent my morning recovering a corrupt database for one of my own customers, but other than that, I had little to do. The revolution of more user-friendly software had caused my business to drop off somewhat. Fortunately, I still served a relatively stable niche market and wasn't feeling the effects too severely. In fact, the additional free time was welcome. Of course, I'm sure I would enjoy it more if I found something to fill it that didn't involve serial killers or talking to the dead.

Emily, our calico, had been doing her best to trip me up for better than five minutes now. Weaving circuitously through my legs as I shuffled back and forth between the refrigerator and the counter where I was preparing lunch. Now and again she had let out a plaintive "mew" in a bid to get my attention. Finally, deciding that tactic had failed, she rose up on her haunches and began pawing at my leg.

"What?" I asked, stopping and looking down toward her.

She screeched out a fresh meow then dropped back to all fours and trotted toward the doorway. Stopping, she looked back at me and squeaked again.

"Here," I told her as I stepped over to the back door and swung it open. "You want out?"

Instead of making a dash for the opening, as was her usual response, she turned and seated herself. Still staring at me, she issued a vocal demand once again.

"I don't speak cat," I told her, swinging the door shut and returning to the counter. "Here's the deal. You learn to speak English, I'll learn to speak cat."

It wasn't long before she was right back at trying to trip me by weaving through my legs, and this time she was even more vocal. I switched off the burner with an exasperated sigh and turned my attention back to her.

"What?!" I demanded.

She immediately turned and trotted toward the doorway again.

"Did Timmy fall down the well or something?" I quipped for my own amusement.

She stopped at the threshold and squeaked impatiently.

I gave up and followed. She cast a quick glance over her shoulder to make sure I was really trailing behind her then continued through the dining room and living room before finally parking herself at the front door and staring up at me expectantly.

"So, the back door isn't good enough for you?" I asked.

She simply pivoted her ears then "mewed" again.

Rather than continue to deal with her annoying behavior, I stepped over to the door and unlatched it. Once I had swung it open and pushed the storm door out a few inches, she darted onto the porch and scurried down the stairs.

Behind me, the pendulum clock bonged out a single chime, announcing that it was now half past noon. Since I was already at the front door, I poked my head out and glanced at the mailbox. I could see a circular or two peeking up from the top of the receptacle, so I stepped out and gathered up the mail as well as a medium-sized parcel that was sitting beneath it.

Before returning to my interrupted culinary endeavor, I sorted through the pile, separating junk from bills and arranging them in stacks on the dining room table. The rectangular box was addressed to Felicity, care of her company, Emerald Photographic Services, so I placed it beneath her assortment of business correspondence.

On my way back to the kitchen, I detoured into the hallway and called down the stairs to my wife, "Felicity... Lunch in about five minutes."

Her voice floated back up to me. "Okay."

"Oh, and the mail is here," I added. "You got a package."

"Who is it from?" she asked.

"Sorry, I didn't pay any attention. Want me to check?"

"I bet it's that effects lens I ordered," she called back. "Don't worry about it. I'll be up in a minute."

"Okay."

I returned to the stove and set about the task of turning the cold sandwiches into hot ones while the microwave hummed along, doing the same for a large dish of tomato soup. I heard the rhythmic thump of Felicity's feet against the stairs followed by the door to the basement opening then closing.

"Something smells good," she announced in a loud voice. "But, since you're cooking, I guess I'd better reserve judgment until I actually taste it."

"Very funny," I called back.

"Well, *I* thought it was," she giggled. Her voice was a bit closer this time, and I could hear her shuffling through the mail in the dining room. After a brief pause she asked, "So, what are we having?"

"It's a surprise."

"Aye, now I'm worried."

"You're in rare form today," I replied.

I heard paper tearing as she opened the package. Following a half-minute or so of silence, she muttered, "Oh, dammit."

"What's wrong?" I asked, still focusing my attention on flipping the sandwiches in the skillet.

"Well, it's not my lens," she replied, a semi-disgusted tone hugging her voice. "There was a card on top under the wrapping. Listen to this—'Merry Christmas. I just wanted to say goodbye. Hope they fit. Forever at your feet, mat.'"

"Hope they fit?"

"I think the creep sent me a pair of shoes."

"Gods... Well, let's hope he really means goodbye," I returned. "So what would you like to..."

I never got the chance to complete the question as it was unceremoniously cut off by a horrified scream. I started immediately, and the spatula I had been holding fell from my hand and clattered loudly on the floor. For the second time in as many days, I found myself racing from the kitchen with the acrid burn of fear churning through my stomach.

This time, however, I somehow knew it wasn't going to go away.

"So, you just found it on the front porch?" Ben asked, staring at me intently, his pencil poised over his notebook.

We had positioned ourselves in the kitchen, keeping out of the way of the crime scene technician as she worked. While the smoky haze had finally settled, the funk of our burned lunch still hung in the air. Felicity had taken the blackened remnants out to the trashcan a bit earlier, and she still hadn't come back into the house.

At the moment, she was standing on the back deck staring out across the yard, the skillet resting atop the railing next to her. I'd been keeping an eye on her through the window, and she hadn't moved for several minutes. I knew I really needed to be out there with her, but I also wanted to keep as much distance between her and the current situation as possible. Since Ben needed answers, here I was, caught square in the middle. Unfortunately, it was probably an exercise in futility because he had already said he would need to talk to her as well.

My mind flashed on the dish of soup still sitting in the microwave. A defense mechanism, I'm sure. Our brains have a way of seeking out the mundane and normal in the face of horror. Of course, anything resembling hunger was long gone, so my thought was that I really needed to get it out of there and put it in the refrigerator before I forgot about it.

An explosion of light diverted my attention yet again. At random intervals a bright flash would illuminate the dining room as the tech took photos of the atrocity resting on the table. I glanced over out of reflex then looked back to my friend.

"So?" he pressed.

"I'm sorry. What did you say?"

"Ya' said ya' found the box on the front porch? Is that right?"

"Yeah," I said with a nod. "It was there when I went out to get the mail."

"Did ya' see anybody hangin' around? Strange car? Anything like that?"

"I didn't notice."

"Okay, so what time was it that ya' found it?"

"Right at twelve thirty."

"Had ya' been outside before that?"

I shook my head. "No. Not since last night around ten."

He jotted a quick note then glanced into the dining room before looking back to me.

"Well, there's no postage on it, so I doubt the mail carrier delivered it."

I nodded. "You're probably right."

"We'll check it out anyway. But, I'm guessin' Devereaux prob'ly put it there 'erself." He paused for a second then huffed, "Jeezus! If I'd just been able ta' get a unit ta' watch the house... Shit."

"She may have paid someone to deliver it, Ben."

"Yeah, maybe, but somethin' in my gut says no. Either way I'll get the locals to canvass and try to find out if anybody saw anything."

"Yeah," I solemnly agreed. "You might want to check over the yard as well."

"For what?"

"Bone fragments."

"You mean from the victim in Baton Rouge?"

I nodded. "If she actually came here, she probably spread them around. That would be a typical use in a cross. Why not kill two birds so to speak."

"You got one of those headaches again?"

"You could say that."

"You gonna be okay?"

"As okay as I can be given the circumstances."

"Yeah... Lovely. I'll get someone on it."

A fresh burst of light flickered through the room, and I found my eyes wandering back in the direction of the table. The shoebox was still sitting there on the corner, resting atop the torn remnants of the craft paper in which it had been wrapped. The lid was lying on the floor exactly where Felicity had dropped it.

Under different circumstances, the contents, a pair of white, stiletto-heeled pumps, wouldn't have elicited such a terror-stricken response from my wife. However, in this case, they weren't simply a pair of white shoes. They were haphazardly smeared with rusted red. It didn't take a close up inspection to know that the foreign substance streaking the patent leather was blood. But, even as disturbing as that was, it wasn't the worst part. Skewered onto the heel of the right shoe was a limp hunk of pallid flesh that bore more than just a passing resemblance to a human tongue.

I heard some unintelligible mumbling in my ears as I continued to stare. A moment later, I felt a hard poke on my shoulder and heard my friend calling my name.

"Yo... Earth ta' Rowan..."

"What?" I stammered, turning back to him. "I'm sorry."

"Look right here," Ben said, holding two fingers forked and waving them at his own face. "Look at me. Forget about that in there."

"Easier said than done."

"Yeah, I know, but stay with me on this. I need ta' know if you touched any of it, or just Firehair?" he asked.

I shook my head. "Just Felicity. Well, except that I'm the one who brought the package inside."

"Was it still wrapped when you touched it?"

"Yeah," I replied with a nod.

"Did you touch it after it was unwrapped?"

"No."

"How about the card? You pick that up?"

"No. I was more concerned with calming Felicity."

"Yeah. I can understan' that."

His cell phone let out a muted warble, so he dug it out of his pocket and looked at the display. Flipping it open, he pressed it to his ear. "Yeah, this is Detective Storm. Whaddaya got?"

While he was talking, I turned to watch Felicity. She had finally taken a couple of steps forward and was leaning against the railing, but other than what was obvious from her dejected posture, I couldn't tell her current state of mind. Of course, even at a distance, I could feel the anxiety flowing around her. I heard my friend snap the cell phone shut, so I brought my attention back to him.

"Had a unit from County go by and check on Lewis at his apartment," he offered, his tone crisp and official.

"He's dead, isn't he," I remarked as much as asked.

"Yeah," he replied with a nod. "The copper that just called sounded pretty green around the gills. From the bloody shoeprints around the body and what's sittin' on your table, looks like she might've stomped 'im ta' death. Apparently, she made the job Firehair did on 'im look like a minor scratch."

"Don't say that around Felicity," I replied. "I don't know quite how she'd handle the comparison right now."

"I won't," he said. "Martin's on 'is the way over with a crew right now ta' work it. Sounds like a real mess."

"She used him to find us," I offered. "Now she's using him to send a message."

"Yeah, I'm inclined ta' agree with ya'. Yesterday coulda been a big coincidence, but this sure's fuck ain't. Brings it all inta' perspective... Question is how'd she know ta' go after him in particular, and that he could lead 'er to ya'?"

"Miranda."

"The ghost bitch. Okay, how?"

"Felicity's connection to Lewis. The incident in the motel room. Everything that happened when Miranda was possessing her is a part of the *Lwa's* memory now."

"So ghosts got memories?"

"Of course they do."

"That's some screwed up shit, Row."

"It always is, isn't it?"

"Uh-huh. Yeah... That's a fact... Problem is, I can't arrest a ghost."

"So you've said numerous times."

"Yeah, I have because it's true. So..." he paused as he smoothed his hair back. "You still feel like you're safe stayin' here?"

I shook my head. "No."

"Okay, so now I'm not askin' anymore, I'm tellin'. Get Firehair in here, pack a coupl'a bags, an' come crash at my place. I'll wait and you can follow me over."

"It doesn't really matter where we go, Ben," I told him. "As long as we're dealing with Miranda, we're not safe anywhere."

CHAPTER 29:

I draped Felicity's coat over her shoulders then slowly stepped around beside her. I had been standing at the door for better than a minute, watching her at the deck railing while trying to decide if I should intrude or simply leave her alone.

"I thought you might be getting cold," I said softly.

She looked over at me with a weak smile as she pulled the garment tight around herself and held it clasped together at her neck. She didn't say a word. Her gaze simply wandered back to some distant point in the patchy snow-covered yard.

Her cheeks were flushed red from the chilly wind, and that made me even more concerned for her emotional state. She had been out here far too long without a coat, and given how much she hated the cold, I knew that could only mean she wasn't handling this situation very well.

"So… Want some company?" I asked.

"She killed him, didn't she?" she answered with her own question. Her voice was faint and strained. It was as if she was struggling to contain her emotions.

I knew it wouldn't do me any good to lie. I could tell she already knew the answer before she asked.

"Yes," I replied.

Ben was still in the house, and the crime scene technician had been bagging the evidence just before I came outside. At least she wasn't trashing the place like the last crew when they had been dead set on finding something to implicate my wife in all this. I cast a quick glance over my shoulder to check on the progress and saw my friend talking to the tech, so I knew things weren't cleared out just yet.

"Why, Rowan?" Felicity asked.

"She's sick, honey."

"But, why did she send that to me?"

"I don't have a good answer for that, other than I think the first one applies here as well. She's a very sick person."

I waited for a moment, continuing to watch her as she stared out at the yard. Finally, I said, "It will probably only be another few minutes. The tech should be done in there shortly, and we can go back in."

"It doesn't matter. That's not why I'm out here," she muttered.

"Oh," I said, unable to keep a mildly perplexed tone from attaching itself to the words. "I see."

"I'm out here because of the way I feel," she explained.

"I know, honey. I understand."

She remained silent for a long while. Even in profile, I could tell by her expression that she was deep in thought, wrestling with something she wanted to say but couldn't.

Eventually, she whispered, "No. I don't think you do."

"Okay, I can accept that," I agreed with a shallow nod. "I really can't pretend to understand what it is you're feeling. I can only imagine that it might be similar to how I feel."

"How do you feel?" she asked.

I tried to sum up the swirl of emotions in a few simple words. "Sickened. Horrified. Mournful."

"Yes," she mumbled. "Like you're supposed to."

"Honey, I'm fairly certain there's no hard and fast rule with regard to how you're supposed to react to something like this."

"Maybe not, but your reaction is normal."

"What makes you think yours isn't?"

"What would you say if I told you I don't feel any of those things? None of them at all."

"If I also consider the fact that you've been standing out here in the cold without a coat for more than a half hour, I'd say you're probably in shock."

"I wish I was."

"Sweetheart, I'm pretty sure you are."

"I don't think so."

"Why not?"

"If I was in shock then maybe I'd be numb," she offered. "I wouldn't feel anything."

"So…" I asked. "I assume that means you're feeling something?"

"Yes."

"Anger?"

She nodded. "Maybe a little. But, that's not really it."

"Can you describe it?"

"Aye, unfortunately I can."

I waited for her to continue, but after several heartbeats, it became obvious she wasn't going to do so without prodding. "Would you like to tell me what you're feeling?"

"I'm afraid."

"That's perfectly normal, Felicity. So am I."

"No, Rowan." She gave her head a shake then frowned. "I mean I'm afraid to tell you what I'm feeling."

"Why?"

"Because… If I do you'll think I'm insane."

"I don't think that's going to happen."

"You say that now."

"And, I'll say it again after you tell me."

She stewed for a moment, turning her gaze toward the activity at the bird feeders nearby. "The grackles have been eating all the food," she stated, conspicuously diverting the subject. "The rest of the birds aren't getting much."

"We go through that every year," I offered in reply. I wanted to press her for an answer to her earlier cryptic comment, but I feared she might be too fragile at this point. As tough as I knew my wife to be, her current demeanor was worrying me.

"I wish they'd just go away," she mused.

"We can always take down the feeders," I said.

"No," she shook her head. "That wouldn't be fair to the other birds… Besides, I suppose they serve a purpose. Before you came out, a hawk swooped in and had one of the grackles for lunch."

"Nature at work, I suppose."

Finally, she pivoted her head back toward me and said, "What if I told you I feel like he got what he deserved?"

"The grackle?"

"No. Lewis. 'mat.'"

I thought about her comment for a few seconds then said, "I'd still have to say shock. After what happened yesterday you were angry. I wouldn't be surprised if you haven't let go of that yet, even if you think you have. Your mind is probably dealing with all of this by rationalizing what happened to him as some form of cosmic justice."

"You sound like Helen."

"Yeah," I admitted. "I guess I do. Sorry about that."

"Don't be. Maybe you're right. At least, I hope you are. I don't like feeling this way. It's not like me at all."

"No, it isn't. But, I can certainly understand it. You've been through way too much this past couple of months. You've been overloaded with a whole spectrum of emotions, and something eventually has to give. Sometimes our brains just have to take a breather, and that tends to make our psyche's go a little off kilter."

"Is this how you feel? I mean, when you've finally had all you can take?"

"We all feel things differently, Felicity."

"So, that's a no?"

"It's a *we all feel things differently*."

"Aye, I thought so."

She turned back to face the yard. I stood there wondering if I should have simply said yes to the original question in order to help her reconcile what she was going through. Of course, hindsight is twenty-twenty, but at the moment even that seemed more than just a bit myopic.

I looked over my shoulder and glanced through the kitchen window but saw no activity at all. I had to assume Ben and the tech were out inspecting the yard as I had suggested.

Turning back to Felicity I said, "Looks safe in there now. Want to go in?"

"Not just yet."

"Do you want me to leave you alone?"

She shook her head. "No."

I waited a moment, listening to the rise and fall of the wind as it hissed through the bare branches of the trees.

"So, Ben is insisting we come stay at his place until this blows over," I finally said. "I think that might be a good idea."

"We can't leave the animals," she said. "We've done that too much lately. They're already traumatized enough."

"We'll get RJ to take them."

"RJ is out of town."

"Then Joe and Terri. We'll find somebody."

"That isn't the point."

"I know it isn't, sweetheart, but she knows where we live. It isn't safe here."

"There's magick involved, Rowan. Will it really be any safer elsewhere?"

"I don't know," I admitted. "But, we can at least stack some of the odds in our favor."

"We could just ward the house again."

"Wards stop magick. They don't stop people."

"If we stay with him, we'll just have to ward there as well. What will he say when I start salting and smudging his house?"

"Knowing him, probably something about hocus-pocus and la-la land."

She sighed heavily. "Aye, I suppose maybe you're right. Staying here would be too big a risk."

I heard a knock behind me, and I turned to see Ben standing at the back window of the kitchen, rapping his knuckles on the glass. As soon as he had my attention, he waved me in.

"It looks like Ben needs to talk to me," I told Felicity.

"Aye, I'm sure he needs to talk to me as well."

"I'm sure that can wait if you aren't ready."

"No. I should get it over with."

"Okay, if you're sure."

I ushered my wife in through the back door ahead of me then followed her through the atrium and into the kitchen. The warmth of the house made my cheeks tingle as the circulation resumed in my face.

"Hey," I said with a quick nod toward Ben. "We were just talking about coming in to pack some bags."

"Yeah, good idea," he returned, a stoic expression on his face.

"I suppose you need a statement from me?" Felicity asked.

"Yeah," he nodded. "But, why don't ya' get started packin'. We can do that in a bit."

"Aye, are you sure?"

"Yeah." He nodded again.

"Thanks," she replied.

We both started from the room, but Ben tapped my arm as I passed. When I looked up at him, he jerked his head toward the back of the kitchen.

"You go ahead, honey," I told Felicity. "I'll be along in a minute."

"Why? What's wrong?"

"Nothing. I just need to talk to Ben."

She looked at us both then turned and continued through the doorway without a word. When he decided she was out of earshot, Ben raised an eyebrow.

"Not doin' too good, is she?" he asked.

"She's okay," I told him. "Rattled, but that's understandable."

"Want me ta' call Helen and invite her over for dinner so they can talk?"

"I doubt she'd want to come over for dinner only to have to work, Ben. Besides, I'd rather not put any pressure on Felicity. I think she might just need some time to get over the shock."

"You sure?"

"Yeah. For now anyway."

"Okay," he said, looking to the side then smoothing back his hair.

"So, you were right about the bones. Didn't take long ta' find a coupl'a fragments. The tech is taping off the front yard right now, and she just called in some support ta' do a full sweep."

"I can't say I'm surprised."

"So, when we pick 'em up, will that make the curse go away?"

"Not really. For one thing it will be impossible for you to get all of them."

"It somethin' that could kill ya'?"

"Probably not."

"Prob'ly?"

"It's magick, Ben," I explained. "It isn't good, but it's also something I can protect myself against."

"Well, then I guess ya' better do some of your hocus-pocus then."

"Trust me, I will. And, Felicity already has hocus-pocus planned for your house."

"Friggin' lovely. So, how's your head? You're sure you ain't gonna kick off all of a sudden or somethin', right?"

"It hurts, and I seriously doubt it."

"Okay, just checkin'. So, anyway, listen… Do cloves mean anything?"

"Why? Did you find cloves out there too?"

"No. Got a call from Martin. Apparently, Devereaux didn't do any of the regular Voodoo shit we've found in the past. Nothin' obvious anyway. But, there was a big ass container of cloves spilled all over the kitchen counter."

"Hmmm… Clove oil is used in love and lust spells. Are you sure it just wasn't some sort of accident in the kitchen?"

"Well, there's a pile of wax too. Looks like what's left of a red candle accordin' ta' Martin. They also found a dish with what appears ta' be blood in it. He figured I should run it past ya' since I was here."

"Okay, if you throw in the candle and the blood, I'd have to say it sounds like some kind of magick, or at least an attempt at it," I replied. "But I'm not sure exactly what."

"Okay. Just thought I'd check…" He sighed then shook his head.

"So, if ya' saw it ya' think ya' might be able ta' tell?"

"Maybe. It's hard to say."

"What if you were in the same room with it?"

"The odds would be better," I replied. "Ben, are you asking me what I think you are?"

"Look, I know ya' quit and all, but yeah, I'm askin'. You wanna come with me to the scene?"

"Why?"

"Ta' see if all that is somethin' ya' need ta' worry about."

"I'm not really comfortable with leaving Felicity right now. I think it would be…"

"I'll go," Felicity's voice cut me off from the doorway.

Ben and I both turned to look in her direction. I had no idea how long she had been standing there, but it was obviously long enough to know what I was objecting to.

"I don't think that's such a good idea," I told her.

"Why?"

"I think that's pretty obvious."

"I gotta agree with Row on this one," Ben added. "Besides, given your history with this guy, your name on the scene log ain't gonna fly."

"One of us needs to go," she replied. "You can't effectively counter a spell without knowing what it is to begin with."

"You can just ward against magick, Felicity. You know that."

"Aye, well maybe I'm tired of hiding," she shot back. "It hasn't done me any good so far."

Ben looked at me and said with a shrug, "Your call, White Man."

I glanced back to my wife. Her expression hadn't changed and neither had the look of determination in her eyes.

"If I can't go, then you have to," she said.

"What about the whole thing with me being banned from the investigation?" I said, looking over to Ben.

"Fuck it."

"You could get into trouble taking me into a scene."

"Yeah, so?"

"I'm not good with that."

"You don't hafta be."

"Yes, I do."

"Listen, this ain't about the investigation. This is personal. If this bitch is throwin' somethin' down on you, then ya' need ta' know what it is."

"It might not have anything to do with us at all."

"You really believe that?"

I didn't reply.

"Uh-huh," he grunted, adding a slow nod as well. "Thought as much."

"You actually sound like you're starting to believe in magick."

"Right now I believe in makin' sure you two are safe. If this weird ass shit poses a threat, then ya' need to know about it."

"So what could happen to you if I go?"

"That ain't for you to worry about."

"I'm going to anyway."

"Yeah, so now ya' know how I feel."

"Well, like I was saying earlier, I'm not comfortable with leaving Felicity here by herself. Not after this morning."

"Not an issue anyway," Ben offered. "I already called for a unit from the locals to come over an watch the house. They'll be here before the crime scene unit even thinks about clearin' out."

"Aye, I'll be fine," she interjected. "I'll lock the door and finish packing while you're gone."

All of my objections had been met head on, and I really couldn't think of any more. Of course, even if I did I suspected Ben would have an answer for them as well.

Reluctantly, I gave in. "Okay, I guess I'll go."

CHAPTER 30:

News crews were already on site, their vans positioned across the street while reporters performed for the cameras using the activity surrounding the apartment complex as a lurid backdrop. As usual, Ben muttered an expletive or two about them as he hooked his van into the parking lot then nosed it into an empty space. Before climbing out of the vehicle, he slipped his badge onto a cord then hung it around his neck.

When we arrived at the fluttering line of yellow tape, my friend flashed the shield to the officer standing watch at the building entrance then signed in on the crime scene log. He stood by patiently waiting while I added my name to the list.

"Can I see your ID, sir?" the officer asked as I handed the pen back to him.

"He's with me," Ben answered before I could reply.

The officer glanced at my name on the clipboard, back at Ben, then to me. "Which department are you with?"

"He's an independent consultant," Ben replied, once again not giving me a chance to speak. "Like I said, he's with me."

The man cocked an eyebrow and stared at him for a moment then pointed toward the building. "One-oh-three. Down the stairs, second door on the right. Can't miss it."

Inside the door, we both donned latex gloves and paper shoe covers before continuing down the short flight of stairs then along the hallway toward the entrance to the apartment. My mind was already starting to race before we had ever entered the building, and upon reaching 103, it was setting new speed records. Ben started through the door, but I visibly hesitated before stepping across the threshold.

The scent of cloves wafted out of the apartment carried along on the unmistakable metallic funk of blood and fresh death. The bizarre mélange of smells made the ache in my head automatically shift into a higher gear.

The last time I had entered a crime scene where Annalise and Miranda had played their deadly games, I had walked into far more than I was prepared to handle. Granted, I had been alone and too exhausted to properly shield myself from the onslaught, but the memory of that incident was still fresh. Too fresh, in fact, for something that was now over two weeks old.

"You okay?" Ben asked as he stepped back out into the hallway. "I turned around and you were gone. You ain't goin' la-la are ya'?"

"No..." I replied. "I'm just a bit... anxious... I guess."

"I told ya' not ta' worry about that," he said. "I'll deal with it."

I shook my head. "It's not that. It's more like bad memories."

"You wanna take a pass?" he asked. "You can wait in the van if ya' want."

"No. I'm already here. I might as well have a look."

"Long as you're sure. I mean, I want ya' ta' take a look at this whole candle thing, that's the whole point. But, I also don't wanna push ya' over the edge either."

My head was pounding at this point, but I couldn't be sure if it was a product of what waited on the other side of the doorway, or if it was entirely due to this attack of anxiety. I closed my eyes for a moment then drew in a deep breath.

"It's okay," I finally said. "Let's go on in."

Ben watched me carefully for a moment then offered a guarded "okay."

I followed him into the apartment, fully expecting to be set upon by latent feelings of arousal mixed with fear, just as I had been before. Instead, I was slapped full in the face by the psychic residue of blind anger. I felt my face flush as the emotion corkscrewed its way into my head, coursing out through my body and making my skin prickle with a sudden wave of gooseflesh.

This was new, and definitely not what I had foreseen.

I stopped a few steps through the doorway and looked around the room. True to what Ben had been told, the beige carpet was stained with bloody footprints, the shape of which was obviously made by a pair of women's high-heeled shoes. While they radiated out in various directions, the majority of them were clustered around a far more solid stain, upon which the victim's body was currently resting.

Someone had placed an open body bag over the top of the remains. I assumed that party to have been someone from the coroner's office since one of their official vehicles was in the parking lot. Why they had simply covered him and not transported him from the scene, I wasn't certain. In any case, he was still here, and I couldn't help but stare.

The rubberized bag covered his face and torso, but his arms and legs were still exposed. The one wrist I could plainly see was shackled into a wide leather cuff, which appeared to be snugged so tightly as to be biting into his flesh. If that weren't enough, it was attached to what looked to be a metal bar that ran beneath his back. I assumed it ended in a like manner at the unseen hand. A similar apparatus had been used on his ankles, rendering him more or less immobile. She definitely hadn't wanted him to get loose.

Two of the fingers on his exposed hand were bent up at an odd angle, visibly broken. A number of ragged holes were torn in the back of the hand as well as his forearm. His legs hadn't faired any better as they were covered in long gashes that were now crusting over. His knees appeared to be buckled backwards, hyperextended to the point of shattering the joints.

As I stared, the rage continued spreading through me, punctuated by twinges of satisfaction. I knew in that moment, there had been nothing at all sexual about this kill for Annalise. There was no arousal or gratification on the physical level. It was purely emotional.

This had been all about revenge.

I heard a new voice and looked up from the horrific tableau. A man around Ben's age was entering the room from a doorway near the back. "Yeah, bag that but get pictures of the whole thing first."

He turned toward us after completing the statement, and a look of mild surprise flitted across his features. Continuing into the room, he looked over at Ben and said, "Hey, Storm."

"Martin," my friend replied.

The detective glanced over at me with an odd look on his face then said, "Hey, Rowan. How are you doing?"

"Hello, Mike," I replied. "Getting by. And you?"

"Better than the stiff I guess," he grunted then looked back over to Ben. "Storm... Can I see you back here for a minute?"

"Yeah," Ben returned then looked over at me as he followed him deeper into the apartment. "Wait here, Row."

I answered with a quick nod.

Detective Martin was one of a handful of cops on the Major Case Squad who actually took me seriously, so I hadn't actually expected to be getting the "what's he doing here?" treatment. However, that was exactly the look he had on his face, and I knew it probably had quite a bit to do with the fact that I had been banned from the investigation by the powers that be. My reception told me that Ben was going further out on this figurative limb than I wanted, but there was nothing I could do. I was already here, so the damage had been done.

After a handful of minutes, the two of them came back into the main room, Detective Martin trailing along behind my friend. He didn't look particularly excited, but at least he didn't look angry either. I didn't know what was actually discussed while they were out of earshot, but it wasn't hard to guess.

Ben asked, "So, you got anything new?"

"Not much," Martin began, gesturing toward the covered corpse. "We're pretty sure the victim is Lewis, but we don't have a positive ID just yet and probably won't until the M.E. gets done."

"That bad?" Ben asked.

"Not much of his face left," he offered. "Not to mention the missing part you already know about. Rest of 'im isn't much better. If you think what you can see is bad... Well, trust me, you don't really want to look under the bag. I don't think she stopped working him over for a while, even after he was dead."

"I'll take your word for it," Ben grunted. "They gonna transport the body soon?"

Martin nodded. "Yeah. The restraints he's wearing are attached with padlocks, so they went to get some bolt cutters. Until they get those off 'im, he won't fit in the bag."

"Lovely," Ben replied. "So, what about the rest of the apartment? Anything helpful?"

"Well, not really." Martin pointed toward the floor, indicating several points in succession. "As you can see, we have a fairly clear trail to follow. It pretty much gives us an idea everywhere the killer went inside the apartment. Residue in the tub indicates she might have showered or bathed after she killed him. Hell, it looks like she might have even had herself a late night snack."

"Why do ya' think that?" my friend asked.

"There was a gallon jug of milk sitting on the back of the toilet. What little was left of it anyway."

"She didn't drink it," I offered. "She added it to her bath water."

"What makes you say that?" Martin asked, looking over at me.

"Voodoo. Given her religious leanings, bastardized as they are, it's something she would do for purification," I explained.

Ben grunted, "Ain't nothin' pure about this bitch except that she's evil."

"True, but she would have wanted to cleanse herself after this murder."

"I don't remember there being anything like that at any of the other crime scenes," Martin added. "Why this one?"

"There was no need in those cases," I said. "This is different. She didn't kill him for the sexual high like she has with her past victims. She was exacting vengeance, and the ritual bath would be her way of ridding herself of any leftover emotions."

He nodded. "Okay. So, what was she getting revenge for?"

"I'm not sure."

"She sent his tongue to your wife, or at least we think it's his. Do you think it has something to do with her?"

"Possibly."

"Why his tongue, though?"

"That's hard to say. My best guess would be that since the tongue is associated with speech, the obvious answer is retribution for something he said or she feared he was going to say."

"Okay, but why send it to your wife?"

I shrugged. "To frighten her maybe. Again, I'm not really sure. I'm just telling you what I'm seeing and feeling."

"So this is coming from one of your gut instincts?" he asked.

"Some of it. The rest is pretty much just a hypothetical application of what I've studied about Voodoo and hoodoo."

"Okay, well since we're on that particular subject, Storm said the real reason you came here is to have a look at what we found in there," Martin said, as he nodded toward the half wall that divided the main room of the apartment.

We followed him as he stepped around the tented evidence markers that were lined across the floor and headed in the direction of the small kitchen. It was no big surprise that a fading trail of bloody shoe prints marked the path we followed.

Detective Martin guided us through the doorway then pointed toward the counter near the sink. "Don't touch anything," he instructed. "The techs haven't gotten to this yet."

"No problem," I replied, an absent tone in my voice as I scanned the area where he indicated.

Whole cloves were scattered across the floor where they had fallen from a large pile on the countertop. Next to the pile itself was a plastic container lying on its side, the dried flower buds spilling from the open mouth in a dark brown spread. The sharp aroma of the spice was even thicker here in the small room.

I edged around the mess on the floor and leaned forward to peer closely at the other remnants of magick occupying the space near the sink. A slag of red wax with a small piece of blackened wick sat to one side. Near it was a pattern of drips, which at first glance also appeared to be wax but was black and had a much glossier sheen. Upon closer inspection, I could tell they had come from a very different type of candle besides simply the color. Next to these sat a bowl, which contained a rusted red substance that had the distinctive look of slowly coagulating blood. Drops of the dried liquid formed a trail across the surface of the counter. I followed it with my eyes until it ended at a roughly circular spot that was devoid of the scattered cloves.

"Have the evidence technicians removed anything in here?" I asked.

"No," Martin replied. "Like I said, they haven't made it this far except to set markers and take a few pictures."

"Something is missing," I muttered.

"What did you say?" Ben asked.

"Something is missing," I said louder, as I pointed to the clear spot. "Whatever she did, it involved a bottle or a jar maybe. See this round spot here that doesn't have any cloves on it?"

"Yeah," he grunted. "So what'd she do?"

"I can't tell."

"Whaddaya mean ya' can't tell?"

"I mean I can't tell," I repeated. "I've never seen this exact type of magickal working before. The basic components of a lust spell are here with the red candle and the cloves. But, by the same token, you also have blood, which I'm betting once belonged to Lewis. And, see these black droplets here? That's sealing wax."

"You mean like the stuff they put on the back of fancy envelopes?" Martin asked.

"Exactly. Whatever she did, she sealed it in a bottle or jar."

"So it's some kind of Voodoo?" Martin asked.

"Hoodoo, maybe. Even more likely, it's some manner of old folk magick," I told him.

"Okay, well I hate to be a skeptic, Rowan, but what bearing does it really have on this investigation?"

"For the police, probably nothing more than evidence that she was here."

"So it's nothing," he replied.

"No, it's something. I just don't know what because it doesn't make sense."

"Which part?" Ben asked.

"The outward appearance of the spell in general. I don't get why she would be doing some kind of convoluted sex magick because she killed him out of anger, not for the thrill."

"Do you think maybe you could be wrong about that part?" Martin asked.

"I could be wrong about all kinds of things," I replied. "But, I can guarantee you that I don't feel any sexual energy emanating from this apartment, and that has always been the predominant psychic feature of all the others."

"Okay, so then what do you think the bottle or jar was for?"

"Like I said, to contain whatever magick she performed, so that in itself creates another mystery. Sealing a magickal working into a bottle isn't unusual, but it can be done for just about any type of spell, so it really doesn't give us any clue as to exactly what she did."

"But, if I'm followin' ya', you're sayin' maybe she made 'erself some lust in a bottle," Ben interjected.

"On the surface that's what it looks like, but we're talking about blood magick here, so I'm seriously out of my element. Even so, since the container isn't here, I'd be willing to bet she either has it with her or she buried it somewhere."

"And that means what?" Ben asked.

I dipped my head and gave him a half shrug. "Unfortunately, it means we aren't going to find out what it is until it does whatever it's supposed to do."

CHAPTER 31:

"So what do we do now," I asked.

Ben and I had signed out of the crime scene shortly after Detective Martin had showed us the mysterious bit of magick Annalise had worked in the kitchen. My headache still hadn't really subsided at this point, but a good amount of the tension had finally ebbed. The most important thing for me at the moment, however, was that my skin was no longer prickling with the unbridled anger that had been so prevalent throughout the apartment.

"Whaddaya mean?" Ben returned. "It's simple. We go back to your place, pick up Firehair and your luggage, then I take you two ta' my place."

"I know that," I said. "I meant, what do we do about stopping Annalise?"

"Gotta find 'er first, so unless you got some kinda *Twilight Zone* thing tellin' us where ta' look, it's just gonna take police work and a bit of luck."

"Define police work."

"We ask around and hope somebody saw somethin'."

"That's it?"

"That's where the luck comes in," he grunted. "If we're lucky, someone did and will be willin' ta' talk to us about it."

"That doesn't sound terribly promising."

"Welcome to the real world, Row. The majority of the time, that's how criminals get caught," he said with a shake of his head. "That crap on TV is e'zactly that. Crap. Ain't nobody gonna stick a piece of hair under a microscope and suddenly say, 'Bingo! She's standin' at the corner of Fourth and Broadway, go get 'er.' When it comes to this kinda crime, real police work is three parts paperwork, one part luck. Truth is, right now Devereaux is really just a suspect. Until we catch up to 'er and compare the DNA and all that shit... Well, you got the idea."

"It's her. Believe me."

"I do. We just gotta make sure the evidence supports it."

"Okay, so what if nobody saw anything?"

"Then we hope she uses a credit card or somethin', and we get a hit."

"And if that doesn't happen."

"Awfully goddamned negative today, aren't ya'?"

"I'm just worried."

"Yeah... I can tell..."

"So? If she doesn't use a credit card or something?"

"Okay, I'll play. If she keeps 'er head down, doesn't use one of the credit cards we're trackin', nobody saw anything, and nobody calls with a decent tip, then we're kinda fucked until she makes some other move."

"Like coming after me or Felicity?"

"Or killin' some other poor bastard, yeah, that's pretty much about it."

"That doesn't make me feel any better, Ben."

"Hey, you were the one playin' devil's advocate, not me," he replied as he turned the van onto Laclede and accelerated with the flow of traffic. "Who knows, maybe she'll see the error of her ways and turn herself in."

"Yeah, right."

"It's happened before."

"I wouldn't count on it this time."

"Didn't say I was countin' on it," he grunted. "Either way, look at the bright side. Ya' played with your doll, and now the ghost bitch is leavin' Felicity alone."

"Yeah," I answered with a tired sigh. "There is that."

"Look, Row, it's all gonna be good," my friend offered. "We get you two outta sight so you're safe, and Major Case'll do the rest."

"I guess you're right."

"Jeez, mark it on the calendar," he half chuckled. "The injun gets ta' be right for a change."

We rode along in relative silence for a few moments while I digested everything he had just said. I wasn't overly excited about hiding out. I had no reason to believe that doing so this time would end as badly as it had the last, but it still didn't do anything for my anxiety level. I suppose the old idiom, "once bitten, twice shy," was a good description of how I felt about the idea.

Finally, out of idle curiosity, I turned to Ben and asked, "By the way, I'm sure I can probably guess, but what did Mike have to say when you two went in the back?"

"Not much."

"I know better. It had something to do with me being there, didn't it?"

"Yeah, well he just wanted ta' remind me that you weren't s'posed ta' be," he grunted.

"What did you tell him?"

"That I already knew that."

"Do you think he'll say anything?"

"Martin?" He shook his head. "Prob'ly not. I wish he would, but it really doesn't matter. Your name is on the log, so it'll come ta' somebody's attention soon enough."

"What do you mean, you wish he would?"

He simply shrugged in answer.

"Well, how much trouble are you going to be in over this?" I asked.

He shrugged again. "Dunno just yet."

"Could you lose your job?"

"Not very likely. But if I'm lucky I'll get at least a two week suspension."

"At least?"

"It'd be even better if it was a thirty day."

"Better? You aren't making sense."

"Yeah I am. You just don't know it."

"Dammit, Ben, you shouldn't have taken me there."

"I keep tellin' ya', White Man, don't worry about it."

"How can I not? All that came from this was me standing there saying, 'I don't know.'"

"Yeah, but whether ya' realize it or not, now ya' actually do know more than ya' did before, even if ya' don't know exactly what she's up to… If that makes any kind of sense. Either way, it's a start."

"Not enough for you to risk your career."

"Yeah, well, those're the breaks. Besides, I told ya' I ain't gonna lose my job."

"But you might get suspended, and I'm going to feel guilty about that."

"Don't. A suspension for somethin' like this really ain't that big a deal."

"You're being awfully calm about this," I remarked, unable to keep the confusion out of my voice.

"Uh-huh."

"Am I missing something here?"

"Apparently."

I waited for him to expand on his answer, but he simply continued driving in silence. After a moment I prompted, "Well? Would you like to enlighten me?"

"Look, it's simple, Row," he explained. "If I can get suspended, I'll be freed up ta' spend my time makin' sure you and Firehair are safe instead of dependin' on someone else ta' do it while I'm off chasin' dead end leads."

"So you're trying to tell me this is all just part of your grand plan?"

"Somethin' like that."

"You've lost your mind."

"Yeah, probably," he grunted. "That's why I'm hopin' for at least thirty days. I could really use the vacation."

The alarm system began to pulse out its countdown as we came through the front door. I stepped quickly across the room and stabbed in the disarm code on the keypad. It didn't escape my notice that the display was reading that it had been enabled in the "away" mode, which meant the motion detectors scattered throughout the house were live. This certainly wasn't the way it should be set if someone were home, which was supposed to be the case.

"Felicity?" I called out then waited for an answer.

We had been gone for almost two hours, and the crime scene van had no longer been parked in front of the house when we arrived. I had glanced around after climbing out of Ben's vehicle but hadn't seen any local police in the vicinity either, which bothered me quite a bit, given that Ben had arranged for them to be there keeping watch.

Getting no reply, I called out again as I headed down the hallway to our bedroom. I was afraid to admit it to myself, but I knew she wouldn't answer the second time either. The house simply felt empty except for the cats and dogs. I reached the end of the hall and poked my head in through the door. My wife's overnight bag was sitting on the end of the bed, but judging from its misshapen profile it was obvious that she had yet to put much, if anything, into it.

"Yo, Firehair!" Ben bellowed as I started back toward the living room.

I could feel my heart rate beginning to rise. I opened the door to the basement and called down the stairs, "Honey, are you down there?"

Again, there was no response.

I shut the door then stepped into the living room where Ben was still standing. "She's not here," I said, my voice a twisted mix of anxiety and confusion.

"Don't panic, Row," Ben said. "She set the alarm, so maybe she had to run out for somethin'."

"Maybe so," I replied, trying to believe what he was telling me, but my heart rate continued to ramp upward as I felt the thumping in my chest. "But, she hasn't even really started to pack, and we were gone for quite awhile. It doesn't make sense."

I'm sure he could sense my growing agitation, and his words reflected as much. "I'm serious, Row. Don't panic."

"Aren't there supposed to be police watching the house?" I asked.

"Maybe she's with 'em," Ben suggested as he stepped around me and started toward the kitchen. "Give 'er a try on 'er cell phone, and I'll check ta' see if 'er Jeep is here."

I nodded reply then advanced across the living room and snatched up the phone from the bookshelf. With a quick stab at the keypad, I quickly dialed her number. While I waited for the connection to be made, I heard the sound of the back door open as Ben headed out to the garage. After a soft click, the handset began to trill with the audible tone of the ringer. A heartbeat later, as the second ring issued into my ear, a syncopated tune began to play from the vicinity of the dining room. I stepped forward and to my left then looked through the archway. There, on the buffet, was my wife's cell phone.

Ben was just coming back around the corner as I was hanging up.

"Jeep's gone," he said.

"And, she left her cell phone here," I told him, though I was certain he'd heard it.

My heart now advanced beyond a fast jog and directly into a sprint as panic wrapped its icy grip around my gut. Apparently it was obvious in my face as well because Ben looked at me and held up his hands.

"Stay calm, Row. Like I said, she probably just went to the store or something."

"Dammit, Ben, someone was supposed to stay with her!" I spat.

"I'm sure they are, hold on a sec."

He pulled out his cell phone and flipped it open then thumbed in a number. Placing it up to his ear, he waited a moment then began to speak.

"Yeah, this is Detective Storm with the Major Case Squad. Can you do me a favor and radio the unit you had watching the Gant household and check somethin' for me?"

He waited a moment, turning to face me and nodding reassurance. "It's fine, Row," he said. "She probably just needed some girl stuff or somethin'."

"No," I said, shaking my head. "Something doesn't feel right about this."

"*Twilight Zone?*"

"It just doesn't feel right," I repeated.

"Yeah, I'm here," he said, turning his attention back to the phone. "What do you mean you hadn't dispatched a unit yet? I called it in over two hours ago!"

He listened for a few seconds then spat, "Yeah. Thanks."

"They didn't send anyone to watch the house?" I asked, distress rising in my voice.

I knew he wasn't ignoring me, but he didn't respond because his cell phone was pressed up against his ear once again, and he was already talking to someone else.

"Yeah, this is Storm," he barked. "I need ta' get a BOLO out on Felicity O'Brien right now…"

CHAPTER 32:

"**Y**eah, ya' got that? Yeah, Victor, X-Ray, November... That's right, black Jeep," Ben said into his phone.

My friend had made a circuit through the house while calling in the "Be On The Lookout" but hadn't come up with anything he felt necessary to share. He was now standing back in the living room with his cell still firmly planted against his ear.

"Yeah... She's about five-two, around a hundred and five pounds," he continued. "Long red hair. Really long, like waist length. Yeah. Green eyes. Uh-hmmm... No... Right now we aren't sure. We have reason to believe she's being stalked by a woman fitting the same physical description. Yeah, no kiddin'. No, there's no evidence of it being an actual abduction, but we might wanna treat it as a possible. She was last seen at the house in Briarwood, and that was about an hour ago. Maybe an hour and a half... Yeah, by a coupl'a crime scene techs who were goin' over the yard... Yeah, had ta' do with the possible stalker... Yeah. Thanks. Call me at this number if ya' get anything."

My friend folded the device and shoved it into his pocket then simply stared across the room at me. I was sitting on the edge of the sofa, making a concerted effort at remaining calm. So far I had been keeping myself on an even keel, but I wasn't sure how much longer that would last.

"What did they say?" I asked after a long pause.

"In about two minutes, every cop on duty in the metro area is gonna be keepin' an eye out for 'er and the Jeep. It's all good. They're gonna find 'er and she's gonna be just fine."

"I hope you're right."

"Look, Row," he said. "I know you're worried, but it's gonna be fine. I'm tellin' ya' we're pro'bly overreacting as it is."

"I'm all about overreacting when it comes to my wife's safety."

"Believe me, I know that. Hell, ta' be honest I'm impressed your head hasn't spun all the way around yet."

"Give me a minute," I replied. "It could still happen."

"Did ya' check her schedule? Maybe she had an appointment or somethin'."

I shook my head. "There was nothing on the calendar. But, I will admit that she sometimes forgets to write them down where I can find them."

"Well, 'er purse is gone. Could ya' tell if she took any equipment?"

"No," I replied. "I looked, but I couldn't begin to tell you what all she has down there, so she could walk out with a case full of stuff and I'd never be able to tell. Besides, she usually keeps a case in the Jeep as it is."

"Don't worry. It's gonna be fine," he offered again.

I simply nodded then got up from my seat and walked over to the open door. I wiped my hand across the opaque condensation that had formed on the glass of the storm door and silently watched the world continuing on about its business outside.

"You're thinkin' about it, aren't ya'?" Ben asked after a long silence.

I knew all too well the "it" to which he was referring. It was something that haunted me every December, especially on the anniversary, which was only a bit over a week away on Christmas Eve. "It" was the night I had returned home from working an investigation with Ben only to find Felicity missing because she had been abducted by a serial rapist. Given the situation, it was hard not to draw a few disturbing parallels.

"Yeah," I mumbled. "Yeah, I am."

"This ain't the same, Row," he told me.

"Of course it isn't," I replied. "He wanted to rape her. Annalise wants to kill her."

"That's not what I meant, and you know it," he huffed. "There's no real reason to believe Annalise has anything to do with this. For one, Felicity's vehicle is gone. For two, like I said, so is her purse. For three, there's no sign of a struggle. And finally, the dogs weren't locked up. Firehair had to have left here willingly, you know that."

In reality, I knew he was correct. There was absolutely nothing to indicate that Felicity hadn't simply climbed in her Jeep and left of her own accord. But, even if that was fact, something still didn't feel right about it.

"Shouldn't we be out looking for her?" I asked, surprising myself at how even my voice was remaining.

"We can if ya' want," he replied. "You got an idea where ta' start?"

I shook my head. "No. Not really."

"Okay," he replied then waited a measured beat before continuing. "Lemme ask ya' somethin'... You absolutely sure the hocus-pocus with the doll worked?"

I turned to face him. "Yeah, why?"

"Just askin'."

I thought about what he'd asked, and my muddied brain managed to match up the pieces. With an obvious accusatory tone infecting my voice, I spat, "You think she might be heading for that bondage club again, don't you?"

"Calm down, White Man. I was just askin'," he replied.

"I broke that connection," I continued, intent on making sure he understood. "Miranda isn't able to use her as a horse any longer."

"Okay, so what if Annalise did somethin'? Maybe that thing with the candle. Didn't ya' say you thought that's why Miranda brought 'er back here?"

"I don't even want to entertain that thought."

"But, didn't you..."

"No," I spat. "Don't even go there."

He held up his hands in surrender. "Okay. I was just askin'."

I'm not sure if I was being so insistent for his benefit or my own because whether I wanted to admit it or not, the very same thought had already crossed my mind. My friend had simply been the first to vocalize it.

"Actually, there's something else that worries me," I finally said.

"What's that?"

"Shamus."

"Firehair's dad? What about 'im?"

"When Felicity first got arrested, he blamed me. During one of his calls to berate me, he said he had made arrangements to have her deprogrammed once she was out of jail."

"Yeah, I remember you sayin' that. But, I thought I remembered somethin' about your mother-in-law sayin' she'd put the kibosh on that?"

"That's what she said, but I still try not to underestimate Shamus."

He shook his head. "But there's nothing here to indicate she was abducted, Row."

"Maybe he set it up differently," I speculated. "Maybe he called her and she went over to their house and he had them waiting for her."

"With their black helicopter?"

"Dammit, Ben, don't make jokes!" I snapped.

"Look, I'm sorry, but you're soundin' like one of those conspiracy nuts. Besides, your father-in-law didn't call 'er."

"How do you know?"

"'Cause there's nothin' on your caller ID since well before we left the house, and the only incomin' call on 'er cell for the past two days is the one you just made a little while ago."

"You checked that?"

"I'm a cop, Row. Remember? It's what I do."

"What about..."

He interrupted before I could get the question out of my mouth. "Yeah, I checked 'er business line, and yours too. No calls from Dad. But, if it'll make ya' feel better, I can call and have a unit go by to check."

"No..." I said after a moment. "Probably not. Not yet, anyway. If I'm wrong then that will just stir up a big mess all over again."

"I agree… and yeah, you're wrong."

"I just don't get it, Ben. Why would she leave? After everything that's happened. After what showed up here. She knows it isn't safe."

"We're talkin' about Firehair here. You wanna ask that question again or think about it first?"

"I guess you're right," I mumbled then looked back toward the storm door. The condensation had obscured the view once again. "I suppose we're going to look like idiots when she rolls back into the driveway with groceries or something."

"Yes and no," my friend replied with a sideways bob of his head. "When it turns out ta' be nothin', yeah, it might look like an overreaction on the surface; but, under the circumstances, this is all warranted. Besides, ain't a copper I know of who wouldn't rather have a call turn out ta' be nothin', rather than somethin'. Believe me, we live for that shit."

Ben's cell began trilling in his pocket, so he dug it out and answered it.

"Yeah, Storm… Uh-huh… Yeah… Where? North or south? Okay, any sign of 'er? Okay. How's it look? Yeah. That's good. Okay. Thanks."

I was talking before he had even managed to switch the device off. "What? What is it?"

"Firehair's Jeep is sittin' on the north lot at the Galleria. Call just came in."

"That's less than a mile from here."

"Yeah, I know."

"Is she…"

"All they found is the Jeep, Row, but it's parked and locked. No sign of any foul play. Like I said earlier, she's probably inside shoppin'. They're gonna page 'er. C'mon, grab your coat and we'll go over there."

The drive was short; still, with traffic it took us a handful of minutes before we pulled off the main drag into the entrance of the large indoor mall. Ben turned early and aimed his van across the less crowded portion of the front parking lot before cutting over toward the far side of the shopping center.

As we rounded the corner and entered the north lot, I spotted Felicity's Jeep parked at the far end of the first row. Angled in behind it were a Briarwood Police cruiser and a mall security vehicle. As we continued up the aisle, I could see two uniformed officers standing next to the Jeep chatting with a petite woman who was gesturing toward the side entrance.

My heart skipped a beat before starting to race yet again because, other than her small stature, she looked nothing like my wife.

"Why did you do this?" I asked, confusion in my voice.

"I already told you," my wife replied.

"Tell me again."

"Because, I don't want to look like her."

I simply stared at her across the kitchen, unsure of what else to say. As it turned out, I had been mistaken. The woman talking with the two officers on the mall parking lot was, in fact, Felicity. In my defense, however, I had a valid reason for not recognizing her at a distance. The truth is, I even had a reasonable excuse for doing a double take when I got out of the van less that twenty feet away from her.

"I still can't believe you had the police looking for me," she countered.

"Why not?" I asked. "After what happened today? Not to mention that you told me you were going to lock the door and finish packing, but then I come home and you're gone. What kind of reaction did you expect?"

"Aye, you have a point. I suppose I should have left you a note."

"You shouldn't have gone out to begin with."

"You're overreacting."

"Maybe I am, but I think maybe you're under reacting."

She simply shrugged and continued to look at me with her head cocked to the side, a mildly curious look in her eyes. I don't suppose I could blame her. I was still staring at her, just as I had been for several minutes. I couldn't even remember the last time I had blinked.

"It will grow back, Rowan," Felicity announced after a moment then leaned back against the counter and folded her arms across her chest. "Really, it will."

"Yeah, I know," I replied. "But… I don't know…"

Her cascading tresses, which once reached down to her waist, now came to a blunt end just below her shoulders. While there was still a good bit of body to them in the form of a rippling wave, the loosely spiraling curls were all but gone as well. However, radical as those changes were, even they paled in comparison to the fact that her color had gone from fiery red to inky black.

As she looked back at me now, her ivory complexion appeared ghostly white beneath the stark contrast of the straight-banged, retro hairstyle. I knew I didn't have a say in the matter. It was her hair, not mine. But, I'd never seen her with short hair before, much less any color other than her natural red, so I was more than just a little taken aback.

"But what?" she asked, prompting me for the rest of my aborted sentence.

"You just look… Well… Different."

"Good. That's what I wanted."

"Really different," I repeated with added emphasis.

"You don't like it?" she asked.

"It's not that… It's just… I mean… I just think it's going to take some getting used to."

"Gonna be kinda hard ta' call ya' Firehair now," Ben announced from his seat at the table.

"Aye, the color is temporary," Felicity replied, twisting a lock of her new coif around her finger and pulling it up where she could glance at it from the corner of her eye. "It will wash out over the next couple of weeks. Of course, if I decide I like it I can get a more permanent dye job."

"Could we maybe just take things one step at a time?" I appealed.

"Don't worry," she replied. "I was only kidding. I like my natural color."

I tried not to be obvious about my relieved sigh but failed miserably. Fortunately, she took it in stride and merely grinned.

"Well, I'll say this much," I offered. "You definitely seem to be in a better mood than you were when we left earlier."

"Aye, it's amazing what getting your hair done will do for your attitude," she replied with a smile. "Now, what are we going to have for dinner? I'm starving."

"Well, after you two finish gettin' packed, we can pick up somethin' on the way to my place," Ben offered. "I'll buy."

"Oh, I guess I forgot to tell you," Felicity replied. "I changed my mind. We're staying here."

"You're what?" he asked, a healthy note of surprise in his tone.

"Don't worry," my wife replied, her demeanor remaining entirely nonchalant. "I'll still let you buy."

CHAPTER 33:

"**A**re you going to need to run home for some fresh clothes or anything?" I asked.

"No," Ben replied with a shake of his head. "Got an overnight bag in the van for emergencies."

"Emergencies?"

"Yeah, emergencies," he repeated, shooting me an obvious *you know what I mean* kind of look.

"Oh, like when you stay over at Con…"

"Yeah," he said, cutting me off before I could get any more than the first syllable of Constance's name out of my mouth. "Emergencies."

In the context of his profession as a cop, the subject of sex was never a stumbling block in conversations. It was just another part of the job, and he would discuss it with unabashed candor as long as it applied to a crime at hand. When it came to his personal life, and especially that of his friends, however, simply hinting at it could send him into an almost painful fit of modesty.

You just never knew with Ben. On rare occasions, he would make a comment filled with sexual innuendo or even publicly flirt like there was no tomorrow. But, more often than not, even a casual mention of anything remotely related to sex was taboo where he was concerned—even a comment as innocuous as him spending the night at his girlfriend's apartment.

Obviously, tonight was one of those times when the subject was off-limits. It was a good thing Felicity was downstairs in her office finishing up a project for one of her clients, otherwise he wouldn't be getting any peace at all. She always seemed to take great pleasure in making him squirm whenever he displayed his timidity on the matter.

At the moment, my friend and I were standing on the front porch, each with a cigar smoldering beneath a crooked finger. Since Felicity was in the house alone, we left the front door standing open with only the glass of the storm door to keep the cold from seeping in. It wasn't exactly energy efficient, but Ben insisted on having a clear view of the interior. Ostensibly, it was so he could keep an eye out in case Annalise was to elect to come here, somehow slip around us, and break in through the back door. However, I knew such reasoning was nothing more than a convoluted excuse. He really wanted to be sure Felicity stayed put. Ever since her earlier excursion, he had been preoccupied with her uncharacteristic behavior. He hadn't said as much just yet, but I could tell it was coming.

Our attempts to reason with my wife over her decision to remain here had gotten us nowhere fast. She had decided that we were staying here in our own home, and there didn't seem to be anything either of us could say to dissuade her from it. With each appeal, she had countered with any one of several reasons such as work, or the animals. All of which were easily dismissed. However, logic, or at least our version thereof, wasn't something she seemed interested in embracing. She had stood her ground, and in the end it all came down to her stating in a matter of fact tone, "Because I've made up my mind, and that's how it's going to be."

Short of actually placing us both in protective custody, which for all intents and purposes meant *under arrest*, there was little Ben could do other than give in. He did, however, make his own proclamation, that being very simply—if we weren't coming to stay with him, then he was staying with us. Fortunately, my wife didn't seem to have a problem with that compromise.

"Listen, Kemosabe, don't take this the wrong way," Ben started carefully after a lengthy silence. "But, I think your wife has gone right over the fuckin' edge."

Finally, he was dropping the bomb I had been expecting all evening.

"I'm hoping it's just an after effect of the shock," I replied.

"So, it ain't just me? You think she's actin' flaky too?"

"I don't know if flaky is the word I'd use, but she's definitely not acting like herself. And, yeah, I'm a little concerned. Not as much as you though, apparently."

"Jeezus, Row, she went and got all 'er damn hair cut off and dyed black. Then she decided on 'er own that you two are stayin' here, and wouldn't even listen... Sheesh... If that ain't flaky I don't know what is."

I waited a moment, struggling with the memory of my earlier conversation with her out on the deck. I'd kept it to myself, but now it was hard not to mention it.

"I probably shouldn't tell you this," I began, hesitation in my voice. "But, earlier today... Before you and I left for the crime scene... She was having a bit of an emotional crisis."

"Yeah, no shit," he replied. "That's kinda obvious."

I continued. "She told me she couldn't feel sorry for Lewis. In fact, she said he deserved it."

My friend turned to look at me with a deep frown creasing his face. "And you're just now mentionin' this?"

"It may be a symptom of post-traumatic stress," I offered. "She's been through way too much the past couple of months. Put that together with the shock..." I shrugged. "It concerns me, but I'm not sure if it's something to get worked up over or not."

"Your wife told you that Lewis deserved to die?" he posed the question like a statement. "Row, that's just not like 'er."

"I know," I replied. "Believe me, I know. But, Helen told me after everything that's happened, she would probably have some emotional issues for a while. A feeling of disconnection. Possible identity issues. She even said there was a good chance she might have some manic-depressive type of mood swings." After a short pause I added, "She's definitely seen some moments of depression since she's been home. So I have to assume that's what's happening now."

"Well, I guess now we're gettin' the flip side," my friend huffed. "'Cause I'd say manic is a pretty good description of the whole hair thing. Not ta' mention the whole mood thing. Did ya' see the way she just kept smilin' when we were arguin'? She wasn't about ta' give in, but she never got mad about it."

"Yeah, I noticed that."

"Well? Was that weird or what?"

I nodded. "A little. But she does tend to grin when she feels like she's won an argument, and in her mind, she had that one conquered from the outset. So, all I really saw was my wife feeling like she had the upper hand. Maybe I'm just too close to her to see."

"She told ya' Lewis deserved to die," he repeated in a half questioning tone.

"Yeah," I said with a nod. "But, I don't think she really believes that. That was the problem. She knew she was supposed to be upset. She just couldn't make herself feel the remorse."

"I'm tellin' ya', Row, that's fucked up. She's actin' flaky."

"Maybe so, but I also think we need to cut her some slack. Like I said, Helen expected some type of odd behavior from her when the effects of the stress bubbled to the surface. I doubt you could come up with a better trigger for it than the package today combined with the visit from Lewis yesterday."

"Yeah, well speakin' of Helen, what I think is that Firehair needs ta' have a sit down with 'er. Right away."

"I don't disagree with you there, but I can't force her to do it."

"I bet we can. I got handcuffs."

"She'd just use them on *you* if she got the chance," I told him with a half-hearted chuckle.

"Jeez, let's not go there, 'kay?"

"You brought it up."

"Yeah, you're right. My bad."

"Seriously, though. She'll talk to Helen when she's ready."

"Yeah, well let's hope she's ready before she shaves 'er head or somethin'."

"You know, Ben, I get the feeling you're even more disturbed by her change of appearance than anything else."

"It ain't right. She looks like one of those goth chicks or

somethin'," he replied then tucked his cigar into his mouth and puffed. After a second unproductive draw, he pulled it out and inspected the end. "Damn. Went out. Lemme see your lighter."

I dug the device out of my pocket and handed it to him. "Actually, with it dyed black, it's more of a Bettie Page look."

"Who's Bettie Page?"

"She's a pinup model from the fifties."

"Pinup model, huh?"

"Yeah. Her claim to fame was cheesecake bondage and fetish photos."

"Awww, Jeez..." He mumbled, casting me a sideways glance as he re-ignited his cigar. "I shoulda known."

"Uh-huh," I grunted, accepting the lighter back. "But, as shocking as the change is, I have to admit it still looks good on her."

"Well, yeah," he agreed. "Never said it looked bad. It just don't look right ta' me. I mean it's Firehair. She's s'posed ta' have red hair."

"I guess you'll just have to call her something else for a while."

"Yeah. I'm workin' on that, but I got a feelin' she ain't gonna like Blackhead."

"I think you're probably right about that."

I took a puff off my own cigar then rolled the smoke around on my tongue before blowing it out in a long stream on the cold air. The cloud of condensed breath quickly dissipated, leaving behind only the thin, blue-white haze lofting on a gentle breeze.

Looking out into the night, I stared at the neighborhood. It was relatively peaceful and pretty much always had been. Up until a few years ago, that is. But, everything that happened to shatter that quiet seemed to center around this house—and me. We'd never had any sort of close relationship with any of our neighbors, but these days they weren't even interested in waving to us from across the street.

I sighed as thoughts of pulling up stakes and moving crossed my mind once again. Finally, I looked over at my friend and asked, "Do you really think Annalise is going to come here?"

"Dunno," he grunted after a moment of thought. "But, she's been here at least once already."

"You don't know that for a fact," I countered.

"Gut feelin'," he told me. "She was here."

I didn't refute what he said. I'd learned to trust his instincts just as much as he trusted mine. After a moment I mused aloud, "Why does this sort of thing always get so out of hand?"

My friend huffed out what passed for an apathetic chuckle then replied, "Just lucky, I guess."

I was getting ready to tell him that his answer didn't make me feel any better, but as I opened my mouth to speak, I heard a distant echo that sounded almost like my name being called. I left my comment unspoken and cocked my head to the side, listening intently.

A second later, I heard it again, louder. This time it wasn't only my name but Ben's too. And, the voice was recognizable, even through the panic in which it was encased. I looked up at my friend whose expression was a mirror image of my own. A heartbeat later we were both in motion. The only reason we didn't collide was that I started for the door a split second sooner than he.

Felicity was already topping the basement stairs and coming into the hall as we entered through the front door. The look on her face instantly bolstered the rush of anxiety that was already tightening my chest.

"What's wrong?!" I asked, continuing toward her.

"She called," she replied, her eyes wide and face even paler than usual.

"Devereaux?" Ben asked.

"Aye," she replied. "Just now."

"You talked to her?" I asked.

She shook her head. "No. She called my business line, and I just let the answering machine pick it up."

"Did you save the message?" Ben pressed.

"I was sitting there when she called. I haven't played it back yet."

My friend pressed past us and headed downward. We followed only a step or two behind. Hitting the bottom of the stairs, we veered immediately left, past Felicity's darkroom, and then hooked around the corner into her actual office. The answering machine was perched on the corner of her desk, where it always sat, and the message light was winking on and off, demanding attention.

Ben reached over and pressed the play button. The device was digital, so it instantly chirped and an electronic voice announced, "You have one new message. Received... December four...teenth... at... nine thir... ty-two P.M..."

The machine-generated voice was then replaced by the hiss of telephone static and the sound of a single, heavily exhaled breath. On the heels of the sigh, a sweet, Southern-accented voice issued from the speaker.

"Hello, Felicity," it said. "I'm so sorry I missed you. I was just calling to see if you enjoyed the gift. You know, mat was just *dying* to be under them." The voice snickered as if amused at the sick joke. A second later it continued, a stern tone affecting its cadence, "He never should have called me by your name. But, I don't guess we need to worry about him making that mistake again, do we?"

There was a thick pause, and we could hear her breathing, then Annalise spoke again, her words harsh and demanding, "It isn't yours, *chienne*! It belongs to me, and I won't let her give it to you!"

With that, the line clicked and went dead, only to be replaced a moment later by an electro-mechanical announcement saying, "End new messages."

We all stared at the machine for what seemed like a full minute, none of us saying a word. Finally, Ben sighed then reached up to massage the back of his neck.

Leveling his gaze on my wife, he said, "Wanna reconsider your decision ta' stay here now?"

CHAPTER 34:

66 **I**t would appear the call originated from a payphone at a gas station in Northwest County," Special Agent Constance Mandalay said, folding her cell and slipping it into her pocket for what seemed like the hundredth time since she arrived. "The local cops checked it out, but the attendant doesn't remember seeing anyone use it, much less anyone who fit Devereaux's description."

"Yeah, figures," Ben grunted.

Almost two hours had passed since the call from Annalise. The clock was just starting its uphill climb toward midnight, but none of us were particularly interested in sleeping at the moment. None of us except Felicity, that is, who was lying down in the bedroom. I suspected, however, she was really doing more hiding from reality than actual resting.

Ben had called Constance after we listened to the recording a second time, since at this point, the FBI was just as deeply involved in this investigation as the Major Case Squad, if not more so. She had arrived shortly thereafter, but until now any conversation with her had been sparse since she was spending the majority of her time on her cell phone conferring with other agents and law enforcement personnel.

"That's always the way," Constance replied. "To be on the safe side, we put a tap on all your phone lines just in case she calls again."

"She will," I offered. "She'll keep trying until she gets Felicity on the line."

"That's typical," she agreed. "I just didn't want to say it."

"You know you don't have to pull any punches with me, Constance."

"You're right," she replied with a shallow nod. "Force of habit. Put the victim at ease."

"I don't think there is going to be any ease around here until this is over, but thanks for trying."

She smiled briefly before slipping back into her serious façade. "So, obviously we expect her to call again. The real question is when."

"I don't think we'll have to wait long. Honestly, I'm surprised she hasn't tried again already."

"Well, a delay is typical too," she told me. "Stalkers use it to instill fear in their victims. They draw their power from terrorizing their chosen subject, and the waiting game tends to be very effective where that is concerned."

"I know, but Annalise isn't your average stalker."

"None of them ever are, Rowan," she said with a nod. "But, what she has done so far fits the basic profile."

"So far," I said. "But, I'm sure that will change. Soon."

"One of your feelings?" she asked, no skepticism in her voice whatsoever. She was among the few who had come to readily accept without question the intangible evidences provided by my curse.

"That, and something she said," I replied with a shrug. "Her last comment was 'I won't let her give it to you.'"

"The 'it' being the sexual gratification you've mentioned before, I assume?"

"That would be my theory. I'm certain she's livid about Miranda using Felicity as a horse. But, projecting the anger at a *Lwa* isn't going to help. For example, it would be no different than a Christian taking God to task for not giving them the new car they prayed for... Or me blaming the universe for not winning the lottery just because I did a money spell... That's certainly not going to get a positive result. Negativity begets negativity.

"So, for Annalise to vent her anger at Miranda will only further deny her the gratification. In the end it's really a simple matter of transference. Felicity becomes the object of her disdain because she views her as a rival for that which she desires."

"I don't understand. How is Felicity a rival?" she asked. "Ben said you'd done away with the connection that allowed all this to happen."

"I did. But, I believe Miranda brought Annalise back here in order to re-establish that connection somehow. The *how*, I haven't yet figured out, but she may have already done it. I'm hoping not, but I can't really be sure. Either way, Annalise almost certainly knows exactly what Miranda wants, but she isn't about to let it happen if she can help it. And, the only way for her to accomplish that is to remove Felicity from the picture entirely."

"Okay, so that's her motivation," Constance replied. "I suppose you believe that is what's driving the escalation as well?"

"Partly. But mainly I think it's frustration," I said with a nod. "To put it bluntly, I don't think she's getting any, so to speak. Of her most recent two murders, neither has been for the sexual gratification like those prior. One appeared to be for the express purpose of working a cross against me, since I am seen as another of her obstacles. Then, the Lewis homicide was purely out of blind anger."

"*He should never have called me by your name*," she repeated Annalise's words from the tape with an understanding nod.

"Which explains the tongue," Ben added.

"Exactly," I agreed. "Blatant symbolism is common in hoodoo, and most any other magick, so it would definitely fit the way she thinks."

Ben thrust his chin toward Constance with a quick nod. "Speakin' of the Lewis homicide, did you check it out?"

"Not personally," she replied, shaking her head. "But we had a team there. From what I hear, apparently they just missed you and Rowan."

"Yeah, well we were just passin' through."

"I heard," she replied then raised her eyebrow and took on a concerned tone. "You know, Ben, you're probably going to get yourself suspended for taking Rowan there."

"That's the plan."

She sighed. "And you worry about me getting into trouble."

"Yeah, well, that's life. So… Your guys find anything we missed?"

She shook her head again. "Not that I've heard. They're still going over everything, but she didn't seem to leave anything that will help track her down."

"Wunnerful," he harrumphed. "So we're still at square one."

"For now, it looks that way."

"Okay, well, if you two will excuse me, I'm going to go check on Felicity," I said.

Constance gave me an understanding nod. "That's probably a good idea."

I turned to head back to the bedroom, but before I even made it as far as the hallway, the electronic trill of a telephone ringing issued from the basement. A split second later, the cordless handset from Felicity's business line downstairs, which was resting on the dining room table, chirped for attention. I stopped mid-stride and turned around.

Constance looked over to me and asked, "Has Devereaux heard Felicity's voice?"

"Probably on the answering machine," I replied.

"Damn," she mumbled. She stepped over and picked up the handset anyway but simply held it in her hand as it chirped again. "Does she actually identify herself on the outgoing message?"

"I don't think so. I believe she just launches into the standard leave a message spiel."

"Good. Maybe we'll be okay then." She thumbed the talk button then placed it against her ear. Without missing a beat, she said, "Emerald Photographic Services."

She looked toward us and nodded as she continued. "This is Felicity... The message? No, that would be my assistant. Who is this?"

We watched silently as Constance put the impromptu ruse into motion. Behind me, I heard the bedroom door open and Felicity softly calling my name. I turned to see her coming toward me, a questioning look on her face. I held my finger up to my lips, motioning for her to stay quiet.

"I assure you, I am Felicity O'Brien," Constance said into the phone. "But, you still haven't told me who you..."

She shook her head and sighed then pulled the phone away and thumbed it off.

"She hung up," she said as she placed the handset back onto the table. "Apparently she didn't buy it."

"The accent," Ben offered. "Five'll get ya' ten Lewis mentioned it at some point."

"You're probably right," she agreed. "And, then she picked it up from the answering machine too, so there's no way around it."

"You'd best let me answer it the next time, then," Felicity interjected.

"I don't know if I'm comfortable with that," I said.

"Aye, and I don't know if I'm comfortable with her still being out there," she spat. "It's me she's after. I just want it over."

"I understand that, honey, but with the state you're in, I don't think it's such a good idea for you to talk to her."

"And what state is that?" she demanded.

"You're distraught... Understandably so... And, getting on the phone with her is just going to make it worse."

"Rowan's right, Felicity," Constance added, stepping back toward the rest of us. "Talking to Devereaux isn't going to be easy."

"*Damnú!*" my wife snapped. "I don't care! I just want this over! Now!"

"Calm down, honey," I said, trying to soothe her.

"Calm down? Don't you tell me to calm down!"

"Felicity," Ben started. "We're just tryin' ta' protect you."

"Well stop it! I don't want you to protect me!"

Before any of us could respond, the telephone trilled again. Felicity twisted away from me and darted forward, shouldering past Constance as she began to turn. In an instant my wife snatched the handset from the table and had it pressed against the side of her head.

"Hello!" she spat, her tone nothing short of a demand.

All three of us started toward her, but she slipped around to the opposite side of the table, effectively placing it between her and us. We could have easily scrambled around after her, but at this point it didn't matter. The damage was already done.

She barked into the phone, "Yes, this is she, you *saigh*... No, it's Gaelic and it means bitch. Well, I don't speak French either, but I know *bitch* when I hear it..."

Having no other recourse, Constance waved to get Felicity's attention. Once she had it, she pointed to her watch and mouthed, "Keep her talking."

My wife gave her a curt nod, but the hard frown never left her face, even as she continued to speak, "No. That was my assistant. She has a tendency to be overprotective... Yes, I did get them. They were a lovely thought, but the police wouldn't let me keep them."

Constance was keeping her eyes fixed on Felicity, but she had stepped back into the living room and was whispering into her cell phone.

"Aye, what's wrong?" my wife asked. "Not getting the reaction you wanted?... Did you really think a little blood was going to bother me? I'm afraid you're going to have to try harder, then..."

I had once been right where my wife was now. On a phone talking to a serial killer—one that wanted me dead more than anything—so, I knew the drill all too well. Unfortunately, my wife wasn't following it. But, of course, neither had I.

Even so, I had at least tried to keep my emotions in check. However, what I heard coming from Felicity at this moment was a darkness so black that it made me fear each coming word.

"Why would I care?" she spat. "I was done with him. Besides, he deserved it, didn't he?... You said so yourself. He shouldn't have called you Felicity... That had to hurt. Him worshipping me and not you... Really? It's too bad you feel that way. Why not? Maybe she's tired of you, did you ever think of that?... Maybe you just aren't worthy of her... Maybe you're just all used up and that's why she wants me... What makes you think you can stop her? Really? I'd like to see you try... Is that so? Well, you know where I am. Come and get me... Hello? Hello?..."

Felicity allowed the phone to slowly drop down from her ear then switched it off.

"She hung up," she muttered.

"The call was coming from a prepaid cell phone," Constance announced. "They pulled a grid location but didn't get an exact pinpoint. There are units responding to the area right now. Don't worry, you did fine, Felicity. We'll find her."

My wife laid the handset on the table then pulled out a chair and slowly lowered herself into it. I watched as the hard expression on her face began to ease then melt away. She stared across the table at me for a moment, until finally there was nothing more than blankness and a vacant stare in her eyes.

"Honey…" I began.

Before I could get the rest of the sentence out of my mouth, a tear began rolling down her cheek and her lower lip started to quiver as her body trembled. By the time I got around the table to her, she was sobbing in violent heaves.

Across the room I heard Ben say to Constance, "I'm callin' Helen."

CHAPTER 35:

"Anything?" I asked as Constance walked into the kitchen and laid her cell phone on the island with a disgusted sigh.

She shook her head and frowned. "No. Not a thing. They've searched the area, out through a ten block radius. They're still working it but nothing yet. She turned the cell off almost as soon as she hung up, so we can't even track a signal."

"So, we wait," I said.

"And, we keep looking," she agreed. "Remember, she's definitely agitated, so she's far more likely to make a mistake now than if she was calm and calculating. That's a good thing for us."

"She's been making mistakes for a while now," I added as I turned back to fill the coffeemaker and start a fresh pot.

"Yes, she has. Just not the kind we need her to make."

I finished filling the reservoir then slid the carafe in and flipped the switch. Instead of turning around to face Constance, however, I simply leaned against the counter and allowed my head to hang. The chronic thud in the back of my skull was drumming along in unison with my heartbeat, and on top of that, my temples were throbbing with the muddied pains of exhaustion.

I glanced to the side and settled my eyes on the bottle of aspirin that was still sitting on the counter where I had left it days before. I had tried repeatedly to self-medicate with other over the counter pain relievers, following their directions to the letter, but plain old aspirin was the only thing that ever seemed to help. Giving up, I reached for the bottle and popped it open. Instead of my normal handful, however, I limited the dose to four tablets. Whether or not that would be enough to even touch the pain, I wasn't sure, but I didn't need to get back into the habit of poisoning myself.

I popped the pills into my mouth then quickly washed them down with a swig of my cold coffee. Setting the cup aside, I continued to rest against the counter, eyes closed and chin against my chest.

After a moment, Constance quietly asked, "Are you okay?"

"Yeah," I muttered. "Headache."

"That's not unusual for you, I don't guess."

"Yeah. Lucky me."

"Is Felicity still on the phone with Helen?"

"She was when I checked a few minutes ago," I acknowledged, pushing away from the counter ledge and turning, then leaning my back against it. "It's been over an hour now. But, at least it seems to be helping her."

"Good," she said as she slid onto one of the barstools near the island. "I really hated seeing Felicity like that."

"You and me both."

"By the way, Ben is out on the front porch having a cigar. He said to let you know in case you wanted to join him."

"I could probably use that," I replied. "But I don't know if I have the energy right now."

I couldn't help but notice that Constance was eyeing me carefully from her seat. She continued to watch me as I stood there rubbing my temples. I'm sure I looked like a total wreck. I know I felt like one.

Finally, she said, "You look tired."

I sighed, "I feel tired."

"How are *you* doing with all this?"

I let out a sarcastic half chuckle. "Just another day in my fucked up life, I suppose."

"Right," she replied, her own sardonic tone showing through. "So, how are you really? Besides being tired, I mean."

"Truth? Angry. Maybe a little worried."

"A little?"

"Okay, a lot."

"You don't have to worry, Rowan. We aren't going to let anything happen to either one of you."

"I know you believe that," I replied with a careful nod. "But there is only so much you will be able to stop."

"Meaning?"

"Meaning, Annalise is a known quantity. She's corporeal and I know you can do something about her. Miranda on the other hand... Well, she's beyond your control. Maybe even mine..."

"Won't stopping Devereaux stop Miranda as well?"

"I really don't know. But, I doubt it. There may well have been some truth to what Felicity said to Annalise on the phone earlier. Miranda might be looking for new blood. If she is, then she won't stop until she gets it."

"And, since she has fixated on Felicity..." she left the rest of the sentence unspoken.

"Exactly," I agreed. "It will be fine if there is no connection there, but if she finds a way to make one... Assuming she hasn't already...Well... I don't really even want to speculate."

"How could she manage to create a connection, though?"

"That's the wonderful and extremely scary thing about magick, Constance. A little goes a long way, and something very simple can have a great impact."

"So, you're worrying about what they found at the Lewis homicide?"

I shrugged. "I guess I am. On the surface it seems like a fairly innocuous bit of spellwork aimed at lust. I keep trying to tell myself since Annalise isn't getting the satisfaction she wants, she did it for that specific purpose... A stab at re-igniting her own passions... But, it wasn't really hoodoo, which is a little odd. Of course, it had some of the hallmarks of folk magick, which is no surprise and could explain the deviation. I just don't know for sure what it was, and that's the thing that bothers me most."

"Isn't there anything you can do about it?"

"I can protect against it, but not knowing what it is for sure, there's no way to counteract it."

"But, like you said, you can protect against it."

"Yes. I can for a while. But, we're talking about the magickal equivalent of being in a boxing ring. I can dance around in a circle with my gloves up in front of my face to deflect the blows; but eventually I'm going to wear down, and a punch is going to get through, and then another, and another..."

"You don't paint a very positive picture."

"I'm just telling it like it is," I replied. "The only saving grace is that magick doesn't always work. If it did, I'd already be dead after the crossing Annalise did. But, sometimes even when it does work, it doesn't necessarily do what it was intended to do. The binding I did to protect Felicity is a prime example. It was supposed to keep her from harm. Instead, it created the connection between her and Annalise— and by default, Miranda."

"Have you figured out why that happened?"

"Yes, actually. It was blatant stupidity on my part," I replied. "It took me some time to figure it out, but I finally did. The problem is I worked the magick while the moon was *void of course*. That means it was in between aspects of two different astrological signs. I realize that doesn't sound like a rational, scientific explanation to most, but we're talking about magick here. And, any Witch with half a brain knows magick worked during a void-of-course moon almost never does what it is intended to do. It has a mind of its own."

"So you did it on the wrong day?"

"Worse than that. Wrong hour. If I had done it a couple of hours sooner or a couple of hours later, there's a good possibility none of this would have ever happened. Where Felicity is concerned, anyway."

"But not you?"

"I don't know. Annalise and Miranda were already out there. I didn't create either of them. Somewhere along the line our paths probably would have crossed. Maybe not as soon as they did, or with such a direct impact, but eventually it would have happened. Ben would have called me to look at the symbols she was leaving behind, and everything would have been set into motion."

"No offense, but aren't you contradicting yourself? It sounds to me as if you think this would have happened anyway."

"Yes, I think it would have, but like I said, differently. It would have happened to me, not my wife. It's one thing to have this crap coming down on my head… But, Felicity doesn't deserve it."

"And you do?"

"Who knows? I've tried to walk away from it more than once, but it keeps pulling me back in, so there must be a reason."

"That doesn't mean you deserve to have these horrors in your life, Rowan."

I shook my head. "Maybe not, but they're here, and there doesn't seem to be much I can do about it, now does there?"

"Okay, I won't argue that point with you. But, let's get back to Miranda. Isn't there anything you can do?"

"That's the big question. Miranda is a personal *Lwa*. Theoretically, her influence should be limited to the person or persons worshipping her. Felicity initially became involved because of the ethereal connection between her and Annalise. So, if it works the way it's supposed to, as long as nothing is done to bind them together again, Felicity should be safe from Miranda. Maybe."

"Maybe?"

"As long as Annalise is alive and continuing to treat Miranda as a *Lwa*, there is a chance the spirit will try to use her to recreate the connection."

"How?"

"If I knew that, I probably wouldn't be as worried."

"So, you're saying if Annalise is out of the picture, Miranda becomes a non-issue."

"That's one way to look at it."

"I hate to ask this, Rowan, but you aren't thinking about trying…"

I finished the sentence for her. "…To kill her? I won't lie to you. It's crossed my mind. Of course, I had ample opportunity to do so when I was in New Orleans, but I didn't, and she got away."

"But, that was before you'd taken the time to think this through, wasn't it?" she asked.

The coffeemaker sputtered and let out a steamy sigh as it finished brewing. Instead of answering Constance, I twisted slightly to look back at it then turned fully and pulled the carafe from the base.

"Coffee?" I asked, as I turned back to her while pouring some into my own cup.

"You didn't answer my question, Rowan," she replied.

"You're right," I said after a moment. "I didn't."

"Rowan…"

"Okay. Yes, I've had time to think about it since, and looking back, I wonder if maybe I should have been a bit less concerned for her physical well-being when I had my hands on her."

"And ended up in prison?"

I shrugged. "Felicity would be safe."

She held out her cup, and I filled it before settling the pot back onto the burner. She took a sip then set her cup aside and regarded me seriously.

"But, you would still most likely have ended up in prison," she said.

"We all make sacrifices from time to time," I said with another shrug. "But, yes, you're right about that too. So, it all comes back to the question of, would I kill her now if the opportunity presented itself? I think you know me better than that."

"I like to think I do, but that is a paradox in itself because I also know you'll do anything to protect Felicity. Otherwise, you wouldn't even be thinking about it. Not to mention that you are still avoiding the question."

"You're right again," I agreed. "So, I guess it's all a matter of trust. But, then, you and Ben have already discussed this, haven't you?"

"Yes, we have."

"And, I guess you drew the short straw when it came to who was going to ask me?"

"Actually, no. Ben is fairly well convinced you'll kill her if you get the chance. I was on the fence so I decided to ask on my own."

"Are you asking as an FBI agent or as a friend?"

"A little of both, I suppose."

"I see," I said with a nod. "Well, I guess I didn't give you the answer you wanted to hear, did I?"

"No, you didn't. But, truthfully, you gave me the one I expected."

Sleep finally entered the picture sometime around four in the morning. Of course, what little of it there was didn't come in the form of truly restful slumber. Felicity had tossed and turned up until sometime after six when her body and mind finally gave in to the exhaustion. I don't know that my brain ever reached that point. I drifted in and out of a twilight sleep, jerking awake each time I felt her move.

In the end, the fitful attempt at rest only served to make seven A.M. seem to come just that much earlier, especially since the hour was accompanied by a hard knock on our bedroom door.

CHAPTER 36:

"Her cell phone just went active again," Constance said as I swung the door open and blinked.

My grey matter was still huddled in a state of half-sleep, so I simply stared at her as I tried to make sense of what she had just told me. Unfortunately, while I recognized the words, all semblance of cohesion between them escaped my grasp. I shook my head and briefly flashed on the fact that I would probably be far more alert if I simply hadn't slept at all.

After a second or two, which seemed like a small eternity, I managed to grunt, "What?"

"Devereaux's cell phone," she repeated. "It just went active a few minutes ago. We're tracking the signal now."

This time I managed to latch on to the sentence and process it into a mental picture that made sense. I glanced over at my wife who was still sleeping. The pillow she was clutching over the top of her head combined with the mild, lingering pain in my ribs told me she had heard the knock as well, but as usual she wasn't about to let anything roust her from the bed until she was good and ready. As far as I was concerned, that was fine. She needed the rest. I could sleep when this was all over.

I nodded and stepped out into the hallway, gently closing the door behind me. Then I followed Constance into the living room where Ben was perched on the arm of the sofa looking only slightly more awake than me.

"Coffee's already makin'," he grunted.

"If she calls, we already know she is going to want to speak to Felicity," Constance offered. "But, I'm going to take it and see if I can stall."

I shook my head. "Why don't you let me take it instead?"

"Why?"

"She'll have more to say to me than to you. Maybe I can keep her occupied longer."

"That might not be the best idea, Rowan. You're too close to this."

"Of course I am. She wants to kill my wife."

"Exactly my point."

"Look, Constance, signal tracking is only going to get you a general location. You know that. If I can keep her on the call, you'll have a better chance of pinpointing where she is."

"Yes, I do know that, but we have other ways to do this."

"No, you don't. If her phone had a GPS module, you would have already used it."

"There are still other ways."

"Okay. What are they?"

As if on cue, the muffled trill of the ringer sounded in the basement, immediately followed by the handset on the table chirping. Constance and I both started toward the dining room at the same instant. Since I was already a step closer, I reached the phone first, but as my hand closed around it, Constance took hold of my wrist.

"Relax," I said, as I remembered the conversation we'd had only a few hours before. "I can't kill her over the phone."

"He's right," Ben offered. "Better let 'im take it."

"All right," she said, letting go of my wrist. "Just stay calm and keep her talking as long as you can."

"That's the plan," I replied with a quick nod then snatched up the handset, punched the talk button, and began speaking. "Emerald Photographic Services, may I help you?"

A familiar Southern-accented voice rolled out of the earpiece. "Put the *chienne* on."

"Good morning, Annalise," I replied coolly.

She repeated the demand. "Put her on."

"I assume you mean my wife. I'm afraid she's still asleep."

She didn't reply, but I could still hear her breathing at the other end. I waited for the telltale click of the line going dead, but after several seconds, she finally spoke.

"Rowan," she stated in a cold, matter-of-fact tone. "I thought I recognized the voice."

"Yes," I replied.

"How is your arm, little man?"

I unconsciously glanced at the mostly healed bite wound she had inflicted. The stitches had already been removed, and the bruising was pretty much a memory at this point. Still, there was a very pronounced jagged line that was going to leave an interesting scar.

"Fine," I said. "How about yours?"

"You bruised me," she replied. "I really didn't appreciate that."

"Well, if I were you I wouldn't hold my breath waiting for an apology."

"*Va te faire, vous d'une chienne!*"

"I hate to tell you this, but I didn't understand that the last time you said it, and I still don't. I'm afraid you're going to have to speak English, otherwise this conversation is going to be a bit one-sided."

"I said, you fucking son of a bitch."

"See, now that I understand."

As I spoke I glanced over in the direction of the living room. Constance was on her cell phone once again, but she didn't look particularly pleased. Ben was keeping his eyes focused on me. I'm not really sure what they were afraid I might do, but obviously they weren't leaving anything to chance.

"Your wife is taking something that doesn't belong to her," Annalise said.

"That's where you're wrong," I replied. "She's not taking a thing."

"Miranda is giving it to her."

"Wrong again. Miranda isn't welcome here."

"No, it's you who is wrong. You can't stop Miranda. She does as she pleases."

"She does as she pleases, or *you* do as she pleases?"

I waited for an answer but received none. I knew from her extended silence that I had struck a nerve.

"That's why she brought you back to Saint Louis, isn't it?" I continued. "Because I took Felicity away from her."

"Miranda wants her," Annalise finally said.

"Yes, I got that impression," I replied. "But, you can tell her for me that isn't going to happen. She can't have her."

"She already does."

"I'm pretty sure you're wrong about that."

"I'm not. You just don't know it yet."

"What did you do, Annalise? Does it have something to do with the cloves and the candle at Lewis's apartment?"

"I didn't do anything."

"I know better than that, Annalise. I visited the scene."

"I didn't do anything," she repeated. "Ask Miranda."

The answer made my skin prickle as a chill ran through me. There was a peculiar honesty in her voice that I couldn't help but believe. This meant that she hadn't worked the magick, Miranda had. She simply used Annalise as a conduit for it, just as she did for everything else. What new dimension this might add to the spellwork, I couldn't begin to fathom. And, I'm not sure I wanted to.

I forced myself to say, "You'll have to put her on the phone before I can do that."

Her answer was exactly what I didn't want to hear.

"I already told you, she's not with me anymore. She's with the *chienne*. Go wake her up and ask her."

I hesitated as the fear continued to pool in my stomach. Finally, I asked, "How do you know that?"

"Because, she isn't with me."

"That doesn't mean she's with Felicity."

"Yes it does. That's why I have to make her go away."

"Miranda?"

"No. Her."

"Felicity. And, by 'go away' I assume you mean you want to kill her."

"She has to go away."

"And, if you kill her, do you really think Miranda is going to come back to you?"

She whispered, "It belongs to me. She promised."

I could hear an insistent fragility creeping into her voice, and at the same time I could feel a sense of loss mixing with my own cold fear. It was becoming obvious that Annalise was psychologically damaged in more ways than I could begin to imagine. The problem was, I didn't know if that fact was going to make her easier to deal with, or simply just that much more dangerous.

I wasn't sure how much longer I was going to be able to keep Annalise on the phone with this verbal sparring. I already had the feeling I was about to lose her at any moment. I looked up at Constance who shook her head and frowned, which told me the FBI and police weren't having any better luck than me.

With a mental sigh I decided to press on. "So, what do we do now? You know I won't let you kill my wife."

"Do you really think Miranda will let you live?" she asked, her moment of frailty completely gone.

"I could ask you the same thing."

"I don't have the same weakness as you."

"And that is?"

"You love her."

"I wouldn't call that a weakness."

"Of course you wouldn't, little man. You're male. You won't understand the power she holds over you until it's too late."

"And, she holds no power over you?"

"That's different."

"How so?"

"I can fulfill her desires."

"I see."

"They can't protect you forever."

"Who?"

"The police. I know they are there."

She was drawing a logical conclusion, so I didn't think anything of it until she added, "I bet I could make him love me."

I froze, not sure how to respond. After a thick pause I asked, "Who?"

She laughed then said, "The indian with the cigar."

The comment told me she probably wasn't simply casting a line into the water, but I still didn't want to confirm anything in the event I was wrong.

"I have no idea who you are talking about," I replied.

"Of course you do," she returned then paused for a moment before letting out a heavy sigh and taking on a heavily sarcastic tone. "I'm bored now. I'll call back when the princess is done with her beauty sleep."

The phone clicked, and the hollow static of a broken connection filled my ear. I thumbed off the phone and laid it on the table.

"Anything at all?" I asked, looking at Constance.

"Yes," she nodded. "But nothing good. The call didn't come from the prepaid cell phone she used last night. They found it sitting on a park bench about two miles from here, which means she dropped it there as a decoy. What's worse though, is wherever she was calling from she used a phone-spoofing card, so it tracked back to the relay service. We won't be able to get anything out of them until we get hold of their legal department, and even then they are probably going to demand a subpoena, which is going to take time."

I picked up the handset and thumbed the display over to the caller ID log. The most recent call was registered on the screen as coming from Felicity's business line. For all intents and purposes, it looked like we had called ourselves.

"Damn," I muttered. "Well, I'm not surprised they found the cell so close. Apparently she was watching the house last night or at least came by here."

"Did she tell you that?" Constance asked.

"Not in those exact words," I replied. "But, she was somewhere nearby when Ben was outside smoking because she mentioned 'the indian with the cigar' before hanging up."

"Fuck me," my friend mumbled.

I let out a heavy sigh. "Yeah, well, she had something to say about that too."

CHAPTER 37:

L ocal police, along with Constance and a trio of other FBI agents, were making precautionary door-to-door rounds of the neighborhood in light of Annalise's comment about seeing Ben. My friend had pulled the duty of staying in the house with Felicity and me, which he hadn't complained about since it was only a few degrees above freezing outside, and a fairly stiff wind was gusting through the streets.

I watched out the dining room window as the few neighbors who were home would point toward our house as soon as they were shown the photo of Annalise. All of them were making various demonstrative gestures along with insistent bobs of their heads as they spoke. I could only assume they were assuring the police the redhead in the picture could be found right here. I really couldn't blame them. I knew firsthand the resemblance was truly uncanny, and I lived in the same house with the *good sister*.

In the end I was sure it would all become more fodder for the local gossip mill. Everything surrounding us always did.

"She probably just drove past while you were out there last night," I said aloud, continuing to stare out the window. "I doubt she's actually hanging around nearby waiting to get caught. Otherwise I think I'd feel her."

"Prob'ly," Ben agreed. "That's what we're figurin' too, but we need ta' cover all the bases just ta' be safe."

"Yeah, makes sense," I replied, stepping away from the window and taking a seat across from him at the table. "Either way, I appreciate it."

Felicity had been up for a couple of hours now. While she was still noticeably moody, her spirits seemed higher than they had been the night before. She certainly wasn't happy, but she wasn't a basket case either, which was certainly putting my mind at ease. Rather than sit around being reminded of the situation, however, she had sequestered herself in her office downstairs to work. Throwing herself into her job seemed to be a common form of personal therapy in which she would engage. She'd done it ever since I'd known her, so I wasn't going to object. But, just to be sure nothing set her off, we had disconnected her answering machine and were keeping the telephone handset upstairs with us. It was a foregone conclusion that she would be ending up on the phone with Annalise again at some point, but I wasn't about to let it happen when she was by herself, even if that was only for a handful of seconds.

After a moment of studying me silently, my friend asked, "So… Gettin' any *Twilight Zone* shit?"

"No. Well, no more than the usual headache, I don't guess. Why?"

"Just wonderin'. You got that look."

"Which look is that?"

"Just that look," he replied then punctuated the statement by whistling a few patently recognizable notes.

"I see."

"I hate ta' say it, but we could use an edge," he said with a shrug. "We're still tryin' ta' predict Devereaux's next move and I, for one, ain't above a bit of la-la land ta' help."

"Good luck on that. If I get anything you'll be the first to know."

"Well, if it's any consolation, Row, the Feebs think there's only a small chance she'll try ta' make an end run at ya' as long as we're here. Even if she is keepin' an eye on the place."

"Small chance?"

"Maybe twenty-five, thirty percent accordin' to their experts."

"They might be underestimating her."

"Why do ya' say that?"

"Desperate people do desperate things," I replied.

"You really think she's that bad off?" he asked.

"Yes, I do. There is only one emotion stronger than love, Ben, and that's hatred. Right now, Annalise is filled with both. That's a volatile combination. It's just like the jealous lover who proclaims, 'if I can't have her, nobody can.'

"She'll do whatever it takes to keep Miranda and Felicity apart, even if it means sacrificing herself so that Miranda has no one left to possess in the end. I'm sure that isn't her first choice, but I definitely wouldn't put it past her."

"So you're doin' psychoanalysis?" he replied, the words were more verbal observation than actual question. "Now I know you've been spendin' too much time with my sister."

"Yeah. That's what I keep hearing. But, it's not really that academic... Or, arcane either. The simple truth is, I could hear it in her voice. It wasn't hard to recognize."

"Okay," he huffed. "So if you really think she's gonna come after ya' here, then we need ta' move ya' no matter what Firehair says."

"That would just prolong the inevitable. Like I said, I think that tactic will be a last resort on her part," I told him with a shake of my head. "She'll try something else first."

"What?"

"I don't know any more what it might be than the rest of you, Ben. Maybe we'll find out when she calls again."

"Still wouldn't hurt ta' get you two someplace safe."

"I know this is going to sound crazy, but right now I think this is probably the safest place we can be."

"Why? She knows where you are, and if you really believe she'll come after ya' here, how is it safe?"

"It just is."

He reached up and smoothed back his hair then shot me a concerned look. "Okay. So, my turn ta' play shrink. What is it you ain't sayin'?"

"What do you mean?"

"I mean it's been damn near four hours since Devereaux called, and you've been off in your own damn world ever since. Somethin's botherin' ya' big time."

"No offense, Ben, but are you familiar with the expression, 'Duh?'

There's an insane woman out there who wants to kill my wife. Of course something's bothering me."

"Yeah, duh, that's funny. I mean there's somethin' else runnin' around in your head, White Man. Otherwise you wouldn't suddenly be so opposed ta' bein' moved. Was it somethin' she said?"

"You heard the recording when Constance called in."

"Yeah, I did. So, what gives? Are you thinkin' she was right about the ghost bitch and Firehair bein' hooked up again?"

"I don't know if she was right or not," I said with a shake of my head. "But it definitely worries me."

"Well, Felicity ain't actin' like a psychobitch or anything. She's definitely got a bit of wingnut factor goin' on, but I think Helen's got a handle on that."

"True. But, the fact that Annalise doesn't seem to recall what was done with that bit of spellwork at Lewis's apartment is especially unnerving. It means Miranda is directly responsible for the magick instead of her."

"And, so explain it to me... I take it that's a bad thing?"

"It may well be. I'm not sure. I've never gone toe-to-toe with a spirit where the actual working of magick is concerned."

"So stayin' here has somethin' ta' do with that?"

"I can ward against magick anywhere I go... But, the fact remains that I've done a lot of work in recent weeks on this house to protect it against any sort of magickal invasion," I explained. "As long as Felicity stays here, I think I have her protected from Miranda. At least, I hope I do."

"Think that's why your *Twilight Zone* ain't workin' so good in here?"

"Maybe. Probably. But, you know that's really hit and miss as it is."

"But, did ya' just say you could do the hocus-pocus someplace else instead?"

"I can," I admitted. "But, look at it this way—walls constructed over a few hours versus those that have been fortified over a period of weeks. Which would you rather take cover behind when the shit starts to fly?"

"Yeah, okay. I get it. So, it's a Witch thing."

"Yeah, it's a Witch thing."

"Jeez…" he mumbled. "Whatever happened ta' just plain old bad guys with guns and knives?"

I knew he wasn't really looking for an answer, but I gave him one anyway. "Easy. You met me."

He didn't reply, not that I really expected him to. With a lull falling in our conversation, I reached up and massaged my forehead. The chronic throb had worked its way from the back of my skull all the way to the front, setting up shop throughout my entire head. I'd been tempted to tap into the aspirin a time or two already but had decided to save them for when things really got bad. At the moment, I was weighing that decision very carefully, trying to convince myself that I hadn't yet reached that point. I was probably being overly cautious, but old habits die hard, and I now had a healthy fear of that one in particular.

Dropping my hand down, I opened my eyes then reached for my cup of coffee. I picked it up and took a quick swig, only to discover that what little of it that was left had gone cold. I looked over to my friend and noticed his cup was completely empty.

"I'm going to get a fresh cup," I said, lifting my mug into view. "You want one?"

"Sure," he replied, pushing his seat back from the table.

At about the moment we were both rising from our chairs, the front door opened, and Constance came into the house.

"Cold out there?" Ben asked after she had pressed the door shut and stepped farther into the room.

"What do *you* think?" she replied with a return volley of sarcasm while shrugging off her coat and draping it over the back of the sofa.

"I'll swap with ya'," my friend offered. "Where'd ya' leave off?"

Constance shook her head. "Don't worry about it right now. The main houses have been covered. Reynolds and Cobb are still working the side street. Parker and the locals are up the block."

"Nothing so far, I take it?" I asked.

"No," she replied. "We didn't expect much though."

"We were just talkin' about that," Ben said.

"We'll have to make another round when people start arriving home from work," she detailed then looked directly at me. "Maybe our luck will change then. Either way, the bureau has arranged for you and Felicity to stay at a safe house. We can probably move you there within the next couple of hours."

"Uh-huh," Ben grunted, answering for me. "Welcome to the party. We were just talkin' about that too."

"What about it?"

"Rowan says they ain't leavin'."

"First Felicity, now you?" Constance appealed, shooting me a hard glance. "Rowan, I hate to break it to you, but you don't have any choice in the matter. We're moving you."

"It's a Witch thing, Constance," my friend told her.

"What? A Witch th..." she shot us both a confused look and cocked her head. "I don't suppose you'd care to explain?"

"Flyin' shit and big walls," Ben retorted before I could say a word. "You'd hafta ask the White Man."

"Rowan?" she asked.

"Long story short, you have to protect us from Annalise, I understand that. But, I have to protect Felicity from Miranda, who may well be an even greater threat in the grand scheme of things. This is the best place for me to do that."

She shook her head again. "I sympathize, Rowan, I really do. I don't necessarily understand it, but I sympathize. Unfortunately, it's out of my hands. My SAC already made the decision. You two are being moved to a safe house, like it or not. Even if it involves officially placing you in federal custody, which we will do if need be."

"Can ya' like take some of your Witch stuff with ya'?" Ben asked. "'Cause it looks ta' me like you're goin'."

"I guess I'll have to, won't I?" I spat.

"I'm sorry, Rowan," Constance said quietly.

"It's not your fault," I told her. "You're just doing your job. I'll go tell Feli…"

I didn't get to finish the sentence because I was interrupted by an anguished call emanating from the basement, which came in the form of my wife's tear-filled voice screaming my name. If that wasn't enough to stop my heart, the two words that followed were a guaranteed flat line.

All three of us were moving as a plaintive "she's here" echoed up the stairwell.

CHAPTER 38:

"What the fuck?!" Ben exclaimed, as he automatically filled his hand with the Beretta that rode in his ever-present shoulder rig. "I got the stairs!"

"Side door!" Constance immediately called out. Her own hand was already wrapped around her Sig Sauer, and she immediately turned back toward the front door and darted for it.

The side entrance, leading down into our basement, was the only door anyone could have entered without coming past us. It had a reinforced deadbolt and a handset lock, not to mention that it was monitored by the home security system. The only time it was ever unlocked was when we were moving things in and out of the lower level of the house, so I had no idea how anyone could have come through it, but it was literally the only way to get in relatively undetected. To my knowledge, the entrance hadn't been used for quite awhile, unless Felicity had done so, and I simply wasn't aware of it.

My friend was already at the mouth of the hallway, as Constance bounded down the front steps and hooked to the left, her cell phone in her free hand. I was directly behind him, and I yelled out to my wife, "Felicity?"

"Rowan… Help me!" she cried. "She's here…"

I quickly made a move to step around Ben to the partially open basement door. His hand shot out and slammed into my chest, knocking me back against the wall with a heavy thud.

"What the fuck are you doing?!" I demanded.

"You stay right here," he growled back at me.

"Dammit, Ben…"

"I said, stay right here! Let us do our jobs!" he barked, then cast his voice toward the opening as he called out, "Devereaux?"

"Rowan…" my wife whimpered. "Help me…"

Before I had a chance to object again, the front door swung open, and one of the FBI agents who had been canvassing the nearby side street rushed in, his sidearm at the ready. Ben gave him a quick glance, pointed at me then stabbed a finger down the hallway. Without a word, the agent continued past him, roughly taking me by the shoulder and pushing me farther back into the corridor.

From the basement, I heard my wife's sobbing voice call out once more, "Rowan... Please..."

"Get down there before she kills her!" I screamed as I tried to turn, but the federal agent caught the move and pushed me hard toward the end of the hall.

"Sir," he said. "You need to stay out of the way. Let us handle this."

"You might have ta' cuff 'im," Ben told him. His voice was cold, and I knew he wasn't even hinting at a joke.

"Dammit, Ben!" I exclaimed. "The bitch has my wife down there!"

"Rowan!" my friend snapped. "This is what we do! Now stay out of the way!"

I looked back over my shoulder, anger and fear seething inside me. My face was growing hot as I flushed with the swirling emotions. All I could think about was getting to Felicity before Annalise could do anything at all to harm her.

"Annalise Devereaux!" Ben called out again. "This is Detective Storm with the Saint Louis Police. I'm coming down."

He was answered by an amused chuckle and the words "Send Rowan, little man."

A second later, struggling through choked sobs, I heard Felicity moan, "*Caorthann...*"

A cell phone on the agent's belt chirped with a two-way alert tone, and it was followed by Constance's voice.

"Cobb... Reynolds and I are on the side door. It appears to be locked," she said. "Parker and the locals are coming now. They'll cover the front and back."

He snatched the phone from his belt, thumbed a button and replied, "Got it. Storm and I are at the top of the stairs. We're having an issue with the spouse."

The device cricket-chirped again, and Constance replied with no hesitation in her voice whatsoever, "Handcuff him."

What had previously been a threat now became a direct order. Cobb holstered his weapon and quickly slipped out a pair of restraints then brought one metal circlet down against my wrist with a hard snap. With a practiced squeeze, he ratcheted it tight.

"You've got to be fucking kidding me!" I shouted, trying to twist away.

He wasn't quite Ben's stature, but he easily had an inch or two on me, not to mention his training. Before I knew it, he had whipped me back around and shoved me into the bathroom at the end of the hall. I bounced against the wall, but before I could turn back around, he had twisted my free arm behind my back and slapped the other cuff onto it.

"I need you to sit down on the floor, Mister Gant," he ordered. "Now."

"I can't believe you're doing this," I snarled.

"It's for your own safety as well as your wife's, sir. Now, please sit down or I'll sit you down."

I was left with little choice other than to comply. I leaned back against the wall and slid downward until I was seated on the tile floor but not without appealing, "Goddammit, Ben, get down there and help Felicity!"

Cobb left me sitting and headed back to the basement door. Drawing his weapon, he stood to the backside of the barrier and gave Ben a nod. My friend carefully nudged the door the rest of the way open, staying well to the living room side of the entranceway.

"See anything," Ben asked.

Agent Cobb carefully shifted to the right, his pistol stiff armed before him and pointing down the stairwell. After a moment, he slid back and shook his head as he said, "Clear."

My friend mimicked the motion from his side, checking the blind spots the FBI agent wouldn't have been able to see from his angle.

"Clear," he told him then called out, "Felicity?"

I listened intently but heard only my wife sobbing. As painful as the sound was, at least it meant she was still alive.

"Devereaux?" Ben shouted after a few seconds.

We waited, but there was still no verbal answer.

"Annalise Devereaux?" he called again.

"No," a haunting voice carried up the stairs. "Not Annalise."

"Okay," he replied. "So, what do I call you?"

We heard the laugh again. In its wake, the Southern-accented voice said, "You may call me, Mistress, little man."

"Yeah, right, like that's gonna happen," my friend muttered, so low even I almost didn't hear him. Then, he upped the volume and called out, "Look, no one needs to get hurt here."

"Why don't you come down," the voice returned. "I won't hurt you... Much."

"How is Miz O'Brien?" he asked, ignoring the taunt.

"Oh, she's simply lovely," the voice replied.

"Can I speak with her?"

"I don't know, little man, *can* you?" she laughed. "Try again."

"What the fuck," Ben whispered.

"I'm not sure, but I think she's correcting your English," Cobb returned in a low voice.

"Jeezus, so she's a smart ass too..."

The voice echoed up the stairs again. "Come on, little man. Say, 'Please Mistress, *may* I speak to Felicity?'"

"I'm not gonna play games with you, Devereaux. Let me talk to her."

A scant few seconds passed, then my wife's sobbing voice floated up to our ears. "Ben? Is Rowan with you?"

"He's right here, Felicity," Ben replied. "Everything is gonna be fine. You just hang in there, okay?..."

"Rowan!" she appealed, her voice strained but stronger than before. "She's back! Help me!"

"Ben! Help her!" I demanded, rolling sideways against the wall and struggling onto my knees. I shuffled into the doorway and hissed, "Either help her, or let me, dammit!"

I completely lost track of my heartbeats as my chest thudded through the silence. After what seemed like several hours rolled into a single moment, Ben shot a glance my way then looked over at Agent Cobb.

"Tell 'em I'm goin' down now," he said.

"That bottom landing is completely blind," he replied.

"Yeah, but I've been down there before. I can handle it."

Cobb thumbed his phone and relayed the message. No sooner had he finished speaking than Constance's voice came back over the device.

"Ben, we can hear you conversing with her. Is the situation stable?"

"Tell 'er that depends on what the fuck she calls stable," my friend snipped.

Cobb thumbed the button and said, "She's talking, and we've spoken to the hostage."

Constance replied, "As long as she's talking to us, and Felicity is unharmed, stay where you are. I've already called in the HRT."

"You heard her," Cobb said. "Hostage Rescue is on the way."

"Ben…" I appealed again.

My friend shot a glance my way then replied, "Yeah, well tell 'er I'm not waitin'."

The agent relayed the new message and was again greeted by Constance's voice saying, "Storm, as long as the situation is stable, stand down and wait for the HRT!"

Ben looked at Cobb then past him at me. Glancing back, he settled his eyes on the phone for a brief second. Stepping forward through the opening he said, "Fuck the HRT."

Before the federal agent could make a move, my friend had skirted in through the opening and disappeared. I could hear him slowly working his way down the stairs.

"I'm coming down," his voice echoed from the opening.

Blood was rushing in my ears, and my head was throbbing with pain both ethereal and mundane. I leaned against the doorjamb and fought to listen as my friend continued down the stairs but heard nothing other than the thumping of my own heart.

Seconds eked by, each one adding to the next until they drew themselves out into languid minutes that seemed like hours. I closed my eyes and waited out the eternity since it was all I could do.

Finally, I heard muffled voices through the floor, bleeding in through the pounding in my ears. A piercing yelp and a string of curses that sounded as if they came from Ben followed. After that came the sound of a woman laughing then the creaking noise of the side door opening on oil-deprived hinges. A moment later, Ben's voice called up the stairwell.

His tone was calm and held only the barest note of urgency when he said, "Cobb… Uncuff Rowan and get him down here."

CHAPTER 39:

I was already heading for the stairs before Agent Cobb had the handcuffs fully removed from my wrists. I could hear several voices as I headed downward, but my wife's wasn't among them, which firmly seated the panic roiling through my gut. My heart still hadn't stopped racing nor had my head ceased to pound with its bizarre mix of pain. If anything, the headache had grown worse.

As I neared the bottom of the stairs, I was struck full in the face by an all too familiar but wholly foreign sensation. It was a too pleasant tingle I had felt brush against me from somewhere between the worlds while I was more or less held captive in the bathroom waiting for this to be over. Unfortunately, I knew the feeling well. I'd ignored it then, and I tried my best to do so now, even though it was growing in intensity with each step I took.

Skipping the last two stairs, I leapt from the lower landing, following the direction of the voices to the left. When I came around the corner, I found Ben, Constance, and another FBI agent standing a few feet away from the entrance to my wife's office.

"Where's Felicity?!" I demanded. "Is she okay?"

"She's fine, Row," Ben said as he turned toward me. "Physically, anyway."

"What do you mean? Where is she?"

He sidestepped a bit and turned back toward the office. There, just outside the entrance was one of the vertical, eight-by-eight support beams which were spaced throughout the basement. Sitting cross-legged on the floor at its footing, with her chin resting against her chest, was my wife. Her arms were wrapped around the solid post and a pair of handcuffs was securely locked about her wrists, holding her in place. The wood of the upright was gouged and scraped where the connecting chain between the cuffs had been raked against it. Though I was still several feet away, I could see welts, and even some trickles of blood, where she had been struggling against the restraints.

"Felicity..." I breathed as I started toward her.

Ben grasped my shoulder and held me back. It was only then I noticed he had one hand wrapped in a washcloth from our nearby laundry room, and a bright splotch of red was soaking through it.

"Why haven't you taken those off her?!" I shouted.

"Because, it might not be a good idea just yet," Constance replied.

"What?..." I stammered. "What's going on?"

"You're gonna wanna keep some distance for a bit," Ben replied, holding up his wounded hand.

"What happened?"

He cocked his head toward Felicity.

"What? Why?" I stammered, confusion rimming my words. Jumbles of thoughts were bouncing around my head in competition with the odd feelings that were creeping in from elsewhere. I knew deep down the meaning behind the odd rush of pleasure that was fighting to overtake me, but I didn't want to admit it. I glanced around as I chose to let the puzzlement continue its reign over my grey matter instead. Finally I asked, "Where's Annalise?"

"She ain't here, White Man," Ben told me. "Never was."

"Then what's going on?" I demanded.

"Ask her," he replied, nodding again toward my wife.

She slowly turned her face up and stared at me with a wicked grin stretched across her lips. A smear of blood was streaked from the corner of her mouth and down across her chin. I knew without hesitation that it wasn't her own.

She casually tossed her head, flipping her hair back over her shoulder in the process, then settled her gaze back on me. After a moment she said, "Hello, little man. Have you missed me?"

Her tone held the same Southern affectation as the voice with which my friend had carried on the conversation via the stairwell. Up close, however, the ethereal hollowness of it resonated through to my very core. I had no idea if anyone besides me could detect the ghostly echo, but that didn't really matter. As long as I could hear it, I knew exactly who belonged to the words.

"Miranda," I said.

"You remember," she replied.

"You're hard to forget."

"Of course I am."

I glanced over at the FBI agent who was standing with Constance. While I was sure there had been some manner of briefing done, I doubted it came with an instant comprehension of the paranormal, especially as it pertained here. Constance caught my gaze and turned to the agent.

"Reynolds," she said. "Why don't you go let everyone know we're secure. And, have Cobb cancel the HRT."

"Yeah, okay," he replied, casting a baffled look toward Felicity then me before going.

Once I heard his footsteps receding up the stairs, I turned back to my wife and stated in a flat tone, "You aren't welcome here, Miranda."

"Of course I am. I was invited."

"Bullshit."

"You really should not be so rude."

"Coming from you that means pretty much nothing."

She smiled. "Come now. Is that really a proper way to express your love for me?"

"Leave now, or I'll make you leave."

"I was invited," she told me again.

"By who?"

She made a show of visually inspecting herself for a moment before saying, "Your wife, of course."

"I know better than that."

"Do you?"

"Yes."

"Perhaps you only think you do."

"Then why was Felicity crying out for help?"

"Giving in to one's desires can be disconcerting at first. But, she will get used to it."

"I don't think so."

"She will. Annalise did."

"We both know you're lying. Felicity never invited you here. You invited yourself."

She shrugged. "Does it really matter? She is mine now."

"Perhaps you only think she is."

She let out a small laugh that sent icy fingers along my spine. "You are very quick, little man. Touché."

"What did you do with the cloves and the blood, Miranda?"

"Is it not obvious?"

"The effects, yes. But, what did you do?"

"It is a secret."

"What's wrong? Are you afraid I might be able to work stronger magick than you?"

"No."

"Then why not just tell me?"

"I have a better idea. Maybe you should beg me to tell you."

"That's not going to happen."

"Even to save your wife?"

"You'll have to excuse me, but I don't trust you."

"Quick and bright. No wonder you love me."

"This game is over. It's time for you to leave. I'm not going to tell you again."

"Not just yet."

I didn't respond. Instead I simply turned and started toward the stairs.

Ben reached out and grabbed my arm. "Wher're ya' goin'?"

I shot a glance back at Felicity then turned to face him. "I'm sure our guest is thirsty," I said. "I thought I'd go get her a big glass of salt water so she can be on her way. You'd like that, right, Miranda?"

"You do not... want... to do... that," she interjected with an odd faltering in her voice.

The hesitation seemed uncharacteristic based on my previous

encounters with this *Lwa*, but I was certainly no expert in the field, so I wasn't sure what to make of it. For all I knew, it was some sort of trick.

I snapped back at her, "Then leave and I won't have to."

"I… I am…" she started, the hesitation growing worse. "I am not… going… to do… that… just yet."

She appeared to be struggling with something unseen. Not just the words but also something on the order of an outside influence. Her expression changed between each syllable, and her eyes would go from a cold stare to a vacant wandering each time. I started to wonder if my wife was fighting back. I could only hope that she was.

"Then you don't leave me any choice," I said.

I wasn't going to take any chances. Whether Felicity was locked in some manner of ethereal tug of war or not, she needed help. I started toward the stairs again.

"It… will not…" she said then suddenly halted.

"What? Won't work?" I called back to her. "It did before, and I'm betting it will again."

I hadn't gone any more than five paces when a pitiful sob hit my ears. I turned back out of a confused sense of curiosity and saw tears streaming down my wife's cheeks.

"I'm not playing this game, Miranda," I spat before turning and starting away once more just for good measure. As I said, I didn't trust her.

"Rowan… Help me…" she wailed.

This time I stopped dead in my tracks. The voice calling my name held every bit of the Celtic lilt that identified Felicity and not even the barest hint of the Southern accent so prevalent in the *Lwa's* manifestation.

"Row?" Ben breathed, shifting his gaze back and forth between the two of us.

I turned and stepped back toward her. "Felicity?"

"Help me…" she moaned, leaning her body against the vertical support as if she was completely spent.

"Give me the key," I said to Ben.

"What?"

"Give me the goddamned key to the handcuffs!" I demanded again.

He dug in his pocket and fished out a key ring then shuffled through it before handing it to me with one pinched between his fingers. "Try this one. Those aren't our cuffs so I dunno if it'll fit."

"You didn't cuff her?" I asked, taking the keys and starting toward Felicity.

"She was like that when I got down here, Row," he replied then asked, "Are you sure about this?"

"I don't know if I'm sure about anything anymore, Ben," I said.

I knelt next to my wife and slipped the key into one of the handcuffs. From this angle, I could see in through the door to her office, and I noticed a purple overnight bag sitting on her desk. It was the same one that had once been seized as evidence when she had been charged with Annalise's crimes, simply because it was a repository of Felicity's "toys" from when she had been directly involved in the BDSM community well before we had ever met. I hadn't seen it since the last time Miranda had made her presence known through my wife. Obviously, she had tucked it away down here.

Things began to gel inside my pounding skull. One of the last times a possession had occurred, Felicity had tried to kill me and had almost succeeded. She must have sensed this one coming on and decided to make sure that couldn't happen again.

I twisted the key and it unlatched the restraint. I carefully opened it and slipped the metal circlet from my wife's bruised and scraped wrist and then undid the other. Sitting down on the floor, I gathered her up into my arms and held her.

After a moment of stroking her hair as I slowly rocked, I looked up at Ben and Constance and asked, "Would one of you please go get me a glass of salt water before that bitch comes back?"

"I'll get it," Constance offered as she turned toward the stairwell.

"Aspirin, too," I added. "Just bring the whole damn bottle."

CHAPTER 40:

"Rowan, I'm fine," Felicity stressed for the third time as she set about rearranging a stack of clothes she had just placed into her overnight bag.

On the surface, the habitual manner in which she placed, removed, and then replaced items into the bag in a bid to defy the laws of physics would normally lead me to believe her comment was true. But, the image of her tear-streaked face was still playing back inside my head, with her desperately pleading whimper as the background score. If I wasn't over it yet, I didn't know how she possibly could be.

"Fine?" I replied. "Funny, you weren't fine an hour ago."

"Of course I wasn't," she countered without looking up. "But, like you said, that was an hour ago. Time heals, doesn't it then?"

Her voice was confident, but her normal Celtic lilt had given way to a much heavier brogue, which wasn't at all surprising. She had to be just as exhausted as the rest of us, probably more so, and that's when her accent was at its thickest.

"I think they were talking about a little more time than an hour."

"I'm a fast healer."

"Uh-huh... Sure... You know, the last time this happened you checked yourself into a psych ward, or have you forgotten that?"

"The last time this happened I was scared."

"You seemed pretty damn scared to me a little while ago."

"I was," she said with a curt nod. "But, now I'm not. Now I'm just pissed off."

I knew she wasn't just saying that for effect. She meant it. Any sense of fragility that had been coming from my wife in the past weeks was completely gone, replaced in total by a mix of anger and determination. This new emotion burned so brightly behind her eyes that it defied any description I could muster. In a very real sense, her present attitude frightened me almost as much as everything else that had happened.

"Look," I said. "I'll admit that you're probably the strongest person I know, but you have limits. We all do. After everything that's gone on in the past twenty-four hours, not to mention the past month, I find it really hard to believe that you're suddenly okay."

"Well, I am."

"I don't believe you."

"Is that so? Welcome to my world."

"Come again?"

She stopped packing for a moment and gave me a serious stare. "Are you telling me this doesn't sound at all familiar to you, then?"

"Should it?"

"Aye." She nodded. "I'm not saying anything to you now that you haven't said to me yourself time and again. For the record, I never believe you either."

"That's different."

"How?"

"It just is."

Her eyes flashed as she opened her mouth to fire off a retort; but before any words came out, she closed it again and simply stared at me. A few seconds later her expression softened, and she slowly sat down on the edge of the bed and sighed.

"We can't keep having this argument, you know," she told me.

I let out a heavy breath of my own. "Yeah... I guess we've covered this ground before, haven't we?"

"We've worn it barren," she replied with a flat huff.

"I guess we have... And, it doesn't get us anywhere, does it?"

"Of course not. We're both too stubborn."

"Maybe so," I agreed. "But, I still think you have me beat in that department."

"Aye. It's a family trait."

"So I've noticed," I said with a halfhearted grin. I paused then added, "I'm just worried about you, honey. This has gotten to be too much… For either of us."

"I know you are," she replied. "And, I understand why. I really do… And, you're right… It has… I'm just ready for this to be done."

"Me too… So, how do we make that happen?"

"To start with, we don't run from it."

"I'm not so sure I agree."

She shook her head. "You're only saying that because it's me she's after. If it were you then you'd be rushing headlong into it. I know you would. You've done it before."

"I suppose I have," I agreed. "But…"

"That's different?" she interrupted.

"Yes, it is," I said. "But, actually what I was going to say is, at least I was dealing with someone who lived in the same plane of existence as me. Miranda is another story entirely."

"She is," Felicity said with a nod. "But, I think Annalise is the answer to dealing with that."

"How?"

"I don't know." She blinked and shook her head.

"Then why do you…"

She spoke up before I could finish the question. "A feeling."

"A feeling," I repeated.

"Aye. Sound familiar?"

"Unfortunately, yes."

"I thought it might."

A soft knock came from behind me, so I put further comment on hold for the moment.

"Hey," Ben said, a questioning look on his face as I swung open the door. "You two about ready?"

"Close," I said. "Probably just a few more minutes."

"'Kay," he replied. "Get a move on. We need ta' go soon."

"Ben?" Felicity spoke up.

"Yeah?"

"I really am sorry about your hand."

He held up his bandaged paw and gave it a quick glance. As it turned out, the wound had initially looked far worse than it really was. Once cleaned up, it had only taken a bit of homegrown first aid in the form of antibiotic ointment, a gauze pad, and some tape.

"Yeah," he grunted. "Remind me not ta' really piss you off."

"Aye, like that would work?"

"Yeah, right," he replied. "Listen, Row, can I see ya' out here for a minute?"

"Needing to talk about me behind my back, are you?" Felicity quipped before I could respond.

"Yeah, that's pretty much the plan," Ben returned, a joking tone in his voice. "Actually, I really just need ta' verify some stuff."

"Go ahead," Felicity said, looking up at me. "I'll finish up here."

"Okay," I told her. "I'll be right back."

My wife stood up and returned to her prior task as I left the bedroom, swinging the door shut behind me. I followed Ben out to the living room where Constance was waiting for us, a concerned look creasing her features.

"So, how is Felicity doing?" she asked. "Honestly."

"She says she's fine," I told her.

"Do you believe that?"

"For the time being, I think so," I replied with as much confidence as I could muster, given that I wasn't entirely sure if I believed my own words. "The real truth is, she's had enough. We both have."

"What about her episode? Do you think it will happen again?"

I shook my head. "Hard to say. I thought she would be safe from that sort of thing here, but obviously I was wrong. The salt water helped. The *Lwa* seems to have a fear of it, which is good. So, we're going to try it as a preventive as well."

"I called Helen, Row," Ben interjected. "We can move Firehair back to the hospital instead of the safe house if ya' want."

"I'm not going to do that to her," I replied, shaking my head. "And, I think you'd be hard pressed to get her to agree to it. You'd probably have to arrest her."

"I already told you full blown protective custody had been

seriously considered and was always an option," Constance chimed in. "And, I'll be honest, after what happened I'm still not ruling it out."

"That won't fix the problem," I objected with another quick shake of my head.

"But, will it keep you both safe? That's the real issue here."

"In the short run, sure," I said. "In the long run, it's just more hiding."

"There's no shame in that, Row," Ben offered.

"It's not shame I'm concerned about," I said. "What I want is to make this all stop."

"We all want that," Constance said. "But, even though we both believe you about the *Lwa*, we're completely out of our element where that is concerned. We have to deal with what we have at hand, and that is Devereaux."

I nodded. "I understand that. What I need you to understand, however, is that this is coming to a head. And, I'm afraid it's going to take some sort of collision between the three of them to resolve it."

"You mean, Annalise, Felicity, and Miranda?" she asked.

"Unfortunately, yes."

"And, how do you think that's going to happen?"

"I wish I knew."

Constance shook her head. "If you're talking about a physical confrontation, Rowan, we simply cannot allow that. It's our job to protect you, not put you in harm's way. Truthfully, right now, I'm not even willing to put Felicity back on the phone with Devereaux again."

"Believe me, I'm no more in favor of a physical confrontation than you are," I replied. "But it just might be necessary. Perhaps even inevitable."

"Why?"

"To get Felicity clear of Miranda."

"How?"

"That's an answer I wish I had, believe me."

"And, that's the only way?"

"It might be."

Constance fell quiet, a deeply thoughtful look on her face. After a moment, she amended her earlier statement. "Maybe once Devereaux is in custody, we can work something out. But, not before then, that's for sure. It's far too dangerous."

"This some kinda *Twilight Zone* thing, Row?" Ben asked.

"Yeah, but not mine," I said with a sigh. "It's Felicity's."

"So she's doin' la-la land too," he huffed.

"Not exactly," my wife's voice came from the end of the hallway, right where it emptied into the living room. "It's just a feeling."

I turned and saw her standing there, arms crossed. Her expression was actually one of mild bemusement.

"Sorry," she said. "But, you did admit you were going to talk about me behind my back. You didn't really think I wouldn't listen in then, did you?"

"So much for reverse psychology," Ben muttered.

"So, this feeling… Is it like the visions Rowan gets?" Constance asked, apparently unfazed by the fact that Felicity had been eavesdropping.

"Aye, I suppose so. Yes."

"You gettin' anything specific from it?" Ben asked.

"Just that Annalise is somehow key to me getting free of all this."

"I assume you heard what I just told Rowan?" Constance asked.

"I did," Felicity answered with a nod. "But, it's really my choice then, isn't it?"

"No, I'm afraid it isn't."

My wife sighed, looked at the floor for a moment then back up to Constance. "All right then. I know I don't have the right to ask this, but I'm going to anyway. You've both already been breaking the rules. Can't you break just one more?"

"Felicity," Constance breathed, shaking her head. "I understand what you must be…"

"Please?" my wife appealed.

Constance sighed heavily and looked at me with a pained expression before finally turning back to her. "What are you asking us to do?"

"Give her what she wants."

"She wants you dead."

"Yes, I know, but what she really wants is Miranda back."

"How do you propose we give her that?"

"Simple. You give her me."

"Not happening!" I objected immediately. "We'll find another way to get through this."

"Jeezus," Ben interjected. "Are you nuts, Firehair? No way."

"They're right," Constance added, shaking her head vigorously. "That's just insane."

"I don't mean literally," she explained. "I mean set a trap for her with me as the bait."

"I'm sorry, but that isn't even an option," Constance told her. "This is real life, not a mystery novel."

"Aye, then what do we do? Sit around waiting for her to knock on the door?"

"No. We make certain that the two of you are safe, and we keep looking."

"You can't protect me from Miranda, then. Nobody can."

"Felicity," Constance said. "This simply isn't how things are done."

My wife shook her head. "I need this to be over… I need it to be over *now*."

Constance dropped her forehead into her hand and massaged it for a second before huffing out an exasperated breath and looking back up at Felicity. "It's not going to happen. But, maybe I can compromise with you if I can get it approved."

"How so?"

"Again, this hinges on approval from my SAC. If I can get that, when and if she calls again, I'll let you talk to her. We'll have you try to set up a meeting if you can," she said. "But, I'm the bait. Not you."

"Aye, but I still need to see her, or I won't be able to get free of Miranda."

"Once she's in custody, I'll see what I can arrange," Constance said. "No promises. But, I'll do what I can. Take it or leave it."

Felicity nodded. "Fair enough then."

"Okay, let me make a call and see if my SAC will even go for the idea."

"You'd best get yourself a wig if you plan on pretending to be me," my wife added.

"I'm going to be honest with you, Felicity. Even if I get this approved, I don't think it will work. Otherwise I would have already suggested it. I really doubt she'll even agree to a meeting, much less show up."

"Oh, she'll agree," Felicity assured her. "And she will show, I can guarantee it."

"How?"

"You have absolutely no idea what Miranda gives her. Unfortunately, I do."

"Is it really that good?" Constance asked, a mild curiosity in her tone. "I mean, I've studied sexual predators before...but to risk being caught, all over sexual release?"

"Like I said..." Felicity replied. Her voice was a half whisper filled with an almost wistful longing. "You have no idea."

Annalise finally called just before three in the afternoon. As expected, the verbal exchange between Felicity and her was heated for the duration. However, my wife played it well. Of course, when it came right down to it, there was really no acting required. Everything that came out of her mouth was real and uncensored.

Just as Felicity had predicted, it didn't take much for Annalise to agree to a meeting between them. Still, as expected, she remained cautious and unwilling to relinquish control. She refused to commit to a time or place, except to say we should expect another call when she was ready.

The wheels spun quickly into motion, and I could feel the situation gaining speed. Even though Constance and the resources of the FBI were now on deck, deep inside I could feel that none of this was going to go according to any earthly plan, theirs or Annalise's.

I only hoped that when the crash finally came, we would all be walking away from it in one piece. Unfortunately, I couldn't shake the feeling that some breakage was about to occur.

CHAPTER 41:

"How do I look?" Constance asked, inspecting herself in the large mirror hanging over our dining room buffet.

Agent Parker had just finished helping her pin a long, bright auburn wig to her head, and she was primping the spiral curls into position around her face and across her shoulders.

She was clad in a pair of jeans and a button down shirt, much like Felicity would normally wear for a casual night out. The notable exceptions were that my wife customarily didn't have a bulletproof vest beneath her clothes, a wireless transmitter on her belt, or a 40-caliber Sig Sauer riding in the small of her back.

"Close enough," I said. "At a distance, definitely passable. But, once she gets close to you though, I don't know."

"Once she gets that close," she replied. "It doesn't matter anymore."

"Aye," Felicity added. "Don't worry. You look good."

"So," I asked. "What if she's seen Felicity since she changed her hair?"

"Then we're screwed," Constance answered in a purely matter-of-fact tone. "The choice on the wig was a judgment call. They did a psych analysis on the recorded conversations and determination was that she probably would have mentioned something about Felicity's hair if she knew. The behavioral analyst said she would have felt empowered by causing Felicity to make a change in her appearance and therefore would have felt a need to gloat about it."

"I hope they're right."

"They almost always are."

"Almost?" I asked.

"Nobody's perfect," she replied.

The front door opened, and Ben stepped into the house, shoving his cell phone back into his pocket as he entered.

"Hmmmm… Firehair junior," he said once he set his eyes on Constance.

"What do you think?" she asked.

"Can you maybe keep it for later?" he quipped.

"This isn't really the right time for jokes, Ben," she replied.

"Who says I'm jokin'?" he said then turned serious and asked, "She call?"

"No," Constance replied. "Just getting prepared."

"Yeah, okay." He made a show of heaving his shoulders and feigning a shiver. "Friggin' cold out there."

"Aye, you should have worn your coat," Felicity told him.

"Wasn't expectin' it ta' take that long."

"Problems?" I asked.

He shook his head. "No. Just stuff."

"Stuff?"

"Yeah." He gave me a nonchalant shrug. "You know, stuff."

"Okay," I replied.

I didn't press him any further. Whatever the phone call had been about, he felt it necessary to step outside to take it. He wasn't acting particularly concerned, so I had to assume it was nothing earth shattering.

I glanced around the room as the short spate of conversation waned. For all the silence that ensued, there was still a good deal of activity, some important, and some just to expend nervous energy.

Constance was busy hooking the receiver for her wireless around her ear and hiding it beneath the temporary hair, while Agent Parker was helping out by threading the wire down the back of her shirt and making the connections to the small transmitter at her belt. Felicity had her arms folded beneath her breast and was pacing back and forth. The dogs, not wanting to miss anything, were laying in the living room following her with their eyes. Ben was still eyeing Constance but not saying a word. Judging by the look on his face, I had a feeling his initial comment about the wig really hadn't been a joke at all.

I turned and looked over at the pendulum clock on our dining room wall. It was edging toward seven, just like it had been when I checked moments ago. Four hours had gone by, and we were still waiting, a fact that wasn't helping my sense of foreboding in the least.

"You two should relax," Constance said, glancing between Felicity and me as she brushed more hair down over her ear. "This could be a dry run. She might not even call tonight. She might wait until tomorrow, or the next day."

"No... She'll call soon," Felicity replied.

"You need to be prepared if she doesn't," Constance offered.

"No," my wife said confidently. "I don't."

The clock made a loud thunk as if to punctuate her statement. The minute hand had completed its upward journey and the internal spring automatically engaged. The winding released and chattered through the house as it drew back the hammer then proceeded to launch it against the chime. Before the fourth bong had finished reverberating, the telephone started to ring.

"Goddamn Witches," Ben muttered.

Felicity stepped over to the table and picked up the handset. Constance gave her a quick nod, so she thumbed it on and placed it up to her ear.

"I was beginning to think you had second thoughts," my wife said, her voice coated with a thick frost. "Where do you want to do this?"

The last chime of the hour echoed from the clock with a dull finality as we stood waiting. I don't know about everyone else in the room, but I was holding my breath.

"Are you sure?" Felicity finally said. "I thought you'd want it to be someplace more private... I see... Well, that's a big place. Where should I meet you once I'm there? Uh-huh... Aye... I can't wait."

She switched off the phone and laid it back on the table as she turned to fully face us.

"The zoo," she said. "In one hour. She told me to wait for her by the carousel. She also said she'll be watching, and I'd best come alone or she won't show."

"Dammit," Constance muttered. "The zoo has their holiday light displays running, and it's going to be crowded."

"Prob'ly why she picked it," Ben grumbled. "Easier ta' disappear into the crowd than to be out in the open."

"Did you hear anything in the background?" Constance asked. "Anything that might indicate she's already there?"

"No," Felicity replied, shaking her head. "It was quiet."

"She might be there but sitting in a car on the parking lot," the other agent offered.

"Probably," Constance said with a nod.

"Your call," Ben huffed, nodding toward Constance. "Whaddaya wanna do?"

"I don't like it," she replied after a moment. "Not at all... But, who knows if we'll get another chance." She turned to the other agent. "Parker, call it in. Get as many bodies as we can into the crowd, and get SWAT on standby. Also, have someone notify the zoo's park security. Tell them to go about business as usual, but let them know what's going on. Tell them do not approach. We don't need some rent-a-cop blowing this and getting someone hurt. Once I leave, give me about five minutes, then head out, but take a different route out of the subdivision. Catch up with me on Highway Forty, but hang back in case I'm tailed."

"Got it," Agent Parker replied, pulling out her cell phone and starting to dial.

Constance stepped into the dining room then pulled her coat from the back of a chair and quickly slipped into it. Picking up Felicity's keys from the buffet, she turned back to us.

"Ben, you still have two local units outside. If you need..."

"Go," Ben said, cutting her off. "I've got it covered here."

"Constance..." Felicity spoke up with a bit of hesitation in her voice. "Thank you..."

She gave her a nod and replied, "I'll call as soon as this is over. You can thank me then."

She turned and headed toward the back of the house where

Felicity's Jeep was parked. Just before she reached the kitchen doorway, Ben called out, "Connie…"

She stopped and looked back, a surprised expression on her face. I suspected it was due to the nickname, since I'd only seen one other person get away with calling her by it, and this was the first time I'd ever heard Ben use it when she was present.

My friend just stared at her for a second then said, "Be careful. 'Kay?"

She gave him a quick smile then disappeared around the corner. A few seconds later, we heard the Jeep moving alongside the house as she backed it out of the driveway then sped off down the street. As ordered, Agent Parker followed along behind several minutes later.

Ben stood silently at the window, peering through a small crack in the blinds. Every now and then he would glance up at the clock then return his gaze to the opening. After a few minutes, he turned and pulled his jacket from the back of a chair and started shrugging into it.

"Something wrong?" I asked.

"Get your coats," he replied.

"Why?" Felicity asked.

"'Cause it's cold outside," he told her.

"Why are we…"

"Just get your coats," he repeated. "We're goin' ta' break some rules."

CHAPTER 42:

B en exited the highway and pulled the van into Forest Park then moved with the flow of traffic until he could swing into the zoo parking lot. He hadn't been particularly forthcoming with answers to any of our questions, so both Felicity and I had eventually given up and simply rode along in silence. It was obvious to us where we were going. What our taciturn friend had in mind, however, remained a mystery.

He slowly pulled around the lot, bypassing several empty spaces until he came back around and located one with a halfway decent view of the zoo entrance. Nosing in, he shut off the lights and engine then cracked his side window to keep the windshield from fogging over. He simply stared through the glass, watching the entrance without saying a word.

After about a minute, I said, "I take it we aren't getting out."

"Nope. Not yet, anyway," he replied then glanced over his shoulder and said, "Felicity, hand me that bag that's in the seat next to ya'."

My wife felt around in the dark and then passed a paper bag forward. I twisted in my seat and took it from her then handed it to Ben.

"Dinner?" I asked with a note of sarcasm, as he took it.

He opened the top of the bag then pulled out a handheld walkie-talkie and switched it on.

"No. It's stuff," he grunted as he ramped up the volume into the audible range then started clicking through the preset channels.

"...ear so far," a familiar female voice crackled from the speaker. "How's my signal?"

He stopped and listened intently.

"Reading you loud and clear," a male voice replied.

"Okay, I'm approaching the entrance," Constance's voice came back across the air.

"Lawson has a visual on you," the man told her.

Ben upped the volume on the walkie-talkie a bit more then laid it on the console between us.

"Okay, I see you," the man responded a few seconds later. "Washburn will pick you up once you're inside. He'll hand you off to Frye at the Bayou Bullfrog display."

"Good. Any sign of her yet?"

"Negative."

The radio crackled with a burst of static then fell silent for the moment. I looked over at Ben who had directed his stare back out the windshield.

"Where did you get that?" I asked.

"It's police stuff," he replied.

"That isn't your regular radio, Ben."

"I got a new one."

"In a brown paper bag?"

"Recycled packaging," he returned.

"That's not police stuff. It's FBI stuff," I said.

"Real cops got 'em too," he said, verbally hinting at his selective lack of respect for the federal agency.

"Yeah… Why am I not buying that?"

He gave me a half shrug but didn't avert his gaze from the entrance. "Hey, she wasn't gonna be usin' it."

"You stole that from Constance?" Felicity asked.

"Borrowed," he replied. "There's a difference. Besides, ain't you the one who wanted us ta' break the rules?"

"So we came here to listen?" she asked.

"We came here so when they take 'er down, I can get ya' a few minutes with 'er before they throw 'er in a really dark hole."

"Are you serious?" I asked.

"Look, Constance'll try ta' make it happen, just like she said she would. But, I ain't countin' on it. Once the Feebs got their hands on 'er, things are gonna get real tight. She off'ed a federal judge, remember?"

"Yeah," I replied.

"So, the real deal is this might be the only chance ya' get. I'm just evenin' the odds."

"So, how much trouble is this going…"

The radio crackled and he held up a hand to shush me.

"Mandalay is in line at the gate," the earlier voice announced.

"Ten-four," another voice responded.

The device hissed then settled back into silence for the moment.

"What?" Ben asked, glancing over at me.

"How much trouble is this going to cause for you?" I repeated.

"Didn't ya' say this's what it's gonna take ta' get rid of the ghost bitch?"

"In theory."

"Well, then let's hope your theory's right."

"You're still going to get into trouble though, aren't you?"

"Doesn't matter," he replied. "I'm pretty much already suspended."

"The phone call earlier?"

"Yeah. S'posed ta' have a meetin' tomorrow mornin'. But, that's just a formality. Unless I'm completely off base, it's pretty much all over except the paperwork. Lookin' like thirty days, no pay."

"I really appreciate this, Ben," Felicity said.

"Yeah, I'll remember that."

"Just remind me if I try to bite you again," she quipped.

"Uh-huh," he grunted. "What was that you told me? Oh yeah, *like that'd work*. Why don't ya' just make sure ya' invite me over ta' dinner a lot for the next month. And, maybe get me somethin' real nice for Christmas too."

The radio crackled and hissed, then Constance's voice issued from the speaker once again. "I'm in and I see Washburn. Heading for the carousel now."

A new voice followed. "I've got Mandalay. Everything's clear."

My head was starting to throb with a fresh round of stabs in the back of my skull. While, as usual, the chronic ache had never fully subsided, it had at least faded into the background for the most part once Felicity was back on an even keel. Now, it was returning with a vengeance.

"She's here," I said.

"Where?" Ben asked, scanning the distant crowd of people who were still waiting to enter through the gates. "Do ya' see 'er?"

"No," I replied. "But, I feel her."

"Fuckin' wonderful," he replied. "Well, at least we know she wasn't blowin' smoke about showin' up."

A handful of minutes oozed by, and the radio crackled again.

"Frye, you should be able to see Mandalay in about ten seconds."

A female voice answered a moment later. "I've got her. Clear so far."

"Who's covering the carousel?" Constance's voice blipped in.

"Book is on the left at the concession stand," the earlier voice replied. "Tamm is in the seating area making like a mommy."

"I don't like it," Constance replied. "Too many civilians. Especially children. Where's our takedown point?"

"When approached, try to lead her back the way you're coming in. We'll move when there's an opportunity."

"And, if she doesn't follow?"

A long span of silence filled in behind her question. Finally, the radio crackled again and the man replied, "We follow her."

"Acknowledged."

The radio hissed then fell quiet. We simply waited since there was nothing else we could do.

After a couple of minutes, Ben asked, "You still feelin' 'er?"

"Yeah," I replied. "Like a hammer to the back of the head."

"What about you, Firehair?" he queried.

"Mmhmm," she hummed.

I turned and gave her a curious glance. She had been especially quiet for the past few minutes, and a wordless response wasn't like her at all. She caught my gaze and simply raised a questioning eyebrow.

"Are you doing okay, honey?" I asked.

She nodded.

Before I could press her further, the radio crackled again.

"Book, you should be able to see Mandalay now," Frye's voice came over the air.

"Acknowledged. Okay, I see her," a male voice replied. "Tamm?"

"Ten-four. I see her," another woman said, her voice low against a backdrop of the calliope-like music from the carousel.

Fifteen or so seconds passed and the radio burped again.

"Heads up. We have a possible target approaching from the south," came Frye's voice. "Red hair... Black, full-length leather coat at my three o'clock."

"Right on time," Constance said, her voice also now underscored by the bright tune of the amusement ride.

"I see her," Tamm acknowledged.

The announcement served to instantly ratchet up the level of tension in the van. Knowing how I was feeling at this moment, I didn't even want to imagine what it was like for Constance and the rest of the agents.

"I'm on her," Frye announced after a desperately long thirty seconds.

"Make sure you give her some room," Book's voice came across. "If it's her, we don't want her spooked."

"Got it."

Another half minute crept past at what seemed like greatly reduced speed. The hammering inside my skull was starting to make me feel nauseous, and I found myself wishing for an economy-sized bottle of aspirin. I waited, my ears straining to hear anything at all, as if some quiet transmission might escape my notice. I knew I was holding my breath, but I didn't care.

"False alarm," Constance's voice suddenly blipped from the speaker. "Not her."

"Dammit," I muttered, as I allowed the oxygen-depleted air to sigh from my lungs.

I looked at my watch and saw that it was 8:04.

"The real adrenalin doesn't kick in quite yet," Ben offered. "Believe me."

According to my watch, it was 8:15 before the radio crackled back to life.

"Male subject approaching Mandalay," Frye announced. "Brown hair, blue over white jacket."

"Acknowledged."

"Probably some fuck gonna hit on 'er," Ben grumbled.

Three minutes later, the radio burped with Constance's voice, "Subject handed me a note. He said a woman paid him fifty dollars to deliver it. He said she told him to look for someone who looked just like her waiting at the carousel at eight-fifteen and that her name would be Felicity. Sounds like our girl. I guess she wanted to size me up."

"Did he give you a location for her?" a male voice asked over the air.

"He pointed toward the storyteller's area back down the path, but he said that was about forty-five minutes ago. I'm looking but I can't see her. Too many people. But, it's a good bet she's watching from somewhere nearby to make sure the note got delivered."

"Frye?"

"Nothing. I'm moving that way now."

"What does the note say?"

"It's one of the map handouts," she replied, her voice still muddied by the carousel music. "Display number eight has been circled."

"Eight is the Glacier motion simulator. It's closed for maintenance," the male voice said.

"I guess she wants some privacy after all," Constance replied.

"We'll need time to move into position," the voice came back.

"She's sure to be watching," Constance said. "I don't want her to get cold feet, so I'm going to start that way now."

The radio hissed for a moment, then the voice answered, "Don't get in a hurry… We need to reposition. Book, you tail Mandalay."

"Already moving," he replied.

"Tamm, you fall in behind Book."

"It's not going to look right if we have too many people moving into a closed area," Constance announced. "Keep some distance."

"Acknowledged," Tamm said. "Hanging back."

A minute passed then Constance's voice came across in a low tone, "There's a huge crowd at the forest exhibit, and they're blocking the path. It's going to take me a minute to get through."

Book's voice burped in behind hers, but it was partially drowned out by the sound of the aforementioned crowd. All that really came through was, "Dam-t, -st Man-lay."

"Say again?"

"The crowd," he repeated, the transmission somewhat clearer. "I've lost Mandalay. She was…"

Before he finished the sentence, the muffled report of something that sounded far too much like gunshots popped loudly from the speaker followed immediately by panicked screaming.

"Shots fired!" his frantic voice fell in behind.

"Everybody move!" the other voice ordered. "Now!"

Seconds later Book's voice was shouting across the radio again, devoid of all composure, "SHOTS FIRED! MANDALAY'S HIT! OFFICER DOWN! OFFICER DOWN!"

If adrenalin hadn't been dumping into Ben's system before, it definitely was now. He came fully upright in his seat as the frantic chatter continued to burst from the radio.

The device hissed for a second, then we heard Book exclaim, "JESUS CHRIST… JESUS CHRIST… ONE GOT PAST HER VEST! SHE'S BLEEDING BAD! WE NEED PARAMEDICS RIGHT NOW!"

CHAPTER 43:

"**G**ODFUCKINDAMMIT!" Ben yelped the curse as a single word before launching into, "GODDAMN FEEBS CAN'T DO ANYTHING RIGHT! SONOFABITCH!"

I was so dumbstruck that I couldn't make any words of my own come out of my mouth. I simply looked at him with a horrified expression as the radio continued to belch frantic chatter.

"Book! What is your exact location?!"

"Just outside the forest exhibit! Right before the path splits! Hurry!"

"Found the gun," Frye's voice blipped over the air. "But no shooter. The area is clear. She must have dispersed with the crowd."

"Washburn, cover southeast," a voice ordered. "If she didn't go past Book and Frye, then she has to be heading that way. I'm on the main path coming in toward you."

"Acknowledged."

"We're locking down the park," another voice added. "SWAT will be here in two."

The device continued to burp and hiss with various voices for a moment, all of them reporting that there was no sign of Annalise. There was a quick burst of silence, then one of the agents came across the speaker, "I've got something. Red wig in a trashcan outside the restrooms near the stuffed animal workshop… Be advised the subject may have changed her appearance."

"WHERE ARE THOSE PARAMEDICS?!" Book's frenzied words bled through on the heels of the announcement

"Mutherfuck," Ben muttered, a jumbled mix of fear, anger, and desperation wrapped tightly into his voice. He was already half out of the van as he shouted at us, "Stay here!"

He didn't waste time closing the door, and the alarm chime was dinging incessantly to warn of the keys in the ignition, adding its irritating insistence to the already chaotic swirl of voices issuing from the radio. The crash I had felt coming was now exploding around me, and the outcome was as bad as I feared, if not worse.

Sirens were filling the night air as they closed in on the park. Their urgent wails were bold punctuation for the overwhelming despair that was starting to tighten its grip around me.

My heart was clogging my throat as I watched my friend take off across the street at a dead run toward the zoo entrance. I still couldn't manage to form anything resembling coherent sentences out of the distressed thoughts rushing through my already tortured grey matter. I turned in my seat and looked at my wife.

"Gods..." I whispered. "Felicity..."

Instead of finding a similar grief stricken expression on her face as I had expected, what greeted me was a thin smile as she slowly shook her head. She looked into my eyes, then cocked her head to the side and clucked her tongue.

"*Chienne damnée,*" she said with a fluid Southern accent. "I knew she was going to do that."

A fresh dose of panic was injected into my veins as the haunting echo in her voice hit my ears. It dawned on me that I should have seen this coming, and that I now knew the reason Felicity had been keeping so quiet. Her body was here, but *she* wasn't even present—and hadn't been for several minutes. Miranda had seen to that. I can only imagine what my expression must have been as the realization washed over me, but whatever it was, it seemed to amuse her.

"Surprised, little man?" she asked.

Next to me the radio crackled. "This is Frye. I've got an open maintenance gate on the southeast corner. Washington drive, just north of Concourse."

"Lawson, your team has the parking area. Did you copy that?"

"Ten-four. There are maybe twenty to thirty civilians on the lot. Parker, Bates, stay with the lot..."

The rest of the broadcast faded into the background as I made a grab for my wife. I wasn't sure what was going to happen when I got hold of her, but I knew if I didn't, things could only get worse than they already were. As I twisted in her direction, she jumped back, shifting to the left and out of my reach. My seatbelt snapped tight as it achieved the end of its tether with a jarring stop, biting into the side of my neck and preventing me from moving any farther.

Whipping back around, I fumbled with the latch, trying to pop it loose so that I could pull free of the restraint. But, I wasn't fast enough. My wife seized the opportunity to scramble to the right, moving directly behind me toward the side door. At the same moment the catch released and I started swinging around again, the sound of the sliding door wrenching open with a heavy thud added itself to the insane concert of noises.

I twisted back around and grabbed for the door handle, but the door didn't budge. Reaching quickly, I pulled up the lock post, mentally cursing the older van and my penchant for habitually locking doors. The door popped open as I shouldered my way out of the vehicle and stumbled onto the lot. My wife now had a substantial head start, and she was gaining speed.

I took off after her, pushing as hard as I could to catch up. My heart was already racing, but my earlier horror was now replaced by determination as my adrenal gland finally elected to dump its payload into my system.

Felicity was darting across the asphalt, weaving between parked cars with the nimbleness of her petite stature. She didn't seem to be running from me as much as she seemed to be running toward something.

I heard shouting voices coming from various positions around the lot and the street in front of it combined with a sudden rush of heavy footsteps in the distance. I suspected the FBI team had spotted her and were responding.

My wife swivel-hipped around the end of an SUV, aiming herself toward a petite, dark-haired figure that was walking briskly up the aisle just beyond. I tried to follow but misjudged the gap, catching my shoulder hard against a truck's mirror bracket. I stumbled, slamming sideways against another car. In that instant I lost sight of my wife, but I could now hear the angry screams of two women engaged in what could only be a fight. I pushed off and continued between the parked vehicles, hooking around the end of the SUV in the direction of the commotion, and launched myself into the aisle.

As I ran out I could see the source of the screams. My wife and the other woman were rolling on the pavement several yards away. I ran toward them as I heard more shouts and pounding footsteps.

I covered the distance as quickly as I could, reaching out as I ran. When I made it to them, Felicity was on top of the other woman with her hands clasped around her neck. A stream of French was spewing from her mouth, and the only word I could recognize was *chienne*.

Grabbing beneath her arm, I slipped my own in up around her chest and latched onto her opposite shoulder. Using my other hand, I dug my thumb into one of her wrists and wrenched her hand free as I pulled her back.

Annalise coughed hard as I struggled to pull my wife off her. Felicity continued to scream in a mix of French and English, kicking as we fell back. With her free hand, she reached around and took hold of my hair, wresting my head roughly to the side. We both tumbled onto the asphalt, her on top of me squirming and still kicking.

I fought to hold on to her, but the air was suddenly forced from my lungs as added weight forced down on my chest. Annalise landed on top of us, screaming her own barrage of French-peppered verbiage. I heard Felicity begin to gag as the tables were now turned. She released my hair and swung her arm up, digging her nails into Annalise's cheek. I heard her shriek as the claws dug in, but the struggle continued. The shouting voices were now right on top of us, and the footsteps were now shuffling nearby instead of pounding in the distance.

A half second later, I heard Annalise scream, "That's mine, *chienne*!"

My unbearable headache instantly became even worse, and I

tasted blood in my mouth. An unearthly scream echoed inside my skull. It was just like the wail I had heard the day I cut the binding in our back yard. I didn't know what Annalise was claiming as her own, but I knew it had something to do with the connection between her and Felicity.

My wife went limp then shuddered and began to yelp as Annalise continued on the offensive. The disorientation of Miranda's sudden exit had taken hold, and Felicity was no longer fighting back. I loosened my grip on her and, in a panic, I twisted against the cold asphalt in an attempt to pull myself out from under them before Annalise could do any damage to her. Just as I managed to kick my legs around and started to extricate myself, I felt both their combined weights pulled from my chest. In the same moment, I was unceremoniously rolled onto my stomach, and my hands were being pulled behind my back as handcuffs were applied.

"Rowan!" Felicity called from a few feet away, her voice strained and confused.

I turned my head, but I couldn't see her.

Behind me I could hear Annalise still screaming some especially nasty sounding French as the agents wrestled her to the ground.

"Rowan!" Felicity shouted again, the anxiety in her voice audibly stepping up another notch.

"It's all right! It's going to be fine!" I called back to her before I laid the side of my face against the cold pavement and sighed heavily, "It's finally over," I muttered to myself. "It's going to be fine."

Friday, December 16
12:16 A.M.
FBI Field Office
St. Louis, Missouri

CHAPTER 44:

I had been here before. Sitting in this very office, in this very chair, while my wife was being fingerprinted, interrogated, and falsely accused of the crimes that had started this entire ordeal better than a month ago. The blob of metal bits that made up the magnetic sculpture sitting on the edge of the desk in front of me had probably morphed shape a time or two since then, though I couldn't tell it by looking. But, other than that, the office hadn't changed. It was just as I remembered it.

I pushed up from my slouched position and readjusted myself in the chair before letting out a tired sigh and rolling my head to the side to look at my wife. She was curled up as only she could do, with her head lying on her arm where she had draped it across the back of her own seat. Her eyes were closed, and she was breathing evenly, but I knew she wasn't asleep. She looked almost at peace, and that was a sight I hadn't seen for quite some time.

"How are you feeling," I asked softly.

"Tired," she answered, her thick Irish accent applying its inflections to the word.

"Yeah…" I agreed. "How about other than that?"

"Aye, you mean?"

"Yeah, I mean."

"Like I just woke up from a nightmare."

"Uh-huh," I grunted. "Me too."

We sat in silence for a while before she yawned audibly and stretched as she repositioned herself in the chair.

"It's really over, isn't it then?" she asked.

"I think so," I replied. "Miranda, anyway."

I heard a click and turned to see the door behind us swinging open. A blonde woman a few years older than Constance entered.

"Mister Gant, Miz O'Brien," she said, her own voice sounding tired.

"Agent Parker," I returned.

"You're free to go," she said. "I'll be happy to drive you home if you'd like."

"Is there any word on Constance?" I asked.

She bit her lower lip and nodded. "Only that she's still in surgery."

"Aye, but she's going to be okay, isn't she?" Felicity asked.

"All we know is she's critical," she said. "She lost quite a bit of blood. Our SAC and director are both at the hospital now. So is your friend, Detective Storm."

"Do you think you could take us there instead?" Felicity asked.

Parker nodded. "I can do that."

As we both stood up, she said, "Oh, before I forget... I wanted to return this to you, Miz O'Brien." She pulled a small paper envelope from her jacket pocket and held it out toward Felicity. "Devereaux claims it's her necklace, but we saw her yank it from your neck when we were pulling her off you. It looks like an heirloom, so I thought you might want to have it back."

The angry scream, *"That's mine, chienne!"* immediately flitted through my brain, along with the ethereal wail of anger and loss. Behind it came the memory of Ben asking me if Felicity had such a piece of jewelry, all because Lewis insisted she had been wearing it when he met her at the bondage club. The connection became instantly clear.

Felicity reached for the envelope, but I thrust my hand out ahead of hers and snatched it from Agent Parker's fingers. "I'll take that."

Felicity cocked her head at me and furrowed her brow. "Rowan, that's..."

"Trust me, you don't want it," I said.

"But..."

"I'll explain later. Right now, I have a feeling we need to just get to the hospital as soon as we can."

FACT OR FICTION?
A Note About The Legend Of The LaLaurie Family

Some of you may or may not be familiar with the legend of Delphine LaLaurie and the horrific tortures she allegedly inflicted upon her servant slaves. I will not endeavor to go deeply into the legend—or quite possibly *myth*—here, as it would take far too many pages. In fact, it would be a book in and of itself, and has been written by authors other than me. Suffice it to say, the story can easily be found with a simple search on the web or a visit to the library. The newspaper articles recounting the horrors actually do exist. Unfortunately for us, as it all occurred in the early 1800's there is no one left alive who knows what *really* happened behind the walls of the LaLaurie mansion.

Some say that what you read in those articles is the gospel truth. Others say it was only the tip of the proverbial iceberg, and the horrors ran far deeper. Still others say that Delphine LaLaurie and her family were the unfortunate victims of jealousy and "yellow journalism" meant for the sole purpose of besmirching their good name. And, there are those who will tell you that the truth lies somewhere in between, hiding in the murky shadows of the often repeated story. Alas, as I said, we will never know the real truth, but the legend has grown and become one of the timeless "horror stories" of the Crescent City used to entertain the morbid curiosity of tourists. The best advice I can offer is to research the story yourself, if you are interested, and draw your own conclusions. Quite obviously, for the purposes of this novel, I chose to treat the story as a slice of reality.

The tie-in of my novels with this long told legend came about when my dear friend, Dorothy Morrison, introduced me to the story. Later, during my visit to New Orleans, working post-Katrina cleanup, I had occasion to visit the library and become even far better acquainted with the saga surrounding Delphine LaLaurie and, as one would expect, it piqued my own morbid curiosity.

The concept for the *Miranda Trilogy* had started as a one book *Rowan Gant Investigation* centered on a dominatrix as the killer. As you, my readers, have now surmised, the story itself grew well beyond the pages of a single book. When I first began researching facts and settings for the plot—as well as the name Miranda itself—I happened upon an obituary. That obituary was from the *New Orleans Bee* newspaper and was almost word for word the same obituary quoted by Rowan in this novel, including the date the notice was originally published. The notable exceptions to the recounted verbiage are Miranda's age and surname. The real Miranda identified in the obituary was twenty years younger, had a different last name, and to my knowledge was in no way related to the LaLaurie family.

So, in effect, as we novelists tend to do, I fictionalized a small bit of reality. The concept for *Love Is The Bond*—and eventually the *Miranda Trilogy*—expanded to encompass my own somewhat bastardized version of the LaLaurie legend—that being the addition of a sister named Miranda and the tie in with the completely unrelated death notice in a better than 150-year-old newspaper.

All I can say is that our minds work in very strange ways. Well, at least *mine* does…

FICTION

The Rowan Gant Investigations

HARM NONE by M. R. SELLARS
RGI Book #1
ISBN 0-9678221-0-6 / EAN 9780967822105 / $8.95 US

MURDEROUS SATAN WORSHIPPING WITCHES

When a young woman is ritualistically murdered in her Saint Louis apartment with the primary clue being a pentacle scrawled in her own blood, police are quick to dismiss it as a cult killing. Not one for taking things at face value, city homicide detective Ben Storm calls on his long time friend, Rowan Gant—a practicing Witch—for help.

In helping his friend, Rowan discovers that the victim is one of his former pupils. Even worse, the clues that he helps to uncover show that this murder is only a prelude to even more ritualistic bloodletting for dark purposes.

As the body count starts to rise, Rowan is suddenly thrust into an investigation where not only must he help stop a sadistic serial killer, but also must fight the prejudices and suspicions of those his is working with—including his best friend.

NEVER BURN A WITCH
By M. R. SELLARS
RGI Book #2

ISBN 0967822114 / EAN 9780967822112 / $8.95 US

THE RETURN OF THE BURNING TIMES

In 1484, then Pope Innocent VIII issued a papal bull—a decree giving the endorsement of the church to the inquisitors of the day who hunted, tortured, tried and ultimately murdered those accused of heresy—especially the practice of WitchCraft. Modern day Witches refer to this dark period of history as "The Burning Times."

Rowan Gant returns to face a nightmare long thought to be a distant memory. A killer armed with gross misinterpretations of the Holy Bible and a 15th century Witch hunting manual known as the *Malleus Maleficarum* has resurrected the Inquisition and the members of the Pagan community of St. Louis are his prey.

With the unspeakable horrors of "The Burning Times" being played out across the metropolitan area, Rowan is again enlisted by homicide detective Benjamin Storm and the Major Case Squad to help solve the crimes—all the while knowing full well that his religion makes him a potential target.

PERFECT TRUST
By M. R. SELLARS
RGI Book #3
ISBN 096782219X / EAN 9780967822198 / $8.95 US

PICTURE PERFECT

Rowan Gant is a Witch.
His bane is to see things that others cannot.
To feel things he wishes he could not.
To experience events through the eyes of another...
Through the eyes of victims...
Sometimes, the things he sees are evil...
Criminal...
Because of this, in the span of less than two years, Rowan has come face to face with not one, but two sadistic serial killers...
In both cases he was lucky to survive.
Still, he abides the basic rule of The Craft—Harm None.

This predator could make Rowan forget that rule...

THE LAW OF THREE
By M. R. SELLARS
RGI Book #4
ISBN 0967822181 / EAN 9780967822181 / $14.95 US

LET THE BURNINGS BEGIN...

In February of 2001, serial killer Eldon Andrew Porter set about creating a modern day version of the 15th century Inquisition and Witch trials. Following the tenets of the *Malleus Maleficarum* and his own insane interpretation of the *Holy Bible*, he tortured and subsequently murdered several innocent people.

During a showdown on the old Chain of Rocks Bridge, he narrowly escaped apprehension by the Greater St. Louis Major Case Squad.

In the process, his left arm was severely crippled by a gunshot fired at close range.

A gunshot fired by a man he was trying to kill. A man who embraced the mystical arts. A Witch. Rowan Gant.

In December of the same year, Eldon Porter's fingerprints were found at the scene of a horrific murder in Cape Girardeau, Missouri, just south of St. Louis. An eyewitness who later spotted the victim's stolen vehicle reported that it was headed north...

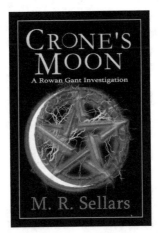

CRONE'S MOON
By M. R. SELLARS
RGI Book #5
ISBN 0967822149 / EAN 9780967822143 / $14.95 US

WHEN THE DEAD SPEAK,
ROWAN GANT HEARS THEIR WHISPERS

A missing school teacher, decomposed remains in a shallow grave, and a sadistic serial killer prowling Saint Louis by the semi-darkness of the waning moon—exactly the kind of thing Rowan Gant has no choice but to face. But, this time his bane, the uncontrolled channeling of murder victims, isn't helping; for the dead are speaking but not necessarily to him. Rowan once again must skirt the prejudices of police lieutenant Barbara Albright as he and his best friend, homicide detective Ben Storm, race to save a friend... and perhaps someone even closer.

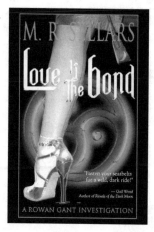

LOVE IS THE BOND
By M. R. SELLARS
RGI Book #6 / Miranda Trilogy Book #1
ISBN 0967822122 / EAN 9780967822129 / $14.95 US

SHE LOVES THEM TO DEATH ...

Of existing serial homicide cases, women make up less than one-tenth of American serial killers. However, among female serial killers in existence worldwide, American women have the dubious honor of snagging better than three-quarters of that total.

Within the characteristics of the Kelleher Typology nine-point categorization of serial killers is that of SEXUAL PREDATORS—those who systematically kill others in clear acts of sexual homicide.

They are sociopaths, sometimes harboring a form of paraphilia, but almost always killing in order to fuel or even validate an ongoing fantasy. In the case of female serial killers, however, this classification is so distinctly rare that there has only been one documented instance of it in the United States.

Still, there are those who wonder if that case was merely an isolated anomaly or in fact a harbinger of what is yet to come.

Rowan Gant is about to find the answer to that question. The problem is, it might just be one he doesn't want to hear...

ALL ACTS OF PLEASURE
By M. R. SELLARS
RGI Book #7 / Miranda Trilogy Book #2
ISBN 0967822130 / EAN 9780967822136 / $14.95 US

PLEASURE IS A RELATIVE CONCEPT...

At 1:52 PM, November 18, Rowan Gant's wife, Felicity O'Brien was arrested and charged with a string of brutal murders.

Due to a number of bizarre and almost inexplicable events leading up to her arrest, even she is unsure of her own innocence, let alone her sanity.

Rowan's faith in her, however, remains unshaken, and he will stop at nothing to find the real killer. The only problem is, the woman he is looking for has been dead for more than 150 years...

All Acts Of Pleasure is the powerful and revealing sequel to the Rowan Gant Investigations biggest cliffhanger to date, *Love Is The Bond*.

NON-FICTION

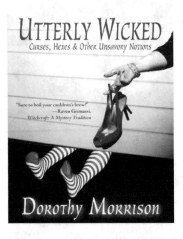

UTTERLY WICKED:
Curses, Hexes and Other Unsavory Notions
By Dorothy Morrison
ISBN: 0979453313 / EAN: 9780979453311 / Retail $14.95

LOOK WHO'S GOT THE RED SHOES NOW...

Hexes, curses and other unsavory notions. Most magical practitioners won't even discuss them. Why? Because they'd much rather find a positive solution that benefits all concerned. And, there's nothing wrong with that.

Occasionally, though, our problems are such that nothing in the positive solution arena will handle them. It's time to make a decision to stand tough, be strong, and take definitive action to defend ourselves. And, if you're ready to do that—*if you're ready to own that action and take responsibility for it*—then Utterly Wicked is the book for you!

A must have for any Witch's bookshelf!

CHASING THE RAINBOW:
Facilitating a Pagan Festival Without Losing Your Mind
By Tish Owen
ISBN: 0967822157 / EAN: 9780967822150 / Retail $14.95

SO YOU THINK YOU WANT TO RUN A PAGAN FESTIVAL ...

Chasing The Rainbow is destined to become the quintessential guide for facilitating Pagan festivals. Author, Tish Owen, draws from over a decade of experience running one of the Mid-south's largest alternative-spirituality gatherings. In her down to earth and often humorous style, she offers sound advice and common sense planning techniques that will help to make any festival coordinator's job a pleasure rather than a pain—be it a small celebration or a large event on a regional scale.

Other Books from WillowTree Press

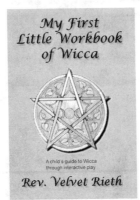

MY FIRST LITTLE WORKBOOK OF WICCA
A Child's Guide To Wicca Through Interactive Play
By Rev. Velvet Rieth
ISBN: 0979453305 / EAN: 9780979453304 / Retail $16.95

WICCA FOR THE KIDS

Containing general educational exercises blended with basic Pagan concepts and symbols, this workbook presents a wonderful introduction to Wicca for young children. Originally produced as a teaching aid for her grandchildren, Reverend Rieth's textbook grew into a project, which was home produced in limited quantities and sold at Pagan festivals nationwide by only a handful of vendors—it very quickly became one of their best-selling items.

Photograph Copyright © 2004, K. J. Epps

ABOUT THE AUTHOR

An active member of **SinC** (Sisters in Crime) and the **HWA** (Horror Writers Association), as well as being an Elder of the **Grove of the Old Ways** coven, M. R. Sellars has been called the **"Dennis Miller of Paganism"** due to his quick wit and humorously deadpan observations of life within the Pagan community and beyond. However, his humor is only one facet of his personality, as evidenced by the dark, unique paranormal thrillers he pens. That face has earned him another name—the **"Pagan Tony Hillerman."** Even with all these comparative monikers, he still likes to think of himself as just another writer trying to eke out a living doing a job he loves.

All of the current Rowan Gant novels have spent several consecutive weeks on numerous bookstore bestseller lists. **The Law Of Three**, book #4 in the saga, received the **St. Louis Riverfront Times People's Choice Award** soon after its debut. The most recent installment in the series, **All Acts Of Pleasure**, the seventh book in the RGI series, (second book in the much touted **MIRANDA TRILOGY**), was released October 31, 2006 and in February 2007 became the recipient of the **"2006 Preditors and Editors Award"** for best novel in a mainstream genre.

Sellars resides in the Midwest with his wife, daughter, and a host of what he describes as, "rescued, geriatric, special-needs felines."

M. R. Sellars can be found on the web at:
www.mrsellars.com and **www.myspace.com/mrsellars**